# THE VENDETTA DEFENSE

# THE VENDETTA DEFENSE

## LISA SCOTTOLINE

HarperLargePrint
*An Imprint of* HarperCollins*Publishers*

For information, address HarperCollins Publishers Inc.,
10 East 53rd Street, New York, NY 10022.
HarperCollins books may be purchased for educational, business,
or sales promotional use. For information, please write:
Special Markets Department, HarperCollins Publishers Inc.,
10 East 53rd Street, New York, NY 10022.

FIRST HARPER LARGE PRINT EDITION

Printed on acid-free paper

Library of Congress Cataloging-in-Publication Data
Scottoline, Lisa
The vendetta defense / by Lisa Scottoline.—1st ed.
ISBN 0-06-018507-4 (Hardcover)
ISBN 0-06-018559-7 (Large Print)
1. Philadelphia (Pa.)—Fiction. 2. Italian Americans—Fiction.
3. Trials (Murder)—Fiction. 4. Homing pigeons—Fiction.
5. Women Lawyers—Fiction. 6. Vendetta—Fiction. I. Title.

PS3569.C725 V46 2001
813'.54—dc21                    00-050556

01  02  03  04  05   RRD  10  9  8  7  6  5  4  3  2  1

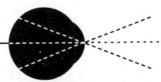

This Large Print Book carries the
Seal of Approval of N.A.V.H.

To the Honorable Edmund B. Spaeth, Jr.,
who taught me, and all his clerks, about the law,
about justice, and about love.

With eternal thanks, and the biggest hug ever—

Thanks, Judge.

# Book One

The conclusion arrived at then has been and always will be the same until I cease to exist; on the score of integrity there is no assault to be made upon me. My political work may be valued more or less, this way or that, and people may shout me up and howl me down, but in the moral field it is another matter.

—Benito Mussolini,
My Rise and Fall (1948)

Italians! Here is the national programme of a solidly Italian movement. Revolutionary, because it is opposed to dogma and demogogy; robustly innovating because it rejects preconceived opinions. We prize above everything and everybody the experience of a revolutionary war.

Other problems—bureaucratic, administrative, legal, educational, colonial, etc.—will be dealt with when we have established a ruling class.

—From a June 6, 1919,
program of the Fascist movement

*I grandi dolori sono muti.*
Great griefs are mute.

—Italian proverb

# 1

The morning Tony Lucia killed Angelo Coluzzi, he was late to feed his pigeons. As long as Tony had kept pigeons, which was for almost all of his seventy-nine years, he had never been late to feed them, and they began complaining the moment he opened the screen door. Deserting their perches, cawing and cooing, they flew agitated around the cages, their wings pounding against the chicken wire, setting into motion the air in the tiny city loft. It didn't help that the morning had dawned clear and that March blew hard outside. The birds itched to fly.

Tony waved his wrinkled hand to settle them, but his heart wasn't in it. They had a right to their bad manners, and he was a tolerant man. It was okay with him if the birds did only one thing, which was to fly home. They were homers, thirty-seven of them, and it wasn't an easy job they had, to travel to a place they'd never been, a distance in some races of three hundred or four hundred miles, then to navigate their return through skies they'd never flown, over city and country they'd never seen and couldn't possibly know, to flap their way home to a tiny speck in the middle of South Philadelphia, all without even stopping to congratulate themselves for this incredible feat, one that man couldn't even explain, much less accomplish.

There were so many mistakes a bird could make. Circling too long, as if it were a joyride or a training toss. Getting distracted on the way, buffeted by sudden bad weather, or worse, simply getting tired and disoriented—thousands of things could result in the loss of a precious bird. Even once the first bird had made it home, the race wasn't won. Many races had been lost by the bird who wouldn't trap fast enough; the one who was first to reach his loft but who stopped on the roof, dawdling on his way to the trap, so that his leg band couldn't be slipped off and clocked in before another man's bird.

But Tony's birds trapped fast. He bred them for speed, intelligence, and bravery, through six and even seven generations, and over time the birds had become his life. It wasn't a life for the impatient. It took years, even decades, for Tony to see the results of his breeding choices, and it wasn't until recently that his South Philly loft had attained the best record in his pigeon-racing club.

Suddenly the screen door banged open, blown

by a gust of wind, startling Tony and frightening the birds in the first large cage. They took panicky wing, seventeen of them, all white as Communion wafers, transforming their cage into a snowy blizzard of whirring and beating, squawking and calling. Pinfeathers flurried and snagged on the chicken wire. Tony hurried to the loft door, silently reprimanding himself for being so careless. Normally he would have latched the screen behind him—the old door had bowed in the middle, warped with the rain, and wouldn't stay shut without the latch—but this morning, Tony's mind had been on Angelo Coluzzi.

The white pigeons finally took their perches, which were small plywood boxes lining the walls, but in their panic they had displaced each other, violating customary territories and upsetting altogether the pecking order, which led to a final round of fussing. "**Mi dispiace,**" Tony whispered to the white birds. **I'm sorry,** in Italian. Though Tony understood English, he preferred Italian. As did his birds, to his mind.

He gazed at the white pigeons, really doves, which he found so beautiful. Large and healthy, the hue of their feathers so pure Tony marveled that only God could make this color. Their pearliness contrasted with the inky roundness of their eye, which looked black but in fact was the deepest of reds, blood-rich. Tony even liked their funny bird-feet, with the flaky red scales and the toe in back with a talon as black as their eyes pretended to be. And he kidded himself into thinking that the doves behaved better than the other birds. More civilized, they seemed aware of how special they were.

The secret reason for the doves' special status was that they were beloved of his son, who had finally stopped Tony from releasing them at weddings for a hundred fifty dollars a pop. Tony had thought it made a good side business; why not make some money to pay for the seed and medicines, plus keep the birds in shape during the off-season? And it made Tony happy to see the brides, whose hearts lifted at the flock of doves taking off outside the church, since you couldn't throw rice anymore. It reminded his heart of his own wedding day, less grand than theirs, though such things didn't matter when it came to love.

But his son had hated the whole idea. **They're not trained monkeys**, Frank had said. **They're athletes**.

So Tony had relented. **"Mi dispiace,"** he whispered again, this time to his son. But Tony couldn't think about Frank now. It would hurt too much, and he had birds to feed.

He shuffled down the skinny aisle, and his old sneakers, their soles worn flat, made a swishing sound on the whitewash of the plywood floor. The floor had held up okay, unlike the screen door; Tony had built the loft himself when he first came to America from Abruzzo, sixty years ago. The loft measured thirty feet long, with the single door in the middle opening onto a skinny aisle that ran the short length of the building. It occupied all of Tony's backyard, as if the loft and yard were nesting boxes. Off the aisle of the loft were three large chicken wire cages lined with box perches. The aisle ended in a crammed feed room, the seed kept safe from rats in a trash can, and there was a bookshelf holding antibiotics, lice sprays, vitamins, and other supplies, all labels out, in clean white shelves.

Tony prided himself on the neatness of his loft. He dusted the sills, cleaned the windows with the bright blue Windex, and scraped the floor of the cages twice a day, not once. It was important to the health of his birds. He whitewashed the loft interior each spring, before the old bird season; he had done it last week, experiencing a familiar pang—the chalky smell of the whitewash and its brightness reminded him of the white liquid shoe polish he used to paint over the scuffs on Frank's baby shoes, when his son had started to walk. Tony remembered the shoe polish—they didn't make it anymore—he would paint it on the stiff baby shoes with the cotton they gave you, stuck on a stick inside the cap like a white ball of dandelion seeds. Even though it dripped it worked okay.

Tony shook his head, thinking of it now, the chalky smell filling his nose like the fragrance of a rose. The bottle of polish had a blue paper label and a little circle picture of a blond-haired, blue-eyed baby who didn't look anything like baby Frank, with his jet black curls and his big brown eyes. Somehow Tony had the idea that if he painted the watery polish on Frank's baby shoes, his son would look like all the American babies and one day come to be one, even though Frank had the black hair and no mother. And when it actually happened and Frank grew up to take his place in this country, Tony was just superstitious enough to think that maybe it was the shoe polish.

Tony had to stop thinking about his son, though he couldn't help it, not this morning, of all mornings, and he tried to concentrate on the first cage of doves, appraising with failing eyes their condition. The doves were settling down, roosting again, and they looked good, no big fights during the night. Tony worried about the fights; the birds were territorial and always bickering about something, and the white birds bruised easily. He wanted them to look especially nice and stay healthy. For Frank.

Tony shuffled down the aisle to the second and third cages, which held the multicolored birds, mostly Meulemans with their reddish-brown feathers, and Janssens. There were other breeds in shades of gray and brown, and the common slateys; a slate gray, their eyes generally the same dark brown. Tony liked the nonwhite breeds, too, the ordinariness of their plumage reminding him of himself; he wasn't a flashy man, not a **brag-gadocio.** He didn't have the strut that some men had, going about like cocks. It had been his ruin, but now that he was old, it didn't matter anymore. It had stopped mattering a long time ago. Sixty years, to be exact.

His thoughts elsewhere, Tony watched the Janssens cooing and stirring without really seeing them. The breed name came from the Janssen family who had bred them, and the other names from the other families who had bred them; Tony had always dreamed that his family would produce its own strain of birds, but he wouldn't name it after himself. He knew who he would name it after, but he didn't get the chance. Many of the best breed stock came from Belgium and France. Italian pigeons also made good racers, but Tony wouldn't have much to do with them, especially the so-called Mussolini birds. Anybody who had lived during Mussolini wouldn't want anything to do with a Mussolini bird. **Chi ha poca vergogna, tutto il mondo è suo.** He who is without shame, all the world is his. **Mussolini** birds!

Tony was an old man with old memories. He wished he could spit on the loft floor, but he didn't want to dirty it. Instead he stood trembling until the anger left him, except for the bitterness in his mouth. Shaken, he idly inspected the Meulemans, and they seemed fine, too. Only Tony had had the terrible morning. An awful morning; the worst he'd had in a long time, but not the worst he'd had in his life. The worst he'd had in his life was sixty years ago. That morning then, and this morning now. Today. Tony had thought he would feel better after, but he didn't. He felt worse; he had committed an act against God. He knew that his judgment would come in heaven, and he would accept it.

His thoughts were interrupted by the Meulemans, cooing loudly, wanting to be fed, and his dark eyes went, as always, to his favorite bird of all, a Meuleman he had named The Old Man. The Old Man and Tony went back eighteen years; The Old Man was the oldest of Tony's pigeons, and to look at him, Tony wasn't sure who was the Old Man, him or the bird. The Old Man roosted peacefully in his corner perch in the second cage, his strong head held characteristically erect, his eyes clear and alert, and his broad breast a still robust curve covering his feet. Tony remembered the day the chick hatched, an otherwise typical slatey, apparently unremarkable at birth except for his eye sign. Eye sign, or the look in a pigeon's eye, spoke to Tony, and The Old Man's eyes told Tony that the bird would be fast and smart. And he had been the best, in his day.

"Come sta?" Tony asked The Old Man. **How are you?** But The Old Man knew exactly what he meant, and it wasn't, "**How are you?**"

The Old Man regarded the old man for a long time then. Tony couldn't help but feel that the old bird knew what he had done that morning, what had been so important as to keep Tony from feeding his birds on time. The Old Man knew why Tony had to do what he had done, even after all this time. And Tony knew that The Old Man approved.

It was then that Tony heard cars pulling up outside his house and in the alley right behind the loft, on the other side of the cinderblock wall. There was the slamming of heavy car doors, and Tony knew that they were police cars.

He had been expecting them.

But the birds startled at the sudden sound, taking flight in their cages, and even though Tony knew that the police were coming, he felt the hair rise on the back of his neck, as it used to so long ago. He froze beside the cages as the police shouted English words he didn't bother to translate, though he could, then they broke down the old wood door in the backyard wall, one, two, three pushes and it splintered and gave way to their shoulders and they burst into his yard, trampling his basil and tomatoes.

They were coming for him.

Tony didn't run from them, he wouldn't have anyway, but he remembered he had yet to feed his birds. He would have to hurry to finish before the police took him away. He shuffled to the feed room even as he caught sight of the police drawing their black guns silently, pointing instructions to each other, and two of them sneaking to the back door of his house like the cowards they were, little men hiding behind black shirts and shiny badges.

Tony's gut churned with bile, and it struck him with astonishment that the deepest hate could rage like a fire for so many years, never burning itself up.

Dwelling with perfect comfort alongside the deepest love.

# 2

"Come on, it's lunchtime! Let's go," Judy Carrier heard the other associates saying as they grabbed their light coats and bags. It was the first day of real warmth after a long winter, and evidently spring fever struck lawyers, too. Everybody at the Philadelphia law firm of Rosato & Associates, except Judy, was escaping. She remained at her desk trying to draft an antitrust article, though the sun obliterated the legal citations on her computer screen and the chatter in the hall kept distracting her. It was hard to work when you were eavesdropping.

Suddenly Anne Murphy, who called herself only Murphy, popped her head in Judy's open doorway. She was one of the new associates, her lipsticked lips expertly lined and her dark hair tied back into its typically fashionable knot. "You wanna go to lunch?" she asked.

"No thanks," Judy answered. She usually gave others the benefit of the doubt, but she was hard-pressed to respect women who drew lines around their lips, like coloring books. Judy wore no makeup herself, and a daily shower was her idea of fashionable. "I ate already."

"So what? Come on, you haven't taken lunch in weeks." Murphy smiled in a friendly way, though Judy suspected it was the lipliner. "It's gorgeous out. Walk around with us."

"Can't, thanks. Got an article to do, on the **Simmons** case."

"You can't even take a walk? It's Friday, for God's sake."

"No time for a walk. I really can't," Judy said, knowing that the walk part was bullshit. Murphy didn't walk, she shopped, and shopping made Judy want to kill indiscriminately. What was the matter with these baby lawyers? Judy didn't like any of them. Graduates of the Ally McBeal School of Law, they thought being a lawyer meant wearing skirts that met the legal definition of indecent exposure. They weren't serious about the law, which is the only thing Judy **was** serious about. She thought of them as Murphy's Lawyers.

"Oh. Okay. Well, don't work too hard." Murphy gave the white molding a good-bye pat and wisely disappeared, and Judy listened to the familiar sounds of the office emptying out, the gossip trailing off toward the elevator banks. The elevator cabs chimed as they left, bearing lawyers into the sun. Rosato & Associates was a small firm, only nine women lawyers and support staff, and for the next hour or so, whatever telephone calls the receptionist didn't answer would be forwarded to voicemail. E-mail would go unopened, and faxes would wait in gray plastic trays. The office fell silent except for the occasional ringing of telephones, and Judy felt her whole body relax into the midday lull that was a long, deep breath before the afternoon's business began.

She knew she was supposed to feel lonely, but she didn't. She liked being on her own. She sipped coffee from a Styrofoam cup amid federal casebooks, stacks of printed cases, scribbled notes, and correspondence that covered her wooden desk and the desk return on her right. Her office was small, standard issue for mid-level associates at Rosato, but the clutter reduced it to a shoebox. Judy didn't mind. She didn't think of her office as messy, she thought of it as full, and felt very cozy surrounded by all her stuff. Nobody needed a nest more than a lawyer.

Papers, memos, law school texts, novels, and copies of the federal civil and criminal rules filled the bookshelves across from her and the shelves behind her, under the window. Three large file cabinets sat flush against the side wall, their fake-wood counter hidden by twenty thick accordion files from **Moltex** v. **Huartzer**, a massive antitrust case, which was redundant. A tower of potential trial exhibits at the end cabinet threatened daily to topple. Blanketing the walls were dog, horse, and family photos, certificates of court admission and awards Judy had received as law review editor and class salutatorian, and diplomas from Stanford University and Boalt Law School. Judy was the firm's true legal scholar, so her office, while a mess, was a highly scholarly mess.

And her friend Mary wasn't around to nag her about it. Mary DiNunzio had worked with Judy since they had graduated from law school, but she was taking time off from work after their last murder case; since then Judy's nest hadn't felt much like home. She took a reflective sip of coffee, eased back in an ergonomically correct chair whose cushions stabbed her in the back and shoulders, and crossed her legs, which were strong and shapely but completely bare. In Judy's view, pantyhose was for Republicans, and now that Mary wasn't here, she was getting away with that, too. Judy and Mary disagreed about practically everything, including Murphy's use of lipliner.

On impulse, Judy pulled open her middle drawer and shuffled through ballpoint pens, parti-colored plastic paper clips, and loose change until she found a red pencil she used to edit briefs; then she dug again in the drawer for the mirror Mary had given her. Judy usually used the mirror to check for poppy seeds between her teeth, but now, her red pencil poised, she appraised herself in its large square:

Looking back at her from the mirror was a broad-shouldered young woman whose bright blue dress, yellow T-shirt, and artsy silver earrings made her look out of place against the legal books. Her hair was naturally blond, almost crayon yellow, and hacked off in a straight line at her chin; her face was big and round, reminding her always of a full moon, and her eyes were large and bright blue, as unmade-up as her lips. Her light eyelashes were mascaraless, her nose short and bobbed. An old boyfriend used to tell her she was beautiful, but whenever Judy looked at herself, all she thought was **I look like myself,** which was satisfying.

She puckered up in the mirror. Her lips were in between full and thin, of a normal pink color. Hmmm. Judy raised the red editing pencil close to her lips. The color match was perfect. And she was a good artist. Watching herself in the mirror, Judy took the pencil, moistened the point, and sketched across the top of her lip. The red pigment smelled funny and felt cold but was blunt enough not to scratch, and she drew a light line on her top lip, out-lined her lower lip as well, and puckered up again for the mirror.

Not bad. You could see the red penciling, but her mouth looked bigger, which was supposed to be good these days, when lips like hot dogs ruled. The phone started ringing at reception, but Judy ignored it. She smiled at the mirror and looked instantly friendly, in an ersatz-Murphy I-ignore-the-phones sort of way. Apparently you couldn't beat office supplies for makeup. Maybe she should take a Sharpie to her eyelids. Paint her fingernails with Wite-Out. Who said being a lawyer wasn't fun? She set down the pencil, picked up the phone, and punched in a number.

"So how do I look?" Judy asked when Mary picked up.

"I got your message about the Sherman Act. Stop calling me about the Sherman Act."

"This isn't about the Sherman Act. Antitrust is easy. Lipliner is hard."

"Murphy was in, huh?"

"She was trying to be friendly so I sent her away."

"You should have lunch with her."

"I don't like her, and she doesn't eat lunch. If I liked her and she ate lunch, I would go with her. Instead I stayed in and drew on my lips. So what do you think? Does Oscar Mayer come to mind?" Judy air-kissed the receiver, and Mary scoffed.

"You're supposed to be making new friends."

"No, I'm supposed to be writing an article and you're supposed to stop slacking off and get your ass back to work."

"I'm fine, and thank you for asking," Mary said, though Judy could hear the smile in her voice. The smile didn't come from Revlon or even Dixon Ticonderoga but was due entirely to a wonderful heart, and Judy felt a twinge of guilt. Attempted murder wasn't a laughing matter.

"I'm sorry. How're you feeling, Mare?"

"Pretty good for somebody who took two bullets."

Judy winced. She had almost lost Mary, forever. She didn't want to think about it. "You need anything? It's only fifteen minutes by cab. Want me to bring you anything?"

"No thanks."

"You sure?"

Mary snorted. "You regret that wisecrack, don't you? If I didn't know you better, I'd say you feel guilty."

"Me?" Judy smiled. It was a long-running joke between them. Mary, an Italian Catholic, held the patent on guilt, and Judy could see that it would never expire. "No way. I'm from California."

"You should be guilty. You were making fun of somebody with ventilation. What kind of friend are you?" Mary laughed, but it got lost in a surprising burst of background noise, which sounded like men talking loud. Mary had been recuperating at her parents' house in South Philly, and the DiNunzios, whom Judy adored, were an old Italian couple who lived very quietly, at least when Mr. DiNunzio wore his hearing aid. Usually the only background noise at the DiNunzio rowhouse was a continuous loop of novenas.

"What's that sound over there?" Judy asked. "Another DiNunzio clambake?"

"You don't wanna know."

"Yes, I do." It sounded like quite a commotion,

with the men now arguing. Judy frowned. "Is anything the matter?"

"You wouldn't believe it."

"Try me."

"My father's friends are here. You met Tony-
From-Down-The-Block."

"The guy he buys cigars with?"

"That could be anybody, but yes," Mary
answered, and the background arguing surged.

"What the hell was that?"

"Feet."

"It didn't sound like feet, it sounded like
voices."

"Feet's his nickname. His real name is Tony Two
Feet. He's shouting. He's an excitable boy, for an
eighty-year-old."

"Tony Two Feet? That's a name? Everybody has
two feet."

"Don't ask me. He's my father's other friend.
They're all upset about Pigeon Tony."

Judy smiled. "Is anybody there **not** named
Tony?"

"Please. It's ten Italian men. Odds are three will
be Tony, two will be Frank, and one will end up in
jail. Pigeon Tony just got arrested. The smart
money was on Dominic."

"Arrested for what?"

"Murder."

Judy's lips formed an imperfectly lined circle.
"Murder?"

"Also my mother sends her love."

"**Murder?**" Judy felt her pulse quicken. "A friend of your father's, arrested for murder? Your father is around seventy-five, isn't he? How old **is** Tony? And who did he kill, allegedly? I mean whom?"

"You can't just say Tony, you have to say Pigeon Tony, and he's close to eighty. He grew up in Italy and he supposedly killed another old man, also from Italy. I was trying to figure out what the hell was going on when you called."

Judy's eyes flared in surprise. She felt awake for the first time in months. "Does Pigeon Tony have a lawyer?"

"Wait a minute. You sound interested. You're not allowed to be interested."

"Why not?" Judy inched forward on her horrible chair. Murder trumped antitrust. Spring had sprung. Her other phone line rang but she ignored it. Ignoring phones got easier with practice. "I can be interested. I have a First Amendment right to be interested."

"My father wanted me to call you, but I don't think you should take the case."

"Your dad wants me to?" Judy's pulse quickened. She would do anything to help Mary's father, especially something she already wanted to do.

"Yes, but I don't, and I don't have time to fight about it. It's **La Traviata** over here. I gotta go."

"Put your dad on the phone, Mare."

"No. Remember the last murder case we took?

Gunfire ensued. Hot lead whizzing around. Lawyers are ill prepared for such things. Stick to the Sherman Act. Besides, I told my father Bennie won't allow it."

"Why wouldn't she? We take murder cases now, and besides, the boss is at a deposition. I'll apologize later if she won't let me take it. Don't make me whine. Put him on!"

"No." The ruckus in the background started again, and Judy could hear Mary's father closer to the phone.

"Now, Mare! Lemme talk to your father." There was a sudden silence on the phone, and Judy could picture Mary's hand covering the receiver, muting the arguing of the men and the softer voice of Mariano DiNunzio. "Mr. D, is that you?" Judy asked, shouting through Mary's hand, as if it were possible. "What's the matter, Mr. D?"

"Judy, thank God you called!" Mr. DiNunzio said. He came onto the line abruptly, and Judy assumed he had taken the phone from Mary. "The police, they have my friend downtown. They took him away, in handcuffs." Mr. DiNunzio's voice was choked with emotion, and Judy's heart went out to him, the gravity of the situation striking home.

"What happened?"

"They say he killed a man, but he would never. He couldn't. He wouldn't." Mr. DiNunzio cleared his throat, and Judy could hear him collect himself. "I would never ask such a thing, a favor, for me. For myself. You know this. But for my friend, my **compare**, he's in trouble."

"Whatever you need, you got it, Mr. D."

"I know you, you're a good girl. A smart lawyer. You know all the ins and outs. You work hard, like my Mary. Will you be his lawyer, Judy? Please?"

"Of course I will, Mr. D," Judy answered, and the words weren't out of her mouth before she was reaching for her briefcase.

And slipping her bare feet into a pair of clunky yellow clogs.

# 3

Pigeon Tony struck Judy as the cutest defendant ever, and she wanted to rescue the little old man the moment she saw him in the interview room of the Roundhouse, Philadelphia's police administration building. He was only five foot four, probably a hundred and thirty pounds, and he startled as Judy burst into the interview room, lost in a white paper jumpsuit that was way too large for his scrawny neck and narrow chest. His withered arms stuck like twigs from short sleeves, and his knobby wrists were pinched by steel handcuffs. His sunburned pate was dotted with liver spots and streaked by only a few filaments of silvery hair. His peeling nose was small and hooked; his eyes a round, dark brown, almost black, under a short brow. Judy couldn't explain his superb tan, but she gathered he was called Pigeon because he looked like one.

"Mr. Lucia, I'm a lawyer," she said, briefcase in hand. "My name is Judy Carrier and I was sent by the DiNunzios. They asked me to come and help you."

The old man's only response was to squint at her, and Judy didn't understand why. Maybe he didn't speak English. Maybe he didn't want a lawyer. Maybe she should have worn pantyhose.

"I'm a friend of Mary DiNunzio." Judy took a seat in the orange bucket chair on the lawyer's side of the counter. Five ratty interview carrels sat side by side. The interview room was otherwise empty, not for want of felons but for want of lawyers. Few attorneys bothered to come to the bowels of the Roundhouse, preferring to meet their clients where the floor didn't crawl. "You know Mary DiNunzio, don't you?"

The old man, still squinting, slowly raised his arm and pointed at Judy with a finger that, though crooked at the knuckle, did not waver. His sleeve slid up his arm when he pointed, revealing a surprisingly wiry knot of biceps and a tattooed crucifix that had gone a blurry blue. But Judy still didn't understand what he was pointing at.

"Mr. Lucia? What is it?"

"Your, eh, your face," he said, his Italian accent as thick as tomato sauce. "Your **mouth**. Is bleeding?"

Judy reddened. The lipliner. The editing pencil. No wonder the cops had recoiled at the sight of her. And she thought it was because she was a lawyer. "No, it's not bleeding. I'm sorry." She wiped her mouth quickly, rouging the back of her hand. "Despite appearances, I'm not a clown but a lawyer, and a fairly good one, Mr. Lucia."

"Mariano tell me. I call him, and he tell me you come. I thank you." The old man nodded, in a courtly way. "Also you calla me Pigeon Tony. Everybody calla me Pigeon Tony."

"Well, then, Pigeon Tony, you're welcome, and I'm happy to represent you," Judy said, then remembered she could get fired for taking on a nice client. Lately she had been representing corporations, ill-mannered entities by charter. "I'll have to make sure that my boss says my firm can take your case. I just came down today to make sure you didn't hurt yourself."

Pigeon Tony's brow furrowed in confusion.

Judy reminded herself to edit her words. Her only experience with broken English had been in the legal aid clinic in law school, and Latin hadn't helped there either. "I mean, hurt your case. Say the wrong thing to the police. You didn't talk to the police, did you?"

"I no talk. Mariano tell me."

"Did the police ask you questions about the murder?" She flipped open the latch of her messy briefcase, wrested a legal pad from the debris, and located a Pilot pen strictly by sheer good luck. So what if her briefcase was a little full? Sometimes you had to carry your nest around. Nobody knew better than a military brat how to pitch a tent.

"**Si, si**, they ask questions."

"What questions?" Judy was wondering if the cops had tried an end-run around the **Miranda** warnings, as they still did. Taking advantage of a little old man, an immigrant even. They should be ashamed. "Lots of questions?"

"I no answer."

"Good."

"I no like."

Judy was getting the hang of the accent thing. "You no like what?"

"Police."

She smiled as she uncapped the pen and flipped through the pad for a clean slate. "Now what else did the police do?"

"Take me to here, take my hands"—Pigeon Tony held up two small palms so that Judy could see the ink on each finger pad—"take me a picture. Take alla clothes, alla shoes, alla socks. Take **blood**. Take everything. **Everything**. No can believe!" His dark eyes rounded with amazement, and Judy gathered he didn't get out much.

"They took your clothes and your blood for evidence. They always do that. It's procedure."

"Evidence?" Pigeon Tony repeated, rolling the unfamiliar word around in his mouth. "What means **evidence**?"

"Evidence is proof against you. Evidence shows you did the crime."

"Evidence? Take **mutandine**!"

"What's **mutandine**?" Judy asked, and Pigeon Tony went visibly red in the face, his thin skin a dead giveaway. **Mutandine** must have meant underwear.

"Forget," he said quickly, looking away, and Judy suppressed a smile. He was so sweet, she couldn't believe the police had arrested him for murder. Were they nuts? She was starting to no like police.

"I understand they're charging you with murder." Judy checked her notes. "The man they say you killed was eighty years old. Named Angelo Coluzzi. Did I say that right? Coluzzi?" She pronounced it like Coa-lootz-see, to make it sound festive and Italian. "Okay?"

"**Si, si.** Coluzzi."

"Good. Upstairs they'll be processing—getting ready—the charge against you. Do you understand?"

"**Si.**" Pigeon Tony's face turned grave. "Murder."

"Yes, murder, and I have to understand the evidence—the proof—they have against you. I'd like to begin by asking you a few—"

"I kill Coluzzi," Pigeon Tony interrupted, and Judy's mouth went dry. She hadn't heard him right. She couldn't have heard him right. She fumbled for her voice.

"You didn't say you murdered Coluzzi, did you?" she asked, her tone unprofessionally aghast. She didn't know what a lawyer was supposed to do when her client volunteered a confession. Probably shut him up, but that wasn't Judy's style. If it was true, it was awful, and she wanted to know why. "Did you say you **murdered** Coluzzi?"

"No."

Judy sighed with relief. It must have been the language barrier. "Thank God."

"I no murder Coluzzi."

"I didn't think so."

"I kill him." Pigeon Tony nodded firmly, his thin lips forming a determined line, confusing Judy completely.

"Let's try this again, Mr. Lucia. Tony. Did you kill Angelo Coluzzi? Yes or no?"

"**Si, si,** I kill him. But"—Pigeon Tony held up a finger, like a warning—"no murder. I no murder!"

"What do you mean?" Judy's mind reeled. Antitrust beckoned. The Sherman Act was a cakewalk compared to an Italian immigrant. "You killed Coluzzi but you didn't murder him?"

"Si."

"That means yes, right?" She wanted to make sure. Clarity would be in order right now, since it was the murder part.

"**Si, si.** He kill my wife, so I kill him. No è murder."

Judy's heart lifted. Maybe it was self-defense. "Where was your wife when Coluzzi killed her? Were you trying to protect your wife at the time? Is that why you killed him?"

"No."

"No?"

"My wife, she dead sixty years. **Murder** by Coluzzi."

Baffled, Judy set down her Pilot pen. "Coluzzi killed your wife sixty years ago, so you killed him today?"

"**Si.**"

It meant yes, but still. "Why did you wait so long?"

"Si! Si!" Pigeon Tony's face went suddenly red with emotion. "Sixty years, alla same. **Occhio per occhio, dente per dente.** Coluzzi big, important man." Suddenly animated, he puffed out his concave chest. "**Fascisti!** You know, **Fascisti**?"

"Yes. Fascists?" Judy racked her brain for Italian history but all she could dredge up was **The Sopranos**. She thought harder. "You mean, like, Mussolini?"

"**Si! Il Duce!**" Pigeon Tony stuck out his lower lip, in imitation. "A murderer! **He!** Not me."

"I don't understand—"

"Coluzzi murder my Silvana!" Tears welled up in Pigeon Tony's eyes, a glistening but unmistakable sheen that he blinked away in obvious shame. His pointy Adam's apple traveled up and down a stringy neck. "So I kill Coluzzi."

"Are you saying that this Coluzzi killed your wife, in Italy?"

"Si, si! He **murder** her!"

"Why did he do that?"

"Because he **want** her and she no want him! So he **kill** her!" Pigeon Tony trembled at the thought, a shudder that traveled through his face and chin, emphasizing his frailty, and Judy felt her heart go out to him.

"So you got him back?"

"**Si, si.**"

Judy understood the scenario, but her chest wrenched with conflict. "So Coluzzi got away with murder?"

"**Si, si!**"

"What did the police do?"

"**Coluzzi** the police! **Fascisti** the police! They no care! I tell them, they do nothing! They **laugh**!" Bitterness curled his thin lips. "The war come, and alla people, they no care about one girl. You think they care? So Pigeon Tony, he get justice! For Silvana! For Frank, my son!" Tony leaned forward, his manacled hands gripping the Formica counter. "We go now. We tell judge!"

Judy put up her hands. "No! We no tell the judge. We no tell nobody. Anybody." The double negative was throwing her, as usual. "You didn't tell the police this, did you?"

Pigeon Tony shook his head. "I no like."

"No like what?"

"Police."

She had forgotten. "Okay, now, after they arraign you—charge you—they decide if you make bail.

Bail means you get to go free, if you pay money. I think you will get bail, considering your age and lack of criminal record." Judy caught herself. "You never killed anybody before, did you?"

Pigeon Tony appeared to think a minute. "No."

"Good. Did you ever commit any other crime?"

"No crime."

"Excellent. If they give you bail, who will bail you out?"

Pigeon Tony frowned again, uncomprehending.

"Who in your family will come for you? Who will pay money for you to be free? Is there anyone, when we go to the judge?"

"Frank. My grandson. He come." Pigeon Tony stiffened. "I tell judge."

"No, you no tell the judge." Judy had a legal duty to protect him and she wanted to get to the bottom of his story before she condemned him, even for murder. "You have to listen to me. Revenge is no defense to murder, outside of Sicily."

"Com'e'?"

"You can't tell the judge. If you do, the police will send you to jail for the rest of your life. You don't want that to happen, do you? You'll never see Frank again." Judy watched as Pigeon Tony's thin lips pursed, the argument seeming to hit home. "Okay, so we agree. Now, let me go upstairs and see when they're going to arraign you. You have to promise me that you won't talk to anybody about this. Do you promise?"

"**Si, si. Io lo fatto.**"

Judy didn't have time for the translation. She wanted to get upstairs fast, to learn the evidence against him. "Promise me now."

Pigeon Tony puckered his lower lip in thought.

"I can't hear you," Judy sang out, cupping a hand to her ear, and Pigeon Tony broke into the first smile she'd seen so far.

"Promise lady with big mouth," he answered, and Judy assumed he meant her lipliner.

# 4

Judy hurried off the elevator at the Roundhouse and followed the oddly hand-scrawled signs to the Homicide Division. They led to a narrow hallway of cheap paneling past a huge black plastic tub of trash sitting right outside a reception area, also cheaply paneled. The small room was covered with signs like POLICE PERSONNEL ONLY and PRIVATE—KEEP OUT, which Judy ignored. The front desk was empty, and she barreled past it. She needed as much information as she could get about the Coluzzi case before she went back to the office and had to account to her boss, Bennie Rosato. She'd been so thrown by Pigeon Tony's confession, she'd forgotten to get the details of the case. Like how he killed Coluzzi, for instance. Little things.

Judy entered the squad room and, because she'd been up here only twice, took a minute to get her bearings. Not that anything had changed—in the last twenty years, for that matter. Water-stained white curtains barely covered grimy windows; most of the curtain hooks were missing and the drapes hung like gaping wounds from cheap metal valances. Six cluttered desks filled the small room, only haphazardly arranged, and in one case covered with breakfast debris of a cold bacon sandwich, the scent of which lingered unaccountably in the air, mixing with traces of cigar smoke. Battered file cabinets lined the side wall, near the two interview rooms. The place was quiet of ringing phones and empty except for two detectives, who were looking through a boxed file on a desk.

Judy wasn't surprised at how quiet it was. She'd been around enough to know that the day tour at the Homicide Division was the sleepy shift, not the other way around. Murders generally happened under cover of darkness—who said there was nothing to do in Philadelphia at night—and most detectives spent at least part of the day testifying in court. Whether it was their court appearances or their occupational machismo, Judy didn't know, but homicide detectives were peacocks. The two in the squad room wore flashy silk ties, well-tailored suits, and too-strong cologne, and they looked up from the file at the same time, staring at the invasion of a young blond lawyer.

Judy stood her ground, even in yellow clogs. Being a blonde was a good thing to be with detectives, good enough to trump being a defense lawyer, and she watched their collective gaze scan her athletic body and stall at her bare legs. But when they reached her footwear, their heads almost exploded, and she was glad she had erased her lipliner.

"I'm a lawyer representing Anthony Lucia," she said, and nevertheless held her head high. It was her first experience with representing a confessed murderer, and she didn't find it easy, even if the killer was a cute little old man. "He's being held in connection with the Coluzzi case."

The detective on the right—a tall, middle-aged man with slicked-back hair—cocked his head. "You work for Rosato," he said, and Judy nodded.

"The firm hasn't entered an appearance," she said, preserving her job. "But I just met with Mr. Lucia. He told me you asked him some questions, and I was surprised at that. You didn't question him without counsel, did you?"

"Perish the thought," the detective said, his smile firmly in place. He turned to the desk behind him, picked up a manila folder, plucked a sheet of paper from it, and handed it to Judy. "Here's the criminal complaint."

Judy skimmed the sheet, which said only that defendant Anthony Lucia had been charged with the crime that occurred on April 17, at 712 Cotner Street, an "unlawful homicide." Judy had thought that was the only kind there was. She needed more information. "You videotaped the interview, didn't you?"

"It's procedure."

"When can I get a copy?"

"Whenever they turn over the other evidence, after the prelim."

Judy gritted her teeth. They were playing my-testosterone-can-beat-up-your-testosterone, and she wasn't as deficient as she appeared. "You study to be this difficult, or does it just come naturally?"

The detective didn't react. "We asked a coupla routine questions, completely within our prerogative."

Judy felt torn. What evidence did they have? How strong was their case? Even the Philadelphia police could convict a guy who actually did it. "What's the basis for the charge?"

"You'll see when we charge him, around three o'clock, Ms.—"

"Carrier, but Judy's fine." She sighed. "Look, I'm standing here and you're standing here. You can't tell me?"

"Ain't the way we do things," the detective said matter-of-factly, and the older detective beside him gave him a nudge.

"The junior varsity's in, Sammy," he muttered, not really under his breath, but Judy ignored it.

"Do you have any physical evidence against Mr. Lucia?"

"You'll find that out, too. Later."

"Are Detectives Kovich or Brinkley around?" Judy knew them from the last case, and they would help if they could. She went up on tiptoe and glanced past the detectives, whose expressions soured.

"The Stan and Reg Show? Not here. They're out of town, and they do things different than I do anyway."

Judy knew what he meant. **If you like them, you'll hate me.**

"In any event, I caught this one. I'm the assigned. I'm the one you have to deal with."

"Listen, Detective—"

"Wilkins. Sam Wilkins."

"Wilkins. Mr. Lucia is not a young man, and I'm concerned about the state of his health. The stress of this—"

"Spare me." The detective snorted. "That old bird's tough as nails. He'll be dancing on my grave."

Suddenly the detectives looked past Judy, and she turned, feeling a presence behind her. A tall, good-looking man in Levi's approached almost out of breath, his jeans jacket flapping to the side in his haste. When he got closer, Judy could see that his eyes were dark with anger, barely controlled.

"Excuse me," the man said brusquely to the detectives. "I'm looking for Anthony Lucia. I heard you arrested him. I want him freed."

Judy realized who it must be, and even recognized a flicker of the grandfather in the grandson, though he was much taller, maybe six foot three, and handsome. "You must be Frank Lucia," she said, extending a hand, but he squeezed it only absently, his grip rough with thick skin, his gaze still burning into the detectives.

"Where is my grandfather?" he demanded. "I want to see him. I want him out of here."

"Relax, pal. Mr. Lucia's in custody, and he'll be arraigned at the end of the day. This is his lawyer, Dr. Judy." The detective gestured in a professional way, and Frank looked over as the introduction registered, his eyes widening with recognition.

"Jeez! You're Judy! I'm sorry, you're Mary's friend. Thanks so much for coming." Frank burst into a tense grin and suddenly grabbed Judy by the shoulders, pulling her easily into a brief hug. An astonished Judy caught a quick whiff of onion breath before she landed in a wall of hard denim. She recovered her dignity only when Frank set her back on her feet.

"Uh, that's okay," she stammered, finger-combing her hair into place, aware of the detectives watching them.

"You know Matty DiNunzio. Mariano. He said you would help." Frank was talking too fast, his emotions clearly all over the lot. "He said you were a terrific lawyer."

"Well, I hope so." Judy swallowed hard. She was getting blocked in on the representation, and of a guilty client. The detectives were taking mental notes. "Frank, maybe we should discuss this in private."

"After I see my grandfather."

"You can't, not yet."

"Where is he?"

"Downstairs."

"You're kidding me. He's right downstairs and I can't see him?"

Judy suppressed her smile. Frank sounded like her, even to her. "Only lawyers can meet with defendants before arraignment."

"Lawyers can meet, but not family? A stranger can meet with my grandfather, but I can't?" Frank's head snapped angrily toward the detectives. "What the hell—"

Judy interrupted, "I saw him, Frank, and he's fine. Now, we really should go." She wanted them both out of there, and flared her eyes meaningfully. Frank wasn't so hotheaded that he didn't get the meaning.

"Yeah, maybe." His glare fixed on the detectives. "Take care of my grandfather."

"Ain't my job, buddy," Detective Wilkins said flatly, and Frank moved instantly toward the detective.

"What did you say?" he demanded, but Judy grabbed his arm before he assaulted anybody wearing a badge or a bad tie.

"Let's go, Frank," she said quickly, yanking him

back and steering him out of the squad room. She tried not to feel self-conscious about her hand on him, since he had already broken the touch barrier. In her experience, Italians didn't have a touch barrier anyway.

She managed to get him down the hall and didn't let go until she had him in an elevator crowded with uniformed cops. Neither Judy nor Frank spoke, and they rode down grimly, with Frank regaining his composure apparently by his looking at his hands. They were unusually thick-skinned for a man his age, which Judy judged to be about hers or a little older. He was built like a weight lifter, though the light in his dark eyes struck her as decidedly intelligent. But maybe that was because he was such a total hunk. She couldn't get a date at gunpoint lately, which was a factor.

His faded jeans looked dusty except for a darker patch at the knee, and Judy guessed he'd been wearing knee pads while he worked. A stonewashed green T-shirt, black beeper attached to his belt, and pocket cell phone didn't give further clues as to what he did for a living. He wore tan Timberland work boots, heavily creased at the ankle and dusted with a fine gray silt, and she tried to figure him out. What he did, who he was. And how he would take the news that his grandfather could die in prison, or worse.

"You did say my grandfather was okay?" he said

softly, almost reading her mind, as they stepped off the elevator. If Frank's eyes were angry before, they were full of worry now, and something else. Fear.

"He's fine, but we should talk. I am concerned about his case."

"Sure." Frank reached the door and held it open for her. "But there's somewhere we have to go first. My truck's in the lot."

# 5

"It can't take long. I have to get back to the office before the arraignment, which will be around three this afternoon," Judy told him, though she was intrigued.

"No problem." They left the Roundhouse and crossed the parking lot in front, which was overflowing with cops and police personnel enjoying the spring weather, even among the squad cars and pool cars. A white Ford F-250 pickup stood out from the dark sedans, in the far space under a WORKING PRESS ONLY sign. Frank made a beeline for it, with Judy only a step behind.

"So you're a reporter?" she asked.

"No. I needed a parking space." Frank yanked a ring of keys from his back pocket, chirped the truck unlocked, and went to the passenger side to open the door. "Climb in, but watch out for the laptop."

"You don't have to keep getting doors for me," she said, and Frank smiled.

"I know that." He walked around the dinged bed of the truck to the driver's side and got in. "I didn't do it because I had to."

Judy withheld comment as she got into the truck, which was an office on wheels. What did this guy do for a living? The front seat was a soft gray bench, but between the driver and passenger sat a desk-size console that held an open Gateway laptop with a slim portable printer wired to the cigarette lighter. There was another cell phone and a walkie-talkie with a stubby antenna. Judy gave up. "You a drug dealer?" she asked, and he laughed as he turned on the ignition.

"Of course not! I'm a stonemason." He picked up the cell phone on the console. "Excuse me just one minute. I have to rearrange my schedule to be able to come at three." He pressed a speed-dial button. "I don't want you to think I'm one of those assholes who's on the cell phone all the time."

"I know how it is," she said, as they pulled away. And she did, which meant that she knew Frank would be on the phone the remainder of the trip, and he was, answering questions, ordering materials, and explaining estimates for retaining walls. At one point Judy held the steering wheel while he printed out a purchase order and argued with ease over a late shipment. She amused herself by checking her own voicemail, not to be outdone in the cell phone department, and calling the recep-

tionist at work to ascertain that Bennie remained
in deposition. The cat was still away.

Judy looked out the window while the big truck
sped smoothly out of the city and into the western
suburbs, where the asphalt turned to strip malls of
Staples stores, Chili's restaurants, and Gap outlets.
Judy had lived in twenty different states growing
up, as her father was promoted within the navy,
and even in her short time had seen how similar
everything had become. Ironically, instead of making her feel more at home anywhere, it made her
feel less so. She kept looking out the window, and
soon the strip malls became green rolling hills
with larger houses. Judy began to like playing
hooky, driving around in a noisy truck with a
stonemason, who was attractive despite his onion
breath.

Frank pushed the cell phone button to end a call
and gave a final sigh as the truck slowed to a stop at a
traffic light. "Sorry about that," he said, braking.
Every time the truck halted, something rolled around
in the pickup's bed. "I wanted to clear the deck completely, and I don't like to leave my guys on the job
without me. Dry-laid is trickier than it looks."

"What's dry-laid?"

"New England dry-laid. Stone walls, no mortar.
That's what I do. That's all I do now. I used to lay
brick and block like my father and my grandfather,
but it's boring. Dry-laid is like fitting a puzzle
together. You use fieldstones or whatever's indige-

nous. You have to think. My guys, they're good, but nobody's as good without the boss around."

"I bet," Judy said, as if it didn't apply to her.

"Now I'm okay for a few hours." Frank turned the truck into a driveway on the right and cruised past the NO ENTRANCE sign. "Here we are."

Judy pushed the button and rolled down the window. They were entering a memorial park, lovely and green, dotted with somber gray monuments. Many of the monuments bore flowers, and some had small flags that flapped in a soft breeze. The air wafted unaccountably sweet. "What are we doing here?" she asked, surprised.

"Showing you why my grandfather killed Angelo Coluzzi."

Frank walked before Judy and stood at the front of the grave with his head bowed for a minute. Judy looked past him to the black granite monument, which sat flush with the grassy carpet:

# LUCIA

## FRANK    GEMMA

*United in life, united in death.*

It took Judy a minute to understand what she was seeing. The graves of Frank's father and mother. The day etched into the glossy granite was a single one, January 25, and the date was last year's. Judy's heart went still. Frank had lost both of his parents. Had Pigeon Tony lost a son?

Frank lifted his head and turned. Pain softened his rugged features, but his eyes remained dry. "Come forward, it's okay," he said, motioning, and Judy stepped toward him.

"I'm sorry."

"Me, too. But that's not why I brought you here." Frank cleared his throat but his voice sounded predictably hoarse. "My parents died last year, in an accident. The truck, it was my dad's old truck, flipped over an overpass on the expressway. It happened late at night. The truck turned into a fireball. They were coming home late from a wedding in Jersey, and the cops think my father fell asleep at the wheel."

Judy remained silent. She didn't know what to say. The breeze was so gentle, the air so fresh. The only sound was Frank's quiet voice, his account continuing tersely.

"Either that or he had a heart attack at the wheel, I don't know exactly. It doesn't matter. I had them cremated, which was . . . well, a necessity. Only that turned out to be a problem, at least as far as my grandfather is concerned."

"Why?"

"See, my grandfather, he didn't believe it was an accident. He thought my parents were murdered.

An autopsy might have proved they weren't. And he blamed himself for their death."

Judy shook her head. "Who would murder your parents?"

"Angelo Coluzzi." Frank scanned the oak trees in the distance, then a sun-dappled lawn that stretched over a small hill. "This goes back so many years, decades, to Italy. My grandfather told you about Coluzzi, didn't he?"

Judy paused. "What your grandfather told me is privileged. It wouldn't be ethical to reveal anything, even to you."

"I respect that." Frank nodded, with a half smile, turning to her. His eyes were an earth brown and the amused crinkling at the corners told Judy he was older than she'd thought at first, maybe forty. "Does this mean you're a lawyer, but with ethics?"

"It happens."

"No it doesn't." Frank laughed, a deep, masculine sound that Judy liked. She always thought you could tell a lot about a man by his laugh, but all she could tell by Frank's laugh was that she hadn't dated anyone in a long time.

"I'm an ethical lawyer, and as an ethical matter, you can tell me stuff. And I can listen. Ethically, of course."

"I talk and you listen? Can women do that?"

Judy laughed, then sobered at the thought they

were flirting, graveside. At least she suspected she was flirting, though she hadn't meant to. In legal terms, she didn't have the intent to flirt; it had sneaked up on her. She realized she'd liked Frank from the moment he tried to deck the cop. "How about you talk, I'll listen? We'll leave the politics out of it."

"Excellent." Frank turned again to his parents' grave, when his smile faded. "Maybe we should take a walk."

"Good idea," she said, and fell into step beside Frank as he strolled down the grassy row between the graves toward a gravel road. He seemed to breathe a little easier.

"My grandfather's wife—my grandmother—was killed by Angelo Coluzzi, in Italy. My grand-mother had been seeing Coluzzi when she met my grandfather, and she accepted my grandfather's marriage proposal over Coluzzi's. Coluzzi could never live it down. He lost face. He hated my grandfather for it. And he killed her. Everybody in the neighborhood knows it."

"What neighborhood?"

"Our block of South Philly. It's one of the most solidly Italian blocks in South Philly, still. The Korean and the Vietnamese, they're right next door, but this block is so solid that everybody came from the same region in Italy, from Abruzzo. All the families knew each other over there and everybody knew the Coluzzis, a wealthy family. A powerful family. Fascists."

"I see," Judy said, hearing an echo of his grandfather's contempt in Frank's voice.

"There was no prosecution of the murder. The Coluzzis had the juice to keep a lid on it. Their power was increasing, and when war broke out, my grandmother, she just got lost in the shuffle." His voice trailed off for a moment, and Judy suppressed the urge to ask him for details. They walked down the gravel footpath as it wound past low-lying hostas, sharp fronds of tiger lilies yet to bloom, and purple alyssum that crept over rocks at the borders. The air under the trees they passed was cool. Frank's Timberlands crunched on the gravel, and Judy was glad for the first time today that she'd worn clogs.

After a time Frank said, "It was a different world then, and another time. My grandfather tried to get her murder prosecuted and almost lost his own life in the process."

"How?"

"They threatened him. Vandalized his house. Fire-bombed his car."

"Who did?"

"Angelo Coluzzi, or men who worked for him. Blackshirts."

"How do you know? Were they caught?"

"Of course not. We just know. Everybody knows, even today."

Judy raised an eyebrow. It sounded like assumption piled on assumption, but this wasn't the time to argue it. She needed information. "So what did your grandfather do about it?"

"He just moved. He didn't retaliate, even when they bombed his car. He left the country with his son—my father, Frank Sr.—who was two at the time. They settled here. Gave up farming, started laying brick, like lots of immigrants from the region. My grandfather tried to accept what had happened to his wife. He went on and raised his son, and his birds."

"Birds?"

"He keeps pigeons. Homing pigeons, but they race. He's amazing at it. You should see. He spends all his time outside with them, teaching them, exercising them, tossing them—"

"Tossing?"

"It means letting them out on training runs, so they learn how to find their way back to the loft. He spends hours sitting with them outside, watching them fly." Frank brightened at the thought, but it wasn't the type of detail Judy needed right now.

"You were saying, about when he immigrated." They walked down the path into the sun, and Frank winced at the sudden light.

"Then there was the accident. My father, my mother. I know it was just an accident but my grandfather, he believed Angelo Coluzzi did it. You must have heard of the family. Angelo, and his two sons, John and Marco. They own a big construction company in South Philly. They build strip malls and have houses in the Estates. Have you heard of them?"

Judy shook her head. She knew next to nothing about construction.

"They're a sick, sick family." Frank was still wincing, and Judy realized it wasn't the sunlight. Duh. "My grandfather believes Angelo Coluzzi bombed my parents' truck, like they had with his car, in Italy. And after they died, he just went downhill. He said it never would have happened if he'd retaliated for my grandmother. He thinks if he'd honored the vendetta, his son would be alive today."

"Vendetta? What vendetta?" Judy had heard of it from the movies but couldn't believe it had any application today.

"It's a blood feud. A vindication of your rights, of your family's rights. An eye for an eye. It grew up in a country where the law was of no help, not to the little guy like my grandfather. He doesn't look to the law to save him, or to punish him. A vendetta has to be honored, in my culture, his culture."

Judy was thinking that Italians raised emotions

to an art form, but didn't say anything for fear of being hit, or hugged.

"And so he just lost it. After my parents died, he became more and more depressed. And he was getting older. It didn't help." Frank stopped short on the path and turned to her, in appeal. "He's a peaceful man. You know, he can't even cull out his own pigeons. He won't kill any of them. He keeps the slow ones and the old ones. He's gentle. You can see that, can't you?"

"Yes," Judy answered, meaning it. "It was hard to imagine him killing anybody."

"He wouldn't have killed Coluzzi if he didn't think he was put to it. He didn't, all those years. Think about that. The Coluzzis moved to Philadelphia, only two blocks away, and every day my grandfather lived with the fact that his wife's murderer was his neighbor. My father lived with that knowledge and took grief from the Coluzzis for years. They practically ruined his business, but my grandfather wouldn't let him take revenge. My grandfather had a **right** to take revenge, and he never used it."

Judy looked over. "Nobody has a right to kill anybody else."

"Sure they do. In war, or in self-defense. To satisfy the death penalty. Even if you're an abused wife. This society, this culture, kills all the time. Isn't that right?"

"But—"

"There's more death, more killing, in America than anywhere on the face of the earth. We justify killing in lots of circumstances. So why not if somebody kills your wife, your son, and **his** wife? Don't you have a right to kill?"

"No, you don't, and in any event your grandfather didn't know that Coluzzi killed your parents. In fact, you think he did."

"But my grandfather takes it as gospel, and for all I know, he may be right. You have to look at it his way, if it's his state of mind you're talking about, don't you?" Frank's eyes searched hers with an openness Judy found disarming, but her legal training resisted his words.

"People can't go around killing each other. That's what a system of laws is designed to prevent."

"But they **do**, in my grandfather's world, go around killing each other. That's what happened to him. And now the ones who wronged him have been punished." Frank shook his head, and a shadow from the long branches of the oak tree above flickered over his pained features. "What good would it do to punish my grandfather? He's not going to hurt anybody else."

"That's not the point."

"No?" Frank looked at the miniature American flags fluttering when a breeze came along. His gaze rested on a monument that read CIARDI, behind a spray of tall, lavender irises, some of their flowers shriveled to brown and curling at the edges. "The man is seventy-nine. This is what's next for him—old flowers and gravestones. This cemetery. Next to his son."

Judy couldn't suppress her sympathy, then forced herself to think like a lawyer, without a trace of human emotion. "None of this will help me defend him."

"Are you sure?" Frank turned suddenly. "I was thinking maybe you could try an insanity defense or something like that."

"The legal standard for insanity is too high." Judy shook her head. "God knows what evidence they have against your grandfather, but if this is his story, it doesn't provide any defense at all. There's no legal excuse for murder that fits here."

"Not even a broken heart?" Frank asked, and he looked at Judy as if it were more than rhetorical.

"Not even that."

"So where's the justice, in the law?"

Judy didn't know how to answer. Her only certainty was that she wanted to take the case.

All she had to do was convince the boss.

# 6

"You did what?" Bennie shouted, and Judy had a déjà vu. Either that or Bennie had said the same thing to her 3,462,430 times before. Judy fleetingly considered putting **You did what?** on a T-shirt, but then she'd get fired for sure. Bennie was that angry. "You went to the Roundhouse? You had no right to do that!"

Judy faced Bennie Rosato in the boss's office, sitting across from a large desk that was almost as cluttered as Judy's. Bennie's office was the same size as an associate's, evidence of her egalitarian ethic, and her bookshelves were stuffed with casebooks, law reviews, and black binders of speeches and articles. Awards from civil rights organizations and First Amendment groups covered the walls. In a far corner sat a pile of running clothes and Sauconys, their rubber-soled toes curled up from wear. In short, it could have been Judy's office. She didn't get it. She and Bennie were more alike than they were different, so why did they fight so much?

"You met with the defendant's family? You went to a grave site? You told him you'd take the case, **at his parents' grave**? And you don't have a single detail of the crime or the evidence against this man!"

Judy swallowed hard. "Bennie, I swear, I made it very clear that the firm hasn't filed an entry of appearance."

"Oh, please! It's just technical whether you entered an appearance. You were there. You **appeared**." Bennie's blue eyes flared, and she yanked off a khaki suit jacket and smoothed it out before she jammed the neck down onto a coatrack behind her leather chair.

"I told the cops it was only temporary."

"Which means nothing. Besides, it's not just the cops, it's the client. It's the grandson. You went to a **grave**?" Bennie ran a hand through a tangle of light hair that fell to shoulders sagging in disappointment under a linen shirt. "We're blocked in. You don't appear and then disappear. At least I don't. How do you think a law firm gets any credibility? Our integrity's on the line. **My** integrity."

"Look, it's me on the line, not you. I got us into this, and I'll get us out. I want to represent Pigeon Tony." Judy felt good taking a stand, but Bennie looked underwhelmed.

"Oh, you do?" Bennie paced beside her chair, too aggravated to stay still. At six feet tall, a muscular ex-rower and all-around tough-as-nails trial lawyer, Bennie Rosato intimidated associates, opposing counsel, and major felons. Everybody except Judy, who had yet to figure out why she wasn't as scared as she should be. Maybe after a childhood filled with lieutenant colonels, she could handle a pissed-off lawyer.

"Ask me if I care what you want," Bennie continued. "I own this firm. I employ you. That means you'll represent who I tell you to represent."

"You said you wanted us to develop our own clients," Judy argued, though she knew she'd be better shutting up, like Ali letting Foreman punch himself out. Yet she couldn't help but swing. Maybe it was the boxing lessons she'd taken. "I would think you'd welcome some initiative. Most firms think it's a basis for partnership decisions."

"In my firm, you bring in the client, then you take it to me, and I decide if you can take it. You don't decide on your own." Bennie glared. "And were you thinking about making partner when you took the case? Is that what you're trying to sell me?"

Judy felt her face flush. What was the matter with her? Why was she making such a bogus argument? "Not really."

"Then don't argue what you don't believe in. Rule number one, in law and in life." Bennie's voice went brittle as ice. Arms akimbo, her hands clutched her hips, wrinkling her skirt. "Now, why did you go down to the Roundhouse? And why do you want to represent Lucia?"

Judy tried to collect her thoughts. This was serious stuff. She had never asked to represent a client before, especially one who was guilty. It felt like the onset of adulthood, but maybe growing up didn't mean automatically resisting everything Bennie said. Judy flashed on her first image of Pigeon Tony, so small in the overlarge prison jumpsuit. Then the granite memorial to the Lucias, so eloquent in its dark silence. And finally Frank's grief at the site.

"Well?"

Judy took a deep breath. "If what they tell me is true, then there is an injustice here, and I think I want to help Pigeon Tony. I mean, if it's true, he's an old man who had a lifelong heartache. He tried to set it aside, and that effort ended up in the death of his own son and daughter-in-law. He chose peace, and all he got was war. Most people who kill are bad men. Instead, Pigeon Tony seems like a good man, who killed someone." Judy heard herself, and only then did she realize that that was how she felt. Insight wasn't her strong suit, but she was learning, and a new certainty steeled her. "Even if you fire me, I'll still take the case."

"You would?"

"Yes."

Bennie stood stock-still. The crease in her fore-head relaxed, and the angry redness ebbed from her cheeks. Judy hoped it wasn't the peace that comes over bosses before they shitcan you.

"Please don't fire me, by the way. I couldn't find another firm that would let me dress as funny."

Bennie laughed softly and sat down in her deep chair. "Oh, well."

"Does this mean I can keep him?"

Bennie didn't answer but picked up a coffee mug from her desk, which read I CAN SMELL FEAR. Judy was pretty sure it was a joke. Bennie tilted it to peek inside. "Empty. What else can go wrong?"

"I'll take care of him. I'll walk him every day."

Bennie half smiled, gazing into the empty mug as if coffee would materialize through an act of sheer will. "Can Lucia afford us?"

"I don't know. I didn't ask."

"Of course you didn't."

"I'll find out, if you let me keep him."

The coffee mug clattered to an upright position. "All right, fine. You win, but you'll do it under my supervision."

"Wahoo!"

"Hold your applause." Bennie waved her into silence. "You'll report to me at every stage of the proceedings."

"Agreed."

"You'll still be responsible for your other matters. You have that antitrust article to do—get a draft to me on time. The journal editor told me they've been waiting on it to cite-check. Don't screw around." Bennie thought a minute. "As I recall, you have seven other fairly active cases, all civil. They have to be worked, just as before. Those clients were there first and they didn't kill anybody."

"Yes, sir."

Bennie ignored it. "Finally, since you didn't bother to see if Lucia could pay for your services, your services to him are free. That means the time you spend on this matter is your own. You bill none of it, to him or to me. That'll teach you."

It took Judy aback, but she saw the rightness of it. "Fair enough. My money where my mouth is."

"And you're on a short leash. Stay in touch on every decision. That's your final punishment for showing initiative. You have to spend time with me."

"What doesn't kill me makes me stronger," Judy said, then ducked as a pencil came flying at her.

"Don't press your luck, Carrier. This firm is doing better than when we started. You ain't the only law review editor in the sea. Now get out of my office. One of us has to make some money." Bennie hit a key on her keyboard, opening her e-mail, and Judy rose happily, despite the situation. She had gotten the case, even if she'd have to work her ass off. But there was a problem, and it nagged at her.

"One last question. What do I do about representing a guilty defendant?"

"Why are you asking me?" Bennie didn't look away from her e-mail. "You took the case, you have to answer it for yourself."

Judy blinked at the sharpness of the response. So much for bonding. "Uh, well, I mean, I know he's entitled to a defense, but I also know he's guilty. It bothers me, even though it's not supposed to, as a legal matter."

"You always were academic, Carrier, so here's the short course." Bennie clicked away, responding to one e-mail after another. "Under the Code of Professional Responsibility, your only ethical constraint is that you can't put him up on the stand and elicit that he's innocent if you know he's guilty. That's suborning perjury, essentially permitting a known falsehood to go to the court. And obviously, Code or no, I wouldn't represent to the jury in your opening or closing that he's innocent."

"I wouldn't do that."

"I didn't think so. You're a lousy liar anyway. I don't know how you got out of law school." Bennie hit "send" and opened the next e-mail, and Judy suddenly didn't know how to talk to her.

"I meant more . . . as an emotional matter. Have you ever represented a guilty defendant?"

"I did in the old days, when I took mostly murder cases. Frankly, it's why I got out." Bennie's large hands covered the keyboard as she typed another response, giving no indication she remembered that anybody else shared the room.

"So how did you handle it?" Judy asked anyway. "Defending the principle, not the person? Innocent until proven guilty?"

"It doesn't matter how I dealt with it," Bennie answered, typing away. "It only matters how you deal with it. You want to defend a guilty man? Do it your way."

Judy detected a change in Bennie's voice. It softened, though she still didn't look up from her computer. "Can you give me a hint or is that against the rules?"

Her fingers poised expertly over the keyboard, Bennie raised her eyes, and Judy was surprised to see them filled with concern, not indifference. "I told you, don't argue what you don't believe in. The converse is also true. Do you believe in him?"

"I think so."

"Figure it out. Figure out if he's guilty or innocent, in your own mind. But don't analyze it as a legal matter or an academic question. That's too abstract, too safe. Don't be a judge, there'll be a judge there already. He's the one in black. You be the advocate."

Judy was understanding. She knew she tended to be a little academic. It had gotten her A's in law school, but nowhere else. "But let's say that I decide that he's innocent, in my own mind. What good does that do him?"

"It will help you build a defense. If you believe in him, your conviction will carry through to the judge and the jury. In your voice, in your manner, in everything you do. If you don't believe in him, Lucia doesn't have a chance." Bennie's attention returned to her monitor. "And you're the worst thing that ever happened to him."

The words shut Judy down, and she stood rooted for a minute, listening to the quiet tapping of the keys. Outside the door, phones rang and lawyers yapped, but the workaday sounds receded. Judy had the sinking feeling she had bitten off more than she could chew—and she had one of the biggest mouths in the city.

"Don't you have an arraignment to go to?" Bennie asked, breaking the silence. "It's tough to get bail for murder. Wear a suit jacket over your dress. And lose the shoes. You can borrow my brown pumps from the closet in reception. I got a whole second wardrobe in there. You're welcome to all of it."

Judy checked her watch. It was almost three. She had to get downtown. She'd have to set aside her angst and her clogs. She murmured a hurried thank-you and let herself out of the office as Bennie returned to her e-mail.

Judy couldn't know that after she left, Bennie spent a long time staring at the computer screen, unable to write a single word.

# 7

The press thronged outside the Criminal Justice Center, spilling off the curb and onto Filbert Street, a colonial street wide enough to accommodate only a single horse and buggy, not reporters and their egos. Both blocked traffic, waiting for something to happen, chatting in the sunshine and blowing puffs of cigarette smoke into the clear air. Judy wondered what case they were feeding on this time.

"There she is!" a photographer with a light meter around his neck shouted, turning to Judy. "Ms. Carrier, just one shot!" "Over here, Ms. Carrier!"

Judy was surprised but didn't break stride. She couldn't, in Bennie's too-big pumps. She hurried ahead, dragging her heels across the cobblestones, feeling like a kid dressing up as a lawyer, in case anybody missed the point. Her thoughts raced ahead. How did the press know about the case? Why did they care? They were all turning to her.

Reporters flicked aside their cigarettes. Cameramen hoisted videocameras to their shoulders. Stringers surged toward her with notebooks in hand. She put her head down and wobbled through the crowd as it rushed to meet her.

"Ms. Carrier, is Bennie Rosato on this case for Tony Lucia?" "Ms. Carrier, is he guilty or innocent?" "Judy, is Mary DiNunzio gonna work with you on the case?" "Ms. Carrier, the Coluzzi family is already on record as saying your client's the killer. Any comment?"

Judy plowed shakily ahead, taking a bead on the brass revolving door at the courthouse entrance. It wasn't the worst thing to be swarmed by reporters. Bennie and Mary never liked it, but Judy had played coed rugby in her time. Reporters jostled her, but she jostled them back. Justice as contact sport. She got bumped in the arm by a TV camera but didn't stop to flip the bird. It might not look professional on tape.

"Ms. Carrier, what do you think about the Commonwealth's evidence?" "Will Mr. Lucia plead guilty?" "Do you think he'll get bail?"

"No comment!" Judy shouted, hustling toward the entrance. Over the door the stained-glass mural caught the sunlight in vivid yellows, blues, and golds, but she didn't pause to enjoy it as she usually did. She had a pigeon to defend, and from the research she had done, it was iffy whether he'd get bail. The case law was against it; her only hope was his age and record. The reporters bumped her around and shouted questions she wouldn't answer, to the amusement of a blue sea of cops in summer uniforms, waiting by the door to be called to testify. A couple of civilians stood nearest the door with them, and Judy had almost tottered to the threshold when she felt a strong hand on her arm and looked over in irritation.

"No comment," she said, but the man with the grip on her arm didn't look like a reporter. He was middle-aged and heavyset, with greased hair and a polyester polo shirt. His eyes were brown slits and his expression looked distinctly unfriendly to Judy. "Let go of my arm," she said, wrenching it free.

"Just wanted to say hello to you, Miss Carrier." He smiled for the cameras. Judy heard the whining of motor drives and the whirring of videotape recording the moment. "My name's John Coluzzi. My father was Angelo Coluzzi. You heard of him. He was murdered by your client."

Judy flushed. There was nothing she could say. It was all true. Her face felt aflame.

"He broke my father's neck, Miss Carrier. Snapped it like it was one of his birds."

Judy's mouth went dry. Was that how Pigeon Tony had done it? It seemed inconceivable.

"I come down here to see what kind of piece-of-shit lawyer you were. You oughta be ashamed of yourself," Coluzzi said, almost spitting in fresh sorrow, and Judy fumbled for words she felt compelled to say, because the cameras were watching them. Her client's life was at stake, and this tape could be Film at 11.

"I'm sorry for your loss, Mr. Coluzzi," she said, and broke away, hurrying for the entrance to the courthouse. Not knowing who was the bad guy, Angelo Coluzzi or Pigeon Tony.

And feeling suddenly that she was worse than both of them put together.

The arraignment courtroom in the basement of the Criminal Justice Center defied the TV stereotype of how a courtroom should look, ironically because it was a TV studio. Philadelphia, like most major American cities, had recently adopted arraignment by television, so that the arraignment courtroom had become a stage set, the same width but only half as long as the conventional courtroom. The bar of the court was separated from the gallery by a wall-to-wall span of soundproof glass, and hidden microphones carried the judge's words to the gallery, though not vice versa.

The courtroom contained the typical judge's dais and counsel tables, but a huge television near the dais dominated the room. The only program playing was **The Defendant Show**. Each defendant appeared in huge close-up on the monitor while the charges against him were read, and he got only

three minutes of face time, less than the average
bank of commercials. Defendants appeared one
after the next, sometimes thirty in a row, and
when they were finished, the bail commissioner
could be heard to say, "Get off the screen."

Judy, entering the slick courtroom set, shuddered at the sight. Not only was it bizarre, it was
unconstitutional; if the defendant wanted to consult with his lawyer, he could do so only by a special telephone in the cell, and his guard would
hear anything he said. Likewise, if she wanted to
advise him, she could use the phone, but the
entire courtroom—including the bail commissioner, her opponent the Commonwealth, and
even the gallery—could hear everything she said.
Judy thought it violated the right to counsel, but
nobody was asking her or had the money to bring
a test case against the procedure, which had
gained nationwide acceptance in all its variations.
The government had gotten away with it only
because arraignments were considered a routine
criminal procedure, but to Judy no procedure was
routine if somebody lost his liberty.

She walked down the aisle, her ankles hurting
and her feeling of unease intensifying. The gallery
was oddly packed, with spectators sitting shoulder
to shoulder, jammed together in light clothes.
Why was everybody here? Could this really be for
her case? And who had told the reporters to come?

She flashed on John Coluzzi outside the courthouse and felt her own face grow hot. Then she
thought of Bennie and what she'd said, **If you
don't believe in him, Lucia doesn't have a
chance.**

Judy shook it off as she caught Frank's eye in the
front row on the right. Turning only slightly in
his seat, his jeans jacket replaced by a corduroy
sport jacket, he smiled with the tension of the
moment, his dark eyes obviously pained. In contrast, Mr. DiNunzio sat next to him in the front
row with a group of older men, and when he spotted her, started pumping his hand with an enthusiasm usually reserved for the President of the
United States. In a better mood Judy would have
laughed.

She strode toward them, noticing that every
head on the right turned toward her. At first she
thought it was her brown pumps attracting the
attention, until she realized that spectators on that
side of the gallery—old men, women, young children, and family of all kinds—were gazing at her
adoringly, as if she were a bride coming down an
aisle. Evidently word had spread that she was
defending Pigeon Tony, and the whole village had
turned out. Luckily Judy reached the bar of the
court before anybody burst into applause.

Mr. DiNunzio rose to his heavy orthopedic shoes
and hugged her instantly, squeezing Frank's head

between them. "Judy, I'm so happy to see you. Thank you so much," he said, though the words got trapped somewhere in Judy's hair.

"That's okay, Mr. DiNunzio. Everything is going be okay." She was thinking just the opposite, but she said it reflexively, breathing in his smell of scented mothballs and fresh starch, and patting his back through the wool sweater he wore no matter what season. It was brown, as they all were, a lumpy cardigan that felt to Judy like a security blanket, even though he wasn't even her father. Under it he had on a white shirt with a knotted tie and old-fashioned brown pants, and Judy had the sense that it was his church clothes. She gentled him back into the pew. "Just sit down and leave it to me. We're on the case officially now."

"Thank God. Thank you. And my wife, she says to tell you hello. She stayed home today, with Mary." He sounded apologetic and seemed not to realize that the spectators in the gallery were craning their necks to overhear their conversation. "She wished she could be here, you know that. They both do. But Judy, you understand."

"Of course I do, my goodness. And thanks for taking such wonderful care of my best friend." Out of the corner of her eye Judy checked the television monitor, but it wasn't showing Pigeon Tony yet. The face of a young black woman filled the screen, and she was tearful. Her lawyer, a public defender, argued her case for bail on the other side of the plastic divider, his mouth moving like a TV on mute.

"I want you to meet my friends, Judy," Mr. DiNunzio said, turning to his right. Beside him sat a row of men easily his age or in their eighties. They were dressed remarkably like him, with sweaters over white shirts and thin ties left over from a working life in a different era. Mr. DiNunzio waved a wrinkled hand at the man closest to him, who was shaped like a friendly meatball. "This here is my friend Tony LoMonaco from down the block. He knows Pigeon Tony from the club."

"The club?" Judy doubted it was the kind of club her parents meant when they said "the club."

"The pigeon-racing club, you know," Mr. DiNunzio said, and Judy remembered.

"Of course. Happy to meet you, Mr. LoMonaco." She shook his hand, catching a whiff of the cigar smoke that clung to his clothes, and surmised that he was Tony-From-Down-The-Block of cigar-buying fame.

Judy itched to finish the pleasantries. She had an arraignment to prepare for, at least mentally, and an unusual case of courtroom jitters. The encounter with John Coluzzi had rattled her, and her peripheral vision had found him sitting in the front row of the gallery on the left side of the courtroom. A shorter man sitting next to him struck a similarly hostile pose, and Judy figured he must be John's brother, Marco, whom Frank had told her about. The two men, John the heavier of the two, anchored the grim-faced crowd around them, with whom she was obviously unpopular. If the right side of the courtroom was the Lucia cheering section, the left was the Coluzzi clan, sitting side by side with only a carpeted courtroom aisle between them, like a modern-day Maginot Line.

Judy felt an intuitive tingle of fear. It struck her that Angelo Coluzzi's death could mean retaliation, as deadly as if the courtroom had been transported to Sicily. And the surviving sons, John and Marco, were very much alive; Marco, in a sharp suit and tie, looked like the more intelligent of the two, and Judy was guessing it was he who ran the business. But it was John's meaty arm that encircled a very old woman in a black dress, dabbing at her aged, red eyes with a balled-up Kleenex. She had to be his mother, Angelo Coluzzi's widow. **He broke my father's neck, Miss Carrier. Snapped it like it was one of his birds.** Judy looked away, her thoughts racing, but Mr. DiNunzio was tugging at her sleeve.

"And this young man here is my friend Tony Pensiera," Mr. DiNunzio was saying. "We call him Tony Two Feet, but you can call him Feet for short." He laughed, as did the man sitting next to him, a thin man who wore glasses with frames like Mr. Potatohead. His feet looked normal to Judy.

"Pleased to meet you, Mr. Feet," she said, drawing a smile from Mr. DiNunzio, as well as from Feet himself and her eavesdropping fans.

"Mr. Feet. I like that. Mr. Feet." Feet grinned, showing a silver tooth in front, which led Judy to wonder briefly why they didn't call him Tooth. The remaining old men in the row edged forward, shaky hands extended with arthritic fingers, trying to meet her, but she begged off with a quick apology.

"I'd like to meet you, but I have to get to the office. We'll talk later, if that's okay." They withdrew their hands and eased back into the sleek pews, nodding with approval. She could clearly do no wrong. They were a brown-pumps kind of crowd. With a quick glance at Frank, she took her leave and buzzed herself into the door in the plastic divider, standing with her back to it until the last case concluded.

Pigeon Tony's face popped onto the screen five minutes later, his appearance giving Judy a start. The close-up magnified every line in his tan face, turning wrinkles into fissures in the brown earth of his skin. The confusion furrowing his brow made him look like Methuselah. His round eyes darted back and forth; he was obviously unsure about whether to look into the camera lens, and disoriented and frightened by the procedure. It was impossible to square the helpless image with someone who would intentionally break the neck of another man. She remembered Frank's words, **You know, he can't even cull out his own pigeons, he won't kill any of them.** But there was no time to puzzle it out now.

Judy moved to counsel table as the public defender stepped deferentially aside. "Your Honor, my name is Judy Carrier and I represent the defendant in this matter, Anthony Lucia," she said, then sat down.

"So Mr. Lucia has private counsel," the bail commissioner said noncommittally as he shifted stacks of docket sheets on the dais. Bail commissioners weren't judges, though this one wore judicial robes, a tie with a collar pin, and the harassed expression of a man who presided over 150 bail cases a day. His light blue eyes looked beleaguered behind tortoiseshell reading glasses. "We're ready to go, Bailiff. Where's defendant Anthony Lucia?"

As if on cue, the TV sound burst to life with a crackle, and Pigeon Tony was whispering, " 'Allo? 'Allo?"

Judy worried that he couldn't understand what was happening, and a ripple of unrest ran through the courtroom gallery as soon as they heard his trembling voice over the microphones; the Lucia side of the courtroom stricken at seeing Pigeon

Tony in jail, the Coluzzi side furious at seeing him alive. Judy's mouth went dry.

The bail commissioner remained insulated on his side of the bulletproof plastic. "This is Commonwealth versus Lucia," he began, reciting the docket number, then looking at the camera facing him, which would transmit his image to a television in Pigeon Tony's cell. "Mr. Lucia, you have been charged on a general charge of murder, do you understand?"

" 'Allo? Who is?" Pigeon Tony kept whispering, squinting at the camera lens.

"Mr. Lucia, this is the bail commissioner speaking to you. I am the judge. Look directly into the camera." The bail commissioner glared into his camera, posing for a fairly cranky photo op. "Mr. Lucia, do you need an interpreter? We have a Spanish interpreter at your location, I believe."

Judy shook her head. "Your Honor, he's Italian. A member of his family could translate if there's no translator available."

"No, that wouldn't be kosher. Let's see if he gets it. Mr. Lucia," the bail commissioner said loudly, as if that would help. "Do you understand that you have been charged with murder?"

"Si, si. Murder. Judge? Is judge?" Pigeon Tony still didn't look at the camera, and Judy's anxiety segued into fear. If Pigeon Tony understood it was the judge, he might blurt out the truth. Anything he said in open court would be admissible at trial. An admission now could kill him.

Oh, no. Judy's hand crept toward the black telephone on counsel table, which would connect her directly to Pigeon Tony. She wouldn't use it unless she had to, since everybody and his dog would hear everything. Pigeon Tony couldn't be counted on to get any hidden messages, and **please don't confess** might tip off the Commonwealth.

"Yes, I am the judge. Excellent, Mr. Lucia." The bail commissioner looked over his glasses at the prosecutor's table. "Is the Commonwealth opposing bail in this matter?"

"We are, Your Honor," answered the prosecutor. Judging from his spiky haircut and black suit, he was a recent law school graduate who had drawn the rotating duty of arraignment court. "As you know, murder is not typically a bailable offense in the county, and this was a particularly heinous murder of an eighty-year-old man. The Commonwealth argues that bail should not be granted."

Pigeon Tony's mouth opened as if he were going to speak.

"Your Honor," Judy said quickly, moving her hand to the phone, "the defense argues that Mr. Lucia is certainly entitled to bail. His criminal record is spotless, and he obviously poses no risk to the population of the city. Nor does he, at almost eighty years of age, pose any flight risk at all."

"Does he have any roots in the city, Ms. Carrier?" the commissioner asked, from the standard checklist for determining whether bail was appropriate.

"He has significant roots in the city, including his grandson, Frank Lucia, who is fully prepared to meet his bail." Judy gestured for emphasis at the right side of the gallery, and they started waving back so wildly she wondered if they thought they were on camera, like a studio audience on **The Jerry Springer Show.** "As you can see, his entire extended family and all his friends support him and are here for this proceeding. He isn't going anywhere, Judge."

"Judge? Where judge?" Pigeon Tony began to fidget in his chair, leaning to the side and peering behind the camera. "Judge, you see me?" He tried to get up out of his chair, exposing the handcuffs that locked him there, and Judy couldn't take it anymore and grabbed the black telephone.

"Mr. Lucia, this is Judy speaking. Pick up the telephone. Answer the telephone," she said quickly into the receiver. The phone should have been ringing in the special cell, and a second later she heard it, then the hollow sound of the turnkey telling Pigeon Tony to pick up.

"Come?" he asked in confusion, turning off-screen to the guard, who finally gave up telling him to pick up and reached across to the ringing phone and picked it up himself. The courtroom TV screen showed a sleeve of tan uniform thrusting a black receiver at Pigeon Tony, and he recoiled as if it were a cobra. With prodding, he reached for the telephone cautiously, only partly because of his handcuffs, and answered it as if he had never answered one before. "**Si? Chi è?**" he said, keeping his distance from the receiver, and Judy translated immediately. It did sound like Latin!

"This is Judy, Mr. Lucia. Remember me, Judy? Your lawyer?" She had to get them out of court, even TV court, fast. The arraignment had already lasted too long. "Listen to me carefully. Please stay in your seat and answer only the questions the judge asks you."

"Judy?" Pigeon Tony burst into a grin of recognition. "Is Judy, with big mouth?"

"Yes! Right!" It was the first time she was happy to admit it, and she could see that the gallery was laughing.

The bail commissioner banged his gavel and addressed the prosecutor. "Counsel, given Mr. Lucia's trouble with the common telephone, I find it hard to believe that he could negotiate the flight schedules of the Philadelphia airport. I find he poses no risk of flight and order bail to be set at twenty-five thousand dollars." The commissioner faced the camera. "Mr. Lucia, you will be free as soon as your bail is paid. You must come back and appear at your preliminary hearing. Please sign the subpoena regarding your next court appearance. It's a paper in front of you. Now, get—"

"Judge? Is judge?" Pigeon Tony started saying into his telephone receiver, and Judy went into action, doing what she did best. Talking.

"That's enough, Mr. Lucia. It's time to go home. Hang up the phone and you can go home."

"Judy? Where judge? **Now** we talk to judge?" Pigeon Tony asked, and Judy's heart stopped. She was about to start filibustering when the bail commissioner banged his gavel again.

"Mr. Lucia, you and I have done enough talking for one day, and we have a lot of cases to get to. This concludes your arraignment. Please sign the paper in front of you before you go back to your cell. Ask the turnkey to help you if need be, sir."

Suddenly Pigeon Tony's face vanished from the screen, which went black, and Judy almost cried with relief. She hung up the phone, grabbed her briefcase, and turned to leave as another defendant materialized on the screen and the public defender reclaimed his desk. She hadn't been so glad to see a TV show end since **Happy Days**. And she had won. Pigeon Tony would be set free. The Lucia side of the gallery was on its feet, hugging each other with happiness.

Judy felt almost high as she opened the door in the plastic divider, and Frank, Mr. DiNunzio, the fragrant Tony-From-Down-The-Block LoMonaco, and glasses-wearing Tony Two Feet Pensiera rushed to sweep her up, thanking, hugging, and congratulating her. She had never experienced such emotion, such total love coming from complete strangers, and she found herself caught up in it, laughing with delight, forgetting every last doubt about the case.

Until the shouting began.

And the first punch was thrown.

# 8

Judy had never witnessed such a scene in any of the conference rooms at Rosato & Associates before, or in any other law firm, for that matter. Seated around the sleek, polished walnut table were a trio of bruised and battered Italian octogenarians, slumping in rumpled and bloodied shirts behind medicinal cups of coffee. Fresh legal pads lay unnoticed in the center of the table with sharpened pencils piled in a ready-for-business logjam, and the state-of-the-art gray conferencing phone went untouched. A huge bank of glistening picture windows showed off a modern skyline of granite skyscrapers and mirrored glass columns, and though it was the best view in the city, the old men around the table hurt too much to be impressed.

Judy surveyed the damage as she doled out Tylenol Extra Strength. At least no one had to go to the hospital. Mr. DiNunzio had taken a mean uppercut to the chin, which swelled unhappily, but he didn't need stitches and had given as good as he got. Tony-From-Down-The-Block had shown surprising agility despite his weight, being the first to respond to the Coluzzi clan's attack, especially aggravated when someone called him a "fat bastard."

Frank sustained a gash over his right eye—luckily the bleeding had stopped—and had been the most effective fighter, largely because he was so tall and muscular, in addition to being the only male under age seventy. He had almost knocked out the more heavyweight John Coluzzi when a combined army of courthouse security and uniformed cops appeared in the courtroom, summoned by a hysterical bail commissioner. The cops broke up the fight, separating the warring tribes and threatening hard time until they dispersed to their separate corners of South Philadelphia. No Lucia had gone to jail only because they had a fairly mouthy blonde on retainer, whose listing to the right was barely detectable.

Judy snapped closed the Tylenol jug and watched Frank apply a butterfly Band-Aid to the bald noggin of Tony Two Feet, who had proved, not surprisingly, to excel at kicking Coluzzis in the shins. Unfortunately, his Mr. Potatohead-eyeglasses had been knocked off in the brawl and nestled broken in his shirt pocket, their dark frames showing through the thin fabric.

And for Judy's part in the battle, she had found

herself relegated to the sidelines, apparently viewed as Switzerland by the Coluzzis. After she'd lost one of Bennie's brown pumps in the fussing, which was no great loss, she helped the cops bring the mess to a close. Pigeon Tony was unscathed only because he hadn't been at the fistfight and had still been trapped in TV custody. Judy was at present rethinking her position on televised arraignments. They were an excellent idea where Italians were involved.

She stood at the head of the table. "Here comes the lecture. First of all, we're damn lucky that the judge didn't revoke Pigeon Tony's bail, and I hope all of you know it. You have to understand right here and right now that we are not going to run this case this way. I may be a slow learner, but I'm getting the idea. The Lucias hate the Coluzzis, and the Coluzzis hate the Lucias. But right now that doesn't matter. I cannot and will not defend Pigeon Tony in this case if you people can't control yourselves." Judy wasn't used to being so dictatorial, but she was starting to like the power femme thing, even though her version of it sounded like a gym teacher. She wished for a whistle on a gimp lanyard, in school colors. "You people have to think a lot more long-term than you have been. You can't be so emotional all the time."

Pigeon Tony blinked. Mr. DiNunzio looked grave. Tony Two Feet hung his head.

Frank smiled, despite a goose egg rising on his

right cheekbone. He stood at the opposite end of the table, resting his hands on the back of Pigeon Tony's chair. "Need I remind you that we come by it honestly?"

"Need I remind you that your grandfather's life is at stake?" Judy watched his smile fade. "Get over yourselves. Being Italian is no excuse for bad behavior any longer. In any event, not with this lawyer. From now on we do this my way, every step of the way, or Pigeon Tony finds somebody else to represent him."

Pigeon Tony stopped blinking and the corners of his mouth went south.

"Pigeon Tony, listen to me." Judy softened her tone, since even gym teachers had a heart. "Do you understand what I'm saying here?"

"Judy, we no start fight. **Coluzzis** start fight." He made a bony fist with his hand and waved it in the air. "They hit, **then** we hit."

Tony Two Feet nodded in agreement, as did Tony-From-Down-The-Block, and Judy realized she had a fairly tough row to hoe.

"Tonys. Gentlemen. Please. I really don't want to hear 'they started it' from eighty-year-olds. You're grown men, not little boys. You should all know better than that, and you're still not getting it." Judy heard herself and wondered when dodgeball was starting. "This isn't a schoolyard game, or a fight, or even a war. It's a legal case. A matter of law."

"In a war," Frank said coolly, sipping his coffee, and Judy bore down.

"Maybe so. But I run this war or I'm outta here." She picked up her briefcase and walked to the door of the conference room, in case Pigeon Tony missed the point. The fact that it was her own conference room seemed a detail compared with the drama of the demonstration. If she kept this up, she'd be promoted to health teacher and could draw fallopian tubes shaped like moose antlers on the blackboard. "We do it my way, or I'm gone."

"No! Judy!" Pigeon Tony exclaimed, his voice thin with anxiety, and she turned at the door, pivoting on one pump, which was a neat trick in itself.

"You want me to be your lawyer?" she demanded, and his sunburned head went up and down.

"Si, si!"

"You gonna be good?"

"Si, si!"

"No more fighting?"

"Si, si!"

"You promise, like before? I was wondering about that promise, back in the courtroom."

Pigeon Tony kept nodding. "È vero. I promise."

"And all the Lucias have to understand the rules, Pigeon Tony. All the people in the gallery today, in the courtroom. All the neighborhood, the whole damn village, the home team. Got it? No more fighting! Or I go."

"Si, si!"

Mr. DiNunzio rose, upset. "Don't go, Judy. You're right, everything you said. I'll make sure there's no more fighting. I swear it, God as my witness."

The leftover Tonys looked properly contrite. "Okay, you win. No more fighting," Tony Two Feet said, blinking unhappily without his glasses, and Tony-From-Down-The-Block gave a grudging wave.

Judy looked at Frank, who was still sipping his coffee. "Well?"

"Well what?" Frank set his Styrofoam cup down on the table. "Will I promise not to fight when they come after my grandfather? The answer is no."

"Are you nuts?" Judy dropped her briefcase in frustration. "You're not in Naples anymore. It was 1900 a long time ago. You're in Philadelphia, in the new millennium. We have the Internet now, and e-books, and boy bands. Microsoft and Britney Spears. Nobody has to go to the well for water in this town, or pound their socks with rocks. If somebody comes after your grandfather, we'll call the friggin' police!"

"No like police!" Pigeon Tony shouted, banging the table with his hard little fist. "**Io non sono Napoletano!**"

Judy couldn't translate. "What did he say?" she asked Frank.

Frank smiled at the outburst, this time with mirth. "He's insulted that you said he was from Naples. He thinks they're all thieves."

Judy groaned. "Is that all **you** got from what I said?"

"No, but I don't agree with you," Frank said, his tone carrying no accusation. "You say this is a legal case, but when I said it takes place in a war, I meant it. You believe there are rules and law, but a vendetta exists apart from the law. It doesn't care about space and time, and it didn't stop in 1900. It's as current as the memories of the Coluzzis and the Lucias, who grew up in another time, in another country, and whose way of living is very much alive, to them, their sons, and their grandsons."

"Are you defending vendettas?"

"No, I'm explaining them. This one, anyway. You have to understand the way it is, before you can represent my grandfather."

Judy fell momentarily speechless. Frank was turning the tables on her, and she didn't like it much. His voice carried authority and weight, and she couldn't let him win, for Pigeon Tony's sake or her own. Frank's words attacked the law she had been trained in, believed in, and had even come to love. Judy's speechlessness stretched into two moments, which worried her.

"John and Marco Coluzzi are not about to let this pass, Judy. They'll come looking for him. That's what sure as hell is going to happen next. What would you have me do then? He's my grandfather. And your client."

Judy threw up her hands. "If that's true, then why did I just get him out on bail? Why didn't we leave him in jail?"

"No, we did the right thing. He'd be in more danger in jail. On the outside I can protect him, and it's my job to protect him. Your laws are going to be useless."

"Why?"

"Because the Coluzzis are too smart for your laws. They have been so far. They have money and power, and they'll get to him if we let them. Your laws can't arrest anybody until **after** they murder somebody, and sometimes not even then."

Pigeon Tony nodded sadly. "**È vero**," he said, and Judy translated. It sounded like the Latin noun **veritas**. Truth. Both men fell equally grave, their mouths set in identical determination and their Lucia eyes glowing darkly. Grandfather and grandson looked so much alike, because of the way similarities of feature and gesture skip generations, that Judy was taken aback. Maybe it was true, what they were saying. She never would have believed it if she hadn't seen the melee in the courtroom with her own eyes. And if all of this vendetta craziness was true, Pigeon Tony would get killed long before she could get him to trial.

"Fair enough," Judy said to Frank suddenly. "I'll give you that your grandfather may be in jeopardy. But we have to investigate this case, to build a defense. We have to go forward. So you protect him your way, and I'll protect him mine. You fight back, only to save him, and I'll use the law."

Frank broke into a relieved smile. "You want to bet on who wins?"

"I can't take your money," Judy told him. "Now let's go."

Judy had no religion per se, but she did believe in karma, Krispy Kreme doughnuts, and Vincent van Gogh. In fact, she was sure it was her terrific karma that had sent her boss out of the office when she had arrived with her battered clients. She hoped she had enough in her reserve tanks to get out of the conference room as cleanly. She had changed back into her yellow clogs to help her escape, and also for obvious style reasons.

She cracked the conference room door to check if the coast was clear. Her eyes swept the office. A square, open meeting area with fancy blue carpet, ringed by lawyers' offices with secretaries' desks in Dilbert cubicles in front of each. Printers were printing. Keyboards were clacking. Lawyers were yapping. Secretaries were doing the real work. All was in order. And no boss.

Judy snuck out of the conference room with Frank and Mr. DiNunzio at her side. The Three Tonys, which sounded like an operatic trio but wasn't, trailed behind. The secretaries averted their eyes pointedly as the injured passed, the way the nicest people avoid gaping at car accidents, but the lawyers contributed to gaper block. Murphy and Murphy's lawyers, wasting time in the hallway, stared as Judy approached. And Murphy's lined lips parted when she spotted Frank, though Judy wasn't sure whether her reaction was due to the fact that he was so good-looking or that he was so good-looking even with an open wound.

"These are my clients," Judy said to Murphy's lawyers, as they passed them. "Please don't drool, stare, point, or laugh. Just say good-bye."

Murphy thrust a manicured hand at Frank. "I would never do such a thing. You must be Frank Lucia. I saw you on TV."

"Yes, you did," Judy said. The courthouse fight qualified as Action News. "Now, say good-bye."

"Hello," Murphy said to Frank, ignoring Judy. She shook Frank's hand, and he shook back, which Judy noticed with disapproval. "That was quite a show you put on at the courthouse. Everybody throwing punches, even outside, when the cops tried to break it up. The news guy said it was the biggest brawl they ever had there."

Frank smiled. "He was just being modest."

Murphy laughed, as did her friends, since that was their job. And the only job for which they were qualified. Judy had had enough.

"Well, we have to go. Say good-bye."

"But aren't you going to introduce me?" Murphy asked, and Judy gritted her teeth. Murphy wasn't interested in meeting The Three Tonys.

"Frank Lucia, this is Murphy. She uses only one name. Nobody knows why. Now let's go."

"Nice meeting you," Frank told Murphy, as Judy took his arm. She wanted to avoid Bennie, and, okay, she was a little jealous of Murphy. She was allowed to have more than one reason for doing something. She was a complex girl.

They headed for the reception room followed by The Three Tonys, who no longer reminded Judy of anything musical but rather of those municipal trucks that were signed SLOW-MOVING VEHI-CLE. They shuffled across the plush carpet, war-weary, and though she felt sorry for them, she wanted to go. They had almost made it to the reception desk when Judy's karma reserves ran out.

"Just the lawyer I want to see!" Bennie boomed, bustling into the office, carrying her heavy brief-case and two newspapers under her arm. She stopped momentarily, introduced herself to Frank and The Slow-Moving Vehicle, and smiled for their benefit. The smile remained fixed as she yanked a newspaper from underneath her elbow and handed it to Judy. "Judy, I have to get to my office, but I thought you might like to have this. You may want it for your scrapbook. And this story is very informative. Looks like your boxing lessons are paying off."

"Thank you," Judy said, also for the clients' benefit, and opened the **Daily News,** Philadelphia's biggest tabloid. UNCIVIL LAW, screamed the banner headline, and under it was a photo of security guards leading her and Frank out of the Criminal Justice Center. Judy thought they made a nice couple, but it didn't seem like the right time to say so. "Yes, the arraignment did get a little out of hand."

"Apparently. This isn't the kind of thing you want to do too often, Judy. Assault and battery in a courthouse, that is." Bennie turned to Frank, and at least she was still smiling. "By way of explanation, we at Rosato and Associates usually confine our felonies to the office."

Frank smiled grimly. "Don't blame Judy for this. It's on me, and she has already dressed us down. I know it doesn't help our case. It won't happen again. Sorry about that."

Bennie waved it away and took off. "No need to apologize," she called back. "Not if you won."

"We did," Frank answered, calling after her, and as Bennie hurried to her office, she shot him a thumbs-up.

It left Judy and The Senior Citizens standing there in amazement, until Judy realized she had to get rolling. She grabbed her telephone messages from the receptionist on the way out and paged through the soft pink slips on the way to the elevator. Three were from opposing counsel in her civil case, one was from the general counsel in Huartzer, and one was from Mary. She'd ignore all but the GC's and Mary's for the time being. Her e-mail would go unread, her voicemail unchecked.

She had Italians to defend.

# 9

Judy was relieved to find there was no press outside the office, and the only congestion was the standard rush-hour traffic on a warm evening. The sun dropped low, a cool, fiery disk edging behind the buildings, filling the twilight sky with a dusky orange wash. Businesspeople flowed onto the sidewalk from the buildings lining Locust Street, their heads bobbing as they moved en masse to the PATCO train station to New Jersey at the end of the street. Couples walked hand in hand, heading for the ritzy shops and restaurants in Center City. Judy noticed Frank's eyes scanning the crowd, his smooth brow a worried wrinkle, and she realized it wasn't the press he was worried about. She edged closer to Pigeon Tony, though it was hard to believe the threat was real.

She and Frank herded Tony-From-Down-The-Block and Tony Two Feet into a cab with Mr. DiNunzio, directing them to their respective houses. She and Frank grabbed the second cab, sliding into the backseat with Pigeon Tony in the middle. Judy and Frank were roughly the same height, but Pigeon Tony, squeezed between them, came only to their shoulders, and Judy felt oddly as if he were their very small, very gray-haired child. He didn't seem as worried about the crowd, and he was completely captivated by the cab, looking around its filthy interior with wonder, his brown eyes recording the greasy door handle, the open and sooty ashtray, and the smudged plastic divider between them and the driver. Judy caught Frank's eye with a smile.

Frank leaned down to his grandfather. "Pop, you ever been in a cab before?"

"Me? Sure!" Pigeon Tony startled as if he'd been awakened by an alarm clock, and his hand flew into the air in a grandiose gesture of a dismissal. "Me inna cab alla time!"

"I thought so," Frank said, and Judy decided then she'd never put Pigeon Tony on the witness stand. He was a worse liar than she was, if that were possible.

The cab lurched off, then came to a quick, nauseating stop, since there was nowhere to go. Frank fell silent, and Pigeon Tony returned to the Total Cab Experience as Judy looked out the window. The driver took a left, going south on one of the number streets, and she watched as they left rush hour behind and the scenery changed. The view going crosstown on the number street was different from that on Broad Street, which was a wide, mainly commercial artery, and the single lane south afforded Judy a perspective of the city she hadn't seen before.

Frank stayed quiet, Pigeon Tony looked drowsy, and the shops and businesses of Center City gave way to rowhouses. Those near the business district were four stories of colonial vintage, their mullioned windows bubbled with old glass, their bricks a soft melon color with a refined white line of mortar. The cab rattled along a few blocks south, passing gentrified houses on Rodman and Bainbridge Streets, which showed off new, modern picture windows and repointed brick. In a few short blocks, only three dollars on the meter, they were into South Philly, where the rowhouses lost their top story.

Judy found it apt, somehow. The houses here were stripped-down, no-frills, working-class, but each was different in its own way. Though they all had a front door and single window on the first floor, with two windows on the second story like wide-open, honest eyes, and each façade had been lovingly customized by the homeowner. Some had plastic awnings, corrugated in orange and green, many adorned with the family's initials, a script **D** or **C**. Some rowhouses sported flagstone stoops, some were of old-fashioned marble, and many were made of brick. Here and there wrought-iron railings had been added, and she saw one railing painted bright red to match the exterior molding. It struck Judy that these differences, whether her taste or not, contrasted with the sameness she had seen in the housing developments, strip malls, and Gap stores she'd driven past earlier the same day. It seemed so long ago now. She felt fatigue creep though her bones, and she still had so much to do.

It grew quiet in the cab except for the churning of the old meter, and Judy kept looking out the window as the sun dipped behind the buildings, leaving the sky a darker haze of clay-orange. The waning light filtered onto the rowhouses, emphasizing the redness of the brick in some and the rust-orange of others, setting the sandstone-hued brick, thin with skinny mortar lines, glowing in the twilight. Judy, who had been painting in oils for most of her adult life, saw the bricks as a gritty mosaic of amber, titian, and apricot, all the more beautiful because they housed people, and families, within.

The cab carried them along, and on each corner of South Philly would be a store, a grocery, a beauty parlor, bakery, a tavern, and all of them named after people. Sam and El's. Juno's. Yolanda's. Esposito's. There wasn't a chain store of any type in sight. The names telegraphed the ethnicity of the owner and, by extension, of the neighborhood. Judy took note that the corner stores grew solidly more Italian as they got closer to Pigeon Tony's house. Only two blocks away she began to feel a weight on her right arm and looked over.

It was her client, dozing on her shoulder, and he had just begun to snore, soft as a puppy.

# Book Two

With arms provided by the Agrarian Association or by some regimental stores, the
blackshirts would ride to their destination
in lorries. When they arrived they began by
beating up any passer-by who did not take
off his hat to the colours, or who was wearing a red tie, handkerchief, or shirt. If anyone protested or tried to defend himself, if
a fascist was roughly treated or wounded,
the "punishment" was intensified. They
would rush to the buildings and . . . break
down the doors, hurl furniture, books, or
stores into the street, pour petrol over
them, and in a few moments there would
be a blaze. Anyone found on the premises
would be severely beaten or killed. . . .

—ROSSI,
The Rise of Italian Fascism (1983)

At the beginning of December, it is time to
mate the birds. . . . All cocks and hens
should be allowed to select their own
mates. A widowhood cock or hen per-
forms better when they are permitted to
choose their mate. Isn't a man or woman

happier if they select their partner than those that are forced into "shotgun" marriages, etc.?

It is a fact that a cock or a hen will perform well in the races for many years. But if one of the pair is lost, the remaining bird never seems to do as well as it did with the old mate.

—JOSEPH ROTONDO,
**Rotondo on Racing Pigeons** (1987)

# 10

As he dozed, Pigeon Tony was remembering the first day he met his wife. He did not know the day exactly—he was never a precise man, but he did know the year because he wasn't stupid either. He was seventeen years old, and the year was 1937. It was a Friday night, in the early spring, in May.

Pigeon Tony, then merely Tony Lucia, was living in the house of his father and mother, in a village outside the city of Veramo, in the mountainous Abruzzo province of Italy. Tony worked hard, helping his father in their olive groves and with the pigeons, spending all his time in the company of birds and old men, having no time, or finding no time, for the frivolities that consumed others. That he was shy was his own secret, or so he believed. That he was also undesirable was something he knew anybody could see.

Tony Lucia was little and skinny, too skinny, his mother said all the time, with his legs like lengths of twine with a knot where the knee would be. His wrists were as fine as a child's. No matter what Tony ate, he never got heavier. No matter what Tony lifted, pulled, or carried, his arm muscles grew no bigger. He had flat feet, which hurt if he walked too far for too long. But that he was strong was beyond doubt; he was the only child of the Lucia family—his mother could bear no more— yet Tony could handle the chores of ten sons, and did.

When he first met his wife, he was doing one of these chores, hauling their pigeons by cart to a shipping for the race on Saturday. It would be a weekend of good flying weather, starting with a warm evening, now on the edge of darkness. Tomorrow would be the first race of the old bird season, and it had taken the day to travel north from Veramo to the city of Mascoli in the Marche province, where the birds would be released, the trip made slower because Tony was on his bad feet. Even so, out of kindness he led rather than drove their pony, an overweight, sway-backed brown creature with a brushy black mane and stiffness in his right hind. The beast pulled the cart gamely, and in back of the cart the pigeons cooed, called, and beat their wings in their wooden cages, sending pinfeathers into the air, transforming the assembly into a swirling cloud of dust.

The pigeons knew they were being shipped to race and anticipated the event as much as they felt fresh despair at having left their mates behind. The Lucias used the widowhood method of racing, leaving the captive hen at the loft, so that the cocks felt eager to fly home faster and so were agitated until they were finally released to be on their way. It didn't help that the dirt road was a rocky one, winding through the hills of the region, and the pigeon cages, piled five on top of one another and tied up with twine, jostled right and left. The birds felt unstable in the creaky cart with the weary pony yanking them along, and Tony couldn't blame them for that.

They all plodded ahead, with Tony barely noticing the terrain, even though he had never been in Marche before on his own. Abruzzo, on Marche's southern border, was considered by the **Marchegiani** to be far less sophisticated than their province. And for their part, the Abruzzese had a popular saying: "It is better to have a dead man in your house than a **Marchegiani** at your door," because the men of Marche had been used as tax collectors by the Romans, and so were universally hated.

But Tony took no notice of differences between men, for all of it sounded like generalizations to him, and he was not the political sort, despite the heated politics of the day. His concerns were his family, his olives, and his pigeons, and he practically walked backward as he led the pony so he could make sure no birds fell off the bumpy cart.

It was the reason he was almost run over by another cart that suddenly came roaring down the curving road, bearing a beautiful woman and a Blackshirt, Angelo Coluzzi.

"Hey! You! Hey! **Stupido!**" Coluzzi shouted to him. Almost out of breath, the Blackshirt pulled hard on his leather reins, bringing his matched brown horses to a stuttering halt, leaving them tossing their heads against the painful bit, their mouths gaping and their nostrils flaring. "Why don't you watch what you're doing, bumpkin? You're hogging the whole road! Fool!"

"Oh, my!" Tony exclaimed, startled. The sudden lurch to a stop set the birds complaining and flapping their wings. He put his hand up to protect the cages from falling. "I didn't see you. The birds—"

"The birds! The birds are no reason to cause a traffic accident! **Cavone! Idiota!**" Coluzzi's face had gone red and he seemed to get angrier as a result of Tony's explanation, not less so. His eyes and mouth were large and his dark hair combed back with brilliantine, making it as black as his shirt, with its gold buttons and pressed epaulets. It identified him as a **squadrista,** one of the elite cadre of Fascists who helped Mussolini rise to prime minister mainly by beating people up, breaking strikes, and destroying all opposition. But Angelo Coluzzi needed no identification in this region, as everybody knew him, or of him, for he had attained high station at only eighteen years of age, mostly because of his father's influence.

"I beg your pardon, sir," Tony said. It cost him nothing to placate the man, any more than a father minds calming a child in tantrum. And Tony's attention was riveted, despite the noisy blowing of the horses and the feather-beating of the pigeons, on the lovely **signorina** sitting beside Coluzzi.

Her eyes were as brown as the earth itself, and her hair was, almost miraculously, the identical color, only shot through with filaments of red, like veins of clay in soil. Bright red lipstick, which Tony knew was the fashion among city women, made her mouth shiny, but Tony would have noticed her lips whether they were painted or not. She smiled at him kindly despite the anger of her companion, and because Tony was not stupid, he apprehended in an instant that she and Coluzzi made a poor match and wondered if she would ever realize it herself. He concluded that she would, because of the intelligence dancing behind her eyes.

"Stumblebum! Why in heaven's name are you leading your broken-down pony along? How can you be so dim-witted?" Coluzzi continued his diatribe; it seemed that nothing could stop him. "Buffoon! Are you so simple you don't realize that man is meant to ride upon his animals and not walk beside them, as a lover?"

Tony ignored the insult, so lost was he in the

eyes of the woman. He contrived to think of a way to make her acquaintance, and then God sent him one. "Please forgive me, sir. My pony is so burdened with his own weight he can't bear even mine after a long day's journey. If I may formally introduce myself, by way of apology, my name is Anthony Lucia, from near Veramo, in Abruzzo. And you, sir, are Signore Angelo Coluzzi, I believe." Tony bowed slightly.

"**Abruzzese!** I knew it! Farmers and nose-pickers!" Coluzzi yanked again on the mouths of his fine horses, who, resigned to his ill treatment, only stamped their feet in response. "**Si,** I am Coluzzi. So you know me."

"Of course I do, sir."

"You are loyal to Il Duce."

"**Si, si**. Of course. As are we all." Tony was hoping Coluzzi would now introduce the young lady in the seat of his cart, but no such introduction was forthcoming. Tony glanced again at the woman, and her smile emboldened him. "I have not had the honor of meeting your companion. She is so lovely, she must be your sister."

"Fool!" Coluzzi's eyes narrowed. "She is lovely, but she is no blood relative. Her name is none of your business. Now, move out of our way. I have already delivered my pigeons and must return home before they do."

Tony bowed deeply, this time to the young woman, and doffed his felt cap with a flourish.

"Well, Miss None-of-Your-Business, my name is Tony Lucia, and I'm very honored to make your acquaintance."

Gentle laughter came from the cart, but Tony was bowing too low to see her laugh. He knew only that the sound made him aware of the exact location of his heart within his chest, something he'd never given a thought to before this moment. He straightened up slowly and whacked his cap against his wrist to shake out the dust before he returned it to his head and shoved it down over his mass of dark, curly hair at an angle he hoped she would find attractive.

"How dare you!" Coluzzi bellowed. "How dare you, show-off! How dare you speak to my Silvana!" In one motion, he raised the long whip he had been using on his horses, snapped it high in the air, and cracked it across Tony's face.

Pain ripped through the young man's cheek, tears sprang to his eyes, and he staggered backward in surprise and shock. Through his tears he saw the horrifed expression of the woman, her bright mouth a red gash of pain. Tony could see she had cried out—for him, yes—though he cowered shamefully. Coluzzi cracked the long whip again, and this time it struck the sweating rumps of the horses and they leaped into the air, clawing it with front hooves, and bolted right at Tony.

He threw himself out of the way, half rolling and half stumbling into the hard ground at the side of

the road, landing on his hip and shoulder before
he came to a stop at the edge of the field. Dust and
small rocks sprayed in his face, and he spit them
out in time to see Coluzzi's cart take off down the
road away from the city. Suddenly Tony's old pony
spooked, then galloped off in blind panic down
the road, toward the city. No!

Tony scrambled to his feet. Pain shot through
his shoulder, and he heard an odd grinding coming from there, the unmistakable sound of bone
against bone. He had broken his collarbone. But
there was no time to lose. His pigeons!

"No! Whoa! Stop!" Tony shouted. Holding his
arm against his side, he ran in agony after the old
pony, who galloped away with the cart, careening
this way and that, using energy he must have hidden from Tony. The cart bounced on the rocky
road. The towers of pigeons cages swayed dangerously. The cart was heading straight for a large
rock. Tony's heart leapt to his throat.

"Whoa!" he cried out, but the pony ignored him
and galloped faster. Tony picked up the pace,
cradling his arm, wincing at each stride.

The cart smashed into the rock. Tony held his
breath. The pigeon cages at the end popped out of
the cart, flew through the air, and crashed when
they hit the road. The other cages quickly followed, toppling out of the cart. "No!" Tony
yelled, but to no avail. He sent up a quick prayer
for the safety of his birds.

The wooden cages, which Tony had carefully constructed but hadn't built to withstand such a calamity, splintered instantly. The twine tying them tore apart. Cages split open all over the road. Tony raced to the cages, his shoulder broken, his feet painful. When he got there he fell to his knees, gasping for breath, as his pigeons struggled to free themselves from their wrecked cages, injuring themselves.

Tony scrambled from cage to cage, breaking them open so the birds wouldn't get hurt further. His shoulder protested the effort and he heard his bones rubbing, but he ignored it. The race was a total loss, a year's training and a day's travel, but there would be other races. He had to save his birds. He hurried to the next cage. Soon passersby came along, laughing at the sight of the young man destroying his own cages and freeing his own pigeons, but Tony didn't care. He finished wrecking the last cage and looked heavenward.

The birds, anxious to return home to their mates, were taking flight one by one, a running river of wings flowing up, defying gravity, soaring high into the clearest of skies, the blue darkening to black. A few flew on bloodied wing, but most looked healthy and sound. Tony's heart lifted with them. Forty pigeons, all slate-gray colored, skated on air currents only they could see, circling just once as Tony had taught them, so as not to waste time, then heading south. He squinted to see them go, holding his hurt arm still. They flapped away, obeying instinct and training, going straight to their mates, and Tony kept watching as they grew smaller and smaller, until they shrank to bright white dots, like stars in the twilight, and then even the stars disappeared. Tony swallowed hard, his heart suddenly full of emotion, and then he understood why.

Silvana. The sound of her laugh was in his ears. Feminine and musical, from her perch on the cart.

Her laughter, right beside him in his ear. He could feel the whisper of her painted lips, then a gentle shaking on his shoulder, which hurt no longer, his collarbone miraculously healed.

"Pigeon Tony," said the woman's voice, and he opened his eyes, to look into not Silvana's earthbrown eyes but the bright blue eyes of another woman. Her mouth had been red the first time they'd met. His lawyer, this Judy.

"Pigeon Tony," she was saying, calling his nickname, one that Silvana never heard. "Wake up, you're almost home."

Then he heard another voice, coming from his other side. He looked up into more familiar brown eyes. Though they weren't Silvana's, they hinted at hers, for they were her eyes passed down to her grandson Frank.

"Pop," Frank was saying with his nice smile. His teeth were white and straight as a wall, like all American teeth. "You okay? Can you wake up?"

"Sure, sure." Tony was awakening only slowly. It took him longer than when he was young. He pushed himself up in his seat in the cab, not knowing when he had slumped down, and shook off his slumber. "Okay, Frankie. Okay, Frank," he said, correcting himself. His grandson didn't like to be called Frankie or Little Frank anymore, like when he was a baby.

But suddenly Frank wasn't smiling and the lawyer wasn't laughing anymore. The cab pulled up at the curb outside his house, where a crowd had collected. Both Frank and Judy had turned toward his house, and they looked so sad. He craned his neck to see around Judy.

Pigeon Tony wasn't at all surprised by what he saw, and he realized that this was both the blessing and the curse of old age.

# 11

It was almost dark and the skinny South Philly street was too narrow for streetlights. Judy could barely see the plastic parti-colored beach chairs that sat outside each house on the sidewalk, in circles of three and four. Neighbors milled on the sidewalk but they were reduced to shadow figures, wearing pink-sponge haircurlers and smoking cigarettes.

Judy threaded her way through the crowd with ease, as they congregated around Frank and Pigeon Tony, and when she got to the front, she looked up. The front door to Pigeon Tony's rowhouse had been sledgehammered from its hinges, and splintered wood blanketed the marble stoop. The two front windows had been shattered, as if by a baseball bat, and lamplight blazed within. Judy stared at the destruction for a minute, uncomprehending, then reached into her purse for her cell phone.

"My birds! My birds!" Pigeon Tony cried, his

voice quavering, and he scurried past Judy to the front stoop, barely grazing the wrought-iron handrail in his urgency.

Frank hurried right behind him but stopped to touch Judy's arm on the way. "Listen, we get my grandfather out of here as fast as possible, understood?" he said in a low voice. "He's in danger if he stays here tonight. He'll put up a fight to stay, and I'll tell him no. You back me up. Got it?"

"Sure," she said, willing to take instructions from a client when she agreed with them. She had already opened her black StarTAC and punched the speed dial for 911 when a woman's voice came on the line. "Hello?" Judy asked, and Frank snorted.

"Good luck," he said as he hurried after his grandfather.

"I want to report a break-in," Judy told her, and gave the address to the dispatcher, who promised that a squad car would be there as soon as possible. Judy palmed the cell phone with some anxiety. She was counting on the Philadelphia police, never a completely safe bet. The score could be Law 0, Old Italian Way 1 unless she did something about it.

She became aware of a tinkling sound and squinted to see a woman in a Phillies T-shirt sweeping shards of jagged glass into a long-handled dustpan. While Judy was touched by the gesture, she couldn't let her finish. "I know you're trying to help, but maybe you shouldn't sweep now," Judy said to the woman, as politely as possible. "The glass could have fingerprints on it, or other evidence. This is a crime scene, technically."

"Oh, sorry." The woman instantly stopped sweeping. Pieces of glass tumbled to a stop across the gritty sidewalk, catching the light from the window. "I didn't know. You being a lawyer, you would know."

Judy didn't ask the woman how she knew about her, from TV or the South Philly network, which apparently was better than cable. "Where are the cops? Did anybody call the cops?"

"I don't know. It's a sin, what they did to that old man," the woman said.

"Who did it?" Judy asked, though she could guess at the answer.

"I don't know."

Judy didn't have to see her face to know she was lying. "You have no idea?"

"No," the woman said, shaking her head.

"Do you know what time it happened?"

"No," the woman answered, edging away.

"Did you hear anything? See anything?"

"No way." The woman disappeared into the crowd, but Judy wasn't giving up. She held up her hands, one containing her cell phone.

"Please! Everybody! I need your attention!" she shouted.

The neighbors, who had been milling around,

stopped and looked at her. She couldn't see their expressions in the dark, but she knew they were listening because they quieted suddenly, and a sea of Eagles caps, Flyers caps, and pink cotton hairnets turned in her direction. Cigarette ends like lighted erasers glowed next to the chubbier, more muted flames of cigars. Somebody chuckled in the back of the crowd, and somebody else shouted, "Yo! What you got in your hand, a bomb?" and everybody laughed, including Judy, who quickly slipped the cell phone back into her purse.

"Obviously, we have a problem here," she shouted. "Somebody broke into Pigeon Tony's house. Did anybody here see who broke the door and windows?"

The crowd remained mostly silent, although some people started talking among themselves and the same joker in the back kept chuckling.

"Look, somebody must have heard or seen something. It takes time to chop down a door and it makes noise to break a window. It had to have happened in broad daylight. Isn't anybody going to help Pigeon Tony out?"

There was no answer from the crowd, which had started to scatter at the fringes. Somebody was still chuckling. Judy wanted to throttle him.

"Wait! Don't go away. You're all Pigeon Tony's neighbors. You care enough about him to clean up the mess. Don't you care enough to help him catch who did this?"

A murmur rippled through the dark crowd, which was growing smaller by the minute. Judy watched with dismay as the shadows disappeared into their rowhouses and shut the doors behind them. Suddenly the chuckling ceased and somebody shouted from the back, "Who the hell do you think did it?"

Judy took a deep breath. It was assumption-upon-assumption time again. "I think I know who did it. In fact, we all think we know who did it. But somebody had to see or hear them do it, to hold them accountable for it. So what we need now, what Pigeon Tony needs now, is a witness."

The crowd quieted suddenly, and Judy understood why. There was something about the way the word rang out in the night that gave even her goose bumps.

"You know what a witness is, don't you? I'll define it for you, since I'm Pigeon Tony's lawyer and it's a highly technical legal term. A witness is somebody with the balls to come forward and tell the truth."

The crowd laughed, this time with her, though Judy noticed they continued their defection. Only four shadows stood before her, and one had to stay because his beagle was rooted to a scent on the sidewalk.

"You don't have to come forward now. You can call me anytime. My name is Judy Carrier, at Rosato and Associates downtown." By the time she finished the sentence, all of the neighbors had gone, except the beagle owner, unhappy at the other end of the leash. "Nice dog," Judy said.

"He's a pain in the ass," said the man, and tugged the beagle away.

Having accomplished nothing, Judy turned and went inside the house. She should have been prepared for what she'd find inside, but she wasn't. The front door, or what was left of it, would have opened onto a small living room, with an old green sofa against the left wall, on which hung a large mirror and several framed black-and-white photographs. There would have been a wooden coffee table in front of the couch, and next to that, at one point, an old overstuffed wing chair, in the same dark green fabric as the sofa. But none of it was recognizable now, the violence well beyond vandalism.

The coffee table had been broken in the middle and looked as if it had been jumped on until its legs gave way. The sofa had been butchered, slashed this way and that, its green fabric rent into shreds. White polyester stuffing had been ripped out and strewn everywhere on the shredded couch and floor. The wing chair had been knifed to death, and somebody had taken a sledgehammer to its frame and splintered the wood as easily as the bones of a human skeleton.

Aghast, Judy looked at the wall. A single blow had shattered the mirror and it hung crazily by one corner. The sledgehammer hadn't stopped at the mirror but had been pounded through the plaster wall behind it, destroying the lath and battering the wire mesh beneath. The only part of the wall left unscathed was a brown wooden crucifix, apparent evidence of the Christian beliefs of the perpetrators.

Judy shook her head. These were rowhouses, all of them connected, sharing a common wall. Of course the next-door neighbors had heard this pounding. It would have sounded like someone was knocking his house down. If they wouldn't talk to her, they'd talk to the cops. Wouldn't they? She couldn't think about it now. She left the ruined living room to look for Pigeon Tony and Frank.

The living room adjoined an eat-in galley kitchen, as savaged as the living room, and the lights had been left on, apparently for full shock value. The kitchen table had collapsed in the middle, taking the brunt of the fury, and lay broken in two. The telephone had been ripped out of the wall. The cabinet drawers, whose white paint looked like new refacing, had been yanked out, the silverware and kitchen utensils scattered willy-nilly. On the wall, all the cabinets had been opened, their doors wrenched off and tossed onto the linoleum floor, and emptied of their contents. Strewn on the counter were packages of lentils, two cans of garbanzo beans, and a jar of yellow lupini beans. Broken dishes, sharp glass, and smashed china littered the tile. The kitchen sink had been stopped up with a dish towel and the faucet left running, so water spilled over the mess on the countertop and ran freely onto the floor.

Judy struggled to understand the mentality of people who would do this. They acted like common thugs, their destruction mindless, their rage spending itself. The only remotely valuable items, a TV and a small radio, were destroyed and not taken. It hardly seemed real, but Judy experienced the same feeling she'd had at the melee in the courtroom. It was real; her eyes couldn't deny the scene.

For some reason she went to the faucet and twisted it off. The silence permitted her to hear Frank's voice somewhere out back. There must have been a backyard. Judy remembered Pigeon Tony's concern about his birds. She headed for the back door, afraid of what she might find.

# 12

It was dark outside but Judy could see the lighted ruins of a little white house that took up almost all of Pigeon Tony's backyard. It must have been the house in which Pigeon Tony kept his birds, but it was unhappily silent. The night was still, except for the city sounds of traffic and a faraway siren. Cinderblock enclosed the yard, which was a small rectangle.

She walked through the darkness to the pigeon house. Judy swallowed hard as she took in the sight. The panels of plywood that made up the bottom of the building had been chopped away from the inside at the far end, so that the end of the house had collapsed onto its foundation, which appeared to be supported by stilts. Judy figured that the stilts would have been chopped away, bringing the whole house down, but the vandals had apparently gone inside the pigeon house and started hacking away, then escaped out the front door. The lights within shone through the openings made by an ax or a baseball bat. Judy could see through the torn and missing screens that Pigeon Tony and Frank were inside.

She picked her way between broken slats of plywood in the yard to what used to be wooden steps that led to an open threshold, the front door dismantled and tossed aside. She stepped inside but neither man looked up. They were kneeling over, absorbed in a common task, and she looked around, appalled. Everything inside the pigeon house had been broken, as if smashed by a baseball bat; cages, perches, chicken wire, wooden frames—all of it had been demolished. A medicine chest at the end of the aisle had been overturned, the medicines spilled. Trash cans that held feed had been dumped and bashed in. Birdseed lay scattered on the floor.

Judy got the impression that as many pigeons as could be caught were killed, brutally. She had no idea how many pigeons Pigeon Tony kept, but she counted seven dead. Some had their necks wrung; some had been stomped to death, a gruesome sight. One slate-gray pigeon had had its head sadistically pulled off, exposing a bloody section of delicate backbone. Sickened, Judy took a step and almost tripped over the lifeless body of a white bird. Its head was a pulpy mass of blood, and it lay on its back, its feet curled in death. A silver band on its pink legs had slid back against the downy feathers of its underbelly. Its blood stained the whitewashed floor. It smelled raw and wasted. Judy felt her gorge rising.

"You okay?" Frank asked, looking at her quickly. He squatted on the floor, helping his grandfather care for a large gray pigeon, mercifully still alive. "Maybe you should sit down."

Judy shook her head no, afraid to speak until her nausea passed. Frank returned to his task, cradling the pigeon expertly in his cupped hands, so that the body of the bird nestled in his palms and his hands gripped underneath its wings. Pigeon Tony deftly wrapped a thin bandage around the top of its left wing, which he had extended. Neither man spoke, but their expressions and their brown Lucia eyes were almost identically strained.

Judy watched and began to feel a little better. She concentrated on the live pigeon. She had never seen one so close up, mainly because she had never bothered to look at them pecking at trash in Washington Square or waddling fast down the street, like Olympic walkers. The injured bird was alert, and its golden eye, with a black pupil like a punctuation mark, darted this way and that. Whitish, wrinkly folds around its eye provided an odd sort of ring, and Judy wondered what it was for. She was surprised at the bird's wingspan, a full twenty inches, with ten pinfeathers at the front of the wing clearly longer than those closer to the body. She wished she had paid more attention in science when they talked about drag and lift, but she assumed that it all made the birds fly better. She didn't really care. She just wanted the pigeon to live.

"Is it going to be okay?" she asked, and Frank looked up.

"Hope so." He managed a grim smile. "There's only the one break. He's young and strong, so I don't think he'll die."

"Good. It's so . . . awful about the house, and the birds."

"We had to destroy two, to put them out of their pain." His mouth tightened. "But most got away. We figure thirty survived, including Jimbo here."

Judy smiled, relieved. "Will they come back, to the house?"

"Loft. After something like this, there's no way to tell." Frank focused again on the bird. Pigeon Tony, almost finished taping its wing, cut the bandage with a bent surgical scissors. "Instinct will tell them to stay away, especially if they left with their mates, which all of them did, except two."

"Which two?"

"One whose mate was killed, a cock named Nino, and The Old Man. His mate died a long time ago."

Pigeon Tony said nothing as he gentled the snipped end of the tape closed, and the pigeon took an ungrateful peck at his finger. A tiny bulb of blood appeared on Pigeon Tony's weathered hand, and he gave an indulgent **heh-heh-heh** when he noticed it, then wiped it on his baggy pants.

Frank laughed, too. "He feels better, Pop."

"**Si, si. Va bene.**" Pigeon Tony smiled, but Judy could see his dark eyes aching with the loss of his birds. He cradled the bird against his sweater, curling his body protectively around it, then rose to his knees, with Frank supporting his elbow. Pigeon Tony nodded and, holding the bird, walked through the debris down the aisle.

Frank gave Judy the high sign, then called after his grandfather, "Pop, we have to get out of here now. Judy thinks so, too."

Pigeon Tony shuffled off, but Judy knew he was only apparently oblivious to them, and she said her line.

"I agree with Frank, Tony. It's not a good idea for you to stay here any longer. You both go, and I'll wait for the police."

"Police!" Pigeon Tony shook his head querulously, picking through the mess in the feed room, righting jugs of veterinary medicines and unused syringes with his free hand. "No like police! Police do nothing! **Nothing!**"

Judy sighed. She kept forgetting that the Lucias lived in Palermo, not Philadelphia. "I had to call the police, I had to report it. What was done here, to your house, to your pigeon house, to your birds, it's a crime. Breaking and entering. Animal cruelty. Malicious mischief. The police will do something about it when they get here."

"Nothing!" Pigeon Tony repeated, but he was preoccupied, pulling a green cardboard box from the wreckage. It read PERONI in bright red and green, and Judy assumed it was a special pigeoner's term until she translated the BIRRA part. Beer, from the Latin, Budweiser. Pigeon Tony opened the lid of the cardboard box, placed the bird carefully inside, then closed the top flap loosely. "I no go. I no go nowhere."

"You can't stay here."

"No." Pigeon Tony slid the scissors from his pocket and poked it into the box top, making an airhole. "I no go."

Frank waved Judy off. "Thanks, but let me try again. This is really a family matter." He turned to his grandfather. "Pop, you have to go with me. The Coluzzis will come back, and you know it. We'll go to my house or a hotel. It's dangerous to stay here."

"I no go." Pigeon Tony made another airhole. "The birds, they come home. The Old Man, he come home."

"You don't know that."

"I know, I know." Pigeon Tony made a third airhole in the box, and the injured pigeon popped his head through the loose top. The bird watched, making no effort to escape, as Pigeon Tony punctured the top again. "Alla time, he come home."

"But you don't know when, Pop. You can't stay here. We shouldn't be here now."

"I no leave." Pigeon Tony kept making airholes for his audience of one. "**My** birds. **My** house. **My** loft. Alla **mine**."

"Pop, it's not safe." Frank raised his voice, his face reddening with frustration. "I'm not going to fight with you about this."

"I no leave," Pigeon Tony shouted. "**Basta**, Frankie!"

"Pop, you can't stay here!" Frank shouted back, and Pigeon Tony looked up from his airholes. The pigeon's head wheeled around.

"I no leave!" Pigeon Tony waved the scissors for emphasis, and Judy knew he had won. An Italian with a sharp object always won, except for World War II.

Suddenly she heard a commotion outside the loft and looked through the torn screen. Two uniformed police were looking around the kitchen. The cavalry had arrived.

Finally.

The five of them—Judy, Frank, Pigeon Tony, and two heavyset, older cops—crowded into the wrecked kitchen. Judy kept Pigeon Tony behind her, so he wouldn't bite, as she talked to the police. He remained unhappily still, clutching his Peroni box, which cooed throughout her account of the events. One cop, whose black nameplate read McDADE, listened critically while the other, named O'NEILL, took careful notes on his white Incident Report pad. Judy knew they wouldn't really understand this situation. Even the Irish were pikers in the grudge department, comparatively. Vendetta was an Italian word for a reason.

Officer McDade flipped his pad closed. "So I have my report, and we'll get right on it. Thanks."

Judy looked around. "When will the mobile techs arrive?"

"Mobile techs?"

"You know, for the crime scene. I see them at murder cases all the time. They dust for fingerprints, photograph everything—"

"We do that for a homicide, but not a B and E."

Judy blinked, vaguely aware of Frank's impatience at her side. "It's still a crime scene."

"We don't have the resources to dust every B and E."

"But this B and E is part of a homicide case," Judy argued, echoing Frank's words from earlier that day. "My client, Mr. Lucia, was charged this afternoon with the murder of the elder Coluzzi, and this is in retaliation."

"I've already told Mr. Lucia here"—he nodded at Frank—"that we'll question the Coluzzi family." Officer McDade shifted restlessly on his shiny black shoes, and his partner started toward the kitchen door. "We'll start with John, the son he mentioned."

"But this is a warning. The Coluzzis are waging war on my client." Judy knew she was pushing it, but pushing it was what advocates were supposed to do. She couldn't leave Pigeon Tony unprotected. The law would take care of him, wouldn't it? "I want whoever did this behind bars. It's the only way Mr. Lucia will be safe."

The cop's blue eyes flared. "No attempt has been made on his life."

"Not yet, but one could be."

"We'll look into it, Ms. Carrier." The officer glanced after his partner, who was leaving. "Now we do have to be getting along."

"But the issue is what happens to him tonight. If you don't believe there's a threat, you can still catch the eleven o'clock news. I'm sure the film of the fight at the courthouse is all over it."

"We have twelve other B and E's to deal with tonight. It's a Friday and a full moon. The whole city is going nuts. We looked upstairs and down. Nothing is missing. Your guy—your client— didn't even lose anything valuable."

"Only his home, and birds he loves," Frank interjected, and Officer McDade turned to him.

"I meant no disrespect to your grandfather, Mr. Lucia, but I just came from an apartment on Moore, near Fifth. That guy's home is a wreck **and** they took everything he owned." Officer McDade touched the patent bill of his cap, a modern-day doffing. "We're doing our best. You'll hear from us as soon as we know something."

Judy couldn't let it go. "So you'll pick up John Coluzzi?"

"Pick up? I didn't say that. I said we'd talk to him and we will."

"Can't you question him at the Roundhouse? Isn't he a suspect?"

"Not legally." Officer McDade frowned. "We have no evidence, only your suspicion. We'll question him, like I said, but we don't have probable cause for arrest. Not on these facts."

"If you talk to the neighbors—"

"We did that already. Nobody saw anything."

"They're just afraid."

"Possibly, but we can't manufacture witnesses, Ms. Carrier. Between us, me and my partner"—at this he nodded in the direction of his now-absent colleague—"have forty-something years of experience in talking to witnesses. We know how to handle this."

Judy fished in her purse, dug for her wallet, and found a business card. She handed it to the cop. "I'll let you know if any of them call me. Will you do the same?"

"Sure, that's standard procedure." The cop stuck her card in his back pocket with his white pad, reminding Judy uncomfortably of a booklet of traffic tickets.

"Thanks," she said anyway, her hopes sinking. Officer McDade shook her hand and Frank's and nodded to Pigeon Tony, who gripped his Peroni box. The cops had been gone only a minute when Judy answered Frank's unsaid argument, "It's a process, Frank. It takes time."

"I understand. I really didn't expect more." Frank didn't look angry to Judy, or even frightened. His brown eyes were concerned, and the stubble on his chin had grown darker. He turned to his grandfather. "Pop, I can't get you to go, so I'm staying."

"You? Inna house? No. No!" Pigeon Tony scowled, his brow creasing with concern, but Frank put up his hand like a crossing guard.

"Yes, and no more fighting. That's it. I'm sleeping on the couch, Pop."

Pigeon Tony nodded only reluctantly, though the Peroni box cooed in happy response.

Home in her apartment, Judy tried to sleep but couldn't. She flopped back and forth in bed because her Patagonia surfer T-shirt, the same blue one she'd worn to bed for the past three nights, had become suddenly bunchy. She yanked it off over her head, then tossed it at the foot of the bed and slid nude under the coverlet, feeling suddenly cold. She refused to put the T-shirt back on, which would involve not only getting out of bed but also admitting defeat, so she leaned over and switched on the electric blanket, at which point she became suddenly hot. Even a pillow cave didn't help. She had a lot on her mind.

Pigeon Tony was across town in his ruined house, in danger. Frank was with him, protecting them both with only a portable copier. The police were changing shifts and proving her faith in them misplaced. She had a murder case to defend and the guy actually did it. Plus she liked the murderer and was developing a crush on his grandson. The thought made her smile, almost, but it faded when she focused on the predicament they were in, then the visions of the smashed house. The slaughtered birds. The pain on Pigeon Tony's face.

She fluffed up her pillow and snuggled deeper into bed, which was queen-size but seemed small. The room was large and messy, with two IKEA bureaus on the far wall, their drawers open and overstuffed, and between them an old rocking chair with sweat clothes piled on it. Her bicycle, a yellow Cannondale, leaned against the wall; her boxing gear sat piled in the corner. She could clean up but that wouldn't improve her mood. She could work the case but she was too distracted. She turned over, facing the opposite wall.

Moonlight streamed through the window, a tall one with mullioned panes, typical of the architecture in this part of town. Judy had moved to Society Hill, the oldest section of the city, as part of her never-ending quest for The Perfect Apartment. The possibilities had narrowed since she got Penny, now a healthy nine-month-old golden retriever, who snored happily at the foot of the bed. No rentals wanted pets and even the largest security deposit didn't help. She'd ended up in this place, her nicest so far and the fanciest, only because she bartered free legal services to the landlord for a year. He had a tricky boiler in one of his other buildings, but like her other clients, he'd have to wait. She had forgotten to call the GC at Huartzer during business hours and left a message only when she'd finally gotten home. And her antitrust article awaited her at the office. The deadline loomed on Tuesday. Her boss loomed constantly.

Judy sat up in bed. She couldn't relax. If she did drugs she'd do them now, but she stayed away from that stuff. She was already addicted to M&M's, a monkey on her back. She could drink a nice chilled glass of pink Zinfandel but that would make her want to dance, not sleep. She had nothing good to read, though the stack of hardcovers on the bedside table threatened to topple. She resolved instantly to buy only books she wanted to read, not books that she should read, and felt suddenly free. Free! She switched on the ginger-jar lamp next to the books and jumped out of bed. Waking, the puppy lifted her head from her oversize paws and put it back down again, knowing where Judy was going and deciding it wasn't worth the trouble to follow.

She padded out of her bedroom and headed for her studio in the adjoining room, where she flicked on the lights. Like her bedroom, it was large and empty, painted white, but there the similarity ended. It contained no furniture but was filled with multilayered wooden trays of acrylic paints in tubes, jars of sable paintbrushes in all sizes, and large-format canvases, most of which were finished, propped against the walls.

Bright, bold paintings of natural landscapes dominated her work, painted from memories and photographs of places she had lived. There were mountains she had hiked in Big Sur from when her father was commissioned at Stanford, and rocks she had climbed in Virginia, near the basic-training facility at Quantico; and green, tropical trails through which she had mountain-biked, outside of Pensacola, where they had moved so he could teach initial flight training. The painting resting on the easel showed a secret stream she had discovered curling through the marsh on the way to the Everglades. She surveyed the verdant greens, dense cobalt blues, and hot orange of the painting without the usual satisfaction. What was wrong with it? Judy confronted her art with new eyes in the still apartment. The dark window across the room reflected the naked form of a tall, athletic woman with tousled blond hair.

The reflection caught her eye. She considered pulling the shade, but there was none to pull, and in any event the city was asleep. The full moon was the only thing peeking into her window, shining off the granulated tar roof of the rowhouse across the street and illuminating the aluminum of the gutter like an outline of light. Beyond the rooftop twinkled the lights of the city and the office buildings uptown. For the first time Judy noticed its gritty beauty, in hues of midnight black, cool silver, and bright white. She remembered the colors of the brick on the way to South Philly, from the cab window. She watched the city shimmer before her, then in her mind's eye, with her own naked form ghosted in the foreground. In time she strode to the easel, picked up the unfinished canvas, and set it aside.

By the time Judy stopped painting, the moon had thinned to a pale shadow in a gray dawn sky, and she caught two hours' sleep before she showered, got dressed, and went to work. She felt peaceful, rested, and even eager, all of which was necessary for where she was going.

# 13

It was another perfect day in Philadelphia, which meant they had used up both of them. The sun was high in the clear sky, and the air felt cool. Judy intercepted a cab heading to the new Society Hill hotels, climbed into the backseat, and retrieved her cell phone from a full backpack. She wanted to know if she still had a live client. It seemed relevant, especially in view of where she was going.

"University City, Thirty-eighth and Spruce," she told the cabbie, intentionally omitting the name of the building. She didn't want him looking at her funnier than he already was.

A young man, he had a line of cartilage pierces, and his red hair had been knotted into ropy Rasta dreads that sprang like palm fronds from the center of his head. He smelled of reefer and was too cool to approve of her Saturday work uniform of jeans, denim clogs, and a wacky-colored Oilily sweater over a white T-shirt. Judy used to like bad boys that looked like him, but she was happily over that phase, having learned the obvious: that bad boys were simply childish men. She punched in the number for Frank's cell phone and examined her nails, fingers outstretched, while the phone connected. Rust-colored acrylic paint rimmed her cuticles and the scent of turpentine overwhelmed the cabbie's pot stink, which was as it should be.

"Hello, Lucia here," Frank said when he picked up, and his voice sounded tired but reassuringly oxygenated.

"Tell me you're both alive and well."

"We're both alive and one of us is well. He's cleaning up the first floor as we speak. He already swept the loft and the second-floor bedrooms. He's the Energizer Bunny of grandpops."

"Is he upset?"

"Yes, because we're out of Hefty trash bags. He wanted to go to the corner for that and coffee, but I told him no."

"And he listened?"

"Of course not. I had to tie him to a chair. What's family for? I didn't think you'd mind."

Judy smiled. "That's false imprisonment."

"Nothing false about it."

Judy laughed. Frank was fun to talk to. His voice was deep and warm. She wondered whether he was dating anybody and hoped he didn't like bad girls. Everybody knew what they were. "Have the cops been over?"

"Are you kidding?"

Their first fight. She let it lie. The cab turned west on Walnut Street, the traffic sparse this morning, before the day's shopping started. "Did the pigeons come back?"

"Not yet."

"So your grandfather isn't leaving the house?"

"He has to. I have a job to go to today, so I'm taking him with me. Did you see the newspapers this morning?"

"I'm avoiding them."

"We're the big story, unfortunately, and there's a whole piece on the Coluzzis and the construction company. Pictures of John and Marco. Speculation about who's taking over now that Angelo's gone. Wait a minute." Frank covered the receiver but Judy could hear Pigeon Tony fussing in Italian. "Sorry," Frank said, when he came back on the line. "He's not leaving my sight today, no matter what he says."

"He wants to stay at the house."

"He's worried about the birds, but he doesn't have to be here when they come home, if they come home. I don't care. I slept on the couch pillows for him, that's enough. He goes with me today."

"I agree." Judy's cab zipped up Walnut. "Why don't you get the Tonys to come over? They can wait for the birds."

"The Tonys?" Frank asked, then laughed softly. "If you think it's weird that they're all named Tony, you're wrong. The only thing that's weird is that they're not all named Frank."

The cab crossed the concrete bridge over the Schuylkill River, which managed to fake a green-blue color today, and reached the Gothic towers of the University of Pennsylvania. They were getting closer. Judy needed information. "Where will you be today, in case I need to see your grandfather?" It was the real reason, but it sounded lame even to her.

"You got a pencil?"

Judy foraged in her leather backpack for a ball-point pen and her little black Filofax. She found both, evidence of her karma returning, and flipped through the onion-thin pages of the Filofax until she found a blank one. The cabdriver clucked at the Filofax, but Judy didn't apologize for it. At least it wasn't a PalmPilot. "Go ahead," she said, and jotted down the address and directions, then flipped the Filofax closed as the cab turned the corner on Thirty-eighth Street. They were only blocks away. Her stomach tightened. "Frank, listen, I have to go. I'm calling you from the cell."

"Where are you?"

"You don't want to know." She looked out the window as the cab climbed University Avenue. The modern building, of low-slung red brick, squatted directly ahead, incongruous against the cheery blue sky.

"Okay, well, stay outta trouble. Don't embarrass me like you did yesterday at the courthouse. Your jab needs work."

Judy laughed, her face flushing warmly. She flipped the StarTAC closed and tossed it into her backpack. "Pull up in front of that brick building on the right, please," she said to the cabbie, who glanced back at her.

"But that's the—"

"I know," she said grimly, and the cabbie's eyes met hers in the rearview mirror with a new respect.

Filofax 1, Dope 0.


Although Judy had impressed the cabbie, she had never been to the city morgue before, much less to an autopsy, and she concentrated on concealing that fact from the district attorney next to her, who had introduced himself as Jeff Gold, and Detective Sam Wilkins, the thin cop from the Roundhouse. They seemed undaunted by the glistening stainless-steel table they stood before, with raised edges all around, surprisingly long because it had a drain in one end and a stainless-steel sink. Judy's gaze ran down the slant in the table toward the drain, and she realized that it wasn't for water but for blood. Her stomach flip-flopped. She would have had to paint forever to get centered enough for this experience. She summoned up images of mountains, rocks, and forest streams from her landscapes, but nothing helped. Autopsy 1, Art 0.

A stainless-steel organ scale was suspended near Judy's face and a huge operating room lamp poised over the table, casting a calcium-white brightness on a lineup of medical instruments on a stand at its head. Shiny scalpels, large scissors with a mysterious bulb at one end, and a tool that looked like a wire cutter gleamed in the light. Next to them rested a hammer with an odd hook on one side, a stubby handsaw with a handle like a gun, and an electric tool with a chubby chrome barrel and a rotating blade. **A power saw.** Judy forced herself to breathe deeply, but formaldehyde and disinfectant cut off fresh air. The operating-room light stung her eyes. Her head throbbed. She gripped the leather strap of her backpack for an anchor, to steady herself for whatever happened next.

The assistant medical examiner, who had introduced himself as Dr. Patel, stood aside as two assistants, both young African-American men in blue scrubs, wheeled over a gurney containing a black body bag. They lifted it from the gurney and placed it on the stainless-steel table with a dull thud that echoed in the quiet morgue. Dr. Patel and an assistant wordlessly positioned the body bag on the table, while the other assistant disappeared with the empty gurney. Judy concentrated on the coroner, not the body bag.

An Indian who spoke with an English accent, Dr. Patel was a middle-aged man with a permanent half smile and steel-framed glasses over brown eyes. He was dressed in blue scrubs and a blue puffy hat with a drawstring, and he wore two pairs of latex gloves. A little gold bump on one finger betrayed a wedding band. His hand rested protectively atop the body bag, which couldn't be denied any longer. The black nylon bag was surprisingly short, with a puff at the end where the head would be and a mound where the feet would be. It smelled of new, cheap synthetics and carried with it the faint chill of refrigeration. Judy's head felt light.

"Are you okay?" Dr. Patel asked her, and though it was kind, she was getting tired of being asked that question. Judy was supposed to be tough. She took boxing lessons. She climbed rocks for sport. She was a lieutenant colonel's daughter.

"I'm fine," she answered, hoping it sounded professional, but knowing it sounded like WATCH OUT, I'M GONNA RALPH! The district attorney and Detective Wilkins looked over. She wanted to run away. "I love it here," she said, and the coroner smiled.

"This is your first time."

No shit. "Yes."

"I understand." Dr. Patel's eyes softened. "Perhaps if I explain as I go along, you can understand what you are seeing and it will diminish your fear."

**No, please, God,** Judy thought. But what she said was, "Thank you."

"Fine. We will begin the external examination." With the help of an assistant, Dr. Patel unzipped the body bag, making a metallic chattering sound. The zipper opened from the top to the bottom and the widening opening at the top showed a V-slit of a gray human mask. The coroner and his assistant made quick work of slipping the body out of the bag and repositioning it on the table, then quickly covering its privates with a white sheet. Judy's nausea surged at the sight. It was the dead body of Angelo Coluzzi.

"This is the case of Angelo Coluzzi," Dr. Patel said, pronouncing the Italian name perfectly as he read it and a case number from a large yellow tag that hung from the body's big toe. The coroner projected his voice in the direction of a black microphone that hung from the ceiling over the body. "Subject was brought into the Philadelphia Medical Examiner's Office on April seventeenth. Subject is an eighty-year-old male Caucasian."

Judy was about to look away again but stopped. She may have been an artist at heart, but she was a lawyer by profession. She had to understand everything about the facts to build her defense. There was a dead body at the crux of every murder case; it couldn't, and shouldn't, be avoided. Especially when this dead body was her client's handiwork. The thought struck her that maybe that was part of the problem, which was also as it should be. It was easier to confront her art than her profession, but she was responsible for both. She told herself, **So take responsibility. Look at the act you're about to defend. Decide if he's innocent or guilty.** Judy's eyes narrowed and her stomach tensed. She took a good look, and it repulsed her.

His face was bone-white in places and gray in the hollow of his cheeks and around his eyes, which were closed so tightly they seemed glued shut. Sparse gray hair sprung haphazardly from his scalp, which was as bald as Pigeon Tony's. His nose protruded from gaunt cheeks, a bulbous shape with a breach at the bridge; it looked as if it had been broken long ago. His lips, flat in death, looked thin. Although Angelo Coluzzi's head rested roughly in line with his backbone, even Judy's untrained eye could see that its location was tenuous. His head wasn't firmly attached to anything; only skin and muscle held it to the body. Judy realized that a broken neck was essentially a beheading. She closed her eyes briefly. How could one human being do this to another? How could Pigeon Tony do this to anyone?

"The first step in the external examination is easy," Dr. Patel was saying. "The body must be measured and those measurements recorded for the case file." He selected a common yardstick from the table of medical instruments and began measuring various parts of Angelo Coluzzi's body, dictating the findings into the microphone. Judy barely listened, except to hear that the body weighed only 155 pounds and measured a mere 67 inches.

As the coroner read his other measurements, Judy's horrified gaze traveled down Angelo Coluzzi's body, which was skinny, his chest almost wasted and his upper arms withered with age. His hands had been bagged in clear plastic with a loose rubber band, but Judy could see they were arthritic. His hips jutted from above the discreet white sheet, and his legs rested slightly open, their calf muscles slack. Blood had collected along the backside of Angelo Coluzzi's body, drawn by gravity once his heart had stopped, making a grim outline around his frail form.

Judy hadn't expected that, hadn't expected any of it. She had imagined that Angelo Coluzzi would be a tall, strong man. A big bully, a brute. But in death he took up only a little over half of the tray table. His were the remains of a bony old man. The body of a frail victim. **Her client's** victim. A wave of emotion swept over her, stronger than the earlier nausea but kin to it, a sensation of ugliness that left her feeling sorrowful and sad. A vendetta was a living thing, and it could kill. It could do **this,** to an old man.

"Now we will note for the record the external abnormalities in the body," Dr. Patel was saying, for Judy's benefit. She watched as he gestured to Coluzzi's broken neck. "There is slight bruising in the neck region, and the neck is at a distinctly abnormal angle in relation to the spine."

Judy blinked, sickened, but the district attorney opened a fresh legal pad. "Wasn't he strangled?" he asked, his pen poised for a note. "Looks like he could've been strangled, with the bruising on the neck and all."

"I think not. Let me explain. Here, see." Dr. Patel turned to an oversize manila folder on the side table, slid a large, dark X ray from it, and with a loud rustling noise tucked the X ray under the clamp on a light box on the near wall. Judy shakily retrieved a pen and a legal pad from her backpack as Dr. Patel switched on the light box. The box illuminated the X ray, a close-up of the miraculous tongue-in-groove vertebrae of the human backbone. But you didn't have to be a doctor to know that something was terribly wrong with this backbone. It was disconnected at the base of a shadowy skull. Dr. Patel pointed calmly to the film. "We took these X rays when he first came in, the same time as the photos. You can see the fracture to the spinal column, at C3. A fracture that high up, death would have been instantaneous."

"But he could have been strangled, couldn't he? I mean, the bruises to the neck look like it was squeezed," the district attorney asked again, but Dr. Patel shook his head, apparently willing only to state facts the science would support.

"No, the neck wasn't squeezed. The bleeding you see is internal. The victim was not strangled to death. In the cases of strangulation, or asphyxia, one always sees petechial hemorrhages on the conjunctiva." Dr. Patel turned back to the body and with a gloved thumb suddenly opened wide the eye of Angelo Coluzzi. Judy startled at the odd sight of the one-eyed corpse, his brown cornea clouded. Dr. Patel was pointing to the flap of the eyelid. "See? There is no blood clotting on the membrane lining the eye, not at all. So there was no loss of oxygen that resulted in death. We are getting ahead of ourselves here"—at this he gave an uncomfortable laugh—"but my initial conclusion is that the cause of death was the fracture to the neck. Death would have been instantaneous. This man did not suffer."

Judy realized where the D.A. was going, and it wasn't concern over the man's suffering. He wanted to prove that the murder was premeditated. The law in Pennsylvania was that premeditation wasn't a question of time, as in weeks or days in advance, but could occur in an instant, as long as death was the intended result. Strangulation was a slam-dunk for premeditation. Judy didn't know if she was allowed to ask questions at an autopsy, but figured if the D.A. could, she could, too. And she had more than a legal reason for asking this one. "Dr. Patel, you said the victim's neck was broken. Is that difficult to do?"

The district attorney snorted. "You can't know that, can you, Doctor?" he asked, while the detective beside him listened impassively. "That's not a pathology question."

Dr. Patel blinked round-eyed behind his glasses, making him look owlish. "Perhaps not, but I am a doctor, sir, and it pertains here. The neck of a man this age would break without difficulty. One forceful snap would be enough. This man's neck was essentially severed by the force." Judy fell into an appalled silence, and Dr. Patel rested a hand on the body's shoulder. "Now. Please, everyone, while I appreciate your interest, allow me to proceed in order, if you would. I must follow our department procedures."

The district attorney made another note, and Judy was having the same trouble the jury would have. **This man's neck was essentially severed by the force.**

"I move next to determine if there are other abnormalities on the body." Dr. Patel took his time reviewing every inch of Angelo Coluzzi's corpse, running his gloved fingers slowly over the skin, bending closer, and recording every scar, mole, and skin lesion. He even described a tattoo on Coluzzi's arm, a crucifix encircled by a blurry crown of thorns and under it a ribbon banner reading ITALY, which Dr. Patel's English accent made sound classy. It made Judy think about Pigeon Tony's tattoo, also of a crucifix.

Judy mulled it over. Angelo Coluzzi and Pigeon Tony were two men, contemporaries, both immigrants from the same country. According to Frank they had grown up not ten miles apart. They both raced homing pigeons. They liked the same tattoos. They loved the same woman. They had more in common than most friends; yet they were enemies. Two little old men, and one had killed the other. Pigeon Tony had killed Angelo Coluzzi, the old man on the table, whose hands were now being slid from sealed evidence bags.

JUDY'S THOUGHTS CHURNED AWAY AS SHE WATCHED DR. PATEL SEPARATE ANGELO COLUZZI'S STIFF FINGERS AND THEN SCRAPE UNDER EACH FINGERNAIL ONE BY ONE, BAGGING CAREFULLY EACH LINE OF DIRT. JUDY KNEW DR. PATEL WOULD SEND THEM TO THE CRIME LAB, WHERE COMMON DIRT WOULD REVEAL DNA FROM PIGEON TONY'S SKIN AND FIBERS FROM THE CLOTHES HE WAS WEARING. ANGELO COLUZZI'S BODY MIGHT EVEN YIELD UP PIGEON TONY'S FINGERPRINTS FROM ITS SKIN; THE LAB COULD DO THAT, TOO, JUDY RECALLED. THE COMMONWEALTH'S EVIDENCE AGAINST PIGEON TONY WOULD BE BOTH SUBSTANTIAL AND SOLID, BECAUSE HE DID IT. HE WAS GUILTY. AND SHE WAS DEFENDING HIM. THE THOUGHT SICKENED HER. THE DEATH SMELL FILLED HER NOSE. THE

ICY BODY CHILLED HER. THE BLACK BRUISES DEMANDED JUSTICE. THIS MAN'S NECK WAS ESSENTIALLY SEVERED BY THE FORCE. JUDY COULDN'T DENY THE ACT ANY LONGER. IT WAS MURDER.

"NOW WE WILL BEGIN THE INTERNAL EXAMINATION OF THE BODY," DR. PATEL WAS SAYING. HE TURNED TO THE INSTRUMENT TRAY AND PICKED UP A LARGE, SHINY SCALPEL. "I WILL MAKE A Y, OR PRIMARY INCISION, INTO THE TRUNK, CUTTING FROM SHOULDER TO SHOULDER, CROSSING DOWN OVER THE BREAST. THEN FROM THE XYPHOID PROCESS, OR THE LOWER TIP, OF THE STERNUM, I WILL MAKE A MIDLINE CUT DOWN THE ABDOMEN TO THE PUBIS." SCALPEL POISED IN THE AIR, DR. PATEL PEERED UNCERTAINLY AT JUDY. "ARE YOU FEELING OKAY? YOU LOOK UNWELL."

BUT SHE COULDN'T ANSWER, BECAUSE SHE FELT HER GORGE RISING AND HAD TO RUN FOR THE NEAREST BATHROOM.

# 14

After the morgue, Judy had planned to go back to the office, but that would have to wait. It had taken her only a minute to decide to blow off work at the office and another half hour to retrieve her car, a new VW Beetle. She had more important things on her mind than antitrust articles. She floored the gas pedal, and warm air blasted through the open window. She was going to talk to her client, the one who could twist another man's neck off and think that was just fine.

The bright green Bug zoomed down the Schuylkill Expressway out of Philadelphia, faster than any cartoon insect should. Judy adored her car but today it gave her no pleasure. Its black vinyl interior reminded her of the nylon body bag. The new-car smell was too close to formaldehyde. The fresh daisy she kept in the glass bottle on the console had wilted. She tasted bile on her teeth and it wasn't nausea, it was anger. At Pigeon Tony for what he had done, and at herself, for being so clueless. She was defending a guilty man. That she could have doubted it scared her. What was she thinking? That he was a cute little guy? That he had a handsome grandson?

What kind of a lawyer was she? The kind who represented guilty people as innocent. The kind who lied to themselves and to the jury. The kind everybody hated, who starred in countless lawyer jokes: How do you stop a lawyer from drowning? You shoot him. What do lawyers use for birth control? Their personalities. What do you call forty skydiving lawyers? Skeet. What's the difference between a woman lawyer and a pit bull? Lipstick. What's the trouble with lawyer jokes? Lawyers don't think they're funny and nobody else thinks they're jokes.

Despite the punch lines, Judy couldn't laugh. She hated that the public made jokes about lawyers, hated that they didn't understand the nobility of the profession, or of the law itself. Now she had become a lawyer joke. She hit the gas.

The Beetle flew west toward Chester County, where Frank had said he'd be with Pigeon Tony. She had intended to go there after finishing her antitrust article, but she still had Sunday and the weekend gave her a reprieve on returning the GC's phone calls. She left the city skyline behind and switched lanes again, impatient even in light traffic. The directions Frank had given her, written in her open Filofax on the passenger seat, fluttered in the wind as the VW accelerated. She'd go out 202 South and west from there. It would take over an hour. Too damn long.

But still not long enough to cool down.


Judy could smell the wetness that chilled the air blowing in the VW's window; though it was sunny outside now, it must have rained west of the city earlier in the morning, and it wasn't only the weather that was drastically different. She glanced around as she steered the car down a winding gravel road flanked by pasturelands. Out here it was country. She checked the directions but she was going to the right place.

A blue sky chased dawdling gray clouds to the horizon, which extended to an expanse of grassy hills so immense she could hardly believe she was still in Pennsylvania. The hills rolled into an unmowed meadow rippling in a gentle, still-damp breeze, and swallows and blue jays sailed above, swooping low to catch bugs the rainstorm had stirred up. Chirping and singing filled the meadow and its overgrown grasses, browning at the top, swaying with chrome-yellow bursts of dandelions, blue dots of forget-me-nots, and clusters of wild honeysuckle. The wildflowers sweetened the air, but Judy rolled up the window. The landscape inspired the painter in her, but a lawyer was in the driver's seat.

Huge pin oak trees towered in a shady grove beside the meadow, and in front of it Judy spotted Frank's white truck and other construction vehicles. They circled the only scar in the perfect landscape: a site that was a large, cleared patch of land the size of a private airstrip. Lush grass had been peeled away like pieces of an orange rind and tons of topsoil surrounded the strip, mounded in triangles smoothed by a bulldozer. Judy aimed for Frank's truck, her VW tires slip-sliding on the wet grass, and as she pulled up she could see that the strip housed a deep trench that ran its length.

The VW bounced off the grass and hit the wet dirt, which clotted Judy's car tires immediately, and Judy wished for four-wheel drive so she could yell at her client sooner. How come they hadn't mentioned that at the VW dealership? She added the car salesman to her shit list, cut the ignition, and climbed out of the car.

Her feet landed in dirt but her clogs felt completely at home. Brown-orange mud lay everywhere and little white butterflies flitted between the wet patches, looking for moisture. Judy couldn't have cared less. She stalked over to Frank's pickup, parked at the far side of the muddy strip, next to a six-foot mountain of rubble. The sun glared off the truck window, and she couldn't tell if anyone was in it at first; when she got closer, she could see that it was empty. She didn't see Frank or Pigeon Tony. A big yellow backhoe was running, but no one was around except a man shoveling more gravel into the trench. Judy thought about yelling at him, but she didn't represent him.

She hurried on, her clogs collecting mud until they looked like snowshoes. It slowed her but didn't stop her. Nothing could. At the far end of the patch roared the John Deere backhoe, big as a dinosaur and equally incongruous, making ferocious grinding and rattling noises. The hoe was engaged, toeing the earth between two hydraulic braces on either side. Judy looked up at the glass cab and there was Frank.

Frowning in concentration, he sat shirtless in jeans, straddling a black console with two black-knobbed levers. He had a palm on each stick, working them independently, so that the immense claw of the hoe feathered the topsoil, extending the trench line. Judy couldn't help but eye Frank's chest, lightly covered with fine black hair and muscular enough to make even his farmer's tan look damn good. She watched him pull the levers expertly, then warned herself not to be distracted by the fact that Frank could operate heavy machinery while naked. Judy's attraction to him confused her, especially since the morgue. She looked around for Pigeon Tony. She hoped the Coluzzis hadn't gotten to him before she could.

The engine to the backhoe stopped suddenly. "Yo, Judy!" Frank grinned and called to her from the cab as he stood up and slipped into a white Nike T-shirt that hung beside him on the console. Now there really was no reason to stick around.

"Where's your grandfather?" she called back.

"Behind the rocks!" He pointed past the rubble pile, and Judy took off. She didn't look back, telegraphing that this was a business call, and after a minute she heard the backhoe engine restart. She tramped in the mud around the rock pile, where she found Pigeon Tony.

He was bent over the rocks, apparently sorting them, in dark baggy pants and a wide-brimmed straw hat that had a makeshift cotton string for a chin strap. A red bandanna was knotted around his neck and a madras shirt hung like a rag from his belt; he toiled as shirtless as his grandson, to a much different effect. His shoulders were skinny and his breasts small and slack, the nipples flat and shriveled against the soft, almost womanish skin. Except for Angelo Coluzzi on the slab, Judy had never seen such an old man so bare. Her throat caught unaccountably, watching him bend over to pick up a rock, setting a golden crucifix around his neck swinging.

The crucifix brought Judy back to her senses. She remembered the crucifix tattooed on Angelo Coluzzi's arm and the skinniness of his gray chest on the steel tray, under the harsh fluorescent lighting. The chilly morgue was a world from this sunlit meadow, but it had a death grip on her, and she

couldn't shake its reach. How lucky Pigeon Tony
was to be alive in this lovely place and how privileged to be drawing breath today. It was a privilege he hadn't afforded Angelo Coluzzi.

Judy looked at her client with cold eyes. He was
examining the rock carefully, turning it over and
over like a tumbler, then setting it down in the far
pile with a tiny grunt. Judging from the size of
the three piles before him, which Judy would have
classified as rocks, rocks, and more rocks, Pigeon
Tony had been making meaningless distinctions
between rocks all morning. When he bent over for
the next rock, he spotted her standing there and
broke into a welcoming smile.

"Judy!" He straightened up, and his hand went
automatically to the back of his belt. He pulled
his shirt out and slipped into it as quickly as
Frank had, leaving it unbuttoned. "You come!"

"I need to talk to you, Pigeon Tony." Judy
shielded her eyes from the sun. "Can you take a
break?"

"Sure," he said, which came out like **shhhh,** and
he set the rock down gently. He slipped his hat
from his head, so that it hung on its cotton string,
revealing that his smile had vanished. "Whatsa
matter?"

"Follow me," she said sternly, and led him to the
shade of the oak trees.

# 15

Sun peeked through the leaves of the oak tree, falling dappled on the tall grass, and a cool breeze wafted through the shady grove. Judy was too angry to sit down but Pigeon Tony perched on the thickly knotted root of a tree in his bumpy madras shirt and baggy pants, next to a Hefty garbage bag he had insisted on fetching from the truck. He had untied his red bandanna and smoothed it out on the grass, then began unpacking the Hefty bag, placing on the red cloth items that were wrapped with what looked like men's undershirts. Judy had no idea what they were or why they were bundled with laundry.

"Pigeon Tony, I need you to listen to me."

"Si, si, I listen." With difficulty he untied the tiny knot in the first item and unfolded it to reveal a generous sandwich on crusty Italian bread—buffalo mozzarella with roasted red peppers. It looked delicious even in underwear, but Judy tried not to notice.

"I want you to look at me when we talk. This is important."

"Okay, okay. Gotta eat." Pigeon Tony nodded, his fresh sunburn obvious now that his straw hat was off, hanging down his back on its cotton string. He unwrapped the next shirt to find a pile of black olives, their rich oil soaked into the soft cotton. "Alla people gotta eat. Work, eat. Work again."

"Fine." Judy sighed. "Can you eat while I talk?"

Pigeon Tony shook his head, no. The next shirt contained a perfect red apple, then Pigeon Tony rummaged in the Hefty bag again and produced a thick jelly glass and a half-full bottle of Chianti. Old-fashioned basket-weaving covered the bottom of the bottle and made a loop at its neck.

"Well, too bad. You have to." Judy lowered herself to the grass, tucking her feet under her. "I just came from the morgue. You know what that is, a morgue?"

"**Che?**" Pigeon Tony twisted the cork from the Chianti bottle, poured it gurgling into the jelly glass, and offered it to Judy. "Drink."

"No thanks," she said, waving it off, but he set it down in front of her anyway. "A morgue is where they keep dead people."

"Ah, **si, si.**" Pigeon Tony picked up the mozzarella-and-pepper sandwich and handed it to her. "Eat."

"I don't want your lunch."

"Not my, is for you. Work, then eat." Pigeon Tony thrust the sandwich at her again. "I make, for you. You work, eat. Work again."

"This isn't your lunch?" Judy didn't understand. She didn't want to understand. She was prepared to ream him out, to call him to account. She had just seen his victim. Pigeon Tony was a murderer.

"No, no, not my. I eat, before." He gestured to the apple and the slick olives. "Alla, for you."

Judy didn't want the sandwich. She set it back down on the undershirt. "Pigeon Tony, I saw Angelo Coluzzi in the morgue. I want you to tell me how you came to kill him. Do you understand?"

"Si." Pigeon Tony frowned, his forehead buckling into leathery wrinkles. "You no eat, Judy?"

"No, now let's talk. Tell me everything. Who else was there, how you found him—everything."

"Talk, then eat?"

"Talk, then eat." Judy sighed. The man could negotiate with the best of them. She imagined him back in Italy, getting the best prices for whatever he grew. Tomatoes, olives, whatever. "But we're going to talk first. Talk now."

Pigeon Tony appeared to think a minute, then his face darkened. "I see Coluzzi at the club, you know? The club?"

Judy nodded. The pigeon-racing club. "What time of day, exactly?"

"Ah, inna mornin'. Friday, eight o'clock inna mornin'." Pigeon Tony nodded, his small mouth tight. "Alla loft, they come to the clubhouse. The birds, they get the bands. Onna legs. Before race. You understand?"

Judy nodded. She was the one who spoke English. She understood. "Who else was there, in the clubhouse?"

"Alla people—Tony, Feet, alla inna club. Me, Pigeon Tony, I go to back, inna back, to get bands and **bom**"—Pigeon Tony's eyes glittered—"I see Coluzzi!"

"In the back? What back?"

"Inna room, inna back. They play cards. You know."

Judy didn't know, but she could guess. "Why were you going in the back room?"

"To get bands, for birds. They have at club. They count, so no cheating. Everybody get bands before race."

"Fine." Judy nodded. Whatever. "Was anybody else in the back room?"

"Coluzzi."

Judy persisted. "I meant anybody besides Coluzzi and you?"

"No."

"So it was just you and him, in the back room." Judy tried to visualize it. She would have to get to the crime scene soon. When would she find the time? What about her other cases? "How big is the back room?"

"Little. Is little room."

"What's in it besides bands?"

"Alla things. Alla for birds."

"Supplies for the birds?"

"**Si, si.**"

Judy could make only a mental note. She'd been so pissed when she got here, she'd left her back-pack in the car. "Okay, so you go in the back room, and there he is. What happens next?"

"I see Coluzzi and I hate him. Hate!" Pigeon Tony's face colored and he clenched his small hands. "I **hate** him, in here. Inside." He thumped a fist on his chest. "Inna my **heart** I hate him. You know, **hate**?"

"Yes, I know," Judy said, though she doubted that anybody whose first language was English knew the hate he was talking about.

"And I kill him."

The words made Judy shudder. "So you just start hating him, and you kill him?" It sounded like spontaneous combustion, but she couldn't begin to translate. "Just like that?"

Pigeon Tony's eyes clouded with apparent confusion.

"I'm trying to understand why you killed him. I saw his body and his neck. It was broken very badly. It was awful to see. I don't know how you could do such a thing."

"**Si, si.**" Pigeon Tony nodded. "I **say** you before. I kill him. He kill my wife. I say, before."

Judy wiped her brow. If this weren't a privileged

conversation, she'd get Frank to translate. Shirtless. "I'm trying to make sense of this. I'm asking, did you just see Coluzzi and then run at him and break his neck?"

"**Si, si,** we make a fight and I break his neck. You know."

Judy did a double take. "What do you mean, you made a fight?"

"**Si, si,** we make a fight." Pigeon Tony cocked his head. "**Come se dice,** make a fight?"

"No, wait a minute." She would have to hire a fully dressed translator. It would be less fun but she could do her job. "We say fight, too, but you didn't tell me you two had a fight. What did you fight about?"

"What he say."

"What did he say?"

Pigeon Tony's dark eyes fluttered. "He say . . . thing."

"Yes, but what?" Judy couldn't keep anger from her tone. "Did he call you a name? What?"

Pigeon Tony didn't answer, his gaze focused on a splotch of sun outside the oak grove. Birds chirped in the meadow but he wasn't listening to them either.

"Pigeon Tony, tell me what he said. You understand more than you let on. You don't fool me."

Pigeon Tony's head moved slowly to face Judy and he seemed to wait a moment until his eyes focused. "He say he kill my son."

Judy felt stricken. "Your **son**? He admitted it?"

"My Frank. And wife, Gemma. Inna truck."

"You mean, the truck accident?"

"No accident! He **do** it. He kill **my son**. He kill **my wife**. He say me, he say me! He say he **destroy** me, because Silvana want me! He say he destroy Frankie. **Alla my family**." His voice broke slightly and tears sprang to his dark eyes, but Judy was struggling for clarity.

"So he told you he killed your son? He said he'd kill Frank, too? Your grandson Frank?"

"**Si! Si!**" Pigeon Tony was looking at her, but lost in the memory. Wetness brimmed in his eyes, refusing to budge. "When he say this, I go **bom**! I **hate him**, I hate him! I run and push him and break his neck! I kill him, for my son! For my wife! For my Frankie! **With my hands I do it!**"

Judy understood. She could almost imagine him, blind with pain and rage, avenging so many murders and saving Frank. "You killed him right then, after he said that?"

"**Si, si!** I kill him and he fall onna floor and they come, from the room. Alla people, come then. Tony, Feet. They see."

Judy found herself thinking like a defense lawyer again. "Did he say he'd kill you?"

"No, no. He no kill me. He destroy me."

Judy understood. The knowledge would make Pigeon Tony's life a living hell. She tried another tack. "When he said this, was it loud? Did the other people hear him?"

"No, not loud. Soft. He make a laugh." Pigeon Tony wiped tears that wouldn't come, and Judy winced.

"Are you sure?" Couldn't one person have heard it? She needed a witness to the conversation. "Was there a door to the room?"

"Si, si."

"Was it closed or open?"

"Close."

Judy considered it. No witnesses, and such a bombshell. "Why didn't I know this? Why didn't you tell me?"

"Ogni ver non è ben detto."

"What?"

"Alla truths not be told."

"What?" Judy hoped she hadn't heard him right. "You tell me everything. You want me to represent you, you be honest with me! You **have** to tell me."

"Perchè?" Pigeon Tony said, and Judy translated from the challenging flash to his eyes.

"Because I said so, that's why!"

"You tell judge?"

"No, of course not."

"Pfft!" Pigeon Tony made a noise that accompanied a twist of his hand in the country air, and Judy figured it meant what's-the-difference. Unfortunately, she couldn't immediately think what the difference was legally, but she still wanted to know.

"Is there anything else you didn't tell me?"

"No, no."

Judy's eyes narrowed. "Promise?"

Pigeon Tony crossed himself, which Judy decided was an acceptable substitute.

Then she remembered something. The conversation with Frank at his parents' gravesite. Frank had said Pigeon Tony suspected it wasn't an accident, not that he was told. Why hadn't Frank told her? Maybe he hadn't had a chance to talk with his grandfather after his arrest. But why hadn't Frank told her since then? Picked up the phone? "Why didn't Frank tell me?"

"I no tell Frank."

Judy's mouth opened slightly. "Why not?"

Pigeon Tony made a quick wave. "Not for him."

"What? It's his family. It's his mother and father."

"**You** no tell. Understand? No tell!" Suddenly Pigeon Tony pointed at Judy so sternly she was taken aback.

"I don't tell him anything you tell me. I can't. But why didn't you tell him?"

"No! I no tell! Why I'm gonna tell? Break his heart?"

Judy agreed. It would hurt Frank, that much was true. Still. "But doesn't he have a right to know?"

"Che?"

"A right. He has a right to know." Judy fumbled for a synonym. How could she explain the concept of a legal right to someone who didn't believe in the law? Or a moral right to someone who thought he was justified in killing? "Frank is entitled to know. He should know. It's his business."

"No! Is for **me,** not Frankie. **I** make vendetta, not **him!**" The gloom vanished from Pigeon Tony's face as he scrambled to his feet with a tiny grunt and motioned to Judy to get up. "Come. **Andiamo!**"

"What?" she asked, confused, but Pigeon Tony grabbed her wrist with surprising strength, yanked her to her feet, and tugged her from the oak trees into the sun. Intrigued, she let herself be led like a child, even though Pigeon Tony was so short he reached only to her shoulder.

They passed the rock piles and stopped when they got to the edge of the muddy construction site, still hand in hand. The yellow backhoe stood at the center of the mud, its huge arm rattling and creaking, toeing the earth among the pale butterflies. Frank was at the controls, absorbed in his work.

"See!" Pigeon Tony pointed at the backhoe with his free hand. "Is sign. See?"

"The sign?" Judy didn't see any signs. She looked around and found a painted strip on the window of the backhoe's cab. LUCIA STONE. "The company sign?"

"Si, si! È vero! È Frankie. Alla Frankie. La macchina, l'automobile, alla. Alla Frank. Alla Lucia Stone." Pigeon Tony's eyes were bright with emotion and his hand squeezed Judy's tight. "See? Frankie, he make—come se dice—he make a—che?" He turned to Judy to supply the English word.

"A company?"

"No. No." Pigeon Tony let go of her hand and waved his impatiently, freeing them. "Frankie make a—"

"A building?"

"No! No!"

"He make a wall?"

"No! No!" Pigeon Tony faced the backhoe and threw his arms up in frustration. "You no see? Judy, whatsa matter you, you no see?"

"I don't know what he's making!" she answered, equally frustrated, but Pigeon Tony turned her bodily to face the construction site.

"See, Judy! See, la macchina. See sign, see alla!"

"I see, I see!"

"Frankie, he make futuro! Capisce? Futuro?"

Judy understood then. It wasn't a company, or a wall. LUCIA STONE. "A future."

"Si, si!" Pigeon Tony almost exploded with relief. "Futuro! Frankie make futuro. Here, for his children. For alla who come."

"I see." Judy's throat caught unaccountably, but Pigeon Tony was wagging a finger at her.

"Understand? No you tell Frankie. About father, my son. Or no futuro for Frankie. Only vendetta. Only murder. Only morte. Capisce?"

Judy nodded.

"Promise?"

Judy couldn't help but smile. She had created an Italian monster. "Yes."

"**Bene.**" Pigeon Tony nodded curtly, then turned to the noisy backhoe, calm coming over him as he watched Frank make his future.

Judy watched, too, the sun warming her back, and after a time, without knowing why, she reached for her client's small, withered hand.


Fifteen minutes later they had piled into two cars, Judy into the green Bug and Frank and Pigeon Tony leading the way in the white pickup, as they snaked from the countryside back to the highway. Judy had replaced her wilted daisy on the console with a fresh spray of blue forget-me-nots, but she wasn't completely sorry to leave the country sights and smells. Now that she had a client again, she had a defense to stage. Not that she had resolved everything.

She hit the gas, whizzing past sunny open country that became cloudy housing developments, but Judy was lost in thought. Images of Angelo Coluzzi in death ran through the back of her mind, but the situation wasn't black and white anymore. As an artist, she knew there were shades of gray and had always counted herself lucky for that. Dark gray underlined a stormy sky in her landscapes; light gray hollowed a human cheek-bone in her portraits. So why couldn't there be shades of gray in a murder defense? She was painter and lawyer both; art and a defense were both her creations. So she could take responsibility for the colors in her cases. She liked the notion.

Judy took a bite of her lunch, crunching through the crusty bread and sinking her teeth into the spongy-soft mozzarella, and she became convinced the sandwich was helping her think. Mozzarella had superpowers. She followed Frank's big truck as it climbed onto the expressway, watching him talk animatedly with his grandfather as they drove. They both used their hands when they talked, and Judy wondered briefly if Italians had more traffic accidents than normal people.

Frank's big hands chopped the air, and she flashed on their conversation at his parents' grave. So they had been murdered. She had been touched by Pigeon Tony's keeping that from Frank, and though she understood his reasons for it, the knowledge burdened her. Judy had grown up in an American family, as patriotic as a military family could be, and she had been trained in law, a code of rights and responsibilities. In her view, Frank had a right to know how his parents had died; it was a truth that shouldn't be hidden from him. And why did Pigeon Tony think it was okay to hide one truth—the way they died—and not the other—the way Angelo Coluzzi died? This case had more cultural conflicts than legal ones, and more ethical conflicts than both. She needed emergency mozzarella.

Judy took another bite. If she ate enough of it, she could figure out how to do all the work she had been ignoring this weekend. She remembered the unfinished article on her laptop; she would have to get to it tonight. Sunday wouldn't be enough time, and she didn't want to face Bennie on Monday. Judy glanced out the window, and the sky was tinged with gray.

She couldn't help but think it was appropriate.

# 16

CONGRATULATIONS, SOUTH PHILLY COMBINE! read a white plastic banner that hung from the flat roof of the clubhouse, oddly parallel with the yellow plastic crime-scene tape that sagged across the front door. The clubhouse, a brick rowhouse used for the purpose, stood by itself on the city block, because the other houses had been leveled and the lots strewn with brick and mortar rubble, bottles, and other debris. Judy climbed out of the truck, and Frank helped Pigeon Tony to the curb.

"See that guy on the corner?" Frank asked, and Judy looked over. A heavyset man sat in a black Cadillac at the far end of the street, apparently reading a newspaper. "That's Fat Jimmy Bello, works for the Coluzzis."

"So?"

"So I told you, I don't like it. He's watching the clubhouse. You sure you gotta go in there?"

"Yes," Judy said. "I have to see it."

"We can't come back another time?"

"No, I have the D.A.'s permission to do it now, and it's best to see the crime scene as soon as possible."

Frank glanced again at the corner. The man was still sitting in the driver's seat, reading a newspaper. "That means you have five minutes in there."

"Why?"

"Because I'm not taking any chances. Hurry. I'll wait here. Go!"

NO BEER OUTSIDE, read a handmade sign on the wall of the small room, which would have been the living room of the original rowhouse. The floors were of lime green and white linoleum, and the walls were lined with chicken wire cages, twelve on a side, their doors double-fastened with plastic clothespins. A makeshift wooden bar sat against the far wall, stocked with cases of beer and soda, with forks and spoons stuck in a chipped mug. Steel folding chairs sat in rows facing a table at the front of the room, as if for a meeting. On all of the walls, like a border atop the cages, hung a line of framed black-and-white photographs, one of men in suits and women in fancy dresses, seated at a roomful of banquet tables, and others in groups. Judy caught one of the handwritten captions as they hurried by. South Philly Pigeon Racing Club, June 14, 1948.

She went into the back room, with Pigeon Tony

ahead of her. She glanced around and realized it had once been the dining room of the rowhouse. "Where was he when you came into the room?" she asked when they were inside.

"There." Pigeon Tony pointed. "Near shelf."

Judy looked where the bookshelves were leaning against the plywood wall and at the supplies and vitamin jugs scattered on the floor. She knew how they'd look in crime-lab photos and blown up as Exhibit B. "Okay, he was standing in front of the bookshelves?"

"Si, si."

"You open the door and you see him. What happens next?"

"I kill him."

Judy winced. "Slow down. Remember the fight you told me about. How exactly did it start? Who spoke first?"

"He."

"How loud was his voice?"

"I **say** you, no loud. Whisper."

Judy nodded. "Okay, what did he say, exactly?"

"He laugh. He say, in Italian, 'Look who come in. A buffoon. A weakling. A coward.'"

"Why did he say that? What did he mean?"

"I no avenge Silvana. I run away, to America."

Judy didn't understand. "That was wrong?"

"**Si, si.**" Pigeon Tony's face reddened, even under his fresh sunburn. "If I honor vendetta, my son be alive."

"You don't know that."

"I know. Coluzzi know."

"But if you had killed Coluzzi, his son would have come after your son. Isn't that how it works? An eye for an eye?"

Pigeon Tony paused. "No matter. I must honor vendetta, like man. Coluzzi come after my son alla way. He come after Frankie."

Judy didn't want to get into it. She had an idea. "Now tell me. He says this to you and what do you do? Besides hate him."

"I hate him and I make a fight."

"Show me."

Pigeon Tony's eyes widened. "You want me to make a fight with you? A woman?"

"**Si, si,**" she said, a close-to-perfect impression, and he smiled.

"Okay," he began, his impression not as good as hers, to her ear. Suddenly his face darkened, as it had back at the oak grove. "I say to Coluzzi, 'You are pig. You are scum. You are worse coward than me, for you kill defenseless woman.'"

Judy wondered how Silvana had died but said nothing. She didn't want to interrupt his story.

"And he laugh, and he say to me, 'You are a stupid fool, you are too dumb to know I destroy you. I kill your son, too, and his wife. I kill them in truck and soon I kill Frank and you will have nothing.'" Pigeon Tony trembled with pain, and though Judy's heart went out to him, she had to keep him on track.

"Then what did you say?"

"I no say nothing. I no can believe. My heart, is full with **odio**. So much hate."

"Did you do something?"

**"Si, si."**

"Show me what you did."

Pigeon Tony thought a minute. "I run and I push him."

"Pretend I'm Coluzzi. Push me how you pushed him."

Pigeon Tony hesitated, then took a step toward her slowly, then another. "I run at him, fast. I no think, I run."

Judy nodded. "I understand."

"And I come to him"—at this Pigeon Tony gripped her arms, reaching only to her elbow—"and I push him, I **shove** at him. I no can believe how hard!"

Judy's idea took shape. "And then he fell back? Against the shelves?"

**"Si, si**. And shelf, is metal, is tin, it falls down. And I make noise, I no can believe it come, and alla people come in—Tony, Feet, alla club. I break his neck!"

"How do you know that?"

Pigeon Tony looked at her like she was crazy. "His neck"—he gestured to the floor—"all crazy, all crooked. Alla people say, 'You broke neck.'"

Judy considered it. This could work. And it was

consistent with what the coroner would say. "Then what did you do?"

"I no do nothing. I look at him. I no can believe Coluzzi dead. Tony, Feet, they take me out, they make me go home. Coluzzi's friend in club, Jimmy, he shout at me. He make a fight to me. He call police. Tony, Feet, they get me, and I go to home. I feed birds and police come."

"So the one push broke Coluzzi's neck." Judy remembered what Dr. Patel, the medical examiner, had said. Pigeon Tony's story would be consistent with it. "His neck snapped?"

"**Si, si.**"

"You didn't touch him again after that?"

"No."

Judy's heart lifted. She had a defense, and it was perfect. One last detail. "How long would you say you were in the room?"

"**Che?** How long?"

"I'm wondering about the time. How many minutes were you in the room before you pushed Coluzzi?"

Pigeon Tony snapped his fingers. "Two, three minute. No time."

Judy tried out her theory. "So maybe you didn't mean to kill him. Maybe you just meant to fight with him, or hurt him, and he fell back and broke his neck."

Pigeon Tony frowned. "No, I want to kill him. I **try** to kill him."

"Did you? Are you sure?"

"**Si, si!** I want to kill him. For Silvana. For Frank. For Frankie. You no **capisce**?"

Judy **capisce**d just fine, but she was visualizing her opening argument. "But nobody will know that you wanted to kill him, from the way it happened. From the way it happened, from what everybody will say, even the prosecution witnesses, you went in the room and you were only in there a few minutes. All you did was push him, and he fell back and broke his neck. That's not murder."

Pigeon Tony broke into a grin of recognition. "**Bravissima,** Judy! Is **no** murder! I say you, before. Is no murder! Coluzzi kill my wife. And my son!"

Judy shook her head. "No, it's not murder because you didn't mean to kill him."

"No! No!" Pigeon Tony bristled. "I kill him! I **want** to!"

"The jury won't know that."

Pigeon Tony cocked his head. "What means jury?"

"Jury. It's the people who sit at your trial and decide if you're guilty of murder."

"**Si, si.** I tell jury. I tell judge. I say I kill him but no è murder."

Judy stilled him with her hands. They were back to square **uno**. "No, you don't say anything. Listen to me. In the law, the prosecutor, or the district attorney, has to prove you intended, or wanted, to kill Coluzzi when you pushed him. In fact, they have to prove you were lying in wait to kill him, for murder in the first degree. They can't prove you meant to kill him from the facts they have. And they can't prove it from the physical evidence." Judy touched Pigeon Tony's skinny shoulder, her excitement growing. "It may be manslaughter, but they didn't charge you with manslaughter. They overcharged, like they always do. They charged you with murder. We're gonna win! You'll go free."

Pigeon Tony looked at her in wonderment. "But, Judy, I **want** to kill him. Is **truth**."

The simple words stung, and Judy felt her face flush. It was the truth, and she was preparing to hide it, to get her client off. How do you explain that to someone like Pigeon Tony? Whose morals were supposedly inferior to hers? Was he guilty or not? What had she decided? They didn't agree on the rationale, but they both thought it wasn't murder. Did it matter? Judy couldn't wrap her mind around it.

But Pigeon Tony was shaking his head. "When I run to him, I say to him, 'I kill you, I kill you, you pig!'"

"What?"

"I say this when I push him. I run at him and say it."

Judy cut him off with a wave. "Why didn't you tell me that before?"

"I forget."

"How loud did you say that?"

"Loud. I scream. How you say 'scream'?"

"We say 'scream.'" Judy's heart sank. There could be witnesses who heard it through the door, but then again, maybe there weren't. "Who exactly was there that morning? Tony, Feet, who else from your club?"

"Nobody."

"Good." Judy hoped they didn't hear it. "Who from Coluzzi's club?"

Pigeon Tony shook his head. "Only Fat Jimmy. He always with Angelo Coluzzi."

"Fat Jimmy. What's his last name again?"

"Bello."

Suddenly there was a knock, and Frank peeked through the open door. His mouth looked tight. "We need to go!"

"For real?" Judy asked.

"John Coluzzi's on his way."

# 17

"You want me to leave my car, in this neighborhood?" Judy asked. She hadn't counted on
that. Her little bug beckoned from its parking
space. **Fahrvergnügen,** it said to her, which she
had learned was Italian for high monthly pay-
ments.

"Go, go, go! Judy, get in the truck." Frank was
hoisting his grandfather into the backseat of his
big F-250, his eyes riveted down the street.
"Coluzzi's man made a cell call two minutes ago
and just got picked up in a black Caddy. My guess
is Coluzzi, he'll show up any minute."

Judy looked down the street, too. There was
nobody in sight except a boxy SEPTA bus. Gray
clouds gathered overhead and a young woman
smoking a cigarette hurried along, pushing a baby
in a plaid umbrella stroller. "Okay, but why can't I
take my car?"

"I want you with me. Get in the truck." Frank
turned to her and grabbed her arm. His grip was

strong, his expression worried. "We'll come back for the goddamn car."

"Promise?"

"No." Suddenly Frank lifted Judy by the waist and hoisted her into the front seat before she could protest. "Any other questions?" he asked, but Judy gathered it was rhetorical, since he slammed the door behind her. She sat slightly stunned. Nobody had ever picked her up before; she didn't know it was possible. She half liked the idea. And half hated it.

"He's bossy, isn't he?" Judy said with an embarrassed laugh, and Pigeon Tony cackled from the backseat.

"My Frankie, he likes you," he said, and Judy couldn't help but blush, wondering if it was true. And surprised that she cared enough to wonder.

Frank jumped into the truck, cranked the ignition, and hit the gas. "Let's get outta here," he said, and the huge engine roared into action. They took off, the truck's wide tires screeching.

Judy's face was still warm as she glanced in the large side mirror mounted outside her window. The SEPTA bus disappeared into the distance. "Nobody back there."

Frank glanced at the rearview mirror. "Not yet." He looked over his shoulder. "Pop, do me a favor and lie down."

"Here?" Pigeon Tony asked. "Inna seat?"

"Yes, just do it, okay? Judy, you, too." Frank's

eyes glittered as they accelerated around the corner, whizzing by rowhouse after rowhouse. People
on the street turned and stared. A woman walking
her poodle shook her fist. Frank gripped the
wheel, controlling the truck with grim determination. Rocks thundered in the back bed, rolling
back and forth. "Both of you, lie down!"

Pigeon Tony obeyed in silence but Judy had
never obeyed anything, in silence or otherwise.
She gripped the handrail in front of her window,
steadying herself as the pickup squealed around
the corner. She was starting to believe that Italians
shouldn't be issued driver's licenses. Next thing
they'd want the vote. "Watch out, Frank! Don't
you think you're overreacting?"

"Lie down!" he shouted, just as an earsplitting
**crack** sounded behind them.

Judy jumped. Was that a gunshot? It wasn't
possible. It was broad daylight. "What was **that**?"
she said, turning reflexively.

A black sedan was bearing down on them. A
man hung out of the passenger window with a
handgun. Holy God. Judy stiffened with fright.
Where had the car come from?

**Crak!** Another shot rang out, louder than the
first. People on the street were throwing themselves onto the sidewalk.

"Get down!" Frank yelled. He palmed Judy's
head, shoved it into her lap, and held it there. The

truck surged forward. "Pop, stay down! They're shooting at us!"

**"They're shooting at us?"** Judy's voice got lost in her skirt. She couldn't believe it. Adrenaline dumped into her system. She tried to stay calm and think. She had no idea where her seat belt was. This was attempted murder. She should call the police. Her cell phone was in her backpack, jostling near her feet on the carpeted floor of the truck. She reached for it with a trembling hand.

**Crak!** Another blast went off, closer this time. The sound shot through her body, shocking her senses. Her backpack slid out of reach when the truck careened around another corner. Her heart pumped wildly. People on the street shouted and cursed them.

"Goddamn it! I can't lose these assholes!" Frank said through gritted teeth. "Hold on!" He wrenched the steering wheel to the right. The tires squealed hideously. Rocks slammed against the truck bed. The truck swerved around the next corner.

Judy was thrown against Frank's side, jolting her upright. She grabbed the console for support. The truck scraped a line of parked cars as it barreled forward. Sparks flew past the truck window like firecracker debris.

Judy glanced back at the dark car. It was only a block away. Close enough for a good shot. "No!"

she heard herself screaming. She twisted forward. The truck was racing toward the intersection straight ahead. The traffic light was red. A Mayflower moving van was already nosing into the grid. In a second they would get trapped between the Coluzzis and the van. They would die unless they could beat the van. In a split second Judy read Frank's mind. "Do it!" she hollered, and Frank floored the gas.

The truck leaped forward like a runaway bull and thundered toward the intersection. Frank threw an arm over Judy's body, holding her back like a seat belt. "I got you," he said, but his words vanished in the blare of the van's horn, blowing like a Klaxon.

The truck zoomed toward the van. The van was almost all the way into the intersection. Judy was close enough to see the driver's horrified face as he tried to stop the van. His brakes screeched. Black smoke came from his tires. His momentum was too great. The opening was narrowing. They wouldn't make it. Judy's heart jumped in her chest.

Frank cut the steering wheel back with a violent jerk. The truck swerved wildly around the van's monstrous hood, then shot past. Its rear end fishtailed as it bounced onto the sidewalk but Frank yanked the wheel back. Judy reached instinctively for Frank's arm across her body. The truck crashed into the parked cars on the opposite side of the narrow street.

"Fuck!" Frank torqued the wheel, regained control of the truck, and tore down the street. The expressway on-ramp lay just ahead. They zoomed toward it.

Judy almost cried with happiness. Safe! Tires skidded and metal crashed on the other side of the van behind them. She looked back. The van blocked the intersection completely, its driver moving and unhurt in the cab. What about the Coluzzis? Were they dead? Judy hoped so. They were killers.

"We did it!" Frank shouted as the truck swerved down the street, ran another red light, and flew onto the ramp for the expressway, eating up the fast lane out of the city. He drove with an eye on the rearview mirror and shifted quickly in his seat to get a view of the back. "Pop, you okay back there?"

"Si, si!" Pigeon Tony squeaked from the backseat, and they both laughed.

"Good!" Frank checked the rearview mirror again. He turned to Judy, his brown eyes bright, and broke into a grin. "How about you?"

"I'm alive," she said, and it felt wonderful. Relief flooded her system. Her breathing eased. Her blood pressure returned to normal, for a lawyer. She wanted to call the police. Frank's arm felt good against her side and he showed no inclination to remove it, now that its purpose had been served. "You gonna move that arm?" she asked with a smile.

"Not unless you tell me to."

"Since when do you listen to me anyway?"

He laughed, and they took off.

The truck traveled away from the city under a cloud-covered sky, turning to a dark, muggy evening. Pigeon Tony snoozed in the small backseat, which fit him perfectly, and Frank drove with his arm resting across Judy's body, making her entire left side feel warm and good. She couldn't remember the last time she had felt like this, when someone's simple touch could set her tingling, and in any event, she had never met a man like Frank. She slid out from behind his arm only to retrieve her cell phone and call the police.

This time Judy bypassed 911 and called Detective Wilkins directly, since he had made the mistake of giving her his card. Lucky for him he was in. "Detective," she said, "I want to report an attempted murder. Of my client, of his grandson, and of a lawyer I like a lot."

"We're on it." His voice sounded flat. "South Philly, right?"

"Yes. We were at the crime scene and were chased several blocks by the Coluzzis. John, we think, and a man named Jimmy Bello, who used to work for his father. They shot at us three times. They tried to kill us."

"We have impounded the vehicle, which crashed into the van. It's totaled. Unfortunately the perpetrators got away. How do you know it was John Coluzzi? Did you see him?"

"Wait a minute. They got away?" Judy shook her head, and Frank looked over from behind the wheel. Concrete highway walls were a blur in the background, the slabs darkened with earlier rain. "How did they get away?"

"I'm already looking into that. We moved quickly once we got the call. Residents called nine-one-one, dispatch got eleven calls, and we were at the scene not five minutes after the collision. The perpetrators had already fled the scene."

Judy frowned. The scenery whizzed by. Frank looked pissed at the wheel. His arm was long gone. Their second fight. She couldn't give up. "But you know who the car was registered to. You can trace that and arrest Coluzzi, right? Or at least Bello?"

"Not so fast. It was a stolen car, owned by a rabbi in Melrose Park. Got pinched three months ago. Why do you keep saying it was John Coluzzi? Can you identify him?"

"I saw them," Judy said, suddenly flashing on the man in the passenger seat with the gun. "At least one of them."

"Was it John Coluzzi?"

She closed her eyes as the truck barreled down the highway. She couldn't remember more. She had seen John Coluzzi only at the courthouse. It had happened so fast. "Not for sure, not yet. I saw a white male. With hair."

"What color hair?" Detective Wilkins asked.

"Brown."

"Anything else?"

Judy thought hard. "No," she had to admit. "Didn't anyone see them run away?"

"The only ID is two white males, one heavyset, but we have no suspects as yet. We have uniformed officers canvassing the neighborhood."

" 'Nobody knows nothin'?' Are you buying that, Detective?"

"What do you want from my life, Ms. Carrier? We're on it. These are major crimes. We're there. We'll call you when we pick up the perps." Detective Wilkins didn't sound unconcerned, and Judy softened. He wasn't the enemy. The policeman was your friend, right? She turned to Frank.

"Can you identify them? Did you see anything?" she asked.

"Sure. Gimme the phone." Frank took the cell phone from Judy. It looked small in his hand. "Detective, here's my description. Got a pen?" Frank paused a minute. "The two shooters, one was John Coluzzi and one was his man, Jimmy Bello, because Marco don't have the balls. You go see John, you'll see a couple guys that look even worse than usual. Those are the bad guys." Frank handed the phone back to Judy with a smile. "Thanks, counselor."

Judy took the phone but couldn't manage a smile. "Detective, what if I could come down to the Roundhouse and look at some mug shots. Wouldn't that help identify them?"

Frank shook his head over the steering wheel. "No, you're not doing that."

The detective was saying, "We do have some shots of members of the Coluzzi family and some associates. It would help if you came down, but I'm not promising anything."

Judy said, "I'll do it."

Frank was shaking his head. "No you won't."

The detective was still talking. "When do you want to come down? I'm on night tour this week. I'm here all night."

"I'll call you later," she said, because Frank was already reaching for the cell phone. He took it from her hand, snapped it closed, and tossed it onto the dash.

"You're not going down there."

"Why not?"

"You'll get yourself killed."

"They're not after me. I'm just the lawyer."

Frank snorted, resting a finely muscled forearm on the steering wheel. The truck sped west. "Those bullets they were shooting, were they going around you?"

"They were trying to hit Pigeon Tony," Judy said, but she was barely convincing herself. "Besides, if I go down to the Roundhouse, I'd go alone. They wouldn't come after me alone."

"Of course they would. You don't get it, do you? What do you think is happening to your car right now?"

Judy's heart jumped. "You think they'll hurt it?"

"No. I think they're too nice to hurt it." Frank laughed, but Judy wasn't kidding.

"What will they do to it?"

"To your Bug? After they pull its little legs off or before?"

"If they so much as touch that car, I'll—"

"Watch it." Frank raised a finger in mock admonishment. "Of course, if they do anything to your car, you will be free to pursue all appropriate legal remedies."

Judy still wasn't laughing. "Now I'm really mad," she said, and meant it.

# 18

When Frank's truck finally came to a stop, it was twilight, the stars just beginning to shine in the country sky, winking behind a thin veneer of dusk. They were back in Chester County, parked in thick grass in front of an abandoned springhouse, painted white. It was on the same property as the construction site, on the far side of the meadow. It had rained here, stirring up the gnats, which flew in dizzy knots outside a windshield dotted with raindrops. Birds chirped loudly, filling the damp air with sound, none of which woke up Pigeon Tony, who snoozed in the backseat.

Judy pushed the button to roll down the truck window. "You think he'll be safe here?"

"No doubt." Frank put on the emergency brake and wiped dark hair from his forehead. "This is a seventy-five-acre property, and the springhouse is in the middle of it, if you look on a topo. A topographic map."

Judy looked around. Not a handgun in sight. They seemed to be in the middle of nowhere, if not paradise. "But where is the house? I mean, don't springhouses provide water to houses?"

Frank pointed past her. "It used to be over there, about fifty yards, but the owners tore it down. They're building a new house on the far side of the meadow. Come on, I'll show you." He climbed out of the truck and closed the door softly enough not to wake his grandfather. Judy followed suit, feeling finally safe again when her clogs hit the grass.

"This is better than people shooting at you," she said, and Frank moved toward her, extending a large hand.

"Am I fun or what? Here, step into my office. It's the best part of my job." He took her hand with confidence, and Judy let him. Her hand nestled happily in his, and she liked the simple connection to him as they walked across the grass. It was long enough to tickle her bare ankles and drench the toe of her clogs, but she felt too good to mind. She didn't know exactly when all the hand-holding and leg-pressing had started, but she was sure that bullets were flying at the time. Frank gestured to the oak trees on their left. "Hope you like what I've done with the place. I don't mean to brag, but those trees over there, they're two hundred years old. And green is my favorite color."

Judy smiled. "I was guessing mauve."

"Nuh-uh. Mauve is for bricklayers."

"My office has law books."

"Too bad." Frank moved easily through the grass, eyeing a tan fieldstone as they passed. "At least they burn easy."

"It also has bookshelves and accordion files and a credenza."

"A credenza! Wow." Frank nodded. "Mine only has the sun."

Judy was enjoying being somebody's straight man for a change. "Plus I have e-mail, voicemail, and two phone lines, right on my desk."

"I have a backhoe, a pickup, and a grandfather. And that used to be all. Now I have something far greater." Frank squeezed her hand, and Judy didn't ask him what he meant, though she had a guess. She didn't want to make a horse's ass of herself or go too fast. She liked him too much. She was in definite like. She glanced at him, hoping for some meaningful interlocking of eyes, but he was looking down at the grass. "See?" he asked, and pointed.

"What?" All Judy saw was wet grass.

"That's the footing wall." Frank nosed the grass with the toe of his big boot, lifting the damp sod and exposing a tan stone. "Valley Forge fieldstone, indigenous to this area of Pennsylvania. This is where the old farmhouse was. See how the grass is lighter, in a line, all around? You can still see the footprint of the house. The stone stays put." He pointed in a line that made a square, and Judy followed his arm, only slightly distracted by the biceps revealed by his polo shirt. It was so pleasant to be standing here, their hands linked loosely, listening to his voice. Its richness told her he loved what he was talking about.

"The farmhouse was built in 1780," he continued. "I saw it last year, before they tore it down. White stucco over centuries-old fieldstone. The foundation was thicker than any I've seen. The windowsills were deep enough to hold two men. The house would have stood forever. It fought to stay up, I swear." Regret tinged his tone, and she understood.

"Why did they tear it down?"

"It didn't have a family room. Or a weight room. Or a place for a spa."

Judy was appalled. "It was historic."

"I'm a professional. I've learned not to judge my clients. How about you?"

Judy laughed. "Enough said."

"History doesn't matter to some people. They want media rooms, hollow doors, and a three-car garage." Frank shrugged. "Anyway, I like their taste in walls. They went to Ireland, and they liked the walls there. Ireland has all dry-laid—they use them for sheep—and England, that's the place where it started. They're the same everywhere and they have been for hundreds of years. And the only ingredients are stone and gravity. They're fun to build. Amazing to build, actually."

"How so?"

Frank paused. "They clear the head, at the same time they engage it completely. Any wall has that effect. Winston Churchill, every chance he got during the war, retired to his country house to build a brick-and-mortar wall, did you know that?"

"No."

"It's true. But it's not always a hobby. In Italy, which of course has the best stonework, the farmers learned to make stone walls for fencing because there weren't enough trees around. Italian masons, when they came to America, built half the dry stone walls in New England and New York. I'll take you out to Westchester County someday. The walls there match the ones you see in Italy."

"Have you been?"

"To Italy? Twice. I went through the hill towns, built almost entirely of stone. Castlenuovo, Spoleto, Pontito, Calascio, Ostuni."

It sounded like a menu, but Judy didn't say so. She was thinking about the Lucia family, and the past. "Did you go to the town where your grandfather came from?"

"Of course I went to the village. It's right outside Veramo, in Abruzzo. I met all my cousins, they're still there. It was great."

"It must have been." But Judy was wondering about the case, and a missing piece. She hadn't wanted to interrupt Pigeon Tony at the clubhouse.

"I have to ask you something, about your grand-mother, Silvana. About her murder."

"Whatever you need," Frank said, and his hand closed on hers.

"How did she die?"

"I told you, Coluzzi killed her because she chose my grandfather over him."

"I know, but how did she die?"

"They still talk about it, over there." Frank cleared his throat. "She was found at the farm, as if she had fallen from a hayloft. Her neck was bro-ken."

Judy startled. "Like Coluzzi's."

"I guess, but there's no connection."

"The jury will think there is, if it comes into evidence." Judy's thoughts hurried on. It would make Pigeon Tony's act look more like payback, strengthening the intent argument for the Com-monwealth. She'd have to keep it out, but she had more questions. "How did they know it was mur-der? I mean, what if she simply fell out of the hayloft?"

Frank shook his head. "The way my grandfather tells it, my grandmother never went near the hayloft. She was probably killed, then taken there to make it look like an accident."

Judy thought a minute. "So how do you know it was Coluzzi?"

"He was seen in town that night, which was

strange enough, since he lived in Mascoli, which is in Marche province, and never came into Veramo, in Abruzzo. It's like being on the wrong block in South Philly. You don't belong. You stand out. Coluzzi was on Lucia turf, and people noticed." Frank's eyes narrowed. "You're going to say that it's circumstantial evidence."

"Exactly. That wouldn't be enough to charge Angelo Coluzzi with murder in this country." Judy nodded, and felt his hand slip from hers. Their third fight. Maybe they were water and olive oil. "It doesn't prove anything."

"But you saw those guys, Judy. They were shooting at **you**."

"Be analytical, Frank. They weren't the same guys. They're not Angelo Coluzzi. The guys who shot at us were his grandsons, his cousins, whoever."

"They're Coluzzis." Frank's eyes darkened. "It's in their blood, Judy. They're crazy. They're all about hate."

"You can't generalize about people as a family."

"Why not? Of course I can. History is filled with families who are murderous, or just plain sick. Whether it's nature or nurture, it just is. What about the Borgias? What about the Gambino crime family? Violence is a way of life for them. It's a family value." Frank spread his palms in appeal. "Judy, you didn't know my father, but I'm not very different from him. And how different am I from my grandfather? I'm taller, younger, with more change in my pocket, but that's it."

Judy couldn't disagree, but Frank was too urgent for her to get a word in edgewise.

"Jeez, isn't that what women are always afraid of? Turning into their mothers? It's the same thing."

Judy thought of her mother, a scholar so proud of her erudition she insisted on being called doctor. Even by waiters. Eeeek.

"Everybody knows Angelo Coluzzi killed Silvana, and he did. I guarantee he thought he was right to do it. And all of the Coluzzis would agree."

Judy focused on Silvana then, the woman who had inadvertently started it all, and felt her loss. If Frank was right, Silvana was a woman who chose her love and paid for it with her life. Judy couldn't imagine not being free to love whom she chose, until she thought of many places in the world outside her own. In the Middle East, Fundamentalist parents chose whom their daughters married. In much of India, women didn't choose their husbands and they still practiced **suttee**, or widowburning. So this stuff really happened, even today. How could it be? Could she do anything to set it right? She didn't have any answers, but Frank was taking her hands in his.

"Judy, this is our war, not yours. Our way, not

yours. After what happened today, I want to find my grandfather another lawyer. I want you out of harm's way. I never should have brought you into it in the first place." Frank's hands squeezed hers, but this time it was Judy who broke the connection.

"No, I can do it. I want to."

"I know you can, but it's dangerous. You could have been shot to death."

"This is my case, and I'll handle it."

"I don't think—"

"I don't care. This is my case and I'm keeping it. End of discussion. If I need protection, I'll get it."

"Oh, really?" Frank's eyes softened, and his crow's-feet wrinkled. He nudged a strand of Judy's blond hair from her face. "I thought I was your protection."

"I haven't had a man protect me, ever."

Frank laughed. "Funny, I protected you pretty good this afternoon."

Shit. "Well. You protected me pretty well." It was her mother talking.

"Good, well, whatever. Remember? The truck, the van? The guy in the driver's seat next to you?" Frank thudded on his broad chest with a knuckle. "That was me."

Judy sniffed. "That was then, this is now. I was unprepared. It won't happen again. And I'm the lawyer. I do the protecting around here. That's why they call it defense."

"You don't get it, do you, cowgirl? If you want

to protect me, that's okay. But please don't get in the way while I'm protecting you." Frank leaned over, and Judy became aware of how close to her he was standing, how near his face was to hers. He didn't have onion breath anymore, but even that she wouldn't have minded, now that that protection crap was out of the way.

"I don't need you to protect me. The most I'll agree to is our protecting each other."

"I'm not negotiating," he said, and his hand moved to cup her face, his finger pads rough on her cheek. "It's not an exchange. I'm a protecting kind of guy. You hang around me, you get protected. You want that or not?"

Judy didn't know. It was too hard to think at the moment. She felt strong and good, the muscles in her body tensed and straining toward him. She could have been on tiptoe but she wasn't sure. She wondered how long she'd have to wait for him to kiss her, then decided waiting wasn't her strong suit. "I don't need to be protected, I need to be kissed," she said.

And so he kissed her.

# BOOK THREE

*Forte e Gentile.*
Strong and gentle.

—The motto of the province of Abruzzo


Dictators ride to and fro on tigers which they dare not dismount.

—WINSTON CHURCHILL,
**While England Slept** (1936)

# 19

Back in the truck, Pigeon Tony had awakened and sat watching Frank and Judy, kissing in the meadow. He had known they would make their way to each other. Pigeon Tony's heart felt happy and full. Frankie had seen so much sadness, too much for such a young man, and it was time for him to stop working so hard, get married, and have sons of his own. Daughters would be okay, too, if they turned out like Judy. Even though she wasn't Italian, Pigeon Tony liked her, and he was realistic enough to know that times were changing.

He looked away from the lovers with a little sigh and eased back into the soft seat of the truck. In a minute his eyes were closed with an image of a kiss, which became a memory he recalled so vividly he could have been experiencing it in that moment, though it had occurred longer than sixty years ago. Pigeon Tony prevented himself from falling back asleep so his memories didn't become dreams and therefore run from his control. Because what he wanted to do now was remember the first time he kissed Silvana.

It had been a night not unlike this, and also in the countryside. The Abruzzese countryside was different from the American, drier and sun-baked, its rocky earth farmed over centuries, its scant nutrients spent. It took a certain quality of man to farm in Abruzzo and many had given up and gone to America, where the soil was said to be like everything else in America; plentiful, rich, and fertile, guaranteeing a life of ease. But Tony and his father remained in the land they loved, **on** the land they loved, and Tony saw his loyalty returned a thousandfold, for the hard earth of Abruzzo had taught him hope, and it was this single virtue that had won him Silvana.

From the night Tony had met Silvana on the road with Coluzzi, he could think of nothing but her, though when he got home his father had scolded him over the loss of the race and the damage to the wooden cages. But the next race of the old bird season was two weeks away, and Tony worked the field and scraped the floor of the tiny loft with a new energy, his mind contriving to see Silvana again at the next shipping. He would not be idle in the meantime.

The very morning after he met Silvana, Tony devised a way to see her again. First he had to learn where she lived. Her manner and dress were those of a city woman, northern, sophisticated, and that meant she was from Mascoli. Also she had been with Angelo Coluzzi, who was from there. Tony rarely went to Mascoli, he had no reason to and had much work at home. He couldn't ask about her in town, for he feared to expose such a personal matter, especially where Angelo Coluzzi was involved. Tony's best hope of finding her was the route he least wanted to take.

That morning Tony repaired the battered cages as quickly as he could, watched only by the pigeons roosting and cooing in the loft, and when he was sure his father had gone to market, he washed his face and hands and rode his chubby brown pony north across the provincial border and into the main street of Mascoli, the Via Dante Alighieri. Mascoli was a medieval city spiked with towers of local travertine, and Tony couldn't help but stare skyward at the sharp peak of the massive Duomo, so tall it seemed to pierce the blue of heaven. The close-together buildings, the shouting and auto horns, and the swarms of city people put him on edge but not in the extreme, since he had once faced down a runaway bull in the olive groves and nothing compared to that.

The only thing that truly worried Tony were the Blackshirts, and so he wasn't surprised that he started to sweat when he turned right onto the Via Barberia. He traveled past the majestic Palazzo Capitani and the Piazza del Popolo, crowded with students who barely seemed to notice the singular beauty of the huge piazza and its sixteenth-century porticos. It seemed to Tony almost obscene that the Fascist headquarters were so nearby, in the office of a leftist newspaper the Blackshirts had put out of business. Tony drew within its sight. Coluzzi would be inside.

Tony urged his pony on, his legs swinging on either side of its rotund belly, and the animal sweating lather in the noonday sun. Automobiles honked behind him, one even driven by a woman, which he found shocking, but the pony was too tired to bother hurrying along. At a distance from the Fascist office Tony dismounted and stood behind the pony, not bothering to find anything to hitch him to. Only a barn fire would get the animal to move again today.

Businessmen hurried back and forth down the street, with their fancy suits and their groomed mustaches, and Tony pulled his sweaty straw hat down over his eyes and pretended to read a discarded newspaper against his pony's damp back, though he couldn't read. He kept an eye on the entrance of the building, seeing the Blackshirts come and go in laughing groups, as if they were factory workers in uniform and not thugs in costume. Their influence was unchallenged. Tony had heard they were now making the schoolchildren dress in little black shirts and do gymnastic exercises, even in the heat, in the schoolyards before class.

He spit on the cobblestones. He shared his father's views that the arrogant Il Duce, his womanizing son-in-law Ciano, and the Blackshirts were a plague of black flies feeding on his country, and, as with flies, only God knew where they came from and only God knew when they'd leave. But Tony and his father kept these views to themselves, as they had to be the only family in Abruzzo who felt this way. The region was friendly to the Fascists, given the vast difference between the aristocracy and the farmers there, and Tony didn't think the black flies were leaving Abruzzo anytime soon, much less Italy. Mussolini had of late joined with the German dictator, and no good would come of it.

Suddenly Tony saw a shiny black car pull up and Angelo Coluzzi emerge from the office, be saluted, and disappear into the back of the car. Tony's mouth went dry. A car! He hadn't thought of that. **Idiota!** He had imagined Coluzzi walking to see Silvana, or at most driving a cart. What had he been thinking? Mascoli was a big place, not a village like his own! Everything was too far to walk, and men drove cars, not carts! He was a bumpkin, it was true! The car was driving away.

Tony had to hurry. He brushed the newspaper off the pony's back but the sweat held the last page in place. **Madonna!** He scrambled onto the pony's back anyway and started kicking him to trot, the newspaper saddle flapping around his legs. The pony didn't budge, hanging his large head low as if in slumber. "**Andiamo!**" Tony called to the pony, who had no name, and a child on the street laughed at the ridiculous spectacle. Tony's face reddened. He had hoped to be unobtrusive, to blend into the city. He should have known. **Stupido!**

Coluzzi's car drove off down the street, heading toward the river, negotiating the heavy traffic. Tony kicked wildly. The pony took root. The car was getting away, down the street. Tony clucked and snapped the rope halter, but the pony stood still. Coluzzi's car turned the corner, onto the Via Maggiore. It was getting away!

Tony had to go. He slid off the pony and left it by the roadside, where it fell immediately asleep, and Tony ran off after the car, holding on to his hat. The businesspeople dismissed him as a country bumpkin, and he picked up his pace and kept his head down. The car was long gone. The corner where it had turned lay straight ahead. Tony sprinted for it, and when he reached it, stopped and clung panting to a building. Unfortunately it wasn't as busy as the main street, and the car was making smooth progress. Tony hurried on, his droopy leather boots soft on the sidewalk. Where was Coluzzi going? Was he going to see Silvana? He had to, didn't he? Sooner or later?

The car turned another corner, and Tony ran after it, keeping his stride even on the crowded sidewalk. It drove down the street, speeding up when it reached its end and turning again, right this time. Tony lost track of the streets but still ran after it. He was getting lost. His feet began to hurt and the sun beat down on him. He whipped off his hat, too far from the car to worry about being recognized. The automobiles clogging the streets made the city hot, and the smoke they spit from their tailpipes filled Tony's lungs. Still he kept running.

The car came to an abrupt stop in front of an older building with a painted sign out front. Tony slowed his pace to catch his breath as he saw Angelo Coluzzi and three other Blackshirts spring from the car and run inside. Tony didn't understand. What could be so urgent inside? Did Silvana work there? Maybe her father owned it? In a minute Tony got his answer.

The Blackshirts burst from the storefront holding a little chemist between them. His white coat was splattered with blood and his head hung low. A woman on the street fled the scene just as Angelo Coluzzi ran from the shop and began punching the unconscious chemist in the face. The chemist's head popped back with each blow and his spectacles flew to the pavement.

Tony couldn't believe his eyes and without a second thought ran down the block to help the man.
Four against one wasn't a fair fight; any man could
see that. The chemist crumpled to the pavement,
and Coluzzi started kicking him in the ribs with
his black boots.

"Stop!" Tony shouted, running, but Coluzzi was
too far to hear. The fourth Blackshirt ran out of
the shop, grabbed Coluzzi, and all of them leaped
into the car, which took off.

"Hoodlums!" Tony screamed after them but the
car sped down the street. He reached the man's
side and cradled him on the sidewalk. One eye was
already swollen shut, fresh blood bubbled from his
broken nose, and his cheeks were a pulp that
repulsed even Tony, who had birthed breeched
calves.

"Sir, wait here while I get you a doctor!" Tony
looked frantically around the street, bewildered. A
pole for a barbershop. A store with Borsalinos in
the window. Offices with signs he couldn't read.
He didn't even know where he was. How could he
find a doctor? "We need a doctor!" he cried out,
but the crowd was dispersing.

"No, no, go away," the chemist said weakly.

Tony assumed the man was delirious. "But
surely, you need medical help!"

"No, forget it, go away, bumpkin! It's none of
your business!" The chemist struggled from a
stunned Tony's arms and managed to pull himself

onto all fours on the pavement, crawling off like a beaten cur. "Leave me alone, boy!"

"Sir, you need help!" Tony shouted as the chemist labored to his feet and staggered inside his shop, slamming the shattered front door closed behind him. Leaving Tony on the street alone, his hands covered in blood, thinking but a single thought: **Dove parlano tamburi, tacciono le leggi**. Where drums beat, laws are silent.

An hour later it was a dazed Tony who found his way back to his sleeping pony, feeling like an adult, seeing the city around him with grown-up eyes. Life went on as if nobody had been beaten senseless on the street. The sun was low in the sky, the business day winding down, and the traffic clogged the streets. Tony's world was the farm, and he hadn't seen what was happening around him, to the land he loved, to his very country. He didn't understand how Italy had gotten to this point, where thugs ran free. Oddly, even the horrifying scene with the chemist couldn't chase Silvana from Tony's thoughts. On the contrary, his attraction to her had grown, for now he was afraid for her safety.

Under his straw hat, Tony kept his eyes trained on the Fascist headquarters. Blackshirts began to leave the office in small groups, walking off to cars and motorcycles, and at the sight of them Tony heard himself growl like a dog. His pony glanced back at the muttering, waking up only briefly.

Finally Angelo Coluzzi came out, talking with a fellow Blackshirt, his clothes neatly pressed and his face washed clean of blood. Tony couldn't hear what they were saying, but his senses told him something had changed. Angelo Coluzzi had the look of a rooster, strutting about. He was a man going to court a woman. Silvana.

Tony's blood felt hot as Coluzzi walked toward a car that pulled up from the curb and was slapped on the back by his fellow as he went around the front and took the wheel. Tony mounted his pony, who roused. The day's rest had done him good and Tony wasn't taking no for an answer, not anymore. He gave a little kick, and the pony trotted on, keeping to the side of the road.

Tony tracked the car with ease, as the traffic was so congested, the horses, carts, and cars making a slow-moving mess. The car threaded its way through the city and to the suburbs, where the cars mixed with farm traffic. Coluzzi honked his car horn, but it was of no interest to the goats, sheep, and chickens that blocked the road. Tony smiled for the first time that afternoon. Even goats had the sense to ignore the Fascists.

The car slowed to a stop, and Tony's heartbeat quickened. Maybe this was near Silvana's house, maybe this was her street. The car stopped at a stone house, which was as neat and clean as the others, though humbler. Tony halted the pony, who didn't need to be told twice. Tony couldn't read the number in the twilight, but he didn't have to. If it were Silvana's house, he would never forget it.

After a minute Coluzzi cut the engine, got out of his car, and rang the doorbell beside an arched door. Neighbors making a **passeggiata** admired the modern automobile and noticed the Blackshirt who emerged from it like a conquering hero. Coluzzi nodded to them as if he knew them, making Tony wonder how long Coluzzi had been coming here. In another minute the front door opened wide.

It was Silvana. Her lovely form appeared in the arch, which made a perfect frame, lighting her from behind. Her waist narrowed above small hips, modestly concealed by the flare of a fancy dress. Her shoulders were narrow, not strong enough for a country girl, but that was a small matter. Silvana wasn't made to carry water or anything heavy. Tony would do all of that for her, and gladly.

Coluzzi swept off his black hat, bowed slightly from the hip, and made a great show of kissing Silvana's hand. Tony watched in amazement. How could a man so brutal put on such a fine show? Dog! Cur! Bully! Had Coluzzi deceived her so completely? Could she possibly love him, if she knew? Tony would have to save her from him.

The arched door closed as Silvana took Coluzzi inside. Tony wanted to cry out in protest, but he remained silent. Coluzzi didn't deserve such a woman, and he could not keep her. Tony wouldn't let him. He would win Silvana from him, and she would be his, and they would be happy forever after, as in a children's story. Now was the time for him to begin.

He slid off the pony, which grunted in gratitude, and ignoring the glances of farmers and goats, Tony reached into his pocket to withdraw his prize. It was wrapped in a white handkerchief he had received as a confirmation gift from his parents, and he hoped it wasn't sacrilegious to put it to such use. He dropped the rope halter, walked quickly across the road, and left the package by the door, so it wouldn't get stepped on by Coluzzi's hateful black boot. Then he hurried back to his pony and remounted, imagining Silvana's surprise when she opened the package the next morning. The image sustained him back through the city and all the way home. And when he arrived home and tried to discuss the Blackshirts with his parents, he was lovingly smacked for worrying them with his disappearance and sent off to bed without any nougat.

The next day, Tony raced to finish all his chores, and then at night, when his parents thought he was asleep, he sneaked out, haltered his pony, and rode out to Mascoli, then through the city and all the way to Silvana's house beyond. Coluzzi's car was nowhere in sight, and all the lights were off. Tony, having no handkerchief save the one he had already sacrificed, pulled the new package from his pocket, wrapped this time in a dishtowel he hoped his mother wouldn't miss. He tiptoed across the road and was about to leave the package when he noticed something.

A small white square sat beside Silvana's front door, where he had left the gift last night. Tony heard himself gasp. It was his confirmation handkerchief, neatly folded and laundered. He picked up the cloth and held it to his nose. It smelled of soap and water and a hot iron. It was the sweetest thing Tony had ever smelled, sweeter even than basil. He held it to his chest, wanting to cherish it, but thought better of it. If Silvana had left it, she was telling him something. So Tony would tell her something back. Quickly he unwrapped his gift, rewrapped it in the handkerchief, and placed it where he had the night before, in the same spot. Then he hurried back to his pony, climbed on, and they trotted home.

Tony couldn't sleep the whole night for thinking about it, and the next day he performed all his chores like a man possessed, pleasing his parents, who told him not to bring up the subject of politics again, that a boy could get shot for it, especially when his mind was supposed to be on feeding himself, his animals, and his family. That night Tony traveled to Silvana's, trotting all the way, and the handkerchief was there, laundered and sweet, as it was the night after that, and the one after that, too. And every night Tony opened the fresh handkerchief and placed inside it the most perfect tomato he had grown that day.

Tony did this for fourteen nights, the same gift every night, until the next shipping of the pigeons, when he loaded his cart for the trip to Mascoli, on the road he knew by now by heart. His brown pony had lost a considerable amount of weight, a condition Tony's parents mistakenly attributed to worms, and trotted with vigor despite the loaded cart. In fact, the pony had grown so well muscled that Tony climbed up on the cart himself and drove him as gentlemen do. For the trip he wore his finest; a clean white shirt, brown pants with a leather belt, and his best shoes. A fedora had replaced his straw hat, because his father had courted his mother in one, and Tony, being so skinny and little, needed all the help he could get.

Tony and his lively pony trotted up to the clubhouse, but Tony didn't see Coluzzi's fine cart and matched horses among the humbler ones that waited outside. Perhaps Tony and his very fit pony had beaten them here. Perhaps Coluzzi and Silvana weren't coming. Tony felt uneasy as he pulled up and hitched his pony to a rail next to the others. That night all twenty lofts in the combine were at the shipping, and it was the usual state of chaos, the pigeoners being enthusiastic but not well organized. Tony got down from his cart and went inside the tiny clubhouse.

Men and their birds filled the small room of the house, which was owned by one of the members; it had an earthen floor and walls of chipped stucco, and behind was another room with a single bed and a sink. Tony's eyes adjusted to the dim light, because there was no money in the combine's treasury for electricity, and he scanned the scene for Coluzzi and Silvana. They were nowhere in sight. One group of men banded flapping birds, another counted lire for entry fees, and a third scribbled the names of the entries on master lists. Where was Coluzzi?

"Tony, we're ready for you," the bander shouted over the crowd, and Tony came over.

"Is the D'Amico loft entered?" Tony asked, though he didn't care. It was a ruse.

The bander skimmed the master lists. A school-teacher, he wore glasses and was one of the few who could read. "Yes, they are coming."

Tony nodded. "How about Coluzzi loft?"

"They, too. Now get your birds, boy."

Tony unloaded his birds, carting his pigeons in cage by cage for banding, barely paying attention. Before a three-hundred-kilometer race he would usually be very nervous, but this time his nerves were for Silvana. It was almost worse knowing she would be here. When would she come? Did she know the tomatoes were for her? And from him? He held the first bird so it didn't struggle while the man slipped a band on his leg.

They made quick work of banding the others, then Tony loaded them on the big cart to be taken to the release. Outside he kept looking around. All the carts were there, the horses grazing and pawing the earth impatiently, but none were Coluzzi's. Where were they? If Coluzzi didn't get here soon he would be disqualified. Almost all the birds were loaded onto the big cart. The drivers were preparing to leave. The sun had almost set. Sundown was the official close of entries, because nobody could see anything in the clubhouse in the dark and the entry fees had a way of getting lost.

Tony stood dismayed as the president of the combine came out of the clubhouse, holding a strongbox with the entry fees. The vice president tucked the master lists under his arm. Now that the hard work was over, the club members laughed and joked, making side bets and having cigarettes and Chianti before the ride back to their homes. Tony felt the weight of disappointment.

"I thought Coluzzi had entered," he said to the president when he passed by.

The president shrugged. "He didn't show up, I guess. **You** be the one to scold him," he added, and the other men laughed loudly.

After a time the members trailed to their carts, mounted up, and clucked to their horses to trot. Night had fallen, and the air was cool and sweet. Tony waited until the last one had left, busying himself with false adjustments to his cart and the pony's halter, hoping Coluzzi and Silvana would arrive. He was worried about Silvana. What if she was sick? Or hurt? What if Coluzzi had found out about his gifts? Was she in danger?

Tony had to know. It was late and his father would worry, but he climbed aboard the cart and they trotted off, the pony knowing the way without being told. They arrived in Mascoli, clip-clopped their way through the city at night, then climbed the dirt roads to Silvana's house. Tony had no gift, having expected to see Silvana at the shipping, but he was too worried to bother about it. He didn't know what he would do when he got to her house; he would decide then. He was driven to make sure she was okay.

Tony slowed his pony to a halt in front of her house, and from his vantage point atop the cart he could see into its second floor. A light was on, shining through sheer lace curtains, and inside he could see the form of Silvana, appearing through a doorway and entering the room.

His heart leaped up at the sight. She was well. She was fine. Her outline was gauzy with lace but he could see her slipping a scarf from her lovely dark hair, as if she had been out that night, and his heart sank. She had been with Coluzzi, to dinner at a restaurant perhaps. Tony heard they did such things in cities.

He looked away from the window. Another man would have thrown pebbles at her window to speak to her. Another man would have pounded the doorbell, demanding to see her. Another man would have made himself known, but Tony did none of these things. He shook his head, hating himself. He would never have her. He didn't deserve her. His gifts were stupid. Only a bumpkin would leave tomatoes on a woman's doorstep.

Tony turned the pony around and they walked home, both downcast. The night was black and starless, so the full moon shone down on them, lighting their way out of pity. The mountain breeze blew cool and sweet, but Tony barely noticed. Moon, man, and cart traveled down the road; the creak of the wheels and the soft thumping of the pony's wide hooves were the only sound. Tony would apologize profusely to his parents when he got home, and on Sunday he would make yet another confession for his disobedience. In the meantime he wouldn't give up on Silvana. Perhaps he needed to leave a fancier gift on her doorstep. Fresh olives perhaps, or a hard wedge of locatelli. Women loved locatelli. At least his mother did.

Tony reached his farm, unhitched the pony, and turned him out into the field with a pat on the rump, then walked to the house. His mother had left a lamp on for him, and he could see both his parents inside, sleeping in their chairs, waiting for his return. His heart softened with guilt and he opened the door. He was just about to go inside when he saw it. There, slightly to the left of the door, was a bright spot in the moonlight. It looked like a small white package.

Tony blinked. Was it true? Was it a wish? He knelt down and looked at it. It was his confirmation handkerchief!

Tony reached for it, though his hand was trembling with excitement. Silvana had put it there. Found his house and left it there. She had done this, for him! Here was where she had been tonight. Not the opera, not the cinema. **Here!** This very spot.

Tony plopped down on the doorstep and unwrapped the handkerchief. Inside was the most perfect tomato he had ever seen. He marveled at it, turning it this way and that, and the shine of its thin skin caught the light from the window. If Silvana had bought it, she was more talented than he knew. If she had grown it, she was a genius. Silvana had given it to him, a gift of love, and so there was only one thing to do with it, which was what he had imagined she had done with hers.

Tony took a big bite of Silvana's tomato, letting its juice and slippery seeds squirt from the sides of his mouth, unmindful that he looked like a complete fool, so besotted was he with its source. He chewed it slowly, savoring the tomato as if he hadn't eaten one before, its taste so wonderful it needed neither salt nor pepper. He gobbled the whole fruit in one sitting, the water running through his fingers in rivulets, and when he was finished, Tony understood that Silvana's tomato was truly one thing and one thing only:

Their first kiss.

# 20

Judy, still warm from Frank's kiss, couldn't fight the feeling that they were playing house as Frank gave her a hand through a broken and weather-beaten door in the back of the springhouse to its second floor. "I'll fix the steps tomorrow," he said.

"I was expecting to be carried over the threshold."

"Don't make me call your bluff," he warned, and Judy felt an unaccountable thrill. She loved how direct he was, and his kiss had been like eating something delicious. Only prudence had stopped her from a full-blown make-out session, that and the nagging worry that her client could be watching. As it was, Pigeon Tony was beaming at her from the springhouse, holding a Coleman lantern aloft like a stumpy Statue of Liberty. Judy didn't need to ask how much he had witnessed; from his expression, he was already picking out a china pattern. She looked away, embarrassed. Her tongue had breached several ethical canons and was contemplating more.

The lantern from Frank's truck cast a bright ellipsis of light. The room had no electricity but Frank was already talking about running a wire from a small fuse box downstairs. Judy could see that the second floor was a single room, large and rectangular, with walls of chipped white stucco that gave off a pleasant chill despite the humid night. They seemed to hold the dampness from the first floor of the springhouse, which had contained a reservoir of stagnant water and two tanks on a cement bed. The side walls of the room had two mullioned windows on louvers, which Judy found charming, and she couldn't help but cross to open one. The floorboards creaked under her heavy clogs.

"This'll do, for a time," Frank said, his voice echoing in the empty space. "I'll work the job here and supervise my other jobs from the truck. I don't need to go home for a while. My whole office is on wheels. Don't you like it, Judy?"

"Sure. I think it's perfect." She cranked open the window, brushed away the cobwebs, and let the night air waft inside. There was a full moon, and the wind rustled through the pin oaks around the springhouse. Frank and Pigeon Tony would be safe from the Coluzzis here, a fact she liked for more than professional reasons. "It seems safe, and you can't beat the commute. How long will you stay?"

"I don't know yet. When's the trial?"

"Six months from now, maybe. But the subpoena said the preliminary hearing is Tuesday, and he'll have to appear at that."

Frank nodded. "I'll get him there and get him back here, right after. I'll talk to the client and see if they'll let me pay something for the use of the place until we can find an apartment." Frank glanced at Pigeon Tony. "What do you think of the new place, Pop?"

"I like."

"Good."

"One night we stay."

Frank's head snapped around. "What did you say, Pop?"

"One night. Then we go home. I no hide. My birds."

"Pop, that's not happening," Frank said firmly. "We're staying here until it's safe for us to go. I'll talk to the owner about it. I bet he won't mind."

"I go home. I feed my birds. They come home."

"Goddamn it, Pop! Don't be so goddamn stubborn!" Frank threw up his hands. "You gotta cut this out! This is life or death here! Forget about the birds!"

"No can forget," Pigeon Tony said quietly, unfazed by his grandson's temper.

Judy couldn't believe it. "Pigeon Tony, they want to kill you. They'll kill you if you leave here."

The old man's eyes went flinty in the lamplight. "I no leave birds."

Judy had an idea. "Fine. I'll get the birds. Then will you stay?"

"You no get birds!" Pigeon Tony exclaimed, shaking his head, and Frank pointed at her angrily.

"You're not getting the frigging birds, Judy. You don't know the first thing about them, and it's dangerous. The Coluzzis will be watching that house. I don't want you anywhere near that neighborhood."

"I have to get my car. I'll get the birds, too, and bring them here. I'll do it tonight, when it's dark. I'll get help if I need it. If I need cops, I'll call them."

Frank's dark eyes flashed in the lamplight. "They'll kill you!"

Judy had had it. The discussion was academic. It was late. Her adrenaline was pumping. Frank's truck was parked outside with the keys in the ignition. Suddenly she turned on her heels, ran for the open door, and jumped out. "Geronimo!" she yelled, but she could hear Frank's heavy feet on the floorboards after her.

"Judy, stop!" he shouted.

She landed on the soft grass outside and sprinted for the truck. It made a large white silhouette in the moonlight, like a toy left in a suburban back-yard.

"Shit!" Frank cursed behind her, and then Judy heard a large crash. He must have hit something going out the door. "Fuck! My ankle!"

She raced for the truck, flung open the door, climbed inside, and locked the door immediately, the way she did in the city. Only this time she was protecting herself from a charging Italian. She found the ignition and twisted it on just as Frank reached the truck and grabbed for the door handle.

"Judy, no!" His hands clawed the door but lost purchase when she hit the ignition, switched on the headlights, and yanked up the emergency brake on the fly.

"Sorry, babe," she said. The truck leaped forward with a kick she hadn't felt since a certain kiss, and she was off, careering through the wildflowers and grasses of the meadow, setting the swallows into panicked flight and the gnats dancing in the high beams, then finally heading for the open road.

Judy checked the digital clock on the truck. It was 2:14 in the morning. The DiNunzios must have known she was coming, because all the lights were on in their brick rowhouse in South Philly. She felt terrible that they were awake at this hour, then realized why. Frank must have called them from his cell phone. She wondered if his ankle was okay and worried fleetingly that auto theft wasn't the best way to begin a relationship.

Judy passed the DiNunzio house, circling the block as a precaution, and when she didn't see any black Caddys or guys with broken noses, double-parked the truck at the end of the street. No harm in playing it safe. She hurried down the street toward the lighted house with the scrollwork **D** on the screen door and was about to knock when it opened.

"Judy!" Mr. DiNunzio said. His few wisps of hair had gone awry and he was wrapped in his plaid bathrobe like a fat homemade cigar. "Come inside!"

"Thank you," she told him, and meant it, as he tugged her into the living room, gave her a warm hug, and led her by the hand past the unused living and dining rooms and into the tiny kitchen, which was the only room the DiNunzios spent time in.

Judy could see why. She loved it, too. It was as close as she had to home. It was warm and clean, with white Formica counters that cracked at the corners and refaced cabinets that reminded Judy of Pigeon Tony's. Easter palm aged behind a black switchplate, and a prominent photograph of Pope John hung on the wall, so colorized it looked like Maxfield Parrish had been in charge of Vatican PR. A photo of Pope Paul hung next to him in a lesser frame, and Pope John Paul didn't even rate a photo op. Apparently, Pope John had been a tough act to follow.

"Judy, come in!" Mrs. DiNunzio called from the kitchen. She shuffled in plastic slip-ons to meet Judy at the threshold. She had thick glasses with clear plastic frames and teased white hair, which looked undeniably like cotton candy because of her puffy pink hairnet. She hugged Judy warmly despite her frailty, and the aromas of her kitchen—brewing coffee and frying peppers—clung even to her thin flowered housedress. Judy realized she hadn't eaten all day, which made her Guest of Honor at the DiNunzios.

"I'm hungry, Mrs. D!" Judy said, smiling as she broke their embrace. "Feed me, quick! I could starve if you don't!"

Mrs. DiNunzio laughed and patted her arm. "Come, sit, you! Come!" She pulled Judy by the hand into the kitchen, where Mary sat at the table in her chenille bathrobe, improbably awake before a fresh cup of percolated coffee. She was sitting up, a big step in her recuperation.

"Jude, you're just in time to eat!" Mary said. "What a surprise! We always eat at two in the morning!" Her hair was pulled back into a ponytail and she was wearing her glasses instead of contacts. Behind them her brown eyes looked bright. If Mary was in pain, she was hiding it well, and Judy hated seeing her like that. She went over and gave her a careful hug.

"Hugging and eating," Judy said. "It's round-the-clock, which is why we love it here. Sorry to get you all up so late."

"No problem." Mary looked at her with concern. "I hear you were dodging bullets. This is not a good thing."

"I tried to play nice." Judy pulled up her chair next to Mary, so her friend wouldn't have to talk loudly. "How'd you hear about it? Frank, right?"

"Among others. The news, the cops, our boss, **and** your new boyfriend. I love a man with a cell phone."

Judy smiled, though her face felt hot. "Wonder how he knew I'd come here."

"He knows you like to eat."

Judy thought about it. "He's smart, you know."

"Oh, yeah. He's a genius. He invented fire. So, you enjoying your work?"

"What a great case. It stimulates me like no other."

Mary snorted. "Really fascinated by the legal issues, huh?"

"Hubba hubba." Judy laughed, while Mr. Di-Nunzio set a fresh cup of coffee before her, on a mismatched saucer, and Mrs. DiNunzio brought her silverware and a plate heavy with green peppers, sliced potatoes, sweet onions, and scrambled eggs, all fried and mixed together. The first time Judy saw this combo, she thought a dog had thrown up on the plate. Now she loved it. Presentation was highly overrated.

"Eat, Judy!" Mrs. DiNunzio said, resting a hand on her shoulder.

"I'll force myself. Thank you, the D family," she said, grabbing an oversize fork and digging in. "Why didn't you tell me about Frank?" she asked Mary, with her mouth full. "I would have shaved my legs."

"Why? Is it Sunday?"

"For him I'd make an exception."

Mary smiled. "You like little Frankie? I didn't think he was your type."

"What, are you blind?"

"Despite his physical charms, I mean. He won't let you push him around."

"I know. He'll get over it." Judy ate hungrily. The green peppers were limp with olive oil, the sliced potatoes were limp with olive oil, the sweet onions were limp with olive oil. Nothing could kill the eggs. In short, it was the perfect meal. "He wants to protect me."

Mary laughed. "Lotsa luck, Frank."

"Can you imagine?"

"No. I don't even want to feed you."

"Your mother does."

"She feeds all strays."

"Good! Good for Frankie!" announced Mrs. DiNunzio, sitting down across from Judy at the circular table of gold-speckled Formica. Mrs.

DiNunzio's English was only slightly less impressionistic than Pigeon Tony's, and Judy remembered that the DiNunzios were almost as old as he was, because they had had Mary and her twin sister, Angie, so late in life. Mary always said they were an accident, but her mother preferred Gifts from God. "We know Frankie when he was baby," Mrs. DiNunzio went on. "Judy, you could have a good man protect you!"

"I protect me!" Judy said, for the record, but Mary was waving her off.

"Don't go so fast. You may need the reinforcements. Bennie called three times today."

"She's a **witch**!" Mrs. DiNunzio said, raising an arthritic finger, and Judy stifled a smile. The DiNunzios blamed Bennie Rosato for all the trouble she and Mary got into, and Judy had failed to disabuse her of that notion. Last thing Judy had heard, Mrs. DiNunzio had put the evil eye on their boss. Judy could only hope it worked.

"Bennie called, here?" Judy asked. "What'd you tell her, Mare?"

"That I don't know you."

"She believe it?"

"No. I think she may actually be concerned for your health and welfare."

"Yeah, right."

"Also she said something about the antitrust article."

"Bingo."

"Hnph!" Mrs. DiNunzio said, which Judy knew was Italian for she-should-burn-in-hell. She was shaking her head, which trembled with age. "She no care about you, Judy. She no care about nobody but **her**!"

"I know, Mrs. D." Judy kept eating. "She expects me to work for my paycheck. She's evil and mean."

"Yes!" Mrs. DiNunzio pounded the table with a hand that wasn't as delicate as it looked. "Yes! She's evil. **Evil!**"

Judy finished the last of her eggs and hoped for seconds. She knew from experience that the thought alone would transmit an instant telepathic message to all Italian mothers in the universe, and one of their representatives would materialize any moment with plates of steaming food. Who needed e-mail? "Bennie just wants to talk to me so she can fire me."

"No," Mary said. "That's not it. She gave me her proxy. You're fired. And stop getting my mother riled up."

"Why? I want her to get her voodoo in high gear. Stick pins in something. Light candles and cast spells. I need an extension of time for that dopey article." Judy smiled, but Mrs. DiNunzio was in the zone.

"That witch, she's **lucky** to have you girls work for her. **Lucky!** I go to her! I **tell** her!" Mrs. Di-Nunzio picked up a serving fork and jabbed the air for emphasis. Judy, who had seen her in action only with her wooden spoon, was properly intimidated. Extreme situations called for extreme utensils.

"You smart girls!" she went on, brandishing the fork. "Very smart girls! You work like **dogs**! You **sacrifice** for her! My Maria, a **bullet** they shot at her!"

Mary looked sideways at her mother. "Ma, please put down the fork. And Bennie's not that bad."

"She's a **devil**!" Mrs. DiNunzio said, quivering with emotion, and Mr. DiNunzio patted her arm heavily.

"S'allright, Vita. S'allright." His eyes were soft with worry. "Mary's gonna be okay. Judy, she's gonna be okay, too. Right, Judy?"

"Right."

Mr. DiNunzio sighed. "I don't know if you should stay on Pigeon Tony's case, Judy. Me, I'm responsible. I asked you to do it. Now look what's happening."

"Mr. D, I would have done it anyway. I wanted to do it." Judy reached across the table and pressed his arm, and he grabbed her hand. He looked like he was about to burst into tears, and Judy panicked. She was way over her emotion quota for the year, in only one day. "Don't cry, Mr. D. It's going to be all right, like you said."

Mary smiled. "Don't worry, Judy. He cries when the Phillies lose. He likes to cry. He's not happy unless he's crying." She turned to her father. "Pop, get a grip. You're upsetting Judy. She's not used to people like us. She's normal."

Mr. DiNunzio laughed hoarsely. "I'm allright, I'm allright. But I'm gonna help you, Judy. I heard about the pigeons, and I got it all figgered out."

"What do you mean?" Judy asked in surprise, and there was a soft knock at the door.

"You'll see," he said, and got up to get the door, just as a second helping of eggs, peppers, and onions appeared on the table in front of Judy.

Message received. Over and out.

# 21

The full moon shone on an unlikely caravan threading its way through the city blocks. Old Chryslers, Toyotas, Hondas, and a battered Ford Fiesta snaked along in a line that lasted ten cars. If it wasn't Raid on Entebbe, it was Raid on South Philly, and it went a good deal slower because it was staffed by septuagenarians, whose night driving wasn't the best. Judy, in the lead, inched Frank's truck down the skinny street, with Mr. DiNunzio navigating in the passenger seat and Tony-From-Down-The-Block and Tony Two Feet in the back.

"Slow down, Jude, you'll lose Tullio," Feet warned, leaning forward. His glasses had been repaired at the bridge with a thick Band-Aid, which couldn't have helped much with visibility.

"Turn left on Ritner," Mr. DiNunzio said, pointing.

Judy turned slowly and braked to five miles an

hour, the truck's huge engine grinding in protest. It felt like walking a tiger on a leash.

"Tullio's still fallin' behind," Tony-From-Down-The-Block said, chewing on a half-smoked cigar that Judy had insisted he put out. Even unlit, it reeked. "It's that friggin' Fiesta he drives. I tol' him to get rid of it. It's a piece a shit."

"He don't listen to nobody," Feet agreed, and Tony-From-Down-The-Block nodded.

"He breaks down, I ain't helpin' him."

"Me neither. He can walk, for all I care. I tol' him the same thing. He's a cheap bastard."

"God forbid he should pick up a check."

Feet clucked. "Never happen."

"**Never** happen." Tony-From-Down-The-Block cleared his sinuses noisily. "You remember, he didn't chip in for the judge's gift at the Newark Futurity. You believe that? For the goddamn **judge**. God forbid he should open his friggin' wallet."

"Never happen."

"**Never** happen. For the **judge**, even. So you tell me. How's his loft gonna do the next race? You tell me. You think he'll **ever** win a friggin' race?"

Feet clucked again. "You think that judge is gonna go out of his way?"

"You think that judge is gonna **forget** the jamoke that didn't chip in? Who didn't even know what the present was? Never."

"Never happen."

"**Never** happen."

Judy rolled her eyes in silence. She had lost track
of who was talking and she didn't even care. "Is Tullio still with us, gentlemen?"

Feet laughed. "He's still alive, if that's what you
mean, Jude. In this crowd, you don't take nothin'
for granted."

Tony-From-Down-The-Block snorted. "He's
movin' now. Musta taken his Viagra." He burst
into phlegmy laughter, as did Feet.

Mr. DiNunzio pointed right as they turned onto
Ritner. "Stay on this for two blocks," he said, and
Judy nodded. On her own she would be lost.
South Philly was a warren of rowhouses, beauty
parlors, and bakeries. If you weren't Italian, you
had to drive around with them. "How long until
we're there, Mr. D?"

Mr. DiNunzio looked over. "At this rate, three
days."

Judy smiled, watching the Fiesta puttering in
the rearview, and even so hardly delaying the rest
of the caravan. Still she couldn't fault them, even
with their blocked nasal passages. They were
members of the pigeon-racing club, each with his
own loft, and they had volunteered to rescue
Pigeon Tony's birds in the middle of the night.
They even had a chart that divided the birds
equally among them, keeping them in their own
lofts until Pigeon Tony could reclaim them. Judy
felt confident the Coluzzis wouldn't attack them

in number, and the old men were all cooperating. The Bar Association should have this much collegiality.

"I tol' him," Feet was saying, "sell the friggin' car, on the Internet. They got eBay, it's free! You don't even hafta put an ad in the paper. My kid told me—eBay, it's called."

"You're shittin' me. You can sell a **car** on it?"

"Goddamn right. And I tol' him, it's **free for nothin'**, Tullio, you cheap bastard."

"But he don't have a computer."

"No way does he have a computer! They cost money, computers. They ain't givin' those babies away."

"You think he's gonna buy one?"

**Never happen**, Judy wanted to say, but didn't. She checked the rearview mirror. The Fiesta now trailed three car lengths behind. She braked again, with a sigh. "If this keeps up, Feet, I want you to take the wheel from Tullio."

"Gotcha, Jude. We'll do like a Chinese fire drill."

Judy winced. "You're not allowed to say that anymore, Feet."

"It's against the law, nowadays?"

"In a way." She watched the rearview. The Fiesta might as well have been in reverse. The pigeons could die of old age before the cavalry got there. "Chinese people don't like it."

Feet shrugged. "So I won't tell 'em."

"I don't even know any Chinese people," said Tony-From-Down-The-Block, and they all cruised forward under the moon.

It was almost four in the morning by the time the last of Pigeon Tony's birds had been stuffed flapping into cages, and the cages were stowed in the ancient cars. It wasn't an effortless fit. The old men crammed birdcages on Honda floors, on the consoles of Chryslers, and even on the dashboard of Tullio's Fiesta. The pigeons panicked the whole time, beating their wings and giving Judy an education on just how loud a pigeon could squawk.

The noise and commotion woke up many of the neighbors, who came in pajamas to their windows and doors to watch the spectacle. None of them said anything, nor did any help, and one of them clapped as the old men shuffled out of a demolished rowhouse bearing pigeon cages, green sacks of pigeon feed, cardboard boxes of pigeon vitamins, and empty spray bottles for disinfecting lofts. The Old Man, which Judy had been told was Pigeon Tony's special bird, hadn't shown up and at this point wasn't expected to. Five more birds had returned. Judy hoped Pigeon Tony would be happy.

She stood outside the front door at the curb and kept an uneasy watch on the dark and quiet street. She was armed with her cell phone, ready to call

911 on speed dial and have the cops arrive an hour later. She had to admit that the authorities weren't exactly on the case. Thirty-odd old men had just emptied a house of its contents, and nobody had said boo.

Short of petty larceny on the part of some very old men, absolutely nothing went wrong. No Coluzzis, no guns, no baseball bats. Not even a rolling pin. Still Judy began to breathe easy only when the last car door slammed and the two Tonys and Mr. DiNunzio climbed into the truck and flashed her a thumbs-up. Judy flipped the Star-TAC closed and hoisted herself into the driver's seat after them. After all, they had only accomplished the first leg of their daring night raid. The second leg was of her devising, and they had agreed. In fact, at Frank's instigation, they had insisted.

Judy started the F-250's engine, which roared in hope but ended up idling in disappointment. She fed it only the slightest bit of gas, and it crept forward, the caravan crawling behind them like a sleepy caterpillar.


Judy's heart leaped up at the sight. Her green VW Bug sat under a streetlight, parked outside the combine's clubhouse, and it had remained untouched. She'd expected to find it the victim of a Louisville Slugger, but it looked as shiny and new as when she bought it. "Wow! Will you look at that!" she exclaimed. Every time she saw the car, she got happy. She couldn't help it.

"It looks okay," Mr. DiNunzio said, surprised.

"Okay? It looks beautiful!" Judy cut the truck engine and opened the door, but Mr. DiNunzio stopped her.

"Wait a minute," he said, his hand on her arm. "You never know."

"You never know what?"

"It could be a trap."

"A trap? Mr. D, it's only a Bug!" Judy said. She was thinking this secret-agent thing had gone too far.

"He's right, Jude," Feet said, in the backseat, and Tony-From-Down-The-Block nodded.

"You can't trust the Coluzzis, Judy. Could be a bomb in it."

Judy's mouth dropped open. "Never happen," she said, but nobody laughed.

"Lemme see, first," Mr. DiNunzio said. He opened his door and eased down onto the black running board and out of the truck with difficulty. Ford F-250s were hardly the vehicle of choice for seniors.

"No, wait, Mr. D." Judy grabbed her backpack and jumped out the driver's side. The Two Tonys struggled out of their half-doors in the back, and they all stood staring at the green Bug from a distance, as if it were radioactive. The caravan had

double-parked in a line down the street and the old
men were getting out of their cars, the night filled
with the slamming of Ford Fiesta doors. Judy
thought the whole thing was silly. "It doesn't have a
bomb or anything."

"Why not? A bomb's easy to make," said Tony-
From-Down-The-Block, and Feet nodded.

"You can find out on the Internet, just like it
was a recipe for gnocchi. My kid tol' me. They
prolly have it on eBay."

Judy scoffed. The Bug gleamed like an emerald
in the streetlight. It was impossible for her to
imagine it exploding. Then she remembered that
the Coluzzis had killed Frank's parents in their
truck and Pigeon Tony's car had been firebombed
in Italy. Still, she wasn't worried, really. "But it's
not me they're after. It wasn't me they were shooting at. I'm just the lawyer."

"Oh, yeah. Everybody loves lawyers," said Tony-
From-Down-The-Block. The old men left their
cars and gathered behind him, Feet and Mr. Di-
Nunzio leading an ocean of bifocals, flat caps, and
black socks.

Feet pushed up his glasses by their Band-Aid
bridge. "I don't like it, Jude."

Mr. DiNunzio was shaking his head. "Don't do
it, Judy. Frank said, 'If the car looks fine, tell Judy
I said she can't get in it. It could be a trap.'"

Judy looked over. "Frank said to tell me I
can't?"

"Yeah, but not in a bad way. I mean, he was worried about you."

Hmmm. Once again there was no point in discussing it. Judy tossed her backpack on her shoulder and strode to the car. She was tired and she wanted to go home to bed. She had a dog to walk. She had a life to live. **Her** life.

"Judy!" Mr. DiNunzio shouted, running after her, but she kept going. She reached the car and dug in her backpack for her keys.

"Don't worry, Mr. D." She rummaged around in her backpack. Given the state of her messy bag, it would take her only about an hour to find the keys. Unfortunately, it gave Mr. DiNunzio enough time to reach her, hustling almost out of breath in his Bermuda shorts and white V-neck T-shirt.

"Judy, we should call the police." Mr. DiNunzio ran a hand over his bald pate, which looked damp. "They have a bomb squad. They could check it out first. Make sure it's okay."

"Mr. D, don't be silly. Everything's fine. It's just a car, and I don't want to wait forever for them to get here. The cops haven't been paying us much attention so far, have they?"

"Leave the car alone, Judy. You don't know it's fine for sure." Mr. DiNunzio's mouth set firmly. In the meantime Tony-From-Down-The-Block had hurried after him, with Feet huffing and puffing at his side. The other old men filled in behind them, encircling the car like a determined Roman phalanx. Mr. DiNunzio looked around in satisfaction and pushed up his glasses. "See, we're all here. If you blow yourself up, you'll blow all of us up."

"Mr. D, you're making too much of this!" Judy felt touched, but the situation had gotten way out of hand. She finally found the car key. All this protection was driving her nuts. "The Coluzzis don't want to kill me."

"Oh yeah?" A voice called out from the back of the car, and everybody's head turned. It was Tullio, rising on rickety knees from the rear bumper.

"What do you mean?" Judy asked.

Tullio frowned. "If they ain't tryin' to kill you, then why they got a pipe bomb on your exhaust?"

# 22

Sunday morning, Judy closed her office curtains against the press that thronged on the sidewalk outside the building, for the first time grateful for windows that didn't open. They sealed out the sound of the First Amendment at work. The sun struggled through the weave in the polyester fabric, and Judy blinked against even that brightness.

She collapsed into the chair behind her cluttered desk, exhausted. She had barely gotten to bed at all last night; there hadn't been more than an hour to conk out and shower before work. And even so she had been too rattled to sleep well. After they'd found the bomb under her car, she'd called 911, but the press, who listened to police scanners all the time, arrived well before the cops. Neither Judy nor any of the men had talked to the reporters, but they'd managed to get photos and videotape of the two uniformed cops who filled out an incident report and the squad that removed the bomb. They had impounded Judy's car for evidence, though she had little confidence it would reveal anything. The Coluzzis were too smart to leave fingerprints, and the crime lab was preoccupied with murder cases on the weekends. An almost-homicide equaled a purse-snatching.

Judy peeled the plastic lid off a cup of Starbucks and let it cool on her desk while she assessed the situation. She was under siege by people armed with pencils and cameras. She had almost succeeded in detonating her best friend's father and an entire parish of wonderful senior citizens. Powerful people were trying to kill her and her client. Plus she had an angry boss who would be in any minute, an antitrust article to finish, and no car to drive for the foreseeable future. Her puppy had forgotten who she was. On the up side, Frank was a great kisser.

Judy sipped her coffee. Her open laptop nagged her about her antitrust article, which seemed so irrelevant now. She idly scanned the introduction, which was all she had written so far: **Section I of the Sherman Act prohibits every contract, combination, or conspiracy in the restraint of trade, and it is a per se violation of the Act to engage in price-fixing. The purpose of this article is to examine the economic implications of vertical price-fixing agreements among competitors and specifically to determine whether conspiracies among oligopolists. . . .**

Judy's eyes glazed over with fatigue and anxiety. She had watched her back on the way into the office this morning and welcomed the sight of the usually cranky security guard in the lobby. Judy had made him promise not to let anyone up with a gun, including her boss, and he had agreed. She even felt uneasy in the quiet office this morning. She had hoped some other associates would be here, but it was a sunny Sunday and nobody but Bennie would be in today. It was both the good and bad news.

Judy's gaze fell on the stacks of correspondence that had accumulated on her desk when she had been out, including the notice of Pigeon Tony's preliminary hearing, set for Tuesday. When would she find the time to prepare? She was too busy ducking bullets. Next to the notice were stacked paperback advance sheets and **The Philadelphia Inquirer**, the newspaper delivered to all the associates every business day. Judy wondered what it had been saying about the Lucia case and reached for the top newspaper, which was Friday's edition.

BLOOD FEUD, read the headline, and Judy cringed. The first part of the article concerned the basics, the time of Pigeon Tony's arrest, and that he was being represented by the women-only law firm of Rosato & Associates, a fact the papers always seemed to pick up on. Other than that, the story seized on the "bad blood" between the Lucias and the Coluzzis but contained none of the details of its history, such as Silvana Lucia's murder, or any speculation on the deaths of Frank's parents, Frank and Gemma. Good. So the neighbors weren't talking to the papers. But they would soon. Judy dreaded to think what today's papers looked like, with the photos of her Bug being towed away by the bomb squad. Then her eye caught the sidebar, a feature about the Coluzzi family:

## THE KING IS DEAD.
## LONG LIVE THE KING!

With the sudden and violent demise of construction king Angelo Coluzzi, speculation is rampant about who will succeed him as president and CEO of Coluzzi Construction, reportedly a $65 million business, with headquarters in South Philadelphia. Angelo Coluzzi was reportedly unwilling to designate a successor, but the contest is clearly between his only children, sons John and Marco.

The older son, John Coluzzi, 45, is chief operations officer of the company and known for his hands-on experience in the construction trades. He supervises the building of strip mall projects that are the main source of the company's revenue. But it is the younger son, Marco Coluzzi, 40, who insiders say will ascend the throne. Marco, a graduate of Penn State and the Wharton School of Business, serves as chief financial officer and is said to exert a great influence over the company's extensive business affairs.

Insiders report that this family feud will have to be resolved soon, with Coluzzi Construction's $11 million bid for a new waterfront mall hanging in the balance.

Judy considered it. This must have been the feature article that Frank had mentioned to her. She hadn't noticed any rivalry between the brothers at the arraignment, but her assessment of their personalities wasn't far off. Marco was the brains, and John was the brawn. Judging from how vicious John could be, Judy was betting on him to become president. Murder was a good way to succeed in business. She skimmed the rest of the article.

"You survived a car bomb **and** the press?" asked a voice, and Judy jumped.

It was Bennie, but that was still a cause for alarm. Judy straightened up in her chair. "I was just reading about the case."

"Me, too." Bennie entered the office with a pile of newspapers and took the seat across from Judy's desk. She was dressed in jeans and a casual white cotton sweater, but her features were anything but relaxed. Her blue eyes crackled with intensity, and her manner was alert and energized. Her long, usually unruly hair was wrapped in a knot and tamed by an oversized tortoiseshell barrette. "Did you see today's paper?"

"I'm boycotting."

"Don't. You'd be surprised what you can learn about your own case from the paper. And what you can plant there." Bennie plopped the stack on Judy's desk, almost catapulting her coffee cup. "The car bomb's the lead story. Did you call your parents? They're in California, right?"

Judy had to think about it. "No, they're on sabbatical, in France."

"You can still call them. They have phones in France. Snotty phones, but phones just the same."

"I don't need to call."

"Wrong again," Bennie said firmly. "If you don't, I will. They're your parents."

"Okay." Judy knew Bennie's mother had passed away recently and she'd never met her father, so she didn't make any parent jokes. She picked up the newspaper on top, which was a tabloid. BOMBS AWAY! screamed the block headline. She set it aside. "So, am I fired?"

Bennie looked surprised. "Of course not. Why would I fire you? It's not your fault somebody wants you dead."

Judy blinked. "Am I off the case?"

"Do you want to be?"

Judy didn't have to think twice. The Coluzzis had tried to kill her car. "No way."

"Good. Then it's still your case. You know the

client and you're much too smart. But I'm on the case with you."

Judy wasn't sure she liked the sound of it. "You mean, you want to work the case with me?"

"Yep." Bennie nodded. "I'm your associate. For one time only."

"Why?"

"Simple. I don't want you to get hurt, Carrier." Bennie got up abruptly and clapped her hands together with finality. "Now, let's get in gear. I got the gist of the case from the papers, but why don't you fill me in?"

"From the beginning?"

"Yes, and don't leave out the grandson. Murphy told me all about him." Bennie smiled crookedly, but Judy didn't.

"Murphy should mind her own business."

"It's **my** business, remember? And I'm not in love with your new love affair with the client's grandson."

"There's no **love affair**, for God's sake. And it's not unethical or anything."

"No, it's just bone-headed."

"You're getting way ahead of the facts, Bennie," Judy said, so she filled her boss in on the details of the case since the arraignment, including the fact that she was attracted to Frank. Bennie scowled at the obvious imprudence of the situation, leaning against Judy's doorjamb with her arms folded. By the time Judy finished, Bennie looked positively cross. "Are you pissed because of Frank?" Judy asked her.

"No, Frank is a distraction. I'm pissed because of the way you talk about this case. You want to work it or not?"

"I do, I just told you."

"Then wake up! You're acting like a victim, which is the best way to make sure you become one. Get it together! Fight back!"

"Against who?"

"The Coluzzis, who else?" Bennie put her hand on her hips. "Haven't you been listening?"

"What should I do?"

"What should **we** do. We'll think of something." Bennie began to pace back and forth, her step lively even in the small office. Judy figured it was because she wore running shoes, not clogs, and considered getting herself a pair. Suddenly Bennie stopped pacing. "I'm hearing a lot about bombs and car chases and guns. What does that have to do with law?"

"Nothing. It's chaos."

"Clearly." Bennie's jaw set in determination. "The Coluzzis are outlaws. Their weapons are nonlegal. They destroy property. They kill people."

"Right."

"And we are distinctly out of our element in the nonlegal world, right?"

"Right." Judy had to agree.

"It knocks us off balance, and scares us, right?"

Judy got a little excited. "Right!"

"It even depresses us, I see."

"Okay, enough." Judy smiled, and so did Bennie.

"Well, it's no different from any other conflict, even litigation. We have to stop playing their game. We have to bring this battle onto our turf. We have to fight with **our** weapons."

"Which are?" All Judy had was a red editing pencil. It wasn't even good lipliner.

"The law, of course!"

Judy deflated instantly. "The cops aren't doing anything—"

"I didn't say the cops. You're a lawyer, Carrier." Bennie leaned over the desk. "Strike fear! Create a scene! Bust some chops! And if they holler, don't let 'em go. Twist 'em, baby!"

Judy was thinking maybe Mrs. D had been right, that Bennie was the devil. "How?"

"Sue the bastards!"

"For what?" she asked, bewildered.

"For **what**? Think, Carrier. They planted a car bomb on you!"

"The cops say they can't prove anything."

"As a criminal matter, they can't. But the same circumstantial evidence can be used in a civil suit, and the standard of proof is lower. Sue 'em civilly, for tort!"

Judy nodded. It was possible.

"They destroyed your client's home! You just

gonna take that? What kind of lawyer are you? Sue 'em civilly for the damages! We'll subpoena the whole goddamn neighborhood. That'll make a stink. Make them take the time to fight you, and get your profile higher, so they'll be less inclined to strike again. Fight them on all fronts. What else you got?"

Judy took heart. "They killed those pigeons. I'm sure there's an animal cruelty statute in Pennsylvania. It might even be criminal, and the press would be terrible."

"There you go! It ain't a home run, but it's all good. Nobody likes bird-killers. Remember those jerks who killed the flamingos at the zoo?" Bennie's eyes glittered. "Now. The Coluzzis are also businesspeople. Coluzzi is one of the biggest builders in the construction industry."

"A sixty-five-million-dollar company." Judy was remembering the newspaper article.

"They build strip malls, mainly." Bennie nodded, obviously thinking aloud. "I've heard of them. They did the one in West Philly, they got the contract over a minority business, and they did one also in Ardmore, I think I read recently. I wonder how many they do a year."

Judy fetched the newspaper from her desk. "They have the contract on a mall at the waterfront pending."

Bennie snapped her fingers. "That's right! So they're politically well connected. They'd have to be to get that big a city contract." She thought a minute. "They must have labor work, tax work, all sorts of business advice. I think they're represented by Schiavo and Schiavo."

Judy would have no reason to doubt it. Bennie knew most of the lawyers in town. The Philadelphia legal community was small, so if you screwed somebody, they could screw you back, and sooner than you thought. It encouraged good lawyer karma.

Bennie faced Judy directly. "Carrier, if we can't make some trouble for a major business like that, we should burn our law degrees."

Judy tried to think. Her gaze fell on the article on her laptop. "At this point I'm only an expert on price-fixing."

"Okay, start there!" Bennie grinned. "These jokers are in the construction business and they get an awful lot of contracts. It's an extremely competitive business. The economy is good, and everybody's building, including the city. I wonder how they do so well."

"You think they rig bids?"

"Anything is possible. They could pay off Licenses and Inspections. They could excavate pools free for union officials. They could inflate their T and E expenses for the IRS. Pour too much sand in the concrete foundations. Keep their mistresses on the payroll. Have mob connections." Bennie's eyes glinted evilly. "Somebody really should investigate these matters. A lawyer, for example."

Judy laughed, delighted. "But what about Rule Eleven? You have to have a factual basis for filing a lawsuit in federal court."

"So get one! You gonna tell me the building trades are **clean**?" Bennie walked to the open door. "I'll handle the torts suits and the animal cruelty. Get busy. We have work to do."

"We have to file soon, huh?"

"No." Bennie paused at the door. "We have to file tomorrow. Lock and load. Any questions?"

Judy thought about it. "How do I thank you?"

Bennie smiled and left, and Judy watched her bounce off in her sneakers. Then she cleared her desk and set to work. She worked all morning and afternoon, breaking only for hoagies they had sent in and for more coffee; Bennie's was even stronger than Starbucks. Judy researched cases on the construction industry, discovering the typical patterns of misconduct that gave rise to damages. It was an education.

Bennie had been right. The construction industry wasn't the cleanest, and Judy's online factual research discovered a number of websites devoted to encouraging contractors to report suspected bid-rigging, fraud, and kickbacks, guaranteeing their anonymity. So there was a clear potential for abuse, but that didn't mean Judy had a sufficient factual basis to sue Coluzzi. A complaint had to be true and specific, especially if it was going to have the maximum terroristic effect on the Coluzzis. For that Judy would need facts, from an insider's perspective.

She checked her Swatch watch. It was almost seven o'clock at night. She didn't have any time to lose.

And she knew just who to call. Or as her mother would remind her, whom.


An hour later Judy was barreling down the expressway in a rented Saturn. She had left Frank's truck parked near the office; she hadn't wanted to risk taking it in case the Coluzzis had wired it for sound, and she also wanted to avoid being spotted by the press. Their numbers had grown outside the office building as the day had progressed, on the correct assumption that Judy would have to come out sooner or later. It had been all she could do to get out of the building through a service entrance in the back, while Bennie gave a diversionary press conference on the sidewalk out front. Bennie could give nonanswers to their questions forever. She was a great lawyer.

Judy hit the gas. She was heading back out toward Chester County. Judy didn't know much about Philadelphia suburbs, but she was learning that all the rich people lived in Chester County and none of them seemed to mind sitting forever on Route 202 South. Judy had finally gotten free of that mess and could breathe again. She was almost there. Frank had agreed to help her, and Judy had to admit to herself she wouldn't mind kissing him again.

Make that **seeing**. She meant **seeing** him again.

# 23

It was dark by the time Judy found the address, or more accurately the mailbox, since the house couldn't be seen for the hedge and trees that blocked it from the road. She turned onto an unpaved drive next to a verdigris mailbox embossed with running horses, and when she saw the white sign that read HIGH RIDGE FARM, Judy knew she wasn't in South Philly anymore.

The Saturn's tires rumbled down a gravel road lined with trees and ending in a circular driveway in front of a huge fieldstone mansion. Judy cruised to a stop in front of the house, which reached three stories and had two wings, one at either end, its banks of windows framed by black shutters. The night was cool and filled with the chirping of crickets. The setting was lovely but Judy was too preoccupied to notice. Where was Frank? How was he getting here, since he was truckless? The springhouse wasn't far on country roads, but it was too far to walk. She cut the Saturn's ignition and climbed out, which is when she got her answer.

Parked in the circular driveway were a midnight-blue Bentley, a champagne-colored Jaguar sedan, and a faded John Deere tractor. Frank was walking toward her with a grin. "Hey, lady," he said softly, reaching to hug her, and Judy wasn't objecting.

"Hey back at you." She let herself be enfolded in his arms and pressed against the warmth of his chest, inside the same thin gray T-shirt he had on yesterday. It smelled faintly of sweat but she secretly liked that; it was a distinctly male scent and at least it wasn't onion. Judy felt her body relax unashamedly in his embrace. It seemed like days since she'd felt this comforted. "If I didn't have to sue somebody, I'd stay here forever."

"You won't get any argument from me."

Judy held him tighter. "How'd you get here? Found a tractor and drove it over?"

"Hell, no. Dan picked me up in the Bentley."

Suddenly the front door opened, and a tall, thin man appeared on the threshold. "Frank, that you out here?" he called, and it broke their embrace.

Frank turned. "Here we come, Dan," he called back. He gave Judy a quick kiss on the cheek and took her hand.

Soft light emanated from a Waterford lamp with a cut-glass pineapple for a base, glowing expensively on Judy, Frank, and Dan Roser as they sat on leather-covered chairs in his book-lined study. Built-in cherrywood shelves ringed the room, while a flat-screen TV, a compact stereo, and a large-screen computer sat recessed in a custom entertainment center, and a wet bar with gleaming nickel fixtures waited to lubricate everybody. It would wait forever. Nobody was in a partying mood, Judy least of all.

A fresh legal pad rested on her lap. "Mr. Roser, tell me something about yourself."

"Please, call me Dan." Roser, in Gucci loafers and pressed suit pants, with a white tailored shirt worn tieless, crossed his legs. Judy judged him to be about fifty-five years old, though he looked younger, with a golfer's tan setting off hazel eyes and light brown hair, worn fashionably long. "If Frank gets away with it, you can."

Frank snorted, and Judy smiled. "Okay, Dan. Gimme the summary."

"Well, I'm a real estate developer," he said, with the easy confidence of the highly successful. "I develop shopping centers, or strip malls if you prefer, in Chester County, Montgomery County, and other Philadelphia and Wilmington-area suburbs. My company does about two billion a year. I ain't Rouse, but I'm getting there."

"So you're not in the construction business, per se."

"God, no." Roser brushed off the thought as if it were lint on his pants. "I hire builders to build my shopping centers. Frank gave me a call because he knew that I hired Coluzzi to build a center for us recently, in South Philly, and it's been nothing but a nightmare."

Judy's pen was poised. "Tell me why."

"The project has been a comedy of errors from start to finish. All along the subs weren't performing—"

"Subs?"

"Subcontractors. See, Coluzzi is the general contractor, and he hires the subs to do the electrical, HVAC, plumbing, and the like. Also site prep, that is, excavation and compaction to receive foundations."

"Compaction?"

"Soil compaction. If the soil isn't compacted properly, it'll fail over time, due to superimposed loads on the foundation." Roser caught himself. "In other words, it'll fall down someday. And in this South Philly shopping center we had an environmental issue, too, because it was on city-owned land, right near the waterfront. Delaware Avenue, or whatever they renamed it to. Soil runoff during construction had to be controlled or the EPA would be all over us."

Judy made a note. "So this was a public contract."

"Yes. It was our first contract with Philly and I hoped to do more, since Rendell and Cohen turned the city around. This was supposed to get me in good with the city. Get my foot in the door. Instead it ended up in my mouth."

"How?"

"I hired Coluzzi because their bid came in lowest, but they didn't lowball me, and I knew they had connections in South Philly."

"Connections?"

"If you mean mob, I'm not goin' there. I got no proof of that." Roser patted his hair back quickly. "But I can and will talk to you about what I know, which is what they did to me. Because I got proof out the wazoo. My tenants are screaming their heads off."

"Like what?"

"Major structural problems." Roser leaned forward and started counting with an outstretched thumb. "The walls crack in the dry cleaners, the floors buckle in the Japanese restaurant, the joints are twisted in the entrance area. The shopping center looks like a fuckin' cartoon. Excuse me."

"No problem." Judy hurried to write it all down.

"The windows were installed improperly, so a breeze goes through the Szechuan restaurant, around table five. The support stairs sag in Blockbuster Video, and an employee fell down last week and broke his leg. The ceilings for all of the tenants—there are fifteen businesses who lease from me—leaked almost from the beginning. We're already on our third roof." Roser picked up a leather portfolio from beside his wing chair and slid from it a thick manila folder. "This is the file I keep of complaints. Hefty, huh? Quite a way to make a reputation with the city." He handed it to Judy, and she opened it up.

NOTICE OF NON-RENEWAL it said at the top, and Judy skimmed the document. It was a written notice by a tenant, given pursuant to a lease agreement. "The tenants are bailing, huh?"

"Correction." Roser pointed at the top. "The **anchor** tenant, Philcor drugstore, is bailing. Now they'll all jump ship. That is, if I'm lucky. If I'm not, I've got the sequel to Society Hilltop on my hands, and it all comes tumbling down."

Judy closed the folder, deep in thought. By Society Hilltop, Roser was referring to a dance club on the waterfront that had collapsed, killing ten people. It had been reported that the tragedy was caused by structural failure. Only one problem. Although what Roser was telling her was terrible, it didn't help her. Shoddy workmanship was only breach of contract, and a contract suit didn't have the counterpunch she needed. But there was still one thing Judy didn't get.

"If the Coluzzis do such lousy work, how do they make so much money?" she asked.

Roser shot Frank a how-naïve-is-your-girl look, then faced Judy. "They're dirty, dear. I looked into those subs they hired, and no way were they qualified to build for us. They got the job because they kicked back to Coluzzi and his sons. Then in order to make any profit on the job at all, they had to cut corners in the construction of my center. They didn't build according to plans and specs. I got left holding the bag."

Judy brightened. Kickbacks trumped breach of contract. She tried to sound more savvy. "What's up with the inspectors? Are they paid off as well?"

"Have to be." Roser nodded. "In any construction project, there are two levels of inspectors. City inspectors, who know what they're doing but don't care, and bank inspectors, who care but don't know what they're doing."

Judy didn't ask if he was kidding.

"Bottom line, Coluzzi pays off the city inspectors at least. The bank inspectors are only a possibility."

Judy was too excited to make any more notes. The city was involved, and major banks. "How do you know this?"

"One of the subs, McRea, who paved the parking lot, just built Marco Coluzzi a new driveway in his house down the shore, in Longport. I heard about it from a friend of mine, so I drove by and saw it. It's got storm drains and all. That's a $130,000 driveway. Now, when I hear it's my sub, who's doing a shit job for me, I put two and two together. The Coluzzis won't hire Irish or black unless they have to. McRea's been ignoring my calls all week."

"You're calling him?"

"Goddamn right I am. But I'll get him, and he'll give. Crooks are like that. Lean on any one of 'em and they'll flip on Coluzzi. There really is no honor among thieves. They'll eat each other alive."

Judy set down her pen. Time to close the deal. Do or die, literally. "Well, Dan, I'll be honest with you. I can think of several major causes of action you could bring against the Coluzzis based on these facts. The most effective would be a suit under RICO, the federal racketeering statute, for bribery, kickbacks, and other offenses. It carries major damages and penalties. I can represent you, and I'd love to. But I can't bring the suit unless you give me the green light."

Roser eased back in his cushy chair and tented thick fingers, then sighed and looked at Frank. "Sorry, pal," he said after a moment. "I know this matters to you, and you almost convinced me on the phone. We've known each other a long time, but the Coluzzis are tough customers."

"I can handle them," Judy blurted out, and Roser looked over in surprise.

"You can."

"I can."

Roser smiled in a condescending way. "Why should I sue the Coluzzis? I took a bath, but I'll write all of it off and I could use the deductions. What do I get out of suing?"

It was an excellent question. Judy scanned Roser's leather-bound books, the brass fastenings on the classy chairs, the costly palette of an oil landscape on the paneled wall. Money damages wouldn't motivate Dan Roser. "There is one thing," she said, and the developer cocked his head.

"Which is?"

"Justice," she answered, and Frank looked over.

"And if justice doesn't do it for you," he added, "how about revenge?"


Baccarat champagne flutes clinked expensively as they met in the center of a merry group that included Judy, Frank, Dan Roser, and his gorgeous trophy wife, Trish. Judy was pretty sure Trish was a recent Student Council member, but didn't say so. She was in too good a mood to let it bother her anyway. Trish was old enough to be out of orthodonture, and love was a good thing wherever you found it. Even with a client's grandson. She raised her flute. "To the law."

Frank raised his. "To Judy."

Roser laughed. "To Trish."

Trish said, "Chugalug!"

Judy even managed a laugh, but didn't take another sip of her champagne. She had to get to work on the complaint. Roser had a file of documents that would be exhibits attached to the complaint, and he had given her the phone numbers and addresses of the subcontractors. She had a sheaf of subpoenas to prepare, not including John and Marco Coluzzi's. She glanced at the polished brass ship's clock on the mantel of the gas-powered fireplace. Eleven o'clock.

"You have to get back?" Frank said to her, and Judy nodded.

"I have tons of work to do. Plus, my boss is working on the same case." Judy thought of Bennie, but it felt different from before. She couldn't leave Bennie in the lurch. "She'll be there all night, too, if we want to file the complaints in the morning."

"Oh, no." Trish buckled her pouty lower lip. "It's such a long drive back to the city. Dan and I hoped you'd stay over in our guest cottage. It's out back, and so romantic. The bedroom ceiling is one big skylight. It's just like sleeping under the stars. You two can have it all to yourself."

Frank was smiling, and Judy thought Trish had been reading her fantasies. A night with Frank? In a romantic little guest cottage?

Dan Roser nodded in agreement. "Take it for a night, why don't you? It's a beautiful cottage.

Trish and I go over there sometimes, just for the Jacuzzi."

Judy's lips parted. Jacuzzi? Did somebody say Jacuzzi?

Frank looked over, his dark eyes cautious. "It's really up to Judy," he said, and she knew she had a choice: love or work?

Judy considered it. Sigmund Freud had said that both love and work were necessary to human happiness, but he never specified the order of priority.

Nobody ever wants to answer the hard questions.

# 24

The conference room at Rosato & Associates had never been so full, especially on a Monday morning. Black microphones clustered under Judy's chin and twenty-odd camera lenses were pointed at her face, focusing. Photographers loaded film, TV anchors yapped on cell phones, and reporters tested the batteries of black Dictaphones. Stringers hovered over the table of cheese Danish, bagels, and hot coffee at the back of the room. Judy waited at the podium in a crabby mood while the WCAU-TV reporter got something he needed.

She tried to suppress her crankiness. She had never held a press conference before but knew it would have gone more smoothly if she had had sex with an Italian last night. Sex with an Italian would have made everything perfect, especially the next morning, when its magic hadn't worn off. The residual pixie dust would have unlocked Judy's inner power and unblocked her nasal passages. Given its obvious benefits, some of which were possibly permanent if not everlasting, who would pass up sex with an Italian in favor of a night of hard work? Only an idiot. Or a lawyer. The cameraman gave Judy a quick thumbs-up, so she tried to stop thinking about almost-sex and cleared her throat.

"Good morning, everyone. Thank you for coming," she said, and tugged her navy suit into place. She wore it with a white silk shirt and Bennie's brown pumps, which had been repaired with packing tape from the mailroom. Her pantyhose fit like a chastity belt, which, Judy reflected, was redundant on her anyway. She couldn't be more chaste if she had wrapped **herself** in packing tape. Damn! What had she been thinking? **No, Frank, I have to work?** She couldn't stop thinking about her stupidity, even with all the freshly shaved and made-up faces staring back at her. They must all have had sex with Italians the night before, accounting for their excellent color, mental alertness, and overall happiness. But she digressed.

"We called you here to announce that this morning, this office filed three separate lawsuits against Coluzzi Construction Company and against John and Marco Coluzzi individually. The first suit is a federal case brought against the Coluzzis for violations of RICO, the Racketeer Influenced and Corrupt Organizations Act of 1970, 18 U.S.C.

Sections 1961 through 1968." Judy let the legalese sink in, and it sobered even her up, chasing images of bulging muscles and V-shaped backs from her brain. Law could kill anyone's mood.

"The lawsuit will be brought by Dan Roser, who developed the Philly Court strip mall located on the waterfront, and who alleges that John and Marco Coluzzi and other officials of Coluzzi Construction, McRea Paving and Excavation, and an array of other subcontractors engaged in a complex scheme of fraud, bribery, kickbacks, intimidation, and other unlawful and corrupt practices in connection with the construction of the shopping center."

Judy took a breath, to let the reporters catch up. "Also named as defendants are the City of Philadelphia and several of its agencies, including but not limited to Licenses and Inspections officials, as well as the two lending institutions on the shopping center, Marshallton Bank and ConstruBank. Subpoenas will be filed and served today against all defendants. In case you missed any of this, you should all have picked up a courtesy copy of the complaints on the back table. They are all public record. Please let me know if you need another."

The reporters started raising their hands and shouting questions, but Judy held up a palm like a traffic cop. She had to stay on message, since she wanted the Coluzzis to get every word of what she was saying.

"We'll take questions after the statement, please," she said, and noticed Bennie slip into the back of the crowded room. They had agreed Judy would run the show, with Bennie joining her to answer questions. Judy welcomed Bennie's confidence in her, as much as she was surprised by it. It was Bennie's drawing power that got the crowd this morning. In a way, Bennie was putting her life on the line, too.

"I am also filing, on my behalf, a lawsuit in state court against John and Marco Coluzzi, as well as members of their family, for torts against me, including but not limited to attempted murder by incendiary device . . ."

Judy went on to describe briefly the particulars of the state law claims, holding her head high. She felt less and less afraid of the Coluzzis the more she went on, empowered by the law itself. She was upping the ante, she could almost feel it, and as risky as it felt, it was exciting. When Judy finished her statement, Bennie came and stood beside her, and they faced the press, the TV cameras, and the Coluzzis, in identical brown pumps.

"Any questions?" Judy asked, and the barrage commenced. One tall reporter in the front was waving wildly. "Yes?" Judy said, since that's the way they did it on TV.

"Ms. Carrier, isn't this really some kind of retaliation, or revenge?"

Judy gritted her teeth. "The suits are valid and are being brought to vindicate legal wrongs, under both federal and state law. This office will continue to vindicate any and all legal wrongs which may be perpetrated against me in the future."

The reporter scribbled quickly. "Aren't you trying to send a message to the Coluzzis?"

Judy hesitated only a minute. "You're damn right I am."

After the reporters had gone, empty Styrofoam coffee cups dotted the conference room table, and spare copies of the federal and state court complaints were scattered about. A leftover newspaper lay on the table, next to Judy's bare feet, propped up there. The show was over, so she had kicked off her pumps and molted her pantyhose like a garden snake.

"Well, that was about as good as it gets," Judy said, and Bennie crossed to the small white Sony television on the credenza near the telephone. "Lotsa questions, huh?"

"Plenty, and we handled them well. We're making noise with this thing, I promise you. If we don't make the twelve o'clock news, I'm losing my touch." Bennie switched on the TV, and the

Action News logo popped onto the screen. "Here we go." Bennie sat on the edge of the table as a pretty African-American anchorwoman appeared on the screen, her foundation sculpting her face into beautiful curves and her mouth glossy with blackberry-colored lipstick.

The anchor said, "The top story on Action News is the continuing vendetta between South Philadelphia's Lucia and Coluzzi families. The police have charged no suspects in the attempted murder of criminal lawyer Judy Carrier and her client, defendant Anthony Lucia, and so it seems the attorney has taken the law into her own hands, filing a series of powerhouse complaints in retaliation."

"Retaliation?" Judy groaned as the footage from the conference began to roll, with her looking fairly stiff in her navy suit, but Bennie waved her into quiet. In the next second, the screen had changed, and a reporter was interviewing an assistant city solicitor, a bright-looking young man with short hair, who appeared on the screen with an expression of official concern.

He was saying, "We will be investigating the allegations of the complaints immediately, beginning with the Bureau of Licenses and Inspections. Any wrongdoing there will be met with termination and possible suits for damages. The city wants to reassure the citizens of Philadelphia and our friends in the business community of the

integrity and fairness of its construction contracts."

Judy grinned. "They're worried."

Bennie nodded. "They should be. They're
exposed, big-time."

Next on the screen was a well-dressed businessman, wearing a three-piece suit and sitting behind a
huge glass desk. Crystal awards were reflected in its
gleaming surface. Judy clicked up the audio and
heard the businessman saying, "As one of the city's
largest construction lenders, we at ConstruBank are
reacting to these allegations with a great deal of concern, and we will investigate them fully."

Bennie smiled. "Now they'll begin to separate
themselves from Coluzzi. The deniability defense
is about to begin. The shit is hitting the fan." She
raised her hand for a high-five, and Judy slapped it
decisively.

"We did it!" she said, her crabbiness lifting.
Maybe litigation was better than sex? Nah.

"Way to go. You worked hard and it paid off."

"You too, Coach."

"Hey, look," Bennie said, pointing happily at
the TV. "Enemy territory."

Judy watched. The last shot was of the anchorwoman, standing on the sidewalk outside a modest
brick building squeezed behind a sandwich shop
and a bakery in South Philly. An old painted sign
read COLUZZI CONSTRUCTION, but it was draped in

black crepe. The anchorwoman held the bubble mike to her glossy mouth. "We tried to reach officials of Coluzzi Construction for comment, but they did not return our calls. Their offices were closed today, in observance of the services in the death of their founder, Angelo Coluzzi."

Bennie's eyes widened an incredulous blue. "No! What services? Is there a funeral today? I didn't know about that, did you?"

"No, but we couldn't have delayed anything. We had to react fast, like you said."

"Goddamn it!" Bennie tossed her empty Styrofoam cup at the wastebasket so hard it had to miss. "They're at their father's viewing at the same time we file suit?"

Judy didn't understand Bennie's reaction. "Okay, so it doesn't look that good—"

"It's not about how it looks!"

"We didn't have a lot of choice, Bennie. The Coluzzis were shooting at me when they should have been picking out caskets."

Bennie stood up. "You know, you're right. We had to file first thing Monday, but I don't feel good about it. And, God forbid, when you bury your parents, you won't either." She walked to the discarded coffee cup and tossed it into the waste can. "Did you call them, by the way?"

"My parents? Not yet."

"Do it," Bennie said, and strode unhappily from the conference room.

Judy watched the remainder of the broadcast, distracted as the news segued into labor strikes and warehouse fires and an early-summer boating accident. She felt they'd done right in filing the lawsuits. Did it really make a difference that the service was today? These people were killers. They had put a bomb under her car. Judy sighed. Her gaze fell on the newspaper near her bare toes, which had been squeezed unfortunately into little flesh blocks by being shoved into wooden shoes all the time.

Her mood was going downhill again. She had passed up sex with an Italian, now for no reason. Was there really a funeral today? She reached the leftover newspaper with her bare foot and slid it toward her hand. She opened it, turned to the obituaries, and found Angelo Coluzzi's.

**Loving father,** it began, which got Judy right there because she had never had one. She imagined her father's obit. **Stern father. Militaristic father. Bad father, but really good lieutenant colonel.** She decided on the spot against making the phone call that Bennie had ordered. If the Colonel hadn't read that his daughter had been fired upon and almost killed, she wouldn't ruin his roast-beef-and-butter sandwich.

Judy skimmed the rest of the tiny print but felt no guilt. How could they say all these nice things about such a rotten person? How could the surviving sons be bereft when they spent their spare time using little old men for target practice? The last line said that donations may be made to Our Lady of Sorrows Church, and a viewing would be held at Bondi Funeral Home in South Philly, with a funeral mass there today.

It gave Judy an idea.

# 25

The Bondi Funeral Home was one of several that lined South Broad Street, the main thoroughfare of the city, and Judy stood in the midst of the growing crowd across the street. Dressed in a black silk scarf, oversized sunglasses, and black raincoat from the spy wardrobe in the office closet, Judy looked more like Boris's Natasha than a mourner, but at least she didn't look like the lawyer suing the bereaved. She might not be welcome at the viewing.

Cigarette smoke blew past her face, and the man standing next to her swilled wine from a bottle inside a bag. Two old women behind her were gossiping about a neighbor, but a couple of students who had stopped on their way to the College of Art were talking about the car bomb. Judy flipped up her raincoat collar. No doubt that the morning's press coverage had attracted residents, onlookers, and the press to the viewing, which wasn't set to begin until three o'clock, according to the obit. Judy checked her watch. It was only two, and uniformed cops were already arriving to control the crowd.

"Back it up, folks," called out one of the cops, stepping out of a squad car and signaling to a slow-moving municipal truck that followed. He and a cadre of other policemen hurried to unload blue-and-white sawhorses from the tailgate of the truck and set them up in front of the curb to prevent the crowd from spilling onto Broad Street and getting hit by cars. Judy could never understand the South Philly tradition of locating funeral homes on the busiest street in town, ensuring either congested traffic or dead mourners, or both, but there was much about South Philly she didn't understand. Twirling your spaghetti and attempted murder, for starters.

"Yo, back it up, sports fans," the cop said again. The art students edged back, leaving Judy standing next to them at the opening between two sawhorses, giving her a clear view of the entrance to the funeral home. She was hoping to see the Coluzzis, to get a bead on how John and Marco were getting along, and also to learn anything else she could. She didn't know what could happen, and even attending a viewing was better than calling her parents.

A murmur ran through the crowd, and Judy followed the heads turning south down the street. From the oohs and aaahs she would have expected the Mummers Parade, but it was an inky line of shiny black limos snaking their way to the funeral home. Judy stood on wobbly tiptoe. It had to be the Coluzzis. Her pulse quickened.

Gray-jacketed men from the funeral home scurried down the marble steps and took stations at the bottom of the stairs as a limo pulled up, a triple stretch with curved smoked glass more suited to Elvis than a contractor. Its mammoth engine idled at the curb awaiting the others, which pulled up slowly behind it, inadvertently building interest in the crowd. Press cameras flashed, and one of the students next to Judy giggled as she raised a disposable Kodak camera.

Judy looked over. That could come in handy. "I'll give you twenty bucks for the camera," she said to the student. The woman had a cartilage pierce, a nostril pierce, and a lower lip pierce, and Judy, who had considered herself counterculture until this moment, felt very sorry for her.

"It **cost** twenty bucks," the art student retorted, but Judy was reaching into her backpack for her wallet.

"You can punch a lot of holes with this." Judy opened her wallet, extracted a fifty, and handed it to her.

"Whoa," the student said, and she and her friend left.

Judy raised the camera just as the doors of the first limo opened and John Coluzzi stepped out, his stocky frame encased in an expensive suit, and reached a hand out to help his mother, wearing a black dress and a shawl like Judy's, and then his wife, a petite woman in a trim black suit with a black lace doily pinned to the top of her stop-time bouffant hairdo. Judy snapped a picture, and only a half second later another limo arrived. The smaller Marco Coluzzi climbed out with his wife, a corporate version of John's wife with normal hair and two young boys in Holy Communion suits holding on to each of her manicured hands.

Judy took another picture, remembering the newspaper feature about who would be king of Coluzzi Construction. You didn't have to be Italian to know that the son with the sons would make a better successor, since the royal line would be assured. Judy took another photo.

The third limo pulled up and a group of men and women Judy didn't recognize got out. She snapped a few photos on the assumption they were named defendants, and then the limos started coming down Broad, fast and furious as string bands. Judy shot all of them, at least in profile, and got lots of photos as mourners arrived in a black river that moved as slowly as tar through the crowd and traffic.

But as the mourners went inside, she began to feel sidelined, even as she snapped away and finished the entire roll in the camera. The viewing was open to the public, and Judy could go in if she wanted to. It was risky, going into the belly of the beast you were suing blind, but she hadn't been recognized so far, even by the art students, who had read about the car bomb. And if she got inside, maybe she could overhear something. Judy slipped the camera into her raincoat pocket, ducked through the sawhorses, and hurried across the street.

Her heart beat faster as she ascended the marble steps to the funeral home, under a gray plastic awning whose scalloped edges flapped in the wind whipping down Broad Street. Mourners filed up the stairs next to her, meeting a bottleneck at the top as people greeted each other, talking and plunging cigarettes into tall ceramic urns filled with sand. Judy waited for the crowd to move, her eyes on the cigarette butts that stuck like a nightmare forest from the sand. She had never been to a viewing before, much less an Italian viewing, and told herself to stay cool and go with the flow. When in Rome and all.

The crowd edged inside and when it hit the thick red carpet, filed to the left. Judy couldn't see ahead of the burly man in front of her. A surreptitious scan of the male mourners revealed a collection of rough-hewn faces weathered from outside work and large, hammy hands bearing high school rings. The men looked even less accustomed to their stiff suits than Judy was to hers, and her stomach tensed as she realized that they had to be subcontractors on the Philly Court strip mall and other Coluzzi projects. Unless she missed her guess, they would be very jumpy today, looking to the Coluzzis to protect them. It could be a lawyer's gold mine. She tried to keep her head down, her ears open, and her eyes attuned to detail. The first detail she noticed was that nobody around her was crying.

The line flowed slowly into a room on the left, and Judy took it in quickly. It was a huge room filled with folding chairs that faced toward the front, which she couldn't see for all the people milling around, clapping each other on the back and laughing. The metal folding chairs were covered with slipcovers of ivory plastic, matching the ivory-colored walls of the room, which were flocked with curlicues of gold velveteen. The air was thick with the scent of refrigerated flowers and Shalimar knock-off. Judy tried not to breathe.

The line edged forward, and she could hear snippets of conversation from the seated areas. "Yo, Tommy, I only see you at wakes and weddings." "So, Jimmy, you back on the Atkins shit?" "I tol' him, the Eagles don't get themselves a new RB, they're fucked." "They never shoulda got ridda Reggie." "She's a real nice girl, real nice. Goin' to Villanova inna fall."

Judy kept listening, but so far it wasn't promising. Maybe nobody was going to chat about confessing today. The line shifted forward along the fuzzy wall. It was almost at the front of the room, and Judy peeked up. A gleaming bronze casket with chrome handles sat on a massive dais of roses, freesia, gladiola, and white carnations spray-dyed rainbow colors. To the left of the casket in front of a similar floral backdrop stood a somber John and Marco Coluzzi, stiff as bookends that didn't match. They didn't say a word to each other, nor did they stand close, but Judy was suddenly too preoccupied to notice more about their body language. The line of mourners flowed directly to the casket, and the people were kneeling in front on a padded knee rest and making the sign of the cross on their chests, then moving on to speak with the Coluzzi brothers.

Judy's eyes went as wide as her sunglasses. She was in a receiving line! She didn't want to kneel in front of Coluzzi's casket. She didn't even know how to cross herself. If she didn't get out of the line fast, she'd be shaking hands with the men who were trying to kill her.

She looked around wildly. There was nowhere to go but the seats on the left and moving there at this point would be dangerously obvious. Nobody in the line was breaking ranks before paying proper respect to the dead. And anybody who had seen **The Godfather** knew that respect counted in this crowd.

The line shifted forward two rows, bringing Judy only twenty feet from the front of the room. She didn't know what to do. She thought fast.

Only one excuse was acceptable on this occasion. "Excuse me," she said loudly. "Does anybody know where the ladies' room is?"

An older woman two couples up turned around and pointed right with a slim finger. "Other side of the hall," she said sympathetically, and Judy nodded.

But the only exits were back the way she came, or to the right of the casket. Only one way to go. If Judy acted suspicious, the Coluzzis would suspect her. She held her stomach as if she'd had a sudden attack of dysentery and hurried to the front of the room, took a quick right at the red gladiolus, and looked for signs to the ladies' room.

LOUNGE, read one softly lighted sign, and she followed the euphemism to the ladies' room. But when she opened the door, it wasn't a bathroom at all but a large, gold-flecked room ringed with covered folding chairs, supplied with prominent boxes of Kleenex, and occupied completely by crying women. One group sat in one corner weeping theatrically and clutching soggy tissues, and the other sat in the other corner sobbing even louder. Judy looked from one to the other and wondered fleetingly if it was an Italian Battle of the Bands.

"Oops, sorry," Judy said, but nobody took notice except a strawberry-blond woman with bright blue eyes. Tall and very pregnant in a black linen maternity dress, she stood alone by the door, examining the bad prints.

"You needn't be sorry," the woman said, with a heavy Irish accent. A light sprinkling of freckles covered her nose, and her skin was a poreless pale pink.

"I was looking for the ladies' room."

"It's down the hall." The woman leaned over, her blue eyes dancing with mischief. "I made the same mistake. You're not Italian either, are you?"

"How could you tell?" Judy smiled, nervous that the Irish woman would recognize her.

"Why, you're nice and tall, too, and I can see under your scarf that you're a blonde."

Renewed sobbing surged loudly from the groups of women in the corners, like tears in stereo. Judy considered leaving the room, but the woman was so obviously alone, a clear outsider. Judy leaned to her and whispered, "We're the only women in here not crying. I think it's the price of admission."

The woman laughed softly. "Now that's the difference between the Italians and Irish. We Irish know how to throw a grand wake. Everybody has a good time. The whole point is **not** to cry." Her eyes lit up. "Wakes last for days in Ireland. County Galway, where my family's from. Do you know it?"

"No," Judy told her, counting it as a measure of the woman's naïveté that she would expect an American to be familiar with Ireland's counties. Judy had always felt guilty she knew no geography but America's own.

"It's a lovely place, lovely. I'm from a town called Loughrea. I came over only two years ago, after I met my husband, Kevin. I'm Theresa, by the way."

"Great to meet you," Judy said simply, and got away without supplying her own name, in Theresa's enthusiasm for someone to talk to.

"Well, my husband, Kevin, he's American. He came to town on holiday, and he was looking for the ATM machine. You know, the MAC machine, you call it? And I told him it was right in front of him, pretty as you please, on Dublin Road. We fell in love right there."

" 'Where's the MAC?' Quite a pickup line," Judy said with a smile, and Theresa laughed warmly.

"It was. We got married and now we're having the baby, and it's been grand." She paused, uneasy. "Not that it hasn't taken some getting used to, a new marriage and all, and the way things are over here. Of course I'd read so much about America, we have all your TV shows and movies and your books, and I thought I knew what to expect. But then again, you can never tell what turn your life will take, can you?" The woman shook her head as if in a memory, and a sudden wetness sprang to her eyes.

"You want to sit down?" Judy asked, taken aback, and helped the pregnant woman to a shaky seat near the door.

"I'm sorry, I'm being so silly. It must be my hormones."

"No, that's okay." Judy yanked for a Kleenex from a box left on the seats and handed it to her. "You're in the crying room. You might as well cry."

Suddenly the lounge door opened, and Judy froze. John Coluzzi stuck his head inside, as if he were looking for someone. He hovered right over Judy's shoulder, so close she could smell his heavy aftershave. Was he looking for her? She could be dead if he found her. She threw her arm around Theresa and quickly yanked her close, comforting her. Judy hoped they'd look like more crying women in the crying room.

Coluzzi lingered a minute more, but Theresa only cried harder, and Judy hugged her tight. Then Judy heard the door close behind her back. Coluzzi must have gone, leaving behind the faint scent of Calvin Klein.

Theresa was saying, through her tears, "You're so nice. It's so nice . . . to make a friend here. Americans . . . or maybe Philadelphians, I don't know . . . they're not always so friendly to new people."

"I know what you mean," Judy said, and she did. She had made only one friend in Philly, Mary, but she had always blamed herself. Maybe she should start blaming other people, which would be easier.

"Everything's going so wrong, just when it should be . . . so right. We're under so much strain now, and my hormones, the doctor said . . . they're going crazy."

"I'm sure things will get better." Judy held Theresa while her shoulders shook with sobs, her heart going out to her, especially because Theresa had just saved her life. "And soon you'll have a new baby."

"But we're in trouble . . . with money, I mean. Things are so expensive here. Not like at home. I think I'm just so . . . what do you call it? Home-sick."

This feeling Judy didn't know. "I'm sure it'll pass."

"We're just building our new house . . . and my husband's business was going so well. He was doing work for the Coluzzis . . . and we were finally going to get out of the apartment . . . and we need, you know, a nursery." Theresa heaved a mighty sob. "They were even talking . . . about buying his company. They wanted to . . . expand or something, and they wanted to pay so much. But then . . . Angelo Coluzzi got killed and now there's . . . a lawsuit against the company and I don't know what's going to happen. We could lose everything."

Judy felt stricken. Theresa must be the wife of one of the subcontractors. Judy had caused all this pain, to a pregnant woman. She didn't focus on the fact that making the Coluzzis' life a living hell meant making a living hell of lives like Theresa's. "I'm so sorry," Judy said, meaning it.

"Kevin says not to worry, but I can't help it. We can't lose the new house, not with the baby on the way."

Judy's thoughts raced ahead. As bad as she felt for Theresa, maybe this was the opportunity she'd been waiting for. What was it Roser had said? **Coluzzi won't hire Irish or black unless they have to.** Was Theresa the wife of McRea, the paving contractor? Judy couldn't remember his first name from the complaint. "It must be so frightening for you," she said.

"It is awful . . . and it couldn't come at a worse time. I don't dare tell my parents for fear they'll tell me . . . to leave Kevin and come right home. I want to go home, but I don't want . . . to lose my marriage."

Judy grabbed the entire box of Kleenex, hating that now she had an ulterior motive. But she had a job to do, and lives were at stake. "Please stay calm, but I have to tell you something surprising. I think I can help you and your husband."

"What . . . did you say?"

"I'm a lawyer, and I can help you. I know about the lawsuit, and your husband isn't the target." Judy handed her a fresh tissue, and Theresa dabbed at her eyes.

"Of course he isn't. He can't be. He hardly

knows . . . the Coluzzi family. We don't know . . . any of these people here. He never worked for them before."

"I figured that."

Theresa blinked her puzzled eyes free of tears. "But however do you know that?"

"My name is Judy Carrier, and I'm the lawyer who filed the suit."

Theresa gasped, but the sound got lost in the wailing broadcasted in Dolby sound from the two far corners of the room. Theresa began to open her mouth, as if to yell or call someone for help, but Judy grabbed her hand and held on to it.

"No! Please don't betray me. These people will kill me."

"**What?**" Theresa's eyes searched Judy's, even through the sunglasses. "What are you talking about?"

"They're killers. They're dangerous people. They're not what they seem, to you anyway."

"Then what are you doing here?" Theresa looked at Judy as if she were crazy, which was a distinct possibility.

"I was hoping to get to your husband or one of the other subs. Your husband, is he Kevin McRea?"

Theresa nodded in teary shock, and Judy kept her grip on her soft hands.

"Listen to me. Kevin's in trouble as long as he stays with the Coluzzis. I know he built them a driveway in return for getting the excavation and paving contract for Philly Court."

"I don't know anything about Kevin's business."

"I'm not saying you knew, but what he did was against our law." Judy felt a twinge of guilt at terrorizing her, but it was all true. "I don't want to go after Kevin, or you." She lowered her voice so as not to be heard by the other sobbing women. "The Coluzzis are the bad guys here and they won't help Kevin when push comes to shove, believe me. They're dangerous people and they stick together. They'll hang you all out to dry."

Theresa's eyes brimmed with new tears, but Judy couldn't stop now.

"You can reach me at my office in town, anytime. I promise you that if you talk to me and get Kevin to cooperate with me, I'll let him out of the lawsuit. I'll drop him, just like that, and your troubles will be over. I won't tell anyone that he called until we have to go to trial. I don't want to take your baby's nursery, okay? Will you do it?"

Tears clouded Theresa's eyes, and she withdrew her hands. "You don't care about my baby. You're just trying to use Kevin, to help your case against him!"

"No, I do care, but that doesn't matter. Given what Kevin has done, I'm the best chance he has of getting out of trouble. Tell him we spoke. It's his only chance, and yours."

But before Theresa could answer or expose her,

Judy rose and left through the lounge door. She wanted to get out of the funeral home, fast. She had accomplished more than she'd hoped to. As the lawyers say, when you win, shut up and get out of the courtroom.

She found herself in a hallway filled with Coluzzi mourners, talking, laughing, and filing outside for cigarette breaks. Judy wedged her way through the broad backs and thick necks and had almost made it through the entrance hall when she felt a pair of eyes on her, from a heavyset man beside her. She looked over, shielded by the big sunglasses.

She had seen him before. It was Jimmy Bello, John Coluzzi's man, who had been on the corner watching the clubhouse the other day. He was surrounded by mourners, but he was looking right at her. Did he recognize her? Judy wasn't waiting to see.

She hustled toward the open entrance and ran out the door.

# 26

"You did what?" Bennie said, and Judy decided she was definitely ordering her boss that T-shirt. They were back at the firm, and the only difference between this and their last **you did what** conversation was that this time they were sitting in Judy's office and the good guys were finally winning.

"So it was a little risky, Bennie. So what?"

"What do you mean, 'so what'?" Bennie was shouting, but Judy felt too good to even be bothered.

"Look what we got out of it! The woman was McRea's wife. I live right, don't I?"

"Keep it up and you won't be living long." Bennie's mouth was tight, her blue eyes washed out with fatigue, and her khaki suit rumpled from a long day. On the other side of the closed door, the business day was winding down. "Don't ever do anything like that again, Carrier. Going to their viewing? It was **insane**."

"I know, but—"

"You don't go to somebody's **family viewing**."

Judy didn't get this quirk of Bennie's. She'd drag somebody out of bed to depose them. What was the difference with a viewing? "The FBI does it all the time. They were probably at this one, too."

"You're not the FBI. They have guns. Don't antagonize the Coluzzis."

Judy laughed abruptly. "We're suing the shit out of them!"

"Suing them is one thing, crashing their viewing is another. These people are killers!"

"I had it in control. I was careful!"

Bennie leaned forward on Judy's messy desk. "You say John Coluzzi may have seen you, and this Jimmy Bello."

"I got out in time. I can take care of myself."

"Oh, really. Tough talk. Can you take care of that woman, the one you liked so much? McRea's wife?"

"What do you mean?"

Bennie cocked an eyebrow. "Coluzzi may figure out that it was you McRea was talking to in the lounge. He knows he's exposed on the driveway. It's in the complaint, and it's the only example of a kickback we have the specifics on. So what do you think Coluzzi will do to the McReas, if he thinks they're talking with you? At best, he'll squeeze the shit out of them not to talk. That's the best-case scenario. Can you guess the worst?"

Judy's mouth went dry. The truth struck horribly home. She had placed the McReas in the line of fire. Having first sued them, Judy had just made it worse. She fell quiet. Her face went hot.

"I see I've made my point. Let's hope the McReas call us before the Coluzzis call them." Bennie sighed and stood up, crossing her arms. "Meantime, the GC in Huartzer really wants to talk to you. I'll cut you some slack on the antitrust article, because we can make the next issue, but you have other cases. If you hadn't been running around funeral homes, you could have been doing your job."

Judy felt a headache coming on. She hadn't eaten in hours. She hadn't slept in days. She hadn't had sex in a year. She'd never had sex with an Italian, and it was looking like she never would.

"Also. You have a preliminary hearing tomorrow in Lucia and you have to get ready for it. Did you call your parents?"

"No."

"Do it now. And tell me if McRea calls you. I want to be in on it. And don't forget your parents! They're first!" Bennie barked, and left the office.

Judy flipped open her Filofax, found the number, and punched it in. It was the number her parents had left on their itinerary, which they had e-mailed to the kids before they left; Judy had a brother teaching law in Boston and a sister in the Sydney office of a brokerage house. If it weren't for e-mail, they'd never see each other.

An answering machine picked up the call. As much as Judy wouldn't have minded hearing her mother's voice on the machine, even recorded, it was one of those mechanical samplings offered by the phone company. She waited for the beep. "It's me, Judy. Just wanted to say hi and that everything's fine. Take care. Love you." That about covered it, she thought, and hung up the phone.

Judy's second call was to the general counsel in Huartzer, and she got voicemail. "Rick, this is Judy Carrier. Sorry I haven't returned your call, but I haven't been in. Feel free to call anytime and I'll get back to you right away."

Her last call was the only one she wanted to make. She pressed the numbers with anticipation, envisioning Frank on the other end of the line, stacking stone in the sun with his shirt off, the long muscles of his back slick with sweat. His cell phone would be ringing in his pocket. He would feel its telltale vibration, a tingle that told him love was calling. Judy heard a click on the line. "Is that a cell phone in your pocket, or are you just happy to see me?" she said.

But it was only Bell Atlantic. "The cell phone customer you have called is unavailable. Please leave a message at the sound of the tone."

Disappointed, Judy waited for the tone and thought of a good message. How about I filed our lawsuit, but I may have jeopardized our best witness? Or I'm sorry I turned you down last night, but at least it was in front of your friends? Or best yet, Everything's fine except that your grandfather has to come to court tomorrow, exposing him to life-threatening danger?

**Beep,** went the tone, and Judy spoke from the heart:

"Call me. I think of you every minute," she said, and hung up.

It was dark outside Judy's office window, and the law firm was quiet. The receptionist and secretaries had gone home, as had all of the lawyers except Judy. Bennie had gone to give a speech to the local ACLU chapter, but said she'd be calling to check in. Judy knew she was worried about her safety, which was a nice feeling, since Judy was worried about her safety, too. She'd taken the scissors from her office drawer and set them conveniently on her desk, just in case she had to make paper dolls of a crazed contractor. Between makeup and her personal defense, Judy was finding whole new vistas for office supplies.

She slurped the last of her take-out lo mein out from a white carton and put out of her mind that nobody she was lusting after or suing had called her back. The phone hadn't rung for hours, but she was going to stop thinking about it. That resolved, Judy scrutinized the thirty-two photos tacked to the corkboard on an easel in front of her.

It was an array of the photos she'd taken in front of the funeral home this afternoon, which she'd had one-hour-developed across the street. She'd posted them in the order in which she'd taken them, and they made a story in still pictures of the people arriving at the Coluzzi viewing. Judy finished eating as her gaze went from one shot to the next. It was dinner theater for lawyers.

She set down her pull-apart chopsticks and got up. The first shots were of the Coluzzis, John and Marco, and their wives, then, evidently, other family, then mourners arriving in cars and on foot. There were shots of mourners parking in the lot beside the funeral home and on the median on Broad Street. There were crowd scenes on the sidewalk, and many more of them mounting the long marble stairway to the entrance or gathering in groups out front or at the top of the stairs. Interestingly, the camera had recorded much more than Judy had realized she had seen. It was the power of the art, and it was working for her.

Judy scanned the dark images. She didn't know the faces, but by the end of the case she would. She walked back and forth before the photos, trying to fix each image in her mind. She'd already had the full set scanned and e-mailed to Dan Roser, who would be able to identify many of them, hopefully subs on the Philly Court project. She'd put in two calls to Roser but he hadn't gotten back to her yet. Not that she'd sit on her hands in the meantime. She shoved them into her skirt pockets and stopped before the fifteenth photo.

A flash of strawberry-blond hair appeared in the photo, an unusually bright spot in a canvas of dark hair and black suits, apparently of men at the top of the stairs to the funeral home. Judy leaned over and squinted at it. The awning cast a shadow that obscured the people, and the image was way too small to make out. Judy couldn't see it well enough and she didn't have a magnifying glass. But she did have a computer.

She hurried back to her desk, logged on to her e-mail, and called up the scanned computer photos she'd sent Roser, pausing at the fifteenth. There was the tiny strawberry swatch. Then Judy opened the Photoshop program, marqueed that section of the photo, and enlarged it once, then again. The strawberry head filled up half the screen. It was Theresa McRea, as Judy had suspected. But who was Theresa with?

Judy moved the photo to the man beside her and clicked the magnifying-glass icon to enlarge the image. The pixels went blocky on her and she stepped it down. A dark-haired man held Theresa's hand. He had to be her husband Kevin. She clicked the icon again. His forehead was wrinkled, and his head close to another man's, as if in confidence. Then Judy rotated the image to see who they were talking to. Only his profile was visible to the camera's eye. Judy clicked the icon, and the image grew into itself, like the child to the man.

The man was Marco Coluzzi. Judy eased back in her chair. She had a shot of Kevin McRea talking to Marco the day the complaint was filed against them. And Marco had evidently come out of the viewing to greet him. Judy moved the image down and spotted a white line at the bottom. A cigarette, in Marco's hand. He had wanted a smoke, but he was also, in the vernacular, showing McRea respect.

McRea had built the driveway for one of the Coluzzis, but Judy couldn't remember which brother; she'd been so tired when she drafted the complaint. She closed Photoshop, opened Microsoft Word, and found their complaint, then skimmed down to allegation 55: **It is alleged that the above-named defendant Kevin McRea did excavate, construct, and pave a driveway for the defendant Marco Coluzzi, at an estimated value of $130,000, in return for . . .**

So it had been Marco, not John, who got the fancy driveway. Judy reasoned it out. It made sense that Marco had the alliance with Kevin McRea, not John. After all, John apparently hadn't recognized Theresa as Kevin's wife when he stuck his head into the lounge, or he might have wondered why the wife of one of his subs was so broken up over his father's death. Or maybe he had and didn't want to show his hand. Judy had no way of knowing, which made her worry for Theresa.

Judy glanced at the phone. Theresa hadn't called. Judy was worried that she wouldn't and equally worried that she would. What had she gotten the McReas into? Judy squirmed in her seat. She didn't like waiting for witnesses to call any more than she liked waiting for men to call. Not that she was waiting for a man to call. Damn!

Judy scrolled to the top of the complaint, to the caption naming the parties. There was Kevin McRea's name, right over his address. He lived in Glenolden, Delaware County, which wasn't that far from the city. She considered going there, but Bennie would kill her if the Coluzzis didn't. Judy opted for the safer and more boring approach. She picked up the phone, called information, got the McReas' phone number, and called it.

Her heart was pounding as a woman picked up, but she didn't have an Irish accent. Judy paused. "Hello, may I speak to Theresa or Kevin McRea?"

"They're gone," the woman said flatly, and Judy started.

"Gone? **Gone**? What do you mean?"

"They just moved out. Right this afternoon. I thought their new house mighta been finished early but it ain't. They left all of a sudden."

Judy felt only slightly relieved. "They moved out? I don't believe it."

"Believe it, baby. I'm the landlady, and I'm just as surprised as you."

"But Theresa's a good friend of mine. I just saw her today. She didn't say she was moving."

"Well, she's gone. They came home together this afternoon, packed their clothes, and left. Paid off the whole year lease plus the security deposit, and I got no complaint with that. They were in a real big hurry. Left all their furniture and kitchen stuff, and they're payin' me two hundred bucks to pack it up and put it in storage."

Judy tried to think. Theresa must have told Kevin that Judy had approached her at the viewing, and they got the hell out of Dodge. He didn't want to get caught between the Coluzzis and the lawsuit. "Did they leave you a forwarding address, or a phone number where they can be reached?"

"Nothin'. Said they'd call later. Now, no offense, I got to get back to work here. Theresa kept a real neat house, but she had knickknacks out the wazoo. Shamrocks. Linen tea towels. Leprechauns carved outta Connemara marble, whatever that is."

Judy thanked the landlady and hung up, thinking about leprechauns and shamrocks. Unless she missed her guess, Theresa and Kevin were halfway to Ireland by now. Judy smiled in spite of her lawyerly instincts. The McReas were out of harm's way, and she'd find another way to win her suit. She sat motionless with her hand on the phone, trying to process this new information. It made sense they'd take off, because a baby was portable, but how about a business? How could Kevin McRea leave his business? And for how long?

Judy turned again to her laptop, logged on to the Internet, and ran a Google search for McRea Excavation and Paving. Sure enough, it had a website, since everybody had a website now. Judy was hoping that www.sexwithanitalian.com was still up for grabs. She clicked the link, and onto the screen popped an amateurish but effective piece of brochureware. There were pictures of backhoes and front-end loaders, ghosted over a clunky MCREA logo. The copy was badly written, but Judy was a lawyer, not a critic. She read:

> McRea Excavation and Paving is a complete, full-service company meeting the excavating and paving needs of numerous residents and commercial businesses in the tristate area for the past twenty years, with annual revenues of two million dollars. Kevin McRea is the CEO and sole proprietor of the company, and he supervises a workforce of 63 full-time employees, many of whom have been with the com-

pany for all of its 21 years in business. McRea never loses time on your construction job because of faulty or leased equipment. McRea owns all of its own equipment, and with it and its able workforce, McRea can meet any and all of your excavation and paving needs.

McRea's business was a going concern, with a very healthy income stream. Kevin couldn't leave it forever, could he? Then Judy remembered something Theresa had said, through her tears. That the Coluzzis had wanted to buy his business. McRea Excavation was a $2 million company, so that would be a major corporate decision, not a routine expenditure. Judy stopped to think, her gaze coming to rest on the photos tacked up in front of her. Why would they be talking about buying a new business with the leadership of the company thrown into doubt? Or, more to the point, who would be talking about buying a new business?

Judy's eyes ran restlessly over the photos. Marco and John. John and Marco. It was Marco who came to greet Kevin, not John. It was Marco who got Kevin's driveway, not John. What if Marco was the one who had tried to buy McRea Excavation, not John? And then Judy noticed something about the photos. In none of them did John Coluzzi appear with Marco or was he even shown speaking to him. They had arrived in separate limos. Their families weren't speaking, even on the sidewalk. Or beside their father's coffin. It was obvious there was a rift, and if the newspaper accounts were correct, it had to be over succession of the company. What else would divide two Italian princes but the kingdom?

Something Judy had heard recently came to mind. **There really is no honor among thieves. They'll eat each other alive.** She remembered Roser had said it, talking about the subcontractors. But didn't the same truth apply to John and Marco Coluzzi? Would their rift turn into war? And could Judy do anything to make that happen? It could be a weapon more potent than any lawsuit. It would turn brother against brother, blood against blood. It was so, well, Italian.

Judy picked up the phone. She was hoping you could still make trouble for bad guys, even from behind a desk.

# 27

The sun shone bright Tuesday morning, in an almost impossible run of good weather in Philly, but Judy was too psyched to care. She couldn't see the blue sky for the TV and still cameras, tape recorders held high, and klieg lights. She couldn't breathe the fresh air for the reporters exhaling coffee in her face. It was a Starbucks contact high.

Judy plowed in her navy suit and lucky pumps through the press outside the Criminal Justice Center, with Pigeon Tony wedged between her and Frank. For the first time, she not only tolerated the reporters, she welcomed them. She felt safer for all of them with 384 witnesses on the scene, and the media was key to Judy's new and improved plan.

"Ms. Carrier, any comment about Kevin McRea's disappearance?" "Judy, over here! What do you say to reports that Marco Coluzzi was trying to buy McRea Excavation?" "Ms. Carrier, do you believe Kevin McRea has met with foul play?"

"No comment," she shouted. She threaded her way to the courthouse entrance, putting on a professional mask to hide her glee at their questions. Obviously her late-night telephone calls, placed anonymously to any newspaper that would pick up, had worked like a charm. She had planted the story about Marco Coluzzi's attempted purchase of McRea Excavation, and eager reporters had investigated the facts and gotten sources to confirm. It had been a year or two since a Philly paper had won a Pulitzer and nobody was forgetting it.

"Ms. Carrier, do you care to comment on Marco Coluzzi's expansion into the concrete and quarry business?" "Judy, who you gonna call now that Kevin McRea's out of the picture?" "Ms. Carrier, what goes into a $130,000 driveway anyway? Gold?"

Judy didn't break a smile. Headlines on the morning newspapers had read DEFENDANT DISAPPEARS, with sidebars like "Marco Coluzzi's Expanding Business Empire," and Judy couldn't have written them better herself. Reporters had interviewed the McReas' landlady and, more important, had unearthed Marco's tax records and SEC filings, which showed an increasing concentration of power in the construction industry, much of it through shell companies that disguised their true ownership. Judy was hoping the acquisitions had been hidden from John Coluzzi as well, and that he would feel surprised and threatened by Marco's growing might.

She looked quickly around, wondering when and how the Coluzzis would arrive. Together or apart? At peace or at war? She couldn't stay to find out, because she had a murder case to defend.

"Ms. Carrier, come on, cut us a break!" "Ms. Carrier, is Pigeon Tony gonna get off?" "Ms. Carrier, did he do it or not?" "Judy, did you hire a bodyguard yet?" "Judy, how's your car?"

Judy exchanged glances with Frank, who grinned, his teeth white and even against his freshly shaved olive skin. He looked handsome dressed up in a white oxford shirt, casual rep tie, and light tweed jacket he'd bought during a trip to the King of Prussia mall, when he was supposed to be calling his lawyer. But Judy could forgive men their shopping. They loved it so.

"Did I tell you how much I liked your phone message last night?" Frank whispered in her ear before he went through the revolving door.

"No comment," Judy said, because it was time for work, not love. These Italians would never get it straight. She took Pigeon Tony by the hand and tucked him inside the courthouse.

The courtroom, though modern, was one of the smallest in the new Criminal Justice Center, and its size contributed to the uneasy hostility that filled the room, as if the tigers and the lions had been mistakenly placed in the same tiny cage. The Coluzzi family and friends sat on the Commonwealth's side of the courtroom, with Marco and John sitting unhappily together, and the Lucia family sat on the right, with Frank, Mr. DiNunzio, Feet, and Tony-From-Down-The-Block in the front pew behind a sleek black panel. The scene was an unfortunate carbon copy of the arraignment, except that it was staffed by double the blue-shirted court officers, for security. Judy wished for the National Guard and a bumper sticker that read MY ITALIANS CAN BEAT UP YOUR ITALIANS.

She put the drama in the gallery behind her and took a seat at the counsel table next to Pigeon Tony. He seemed unusually quiet, but it could have been discomfort in the new striped tie and brown jacket that Frank had made him wear, over protest. They'd come from the boys' department at Macy's because Pigeon Tony was so small, and Judy, sitting next to him, felt more baby-sitter than lawyer. And she had wanted to get him a translator for court, but he had adamantly refused. Judy wondered if Pigeon Tony was turning into a problem child, in a clip-on tie.

"Let's begin, people," Judge Maniloff said, from the sleek, modern dais with a gray marble front. Judge Randy Maniloff, a middle-aged gold-spectacled judge, had been picked by computer for the hearing, but Judy preferred to think it was her lawyer karma at work. Maniloff was one of the smartest judges on the municipal court bench, which heard preliminary hearings on murder cases and held misdemeanor trials. He wouldn't be the ultimate trial judge, but he'd be fair at this level. "We have a crowded docket today for a change, and we can't waste any time." He banged a gavel loosely. "This is the matter of Commonwealth versus Lucia. Who's here for the Commonwealth?"

"Joseph Santoro for the Commonwealth, Your Honor," said the district attorney, and he stood up. He was on the short side but powerfully built, with dark wavy hair and a black walrusy mustache. Santoro was the top assistant in the D.A.'s office, which was undoubtedly why he was picked for this high-profile case. His Italian surname wouldn't hurt either. Judy resigned herself to being a minority for the duration.

Judge Maniloff acknowledged Judy, swiveling in his black leather chair. "I see we have Ms. Carrier here for defendant Anthony Lucia. Welcome, Ms. Carrier." He smiled pleasantly, and Judy stood up briefly.

"Thank you, Your Honor."

"Now that we're all friends, Mr. Santoro, call your first witness," Judge Maniloff said. He turned his attention to some papers on the dais, as Santoro stood up again.

"The Commonwealth will present just two witnesses today, Your Honor, and we would first call
James Bello to the stand," he said, and in the front
row the heavyset man from the funeral home
wedged himself from the right side of John
Coluzzi, moved with difficulty down the pew, and
came before the bar of court. He took the witness
stand heavily and was sworn in as the D.A. took
the fake walnut podium between counsel tables.

"Mr. Bello," Santoro said, "please state your
name and address for the record."

"My name's James Bello, but they call me Fat
Jimmy," he said matter-of-factly, though Judy
wasn't sure it was what Santoro had been
looking for.

"And your address?"

He rattled it off.

"Fine, Mr. Bello. Let's move directly to the
morning of Friday, April seventeenth. Were you
present at about eight twenty-three A.M. at 712
Cotner Street in South Philadelphia?"

"Yeh." Bello wore a black knit shirt with suit
pants, and his thick wrist bore a gold Rolex. His lips
were puffy, his nose a pockmarked bulb, and his eyes
large, round, and unforgettable if they were glaring
at you in a funeral home. If he recognized Judy, it
didn't show.

"And that address is a clubhouse for a pigeon-
racing combine, correct?"

"Yeh."

Judy opened her legal pad to a fresh page and shifted forward on her seat. At a preliminary hearing the Commonwealth had to prove only a prima facie case of murder, and the D.A. would have more than enough in this case. The hardest punches at a prelim were thrown beneath the surface, because the Commonwealth was trying to reveal as little as possible about its case, and the defense was trying to find out as much as possible. It was a legal fistfight, and only apparently civilized.

"Mr. Bello, please tell the court who else was present in the clubhouse on the day in question."

"Mr. Tony LoMonaco, Mr. Tony Pensiera. Angelo Coluzzi was in the back room, and Mr. Tony Lucia, the defendant, went in there, too."

"Was anybody else in the back room except for Mr. Coluzzi and Mr. Lucia?"

"No, Angelo and me opened the place that morning. He was the only one back there until Tony went in."

Santoro nodded. "Mr. Bello, please tell the court what happened next, if you would."

"Sure, yeh." Bello cleared his throat of smoker's phlegm. "Mr. Lucia went in the back room and there was a scream, and then we heard like a crash. And we went in and there was Angelo dead on the floor and Tony, Mr. Lucia, was standing over him, all worked up."

Judy held her breath to know what Bello had heard, or what he'd claim he heard.

Santoro shifted closer to the microphone at the podium. "Mr. Bello, you said you heard yelling. What did you hear?"

"I heard yelling, in English and Italian."

"Do you know who was doing the yelling?"

"Mr. Lucia."

"Mr. Bello, what did you hear Mr. Lucia yell?"

"He yelled, 'I'm gonna kill you.'"

Judy made a note, only apparently calmly. It would be home run evidence at trial. Worse, it was true.

"Mr. Bello, did defendant Lucia yell this in English or in Italian?"

"In Italian. Definitely, Italian."

"And you understand Italian?"

"Very well. Been speakin' it since I was a kid. Now, Angelo, he didn't like to speak it. He wanted the old ways behind him. He wanted to be a real American. He didn't have no accent either. Hardly."

Santoro nodded, his soft chin wrinkling into his stiff white collar. "So you are sure it was Mr. Lucia's voice and not Angelo Coluzzi's?"

"I know Angelo's voice and also, he's the one who ended up dead."

Santoro didn't blink. "Then what did you do, Mr. Bello?"

"I got up and ran into the back room and there was Angelo, lyin' on the ground, with the shelves over him and a big mess onna floor. I checked Angelo out but he didn't have no pulse and his head was lying funny."

"Where was the defendant at this time?"

"Standin' over Angelo."

"What did Mr. Pensiera and Mr. LoMonaco do then?"

"Objection as to relevance," Judy said for the record, but Judge Maniloff overruled her.

"They said to Mr. Lucia, 'Let's get outta here,' and they got him out and they left."

"Then what did you do?"

"I called 911 and they came and took Angelo away, and that was that."

Judy made a note. It was the least emotional account of a murder she could imagine. Santoro would have to offer Fat Jimmy a dozen ravioli to shed a tear or two at trial, but for the time being the D.A. nodded in satisfaction, returned to counsel table, and sat down.

"I have no further questions, Your Honor," he said, and he didn't need any.

Judy stood up to pick Fat Jimmy's brain for cross-examination, though she couldn't win here anyway, and as a defense lawyer, wouldn't want to. If the defense won at a preliminary hearing, the Commonwealth could rearrest the defendant and retry him, because double jeopardy hadn't yet attached. Not that winning anything was in the cards today. Judy approached the podium.

"Mr. Bello," she began, "describe where you were sitting when you allegedly heard Mr. Lucia yell, 'I'm gonna kill you.'"

"I just come into the room from the bathroom, and sat down at the bar, when I saw Mr. LoMonaco and Mr. Pensiera. They told me that Pigeon Tony, Mr. Lucia, had gone in the back room."

Judy recalled the layout of the racing club. "So you were at the bar."

"Right."

"How far is the bar from the back room?"

"About ten feet."

"Which seat were you sitting in at the bar?"

"In the middle."

"Were you having a drink?"

"I was gonna but I didn't get to."

"What was the drink?"

"Coffee."

Judy made a note. It was good to take notes in court because it made you look as if you were getting somewhere. This note said NICE GOING, BUCKO. "Anything alcoholic in the coffee?"

"No."

Judy made another note. OUTTA THE PARK, LOSER. "Now, you said you heard yelling. Did you hear anything else other than Mr. Lucia allegedly yelling, 'I'm going to kill you'?"

"No."

"Are you sure about that?"

"Yeh."

"You didn't hear Angelo Coluzzi say anything?"

"No."

Judy made a note. NOW WOULD BE A GOOD TIME TO TELL US YOU HEARD ANGELO COLUZZI CONFESS TO A DOUBLE MURDER. Santoro looked over at Judy from his counsel table, and she knew she had him wondering what else had been said in that back room, and if it made a difference. Let him sweat. "Let's change gears, Mr. Bello. Are you married or single?"

"I'm, uh, divorced."

"I see. And are you related to the Coluzzi family in any way?"

"Yeh."

"How so?"

"Uh?"

ENGLISH, PLEASE. "I mean, how exactly are you related to the Coluzzis?"

"I'm a second cousin, twice removed. I think. My father Guido married somebody's second cousin."

GUIDO, NOT TONY? "I see. And how long have you worked for the Coluzzi family?"

"Objection, no foundation, Your Honor," Santoro said, popping up, but Judy waved him off.

"I'll rephrase. Mr. Bello, do you work for the Coluzzi family?"

"Yeh."

GLAD WE CLEARED THAT UP. "What is your job, Mr. Bello?"

"Office."

"You work in their construction office?"

Jimmy seemed unsure. "Yeh. I help out."

"How?"

"Whatever Angelo axed me to do, I do."

"Like an assistant?"

Santoro stood up again. "Objection as to relevance and beyond the scope, Your Honor."

"Overruled." Judge Maniloff looked up from papers he had been reading. "I think the defendant is entitled to know something about the primary witness against him, don't you, counsel?"

NO, HE DOESN'T, Judy wrote, but Santoro didn't answer and sank into his seat. She cleared her throat. "So, Mr. Bello, did you say you were a personal assistant?"

Jimmy frowned at the term. "Kinda."

"And were you a personal assistant to Angelo Coluzzi, or are you to John Coluzzi, or to Marco Coluzzi?" Then she added, because she couldn't resist, "In his various businesses?"

"I guess, the whole family now. I'm like an office assistant." Jimmy looked over at the front row uncertainly, and Judy acted like she didn't notice. She didn't want him coached out of it; she wanted him to repeat it in front of the jury, when she could get mileage out of it.

"And how long have you been an office assistant to the Coluzzi family, Mr. Bello?"

"Thirty-five years."

Judy made a note. NOW WE'RE GETTING SOMEWHERE. "I see. And how much do you currently earn as their office assistant, Mr. Bello?"

"Objection!" Santoro said, shooting up like a booster rocket, but Judy wasn't having any.

"Your Honor, how can it be of no relevance that the primary witness is on the family payroll?"

Judge Maniloff arched a graying eyebrow. "I'll allow it, tiger, but do finish up here."

Judy smiled. "Thank you, Your Honor." IT'S GOOD WHEN A JUDGE CALLS YOU TIGER. "Mr. Bello, you were telling us what the Coluzzis pay you. Please proceed."

Jimmy paused, undoubtedly trying to remember the difference between what he earned and what he reported. "Fifteen grand a year."

EEEK. YOU NEED A LAWYER. Judy closed her pad and stepped away from the podium. "I have no further questions, Your Honor."

"Excellent," Judge Maniloff said, nodding at the district attorney. "Mr. Santoro, your next witness?"

"Commonwealth calls Dr. Patel to the stand." Santoro stood up, turned to the second row, and gestured like Vanna White to Dr. Patel, reducing the distinguished medical examiner to the status of a free refrigerator. The medical examiner took the stand, raised his hand politely, and was sworn in.

"Please identify yourself for the record, Dr. Patel."

"My name is Voresh Patel," the coroner said, his voice soft and professional. He had the same kind brown eyes and steel-framed glasses Judy remembered from the autopsy, and he wore a trim brown suit. She would have to question him with care, because she didn't want to show her hand.

"Dr. Patel, what is your profession?" Santoro asked.

"I am an assistant medical examiner for the County of Philadelphia."

"I see. And did you perform the postmortem examination on the body of Angelo Coluzzi?"

"I did."

"And when did that take place, Dr. Patel?"

"The day after the body was taken to the morgue." Dr. Patel thought a minute, his eyes rolling heavenward. "April eighteenth, I believe."

Santoro nodded, rolling a pencil between his fingers. "And did you form an opinion about the cause and manner of Angelo Coluzzi's death, Dr. Patel?"

"Yes, it is my opinion that the cause of the decedent's death was a homicide and the mechanism was a fractured vertebrae at C3."

Santoro gripped his pencil. "In common parlance does that mean a broken neck, Dr. Patel?"

"Yes."

"I have no further questions, Dr. Patel." Santoro moved aside and sat down, as Judy rose with her legal pad. She stepped behind the podium.

"Dr. Patel, there has been testimony that the decedent fell against a bookcase. Just so the record is clear, did that fall have anything to do with Mr. Coluzzi's death?"

"Objection, beyond the scope," Santoro said, half rising, but Judge Maniloff was already shaking his head.

"Overruled, counselor. Please, let's move along."

Dr. Patel looked at Judy. "No, the decedent was dead by the time he fell."

Judy wanted to nail him down. It would avoid sympathy for Coluzzi later, at trial. "And you can be sure of that?"

"Yes."

"I have no further questions, Dr. Patel." Judy grabbed her pad and sat down as Judge Maniloff reached for the next case filed and opened it.

"Mr. Lucia, I find that the Commonwealth has proved a prima facie case of murder sufficient to support their indictment on a general charge of murder, and I order you held over for trial. Your attorney will inform you of the schedule of further court appearances, sir."

"Thank you, Your Honor," Judy said, almost at the same time as Santoro. It was the last time they'd show any unanimity. She looked over at Pigeon Tony. "Now all we have to do is get you out of here." As they had discussed, Frank left the gallery instantly to stand behind Pigeon Tony, and two courthouse security officers came from the side to flank him, as they would a prisoner in custody. They'd escort him out the secured exit to a waiting car Frank had rented. "I've made arrangements to get you out a secure way, where they take prisoners, so you'll be safe."

"I no afraid," Pigeon Tony said quietly, but even with the precautions, Judy found herself wondering if they made bulletproof vests in a size 6X. The Lucia side of the gallery was lingering, evidently making sure that Pigeon Tony got out alive. The Coluzzi faction also filed out slowly, with Marco going with his mother, and John stalling, ostensibly to join Fat Jimmy. Each man eyed Judy pointedly, and if looks could kill, they'd already be in handcuffs.

Judge Maniloff began banging his gavel, loudly this time, his voice more urgent than during the procedure. "Clear the courtroom, please. Clear the courtroom immediately!"

Judy stood guard as Frank guided Pigeon Tony from his chair, and the guards flanked them quickly. "You got him?" she asked Frank, who smiled tensely.

"Don't worry about him, worry about you." He

glanced back at the gallery, where John Coluzzi stood with Fat Jimmy, his dark gaze morphing into an undisguised glare.

"We're ready to go, Mr. Lucia," said one of the security guards, but Frank's jaw clenched with anger.

"We go nowhere until that asshole is gone and she's safe."

"Frank, I'm fine," Judy said, but the court security officer was already looking in the direction of Frank's glare.

"Move it along, Mr. Coluzzi," the guard called out. "We don't want any more trouble from you."

"Tell **him** that!" Coluzzi bellowed, drawing Judge Maniloff's gavel.

**Crak!** it sounded, loud. "Clear this courtroom right now, Mr. Coluzzi, or I'll find you in contempt! Bailiff?"

The bailiff hurried to the gallery, but two other security guards were already in motion, escorting Coluzzi and Fat Jimmy to the door.

Frank was looking at the guard. "You'll follow her out, right?"

"Fine," he said reluctantly, but Judy knew she'd lose him outside the courtroom. She'd been watching her back since she left the office and she'd be doing it until the day of trial. "Better get going," she told Frank.

"Okay." He nodded quickly and slipped an arm

around Pigeon Tony. "I'll call you, and thanks for everything today, **tiger.**"

"Grrrr." Judy managed a smile, wondering when she'd see him again as the guards led them away.

# BOOK FOUR

By 1870 . . . these somewhat self-contained communities were becoming the neighborhoods, or "urban villages," of modern America. The Italian case had also attained a peculiar sociological anomaly that tends to mark most ethnic groups in complex societies. With its own internal order and partial autonomy, the Italian community in South Philadelphia formed a distinctive and separate social system in itself.

> —RICHARD JULIANI,
> Building Little Italy:
> Philadelphia's Italians Before
> Mass Migration (1998)

*Fratelli, flagelli.*
The wrath of brothers is the
wrath of devils.

> —Italian proverb

# 28

Tony caught the look on Judy's pretty face when she said good-bye to Frank, and he felt sad for them, lovers who were not yet lovers, because it was a feeling Tony knew well, its memory deep in his bones. He wanted to tell Frank to go back to her, to run to her, that he would be fine, but there was no time to speak, for the guards had clamped their hands on his arms and were rushing him along roughly, as police do even when there is no need. Frankie, who walked behind, where Tony couldn't see him, had said that the police were working **for** them this time, helping them stay safe, but Tony had seen things in the world that his grandson never would, and he knew that in the end, police never worked for anyone but themselves, and that they were rough with others because they enjoyed the sensation it gave them, as the Coluzzis welcomed the pain they inflicted, their depravity so deep it coursed even in the blood.

The police hustled Tony down a plain white corridor, then another, which took a sharp right turn, then a sharp left, then down a flight of white stairs, bearing Tony along so swiftly he soon grew dizzy with the twists and turns, with no landmarks to orient him, or to make one corridor different from the next, and he became a field mouse in a pasture, vulnerable and confused. Fear grew in his stomach, anxiety rising from the police taking him away, and his knees grew weak and his palms damp, as they had so long ago, when his terror had been so real, but then it hadn't been for him but for Silvana.

It was the second Sunday in August, he could not forget it because nobody could; the second Sunday in August was the Torneo della Cavalieri, a festival in Mascoli since the fifteenth century. Although Tony had heard of the Torneo, he had never been to see it, for he had no time for such diversions and would not have been at this one except that he knew Silvana would be there. In the two months since they had shared their kiss wrapped in a kerchief, they had in fact kissed, as man and woman, seeing each other on a regular basis.

Tony would pack a basket of hard cheese, olives, fresh-baked bread, and juicy tomatoes, with a bottle of home-pressed chianti, and Silvana would meet him, leaving her house with some excuse, but only during the daytime. They would spread out a blanket in the hills around Mascoli, and while their ponies grazed, talk the entire afternoon, confiding in each other, kissing and laughing, and Tony grew to love the hills of Marche as his own, almost as much as he loved Silvana. In these talks, Silvana told Tony that she also saw Coluzzi on some nights for dinner, and that she appreciated the Fascist's strength and cunning in ways Tony could not comprehend, so that in time the three of them—Tony, Silvana, and Coluzzi—were dancing that delicate tango that occurs when a woman is trying to make up her mind between two suitors.

It drove Tony crazy, waiting for Silvana to make her choice, but he knew it was folly to force her hand. His mother, being Abruzzese, had a proverb for everything, and counseled him to wait: **Amor regge il suo regno senza spada**, Love rules his kingdom without a sword. And his father, who knew more about politics, worried that the third leg of the triangle was a Blackshirt, and had a proverb of his own: **I guai vengono senza chiamarli**, Sorrow comes unsent for. He told Tony to forget Silvana, but Tony could not, and so he waited, withholding even the marriage proposal that was on his lips with each kiss, sensing that it was too soon. Then the Torneo was upon them, and Tony knew Silvana would be there with her family and so he journeyed to Mascoli to catch sight of her, and perhaps to meet them, to press his suit.

It was sunny that day and Tony arrived in Mascoli to find even its outskirts thick with revelers, honking automobiles, drunks on bicycles, and neighing horses. He tied up his pony for fear the beast would be terrified and made his way on foot through the raucous crowd to the Piazza Santa Giustina, where the opening ceremonies were held and the procession through the streets would begin. But Tony was late getting there, having spent much of the route trying to find Silvana, so he joined the procession at its raggedy end. Ahead of him, to clarion blasts and noisy drum-beats, strode the town mayor, in the role of Magnifico Messere, then the high magistracy, represented by local officials, all in colorful fifteenth-century costumes, surrounded by hundreds of costumed people and actors, all making merry. Groups of Blackshirts paraded in dress uniforms, laughing at the townspeople, delighted at the celebration encouraging Italian pride, but Tony didn't see Angelo Coluzzi among them.

Tony started out following the procession but soon found himself borne along by it, his head swiveling this way and that to find Silvana, which he could see was a fool's errand. The processants were in makeup and costumed as medieval knights, pageboys, ladies-in-waiting, and captains, and Tony had no idea if Silvana was masked as well. On all sides men juggled burning torches, swallowed swords, twirled flags, and performed magic tricks of every sort. Trained dogs did somersaults on a man's shoulders, to the delight of Fascist schoolchildren dressed in little black shirts, black shorts, and black kerchiefs. The procession swept down one street, then turned at the next, then made a sharp right, and Tony was shoved from behind by a drunken knight. Tony picked up his pace, ignoring his flat feet, anxious lest the Torneo be over by the time he got there and Silvana gone.

The procession ended in the Piazza del Popolo, but even in its huge expanse Tony could barely breathe for all the people. He looked everywhere, but Silvana and her family had to be lost in the crowd, which was roaring for the tournament to begin. At the center of the piazza stood the Saracen, the false knight and horse constructed on a wooden frame and covered with rich velvet fabric, and standing to the side, representing the six ancient sections of Mascoli, were six knights on horseback, their costumed horses pawing the cobblestones and gnawing their bits to begin the contest. Each knight would have three runs at the Saracen, to try to hit the center of his shield with their lances in the shortest possible time. Tony knew there was a prize, the Palio del Torneo, but he didn't care. He wanted to see Silvana, but it seemed he couldn't stand in one place long enough to look around, there was so much pushing and shoving.

Tony wedged forward to the very front of the piazza to get away from the unruly revelers behind him and breathe easier, which was when he spotted Angelo Coluzzi. The **squadrista** stood on a black-draped dais at the near side of the piazza, in the forefront of a cadre of Fascists and their families. Coluzzi was frowning in emulation of Il Duce himself, his jaw thrust forward as if he were surveying parading troops, not pretend knights and toy horses. At the sight Tony recovered his footing, just as a shout went up from the crowd. The first knight was galloping full-tilt toward the Saracen, and his lance struck the shield with a loud **clonk**, setting the bogus Saracen spinning like a top and the crowd cheering wildly, especially residents of the knight's district.

Coluzzi nodded in approval and turned to talk to his fellow, which was when he spotted Tony. Tony knew it the moment it happened, his gut told him before his two eyes did, and across the wildly cheering piazza, the two men locked glares; the farmer and the Fascist, in love with the same woman. The second knight spurred his horse leaping to a gallop and they thundered across the cobblestones, but neither Tony nor Coluzzi broke his gaze. The lance missed its target, to the disappointed **aahs** of the crowd, but Tony would not look away, nor would Coluzzi. The third knight was already off and racing flat-out toward the Saracen, and his lance struck boldly, making a dervish of the wooden target, obscuring Coluzzi from Tony's view, and when the knight had passed, reveling in the crowd's affection, Coluzzi had gone.

Good riddance. Coward. Pig. Filth. Tony thought Coluzzi was like the false Saracen, a hollow soldier waiting to be knocked down. How could Silvana see anything in such a poppet? Women apparently liked men who had strut and power, who wore confidence as thin as a uniform with epaulets. Though Tony had told her that Coluzzi had beaten the chemist, she had insisted that the chemist must have done wrong. Tony searched the crowd for her at the same time that the fourth knight was charging the Saracen, his lance raised, and this target struck the shield. A shout went up, and Tony felt hands suddenly clamped all over him and his neck yanked back by his collar.

"**Come?**" he said, not understanding at first, but Tony's words were choked from his throat and the next thing he knew he was surrounded by black wool and strong hands were grabbing his arms and muscling him from the piazza. He cried out in alarm but a swift punch to the cheek brought blood bubbling to his mouth, and the next fist, expertly delivered, set pain arcing through his jaw and knocking him almost senseless.

There must have been ten Blackshirts and they hauled him off by his arms, his toes dragging on the cobblestones as the shouts of hundreds went up, cheering for the knights and drowning out the gurgling from his throat. Tony had to save himself. Nobody else would help him. He saw what had happened to the chemist.

He torqued in their grip but they hit him again and he was in such agony and shock that he was almost insensate as they dragged him back along the processional route, littered now with bottles and drunks retching on the sidewalk. The cobblestones rubbed off his farmer's boots and flayed the skin from his bare feet as the streets grew quiet and they left the piazza, where celebrants could have borne witness.

They rushed him twisting and turning through streets as narrow as corridors, and Tony knew from their grunts and curses that they were loving this business, which sickened him to his stomach. He didn't know where he was, or where or even why they were taking him, and the medieval streets all looked the same, each one like the next, which for some reason scared him more than the beating.

Then the rushing stopped and they began hitting him in earnest, raining blows everywhere on him all at once, to his back, his head, his gut, and he tried to raise his arms and cry out but they socked him in the stomach so hard he couldn't breathe, and he crumpled to the ground, where they began kicking him with hard boots in his ribs, his legs, and his kidneys, so that he was thrashing and rolling in agony on the hot and gritty cobblestones. The hope of the Abruzzese lifted in his chest until more kicks came and Tony realized all that screaming was coming from him, and then even he began to lose hope, his limbs fighting back no longer. He barely remained conscious and gathered with peaceful resignation that he would die at their hands.

But just then the kicking came to an abrupt stop and everything went completely still. The air felt suddenly cool as a balm. Tony thought surely this was his death. His body had gone numb. He felt no pain. He didn't think he could move, nor did he care to. It was so calm and nice lying here, like being in the hills under the trees where he and Silvana would have lunch. There was no sound. Tony opened his eyes to see at last the full glory of God.

Above him stood the outline of a helmet, shoulders with epaulets, and a chin like a dictator's. The sun shone behind the outline, casting its long shadow on Tony. It wasn't God, it was the Devil himself. Angelo Coluzzi.

"Congratulations, my friend," Coluzzi said, laughing softly, but Tony didn't understand.

"Che?" he croaked out incomprehensibly.

"I have excellent news for you, farmer. You would never guess it in a million years. Let us play a game, a guessing game. Can you guess my news?"

Tony was too weak to speak, and Coluzzi dealt him a swift kick in the hip, which sent agony through his spine.

"Speak, cur! Ask me what is my news!"

But Tony couldn't, so Coluzzi kicked him again and again until he cried out in pain, but not for mercy. That he would not do.

"Good dog!" Coluzzi exclaimed. "Here is my news. Our whore has chosen you."

What? Tony couldn't believe his ears. Silvana had chosen him? Silvana had chosen him! The knowledge tasted like the most succulent of fruits. And then Tony closed his eyes, realizing that the taste on his tongue was his own warm, salty blood, and that this, the sweetest moment of his life, was also the bitterest. For in that moment he understood that if Silvana had chosen him, Angelo Coluzzi would not let her live. Tony should have foreseen this, but he hadn't. He wouldn't have courted her if he had realized. And now it was too late. Tears for Silvana sprang to Tony's eyes, and his heart burst with fear, and with his last breath before he lost consciousness he screamed:

"No!"

"No!" Pigeon Tony struggled in the strong arms of the guards, his heart beating wildly and his breath coming only in short bursts, but the guards held him tighter. There must have been ten of them.

"Pop! Pop!" Frankie cried. "What's the matter, Pop?"

"No! No!" Pigeon Tony kept shouting, screaming in Italian, panicking, surrounded by police in uniform. "No!"

"Let him go, you're scaring him!" Frank shouted. "Let him go!"

Suddenly the grip released and Pigeon Tony felt the guards pushed aside and his grandson Frank holding him, talking to him in his ear, whispering in Italian like music, his voice as soft as his father Frank's used to be, as a boy. The lullaby reached Tony's heart and soothed him from the inside out, relaxing every muscle in his body, easing even the deepest grief within him, so that he allowed himself to be cradled as unashamedly as a child, and he dreamed in that moment that his own son Frank was still alive, as was his Silvana, and Frank's wife, too.

And he dreamed that all of them lived together in eternal sweetness, as a family, whole again and full of love.

# 29

After the prelim, Judy hit the office running, with a lot of work to do. The trial was a few months away, but she had learned something at the prelim and there was no time to waste. Also she had other cases she'd been neglecting, not to mention a general counsel who would fire her any day now. Judy stopped at the reception desk in the entrance room of the firm.

"They in there?" she asked the receptionist, as she picked up her correspondence and thumbed through her phone messages. There were twenty in all. **The Daily News,** the **Inquirer,** the **New York Times**. The Coluzzi story was white-hot. She'd return the calls later on the cell phone, to keep the Coluzzis' feet to the fire.

"Sure, they arrived about ten minutes ago."

"Will you tell 'em I'll be right in? I want to drop this stuff at my office."

"Sure."

"Thanks." Judy tucked her things under her arm

with her briefcase, powered past associates and secretaries to her office, only to find Murphy sitting behind her desk.

"Huh?" Judy said, and Murphy shot up self-consciously. Her dark hair was slicked back, her lips properly lined, and she wore a white silk T-shirt with a yellow skirt the size of a Post-it. Murphy looked wrong, not to mention naked, behind Judy's desk. "What are you doing in my office?"

"I wasn't snooping or anything." Murphy stepped away from the desk quickly. "I was leaving you something."

"What?" Judy dumped her stuff on her already cluttered desk and walked around it. Next to a leftover coffee cup and some old correspondence sat the fresh draft of an article. It looked like Judy's article, but it was finished. "That's mine," Judy said, reading her own mind.

"Yes. But I knew you'd be too busy to finish it, given the car bomb and all. I picked up the file and drafted it for you."

Judy skimmed the top page of the brief. A one-paragraph introduction, a statement of the legal issues, a crisp analysis of the law. It was really good. "Where did you get this?" she asked, but Murphy thought she was joking.

"Make any corrections you want and pass it back to me. I'll make Bennie a copy, and if she likes it, I'll submit it."

Then Judy got it. Murphy was trying to make

her look bad in front of Bennie. Judy turned to the last page of the article. The proof would be on the signature line. Judy was just about to shout Aha! when she read it. It was her name on the papers, not Murphy's.

"You don't have to use it if you don't like it."

"Well, jeez, thank you." Judy felt touched. Only Mary did things this nice, and she was a saint. Judy picked it up and put it in her briefcase. "I'll look at it first chance I get."

"Good." Murphy moved to the door. "Anything else I can do?"

"Uh, no, thanks."

"Thank me over lunch," Murphy said, and she left.


Seated around the walnut table in the conference room, still in their best going-to-court polyester, were Tony-From-Down-The-Block LoMonaco, Tony Two Feet Pensiera, and Mr. DiNunzio. They sat behind Styrofoam cups of office coffee, heat curling from each cup, and among the pencils and legal pads in the middle of the table sat a white bakery box the size of a briefcase. On the top it said, in script, **Capaciello's.** "What's that?" Judy asked, and Mr. DiNunzio smiled.

"Just a little something to thank you for what you're doin' for Tony."

Tony-From-Down-The-Block nodded. "You think we'd come over empty-handed? That ain't right."

Feet looked cranky. "Open it already. We all got our coffee here. We been waitin'."

"I'm on it, Coach," Judy said. She pulled the box to her, broke the light string, and opened the lid, releasing a sweet smell. The box was stuffed with pastries, but she didn't recognize any of them. Some large pastries were shaped like flowers of dough, some looked like clams with fruit embedded in them, and others were long slices of flaky cake. God knew what these were. Judy's family ate doughnuts and brownies. "How nice of you. Thanks, gentlemen."

"Hand me a **sfogatelle,** will ya, Jude?" Feet asked, and Mr. DiNunzio shifted forward on his chair.

"I'll take the **pastaciotti,** please."

"Gimme a **crostata,**" said Tony-From-Down-The-Block.

Judy looked bewildered at the box. "Is this a test? There's not even a cannoli, so I could go by process of elimination."

"No cannoli, sorry." Feet frowned behind his Band-Aid bridge, which Judy was getting used to. In fact, she was starting to like it. Some glasses, Band-Aids could improve. "They didn't have the chocolate chip. They don't have the chocolate chip, I don't buy cannoli."

"Not all Italians like cannoli," added Mr. Di-Nunzio. "People think we do, but we don't."

Tony-From-Down-The-Block rubbed his ample tummy. "Cannoli's too heavy. If I eat one, I feel like I'm gonna blow up."

Judy wanted to get on with it. "Okay, gentlemen, which one's the what-you-said?"

Tony-From-Down-The-Block pointed, as did Mr. DiNunzio and Feet, but their wires kept getting crossed so Judy gave up and slid the box across the table. "You're on your own. I called you here for a reason."

"You got dishes?" Feet asked, pastry in hand.

"It's a law firm, not a restaurant." Judy grabbed a legal pad from the center of the table, ripped off the top three pages, and passed them out like plates. "Use these. Now to business—"

"Ain't you eatin', Judy?" It was Tony-From-Down-The-Block.

"No, thanks, I had lunch on the way over. A hot dog."

"So? This is dessert."

"At lunch?"

"People have rights."

Judy blinked. "No thanks."

He paused. "Well, if you ain't eatin', can I have my cigar?"

"No." Judy stood up and went to the front of the conference room, while Mr. D and The Tonys munched away, poured coffee, and slid sugar packs around like bumper cars. The atmosphere was more family wedding than case conference, but Judy knew that would disappear when she started talking. She stood near the easel at the front of the room, which supported her delusion that, except for the pastry part, she was controlling this meeting. "Okay, here's the problem," she began. "Our firm has a great investigator, but he's away and—"

"You want coffee?" Mr. DiNunzio was holding the pot in the air.

Feet nodded, his mouth full of mystery pastry. "We made fresh. The girl showed us how."

"Feet, you're not supposed to say 'girl' anymore," Mr. DiNunzio said, placing his pastry carefully on his sheet of legal paper.

"Why not?" Feet shrugged. "Whatsa matter with 'girl'? I like girls."

"You don't call them girls anymore. They're women."

"Hey, if she's got her own teeth, she's a girl." Feet shoved his pastry into his mouth, and Judy cleared her throat as effectively as a substitute teacher.

"Gentlemen, listen up. We were just in court and we heard lots of testimony. Who can tell me the most interesting thing we heard this morning?" Mr. D's hand shot up, and Judy smiled. Every teacher needs a pet. "Mr. D?"

"I didn't know that Fat Jimmy heard Pigeon Tony say, 'I'm gonna kill you.'"

Judy nodded. "Very good, but it's not the answer I'm looking for. Tell me why that was interesting to you, Mr. D. Did you hear Pigeon Tony say that?"

"Of course. We all heard it, didn't we?" Mr. DiNunzio looked at the other two for verification and they nodded, sure. "I was just surprised that Fat Jimmy heard it. He never looks like he hears anything. I guess it was really loud."

Judy sighed. Case was going down the tubes. That made four—count 'em, four—witnesses to a murder threat by the client, who was, by the way, guilty as charged. "Did any of you hear anything that Coluzzi said, while they were both in there?"

"No," Mr. DiNunzio said, and the others shook their heads, no.

"Why?" Feet asked. "Did he say something we shoulda heard?" He half-smiled in an encouraging way, but as much as she wanted to, Judy wasn't writing scripts for witnesses.

"No, you heard what you heard. Okay, anybody else find anything interesting in the testimony today?"

Tony-From-Down-The-Block raised an unlit cigar. "I thought it was interesting that Fat Jimmy broke up with Marlene. Musta just happened, because I didn't hear nothin' about it. She's a number, that Marlene. She makes a buck, too."

"Not what I was looking for, but that's very interesting."

"It's what **I'm** looking for," Tony-From-Down-The-Block said with a snort, and Mr. DiNunzio gave him a solid shove.

"I thought you had that girl, on the Internet. In Florida."

"She thinks I'm twenty-five. And anyway, I need a real girlfriend. I need Marlene. She's got red hair."

Feet wiped his mouth. "Her hair ain't real."

"So?" Tony-From-Down-The-Block sipped his coffee. "I got a bum ear and a prostate the size of Trenton. I'm gonna throw stones?"

Judy wished for a pointer and something to tap it on. "In any event, Feet, what did you learn in court today?"

"I heard something interesting." Feet rubbed his hands over his legal pad, so that sugar crumbs fell like snow all over the table. "I heard Fat Jimmy say he only got paid fifteen large for blowing Angelo Coluzzi."

Mr. DiNunzio's head snapped angrily around. "Don't say blowing."

Tony-From-Down-The-Block scowled. "Not in front of a girl."

Judy winced. "True, it wouldn't be the way I'd put it, but that's close to what I was looking for. Fat Jimmy said he'd worked for Angelo for over thirty years. That's a long time. What did he do for Coluzzi, besides the aforementioned? Mr. D? Do you know?"

"Not really. I wasn't in the racing club, like these guys. I just know Pigeon Tony."

Feet thought a minute. "Fat Jimmy was with Angelo all the time. He drove him around, went to the clubhouse with him. Showed up at all the races with him."

Tony-From-Down-The-Block was nodding. "He had to take Angelo's shit, that's what. Angelo bossed him around all the time."

"You couldn't pay me enough," Feet said, and Mr. DiNunzio shook his head.

"Me neither."

But Judy had stopped listening. She took a seat at the head of the table. "We all know that Pigeon Tony's son and daughter-in-law were killed in a truck accident last year, and that Pigeon Tony thought Angelo Coluzzi was responsible for it. Tell me what happened with the accident, like where it was."

Mr. DiNunzio looked up. "It was at the ramp off of I-95, you know where it goes high to get back into the city, like an overpass. It's a sin." He shook his head slowly. "They think Frank lost control of the car, maybe he was tired, and the car went over the side and crashed underneath."

Judy tried to visualize it. "Did it hit anybody when it fell?"

"No. That time a night, there was no traffic. They say the Lucias, they died when the truck crashed. They didn't suffer, which was good."

"They were good people," Feet said. "Frank, he'd give you the shirt offa his back. Did free brick work for me and my cousin. And Gemma, my wife loved her." His silver tooth disappeared behind the sad downturn to his mouth, and Judy realized they were all still grieving over the loss of the Lucias, despite their bravado. "They didn't deserve to go like that."

Tony-From-Down-The-Block was shaking his head. "Nobody does, 'cept my ex-wife." Feet laughed, and even Mr. DiNunzio smiled, which broke the grim mood that had fallen in the room.

Judy leaned over. "Well, if that wasn't an accident, but was murder, and we can prove it at trial, maybe we can get Pigeon Tony's charge reduced. And if Coluzzi was responsible for it, I'm betting that Fat Jimmy was involved."

Mr. DiNunzio set his coffee cup down quietly. "Judy, I don't think so. It had to be an accident, didn't it? Maybe Angelo Coluzzi could get away with murder in the old country, in the old days. But here, in Philly? Nowadays?"

Tony-From-Down-The-Block chewed his unlit cigar. "They put a bomb under Judy's car, for Christ's sake. I wouldn't put it past the Coluzzis, not at all. That scum was capable of anything, and he coulda made it look like it was an accident, since it was on the expressway and all."

Only Feet looked grave. "I always thought Coluzzi did it. Always."

"Why?" Judy asked.

"Just because. Coluzzi hated Pigeon Tony. He wanted to ruin him. Coluzzi was an evil bastard, and you know what? The next person Coluzzi woulda killed was Frankie. Frank."

Judy shuddered. "So we have our work cut out for us. I want you all to help, but you gotta make me one promise before I give you your assignment."

"What?" asked Mr. DiNunzio.

"Nobody tells Frank," she said. "Agreed?"

Around the table, each of the old men nodded. Conspirators, covered with confectioner's sugar.

# 30

As soon as Marlene Bello answered the screen door of her brick rowhouse, Judy could see what Tony-From-Down-The-Block had meant. She was wreathed in the scent of a spicy perfume, her dark red hair was wrapped into a neat French twist, and her big brown eyes were expertly made-up. She had a cute little nose and full lips emphasized by chic rust-colored lipstick. Marlene had to be sixty, and it looked womanly on her, as if she had earned honestly the smile lines around her eyes and mouth. "Can I help you?" she asked with one of those smiles.

"Yes. My name's Judy Carrier, and I'd like to talk with you if I can. For just a minute."

"Ha!" Marlene pursed glossy lips sympathetically. "Honey, I used to go door-to-door myself. Whaddaya sellin'?"

"I'm a lawyer. I—"

"A lawyer! You're shittin' me! They go door-to-door now?" She shifted her weight from one slim hip to the other, in black Spandex stirrup pants that clung to shapely, if short, legs. A pink T-shirt with a scoop neck revealed a small, gym-toned waist and a soft, natural décolletage. The whole package registered as European, except for the white letters across her chest that read MARY KAY COSMETICS. "Whaddaya got? Wills, contracts, like that?"

"No, I'm not selling anything, but I was wondering if I could come in. It's private." Judy felt nervous even though she had taken a cab here. Night was already falling. Her eyes swept the skinny city street. Nobody was out, and the beach chairs sat empty, in friendly little circles. The Phillies game was on, and the televisions in everybody's front rooms flickered on the dark street like South Philly lightning. "It's about your husband, Jimmy."

"A lawyer looking for Jimmy? That's unusual." Marlene snorted. "Anyway, he doesn't live here anymore. And you'll never get the money he owes you." She began to close the door, but Judy stuck her briefcase in the way. "Nice move," Marlene said with admiration.

"Mrs. Bello—Marlene—please let me in. I need help, not money. I represent Tony Lucia—Pigeon Tony—against the Coluzzi brothers. I had Fat Jimmy in court yesterday, on the stand—"

"Shit, why didn't you just say that? Any enemy of Jimmy's is a friend of mine." A huge smile broadened Marlene's face, and the front door swung wide open.

Ten minutes later Judy was installed behind a pink mug of instant coffee at the white Formica in Marlene's kitchen. It was the same size and shape as the DiNunzios', but it was modern, lit coolly by an overhead fixture of Lucite. Cabinets of white laminate ringed the room, the counters were of lacquered butcher block, and the table and chairs had an IKEA style, which Judy mentioned to open the conversation.

Marlene laughed. "Are you kidding? I don't **build** furniture. Please." She sat down, tucking a calf underneath her and letting a black leather mule slip from a pedicured foot. "So what do you want to know, Miss Judy?"

Judy smiled. She felt cozy with Marlene, who reminded her of Mary on estrogen replacement. "To get right to it, you probably know that there is something of a vendetta going on between the Lucias and the Coluzzis."

"Sure, everybody in South Philly knows that, but I don't get real involved in the neighborhood anymore, sittin' around with the girls in the coffee klatch like I used to. I have my own business now, with Mary Kay." Her eyes scrutinized Judy's. "You could use a little more foundation, you know. Especially with such a dark suit. What are you wearing, on your face?"

"Nothing."

Marlene's shadowed eyes widened. "**No makeup?**"

"No."

"It's not just a neutral look you got going?"

"No."

"You're shittin' me!"

"I shit you not."

Marlene laughed. "No wonder it looked so natural!"

"I'm an expert on natural. I have natural down to a science."

Marlene laughed again. "That's your problem! I could make you up, make your eyes look even bigger, and bring out the blue. For you, I would go with the Whipped Cocoa on the lid and White Sand up here, on the bone." She pointed with a crimson-lacquered nail. "You could also use a blush, you know."

"Lawyers don't blush."

"Then you need to buy it. We have powder and crème but for you I'd say the powder. Your best colors would be Teaberry and Desert Bloom."

"Are you trying to sell me something?" Judy's eyes narrowed, and Marlene smiled.

"Of course. It shows you what a great saleswoman I am. You come to my door, and I sell **you.**"

Judy clapped.

"I'm an independent sales director now. One of

only eight thousand in the country. Got my pink Caddy and everything. I more than pay my mortgage, all by myself, and it all started with a hundred-dollar showcase. You can laugh, but it's my own business."

"I wasn't laughing. Congratulations."

"It's just an expression. Thanks." Marlene smiled and took a quick gulp of coffee. "Mary Kay is the bestselling brand of skin care and color cosmetics in the United States, six years running. They're great products, take it from me. I'm an old dog under this paint."

"Not at all." Judy laughed.

"It's true. And I wasn't sellin' you. It's just that you seem like a nice girl and I can make you look a little prettier, is all. You wanna know about it, ask me."

"Okay."

"And you could use a crème lipstick. Something neutral. Mocha Freeze. Or Shell. I'll give you a sample before you go."

"Great."

"So what do you wanna know?"

Judy sipped the thin coffee. "We were talking about the vendetta."

"Okay. I see it made the papers, but I've known about it for a long time."

"I get the impression that everybody in South Philly knows everybody else. Is that right?"

"Yes, it's like a small town down here. Everybody knows everybody else's habits, their cars, their kids, their problems. True, South Philly's only an eight- or ten-block square. It used to be all Italian, but now it's Italian plus Vietnamese, Korean, like that, south of Broad." Marlene grabbed Judy's teaspoon and hers and made a shiny line. "This is Broad Street, and you don't cross Broad for the neighborhood. North of Broad is a little different, more like a twenty, twenty-five-block square on that side. It's mostly still Italian, but you got some black. All middle-class, pay their bills. Everybody gets along. Good people."

Judy blinked in wonder. "How do you know all this?"

"It's my territory. You gotta know the territory. Like the Music Man says." Marlene drank her coffee again. "Then you got Packer Park, which is like a place unto itself, and the Estates, which is the same, only ritzier. That's where the Coluzzis live, by the way."

Judy took out a pad and made a note.

"Write down that the homes cost five hundred grand and up. There's a Mercedes in every driveway. Jimmy always wanted to move there, but not me. I'm old-fashioned. I love my house. I don't like the mob snobs there."

Judy smiled. "Mob snobs?"

"Everybody knows it."

"Which Coluzzis live there? John or Marco?"

"All of them, and Angelo did, too. The wife still

does, they all got the same model house, same upgrades, and all. Keepin' up with the Coluzzis."

Judy made another note. "So you probably knew that Pigeon Tony's son and daughter-in-law were killed in a car accident last year, on the expressway."

Marlene thought a minute. "I heard about that."

"I'm investigating that crash, because I think Angelo Coluzzi was responsible for it, and if he was, then I bet Jimmy was, too."

"Frankly, it's possible." Marlene's smile vanished. "Jimmy's business with Angelo, I didn't know much about, and honestly, I didn't want to. I was out all the time, working and building up my business. The less I knew, the better off I was."

Judy sighed. "So you really didn't know anything?"

"Not a thing." Marlene shook her head regretfully.

"Do you know anything about John Coluzzi?"

"No."

"About Marco?"

"Nope."

"Anything about the Philly Court Shopping Center?"

"Sorry."

Judy set down her pencil in disappointment. The visit had been a dry hole. Maybe Mr. D and The Tonys would find something.

"I'd like to help you but I can't. Me and Jimmy

lived two separate lives, just in the same house. He moved out last year, but it was over way before that."

Maybe Judy could get some background. She picked up her pencil. "How did Angelo and Jimmy meet? Were you married then?"

"Sure, and Jimmy was sellin' paint at the hardware store. Angelo used to go in there and they got to be friends, then Jimmy ended up working for him, and was gone all the time. His personality changed. He turned into a big bully. He let himself go. That's when I think he started runnin' around."

"How much was he making working for Angelo, if you know? He said in court he only made fifteen thousand dollars."

"Yeah, right, but that's between him and the IRS. He had to take in at least a hundred grand, but it was all cash." Her eyes glittered with a sudden ferocity, and she pointed at Judy. "And don't think for one minute that I took blood money, because I didn't. I'm no hypocrite. We didn't even file jointly. I made my own money."

Judy clapped again. Even though the visit was pointless, she was happy to have met Marlene. "I have to tell you, I don't see how Jimmy could have left you. I don't think he deserved you in the first place."

"Thanks." Marlene reached across the table and

gave Judy's hand a quick pat. "I don't think he did either, but I didn't know it then. He moved in with his young chippy, I hear. It's supposedly the real thing, this time." She sighed audibly. "It was tough."

"I bet."

"Face it, the man is not good-looking. Who woulda thought? You know how I found out?"

"You didn't catch him, did you?"

"In a way. On tape."

Judy frowned. "What do you mean?"

"I had the phone tapped. I paid a guy to do it."

"You tapped **your own phone**?"

"Damn straight."

"That's illegal. Criminal, even."

Marlene nodded happily. "I was out all the time and Jimmy had the place to himself. He was on the phone, making whoopee with twenty-year-olds. Sometimes he used the cell, but mostly not. I listened to the tape of him talking to the new one. I didn't believe it until I heard it with my own ears, and then I threw his ass out."

Judy thought a minute. "You taped his phone calls, from when?"

"Let's see, he's been out less than a year. So about six or seven months before that." Her eyes met Judy's, and the two women had the same thought at the same time.

"Where are the tapes?" Judy asked, but Marlene was already out of her seat.

A colonial rowhouse, with authentically melony brick, contained Judy's apartment, and she stepped out of the cab in front of the house, her backpack slung over one shoulder, her briefcase tucked under the other, and a big cardboard box full of cassette tapes in both arms. Also a pink bag filled with Mary Kay cosmetics she couldn't resist buying, in gratitude, though she had taken a rain check on the free makeover. She had to get to work.

It was dark out, but the narrow street was full of people. Judy was for once happy to see the summer tourists crawling all over her Society Hill neighborhood, which was chockablock with restaurants, ice cream parlors, clothes and record stores, all open late. She didn't feel safe unless she was in a crowd lately, and sometimes not even then.

Judy glanced around. The traffic was thick, and cars moved down the cobblestone street so slowly Judy could feel the heat from their idling engines. Attractive couples and families walked hand in hand on the sidewalk. Lots of Liberty Bell T-shirts and Bermuda shorts. Ice cream in costly waffle cones and kids holding red, white, and blue balloons. Not a broken nose or a Glock among them. Excellent.

Judy hoisted the box higher, juggled her stuff to the front stoop, and leaned the box against the door while she searched for her keys in her backpack. The box was heavy. Maybe the couple on the first floor could buzz her into the front door. She glanced at the first-floor windows, but they were dark. It was only ten o'clock. They were overworked Penn med students and probably at the hospital. Damn.

Judy kept fishing and looked up. The second floor was dark, too. A couple of gay men who liked to say they were in the cruise business. They had to be out cruising. She dug deeper in the bag. Maybe next time she would take her keys out ahead of time, the way it said in the women's magazines. How had she survived a car bomb? She heard a shuffling noise behind her and peeked timidly over her shoulder. Only a couple in work clothes, walking home. She finally found her key, shoved it into the lock, and pushed open the front door.

"Down! No! No jumping!" Judy yelled, surprised. It was her puppy in the front hall. What was she doing here? How had she gotten out? She was supposed to be up in the apartment, which was locked. Wasn't it?

Judy's gut tensed. She struggled to hold the cardboard box while the puppy jumped up on it, then scooted out the door past her. The street!

"No! Penny! Come!" she shouted, dropping everything and running panicky after the dog. "Penny! Come!"

But she needn't have worried. Goldens chose people over cars every time. Unless the car had a tennis ball. The puppy was bounding over to greet the couple, but they recoiled when she leaked in delight on their shoes.

"Sorry," Judy said, when she reached the pair. "It's not her fault, I left her all day." She grabbed the puppy by the red nylon collar and walked her like Quasimodo back to the front stoop, nervously assessing the situation.

Judy's box, briefcase, and backpack lay in disarray. Her apartment was evidently unlocked. The house was completely empty, and it didn't have the tightest security in the first place. The only blunt instrument in her place was a wooden clog. Her only protection was a drippy puppy. No way in hell was she going upstairs.

She unhooked the strap from her briefcase, latched it onto the dog's collar, and picked up the box. She'd borrow tomorrow's clothes from the office closet, if she had to. Then she gathered her stuff, moved it and the puppy to the curb, and hailed a cab.

The girls were on the move.

# 31

Judy sat on the conference room floor at the office and slipped the tape for January 25 into the office boom box. Penny slept peacefully on the navy rug beside her, with a tummy full of chicken lo mein. They both felt well fed and reasonably safe, given the lock on the conference room door, the double lock on the firm's reception area, and the armed guard at the desk downstairs. Rosato & Associates wasn't Fort Knox, but it beat Judy's apartment, for the time being.

She'd called the cops about the break-in, but Detective Wilkins was on the day tour this week and she'd had to settle for filing a complaint with the desk officer, who said they'd check it out when they could. He didn't know about any follow-up on the car bomb or where her car was. So far the score was Coluzzi Family 1, Golden Lovers 0. It was against nature.

Judy hit PLAY on the tape machine, and Fat

Jimmy's gravelly voice came on the line, by now familiar:

> JIMMY: I need that suit.
> WOMAN'S VOICE: Sir, I told you Tuesday, not Monday.
> JIMMY: So Tuesday, Monday, what's the difference? I need it today.
> WOMAN'S VOICE: Sir, we don't have it. We sent it out. It will be back Tuesday morning. You can get it then.
> JIMMY: Why the fuck did you send it out? I don't see why you had to send it out. Where the fuck did you send it anyway? Camden?
> WOMAN'S VOICE: No, sir, our plant is in Frankford.
> JIMMY: Frankford? So get your ass inna car and go there! I need my effin' suit!

She hit FAST FORWARD. The tapes were hand-labeled by date, but they had been running around the clock, and Jimmy spent more time on the phone than any man in creation. Judy had started listening to them the day before the car crash, on January 25, and gone backward in time from there, in case there was any conversation between Coluzzi and Jimmy that suggested the two men had planned it. She hit STOP, then PLAY:

JIMMY: Is that you?

WOMAN'S VOICE: Who do you think it is? Cher?

JIMMY: I don't like Cher. Cher don't do nothin' for me.

WOMAN'S VOICE: Um, how about Pamela Sue Anderson?

JIMMY: The one with the tits? Her, I like.

WOMAN'S VOICE: Okay, I'm her.

Judy fast-forwarded, with nausea. It made her never want to have sex with an Italian. It made her never want to have sex again, which was turning out to be a given anyway. Poor Marlene. Jimmy Bello was a pig. Judy hit PLAY when she thought she had gone far enough.

MAN'S VOICE: And don't forget the baby oil.

JIMMY: What do you need that for, Angelo?

It was Angelo Coluzzi, and Judy's ears pricked up despite her fatigue. His voice was deep and brusque, and his English much better than Pigeon Tony's. So far there had been just a few conversations between the two men, and they revealed only that Jimmy was a glorified errand boy. He ran personal errands:

ANGELO: I told you, get the Cento. I like the Cento. Sylvia likes the Cento. She don't want

Paul Newman. What the fuck's she gonna do with Paul Newman?

JIMMY: So I forgot, I'm sorry.

ANGELO: What's so fuckin' hard to remember? Cento! Cento Clam Sauce! **White!** What's hard? Cento, that's hard?

JIMMY: Cento, I got it. I'll bring it this afternoon.

ANGELO: Cento, for fuck's sake! It's the only one without the MSG. Sylvia can't take the MSG, I tol' you that. You know that.

He also ran pigeon errands:

ANGELO: You mix oil with the malathion, stupid.

JIMMY: Baby oil?

ANGELO: The oil holds the malathion. You mix it and brush it on the perches. The fumes go in the birds' feathers at night. Kills all the mites.

JIMMY: So you don't want the borax now?

ANGELO: Of course I want the borax. Bring the borax, too! You're so fuckin' stupid! And pick me up at ten tomorrow.

And he wasn't always the best errand boy at that:

ANGELO: The peanuts you dropped off, they're the wrong kind.

JIMMY: What? Whatsa matter with the peanuts?

ANGELO: They're the wrong kind.

JIMMY: They're normal. They're normal peanuts.

ANGELO: You need raw Spanish peanuts, not roasted, no salt. The kind you got, they got at the ballpark. You can't feed 'em to the birds. Why'n't you just bring 'em a hot dog and a Bud Lite, you idiot? And make it two o'clock tomorrow, not three.

He also ran errands for the construction company:

ANGELO: No, stupid, I said 20,000 square feet of plywood, builder's grade. They shorted us, the bastards.

JIMMY: You said 2000 square feet. I wrote it down, Ange. 2000.

ANGELO: 2000? I didn't say 2000! What am I gonna do with 2000 square feet of plywood in a mall, for fuck's sake? And pick me up at nine o'clock, can you get that right? Don't be late.

Judy took notes on every conversation between Jimmy and Coluzzi, but as the tapes rolled on, her hopes sank. There was nothing to suggest that they had caused or planned the car accident with Frank's parents. She flipped back through a legal pad full of notes. The only evidence she'd gotten was on the first tape, for January 25, the day of the crash:

ANGELO: I'll be ready at ten tonight and I'm gonna be thirsty.
JIMMY: You got it. I'll bring the Coke.
ANGELO: Good. Don't be late.

Judy had listened to it over and over, excited when she first heard it. But on her notes she could see it for what it was. Nothing. All it proved was that they were together that night, not that they killed two people together. But still it was interesting, and it motivated her to keep going, despite her growing fatigue.

Judy checked her watch. It was three in the morning. Maybe she could lie down and listen. She put her legal pad on the floor, stretched out on the soft wool of the conference room rug, and curved her back against Penny's, which felt surprisingly warm and solid. It was good to have a dog around, and Bennie couldn't fire her for it, since she did it herself most of the time.

Judy snuggled back against the puppy, who leaned against her in response, then she rested her head on her arm, picked up her pen, and hit PLAY. She closed her eyes and listened to the tape drone on, hoping that, in the still of the conference room, in the middle of the night, she would hear the sound of men planning murder.

A lawyer's lullaby.

The next thing Judy knew the tape had gone silent and the telephone on the credenza was ringing. She must have fallen asleep. Her navy suit bunched at the skirt. Her brown pumps lay discarded on the carpet. She looked at the windows. It was dawn. An overcast sky, with the clouds showing a pink underbelly.

**Ring! Ring!** Judy propped herself on an elbow and checked her watch through scratchy eyes. It was 6:30 A.M. **Ring!** Penny lifted her head and blinked dully, clearly hoping voicemail would pick up.

**Ring!** Judy got her feet under her, sleepwalked to the credenza, and picked up the phone. "Rosato and Associates."

"Judy! You there? It's Matty, Mr. DiNunzio." His voice sounded urgent, and it woke Judy up.

"Sure, what is it?"

"We been callin' you all night, at home. What's the matter with your phone?"

"I don't know, what's the matter with it?"

"It don't work. I called the company, they said there was something wrong with the line, inside the house. They can't even send a guy to fix it, they only fix the outside lines."

Judy felt a tingle of fear. Her apartment, unlocked. Her phone, possibly tampered with. It sure sounded like a trap. Her gaze found Penny, who had gone back to sleep curled into a golden circle on the rug, reminding Judy of a glazed doughnut. The dog had saved her life. Judy resolved to be a better mother.

"Judy, you okay?"

"I'm fine. I stayed here and worked. I got these tapes of Coluzzi and Jimmy, but they're not much help—"

"Judy, I don't have time to talk. I'm at a pay phone and I don't have another quarter and I'm almost out of time."

Judy couldn't remember the last time she'd spoken to anybody calling from a pay phone, but it had probably been Mr. DiNunzio. In fact, the DiNunzios still had a black rotary phone at home, resting on something that they called a telephone table. Soon the whole family would be on display in the Smithsonian.

"You gotta come," Mr. DiNunzio said. "Now."

"Where? Why?"

"Down by the airport."

"Are **you** okay?"

"I'm fine, but we need your help. Come now. Get a pencil." He recited an address as if it were familiar, and Judy grabbed a pencil, scribbled it down, and reached for her clogs lying under the table.

"What's going on?" she asked.

But the line went dead.

The metal scrapyard lay alongside the highway in an industrial section of South Philly, and it was immense, taking up at least three city blocks. Mountains of rusty oil barrels, fenders, bumpers, aluminum duct work, brake drums, and railroad wheels reached like houses to the sky, and between each was a dirt road. It looked like a veritable City of Scrap, and if it was, its city hall sat at its center: a huge metal tower of dark corrugated tin, with a series of conveyor belts reaching to it in a zigzag pattern, like a crazy walkway. Judy had never seen anything like this, except in the cartoon **The Brave Little Toaster**, but she didn't say so. It didn't seem like the sort of thing you'd want your lawyer knowing, much less saying.

Cyclone fencing, concertina wire, and a heavily chained and padlocked gate kept the world out of the scrapyard, although the only world interested in entering was Judy, Tony-From-Down-The-Block, Feet, Mr. DiNunzio, and a golden retriever puppy, sitting patiently and only occasionally nosing Judy's hand to be petted. Judy hadn't wanted to leave her at work without telling anybody, and Penny was already turning out to be useful, finding ossified dog turds where nobody else could.

Three senior citizens, the puppy, and the lawyer stood in a stymied line facing the front gate. Everybody but the dog held a take-out coffee from Dunkin' Donuts, and a half a dozen glazed were left in the car. Judy was coming rapidly to the conclusion that no Italian went anywhere or did anything without a saturated fat nearby. It turned a job into a party, even a job this filthy. Trash lay everywhere, litter clung to the Cyclone fencing, and the increasing traffic on the highway spewed air scented with hydrocarbons. Soon it would be the morning rush hour, and they all would suffocate.

Mr. DiNunzio read the sign on the front gate, a long notice posted by order of the court. "No admittance, it says, and then some court lingo. What's it mean, Jude?"

Tony-From-Down-The-Block snorted, an unlit cigar in the hand with the paper Dunkin' Donuts cup. "It means you can't go in, Matty. Whaddaya think it means, siddown and have a cuppa coffee?"

Judy ignored them in favor of the notice. It had been posted by the bankruptcy court and was dated February 15, a year ago. She juggled Penny and the coffee cup to run a finger along the fine print. "Apparently the business that owns and operates the scrapyard went into receivership, and its assets—the land, the machinery, the equipment—were frozen pending the outcome. In other words, this scrapyard is just the way it was on February fifteenth."

"That's what Dom from Passyunk Avenue said," Mr. DiNunzio added, and Judy looked over.

"Tell me how you found it, Mr. D."

"Well, we figgered that the truck that they died in, Frank and Gemma, was totaled. I mean, the way it went over the overpass, and the fire, it couldn't not be." Mr. DiNunzio swallowed at the memory, his eyes, behind his bifocals, still puffy from lack of sleep. He had a fresh shave, a new brown cardigan, a white shirt, and baggy pants. It was a given that he smelled like mothballs.

"So we knew it had to be sold for junk, and the junkyards everybody uses in South Philly are the ones on Passyunk Avenue, because it's close."

Feet nodded eagerly. "Also that's where you get the best deal. They got five or six there, and you can bargain. You can—"

Judy interrupted him with a wave. "Don't say 'Jew 'em down,' okay, Feet?"

Feet's lips parted in offense. "I wasn't going to say 'Jew 'em down.' I **never** say 'Jew 'em down.' I'm Jewish."

Judy closed her eyes, mortified. "Sorry. I don't use that expression either. I never say it. I just know that some people do."

Mr. DiNunzio cleared his throat. "There are Italian Jews, Judy. Many people don't realize that. They assume all Italians are Catholic, but they are incorrect."

Feet resettled his T-shirt huffily. "Well, I hope you don't use that term, Judy. It's not nice."

"I don't, I swear." Judy crossed herself, backward. This religion thing was so confusing. Maybe she should get one. She turned to Mr. DiNunzio. "Anyway, you were saying, Mr. D."

"So we asked all the junkyard dealers 'til we found the one they brought it to, named Wreck-A-Mend. Ain't that a stupid name? Anyway, the guy's name is Dom and he had a record of the title and he said that he sold it to these guys for scrap, right after they were killed, which was on January twenty-fifth. I know because I still got the Mass card. He said if they didn't scrap it yet, or whatever they do, then the car should still be here."

"Great work, gentlemen!" Judy said, excited. It was more than she'd hoped when she gave them the assignment, yesterday in the conference room. But her bomb theory wasn't panning out. "Did the junk dealer really say the truck was still whole, though?"

"Yes. He said he had enough to sell. Got two hundred and fifty bucks for it, which ain't bad."

"Tullio's car ain't worth that now," Feet said, but Judy was thinking ahead.

"So they couldn't have planted a bomb on it, or there wouldn't be anything left. But if they tampered with it somehow, there should be some evidence of it. Or what's left of it."

Mr. DiNunzio sipped his coffee reflectively. "I still don't unnerstan' why the cops didn't think that, if it's really a murder."

Feet looked over. "They weren't lookin' for it. They thought it was an accident. It's possible that it wasn't, and we'll know when we find it, like

Judy said. She said she'd get it tested, like from a professional car tester guy. Right, Judy?"

"Right. A car tester guy." She nodded, relieved that Feet had apparently forgiven her gaffe. "Way to go, gentlemen." Judy felt a cool nose under her hand and petted the dog, who apparently felt left out of the praise. "So where are the junked cars?" Feet pointed to the left, and Judy looked over with a start. On the far side of the scrapyard, behind piles of dark, shredded metal and bales of crushed aluminum cans, sat junked cars stacked as high as skyscrapers. Judy almost dropped her coffee. "Are you serious? There have to be a zillion cars there."

Feet shook his head. "No, only two thousand forty-four. We counted while we were waitin' for you. We had nothin' else to do."

Judy blinked, astounded. "But how will we know which one it is?"

"It's an '81 red Volkswagen, a pickup. He used it for the construction business. It had a gold Mason emblem on the back, because Frank was a Mason."

Judy smiled. "How do you know their truck, Feet?"

"Frank and Gemma lived down the block from me. We all know each other's cars in South Philly. How else you gonna double-park?"

Mr. DiNunzio nodded. "We were thinking, if

you only look at the red ones, that narrows it down to only 593 wrecks we gotta look at."

"But we gotta check the burned ones, too," Tony-From-Down-The-Block added, "since I think the truck caught on fire."

"How many burned trucks are there?" Judy asked, but Feet shrugged.

"We didn't count. We got tired and ate dough-nuts instead."

Judy smiled and faced the Cyclone fence around the scrapyard. She didn't know how she'd scale it, much less get them over. It was easily ten feet high, and the concertina wire would slice like a razor. "Only one obstacle left. We gotta climb the fence."

"The hell with that," Feet said, and Mr. DiNunzio laughed.

"You think a fence can keep out a coupla boys from the neighborhood?" He hooked an arthritic index finger on one of the fence's wires and yanked. A waist-high door opened in the fence, its metal crudely severed. "I know it ain't right, so don't tell my daughter on me."

Judy's eyes widened. "Mr. D, this is breaking and entering."

"No, it ain't," Tony-From-Down-The-Block said. "We didn't break nothing."

"Let's go." Feet ducked down and shuffled with his coffee through the makeshift gate, and Tony-

From-Down-The-Block went behind him, while Mr. DiNunzio held open the door for Judy, who balked.

"I can't do this," she said, albeit reluctantly. All the Italians were going inside to have fun. Even the puppy tugged at the leash. "I'm an officer of the court. I've never broken the law in my life. It's the only rules I follow."

"Don't be a party pooper!" Tony-From-Down-The-Block shouted from the other side of the fence, and Feet agreed.

"You tol' us to find the truck, we found the truck. Now come on, Jude! It could be in there somewhere. We gotta get goin'."

Judy thought hard. She could petition the bankruptcy court for permission to enter, but that would show her hand, publicly and to Frank, and they wouldn't grant it in the end. Maybe if she called the counsel for the scrap company, but that could take days. She couldn't see any alternative.

"You gotta do it, Judy," Mr. DiNunzio said. "For Pigeon Tony. How's he ever gonna get justice if we don't help?"

Judy smiled at the irony. "Is it okay to break the law to get justice, Mr. D?"

The old man's eyes narrowed, and though none of them had ever discussed the direct question of Pigeon Tony's guilt, Mr. DiNunzio knew just what she was saying. "Sure it is," he said with certainty.

Judy considered it, standing her ground, feeling like a hypocrite, then a fool. It had started as a simple question but had become freighted. Still, an ethical question didn't have to be a momentous one to present the issue; the fact that it seemed minor only eased glossing over the ethics. Judy was confronting the white lie of break-ins.

"Penny, come! **Come!**" Feet shouted suddenly, with a loud clap, and Penny, on the leash in Judy's hand, leaped forward and tugged them both through the gate, lunging for the doughnut Feet was offering.

"No fair!" Judy said, landing confused on the other side.

Mr. DiNunzio came through and patted her on the back. "Let's go save a life," he said, but Feet shook his head.

"What's the big deal, Jude? You may be a lawyer, but you can lighten up a little."

Tony-From-Down-The-Block threw an arm around her, with a cigar between his fingers. "Sometimes education makes you dumb," he said.

Judy wasn't sure she agreed, but she was already on the other side of the fence.

And the gate was closed behind her.

# 32

The toxic wind from the expressway lessened inside the scrapyard, and Judy and The Two Tonys, the puppy, and Mr. DiNunzio made their way to the junked cars, past a thirty-foot-high pile of car parts. "Looks like crab shells," Feet said.

They passed a lineup of used rubber tires.

"Looks like chocolate doughnuts," Feet said.

They passed bales of smashed tin cans.

"Looks like shredded wheat," Feet said.

Judy smiled as they walked by a yellow crane that said KOMATSU on the side in black letters. "What's that look like, Feet?"

"My mother-in-law," he said, and everybody laughed.

They walked on, down one of the makeshift streets of scrap, and in time Tony-From-Down-The-Block took on the role of tour guide. "See, Judy, that thing there"—he pointed at the corrugated tower, his cigar between two fingers—"that's the shredder. It shreds the metal."

"Interesting," Judy said, meaning it. She thought all cars got flattened, like in **The Brave Little You-Know-What**.

"The cars and scrap metal go up the conveyor belts, then inside the tower is a row of magnets, and it separates the aluminum, copper, and brass from iron scrap. Aluminum don't get attracted to magnets, you follow? Also it shoots out the rest of the stuff that's not metal, like car seats and shit like that. That's called fluff."

Feet looked over. "How do you know that?"

"I been around, that's how. A scrapyard this big, they could do three, four thousand cars a day. Usually the cars get collected in the day and shredded at night." They walked past a ten-foot triangle of chewed-up metal, and Tony-From-Down-The-Block pointed. "That's frag. Comes outta the metal shredder like that. Worth a lot of money. They use it in new cars. Recycled metal."

"Looks like fried clams," Feet said, and Penny looked over with interest.

About five miles of trash, scrap, twisted metal, and rusty train wheels later, Judy and Company stood dwarfed before a wall of junked cars, bound by heavy chain. The cars had been stripped of their tires, exposing the brake drums, the headlights had been pulled out, leaving the cars eyeless, and the chrome and the car roofs had been cut off, so that only the bodies remained.

"Looks like a stack of pancakes," said Feet, who

now held Penny's leash. The dog had fallen in love with him on the way over, for obvious reasons.

Judy skimmed the names on the carcasses. Delta 88. Monte Carlo. Sunbird. Ford Granada. They were all old cars, judging from the ridiculous lengths of the car bodies. It was hard to see how earth had room for all the cars in the eighties. "I've never heard of half these cars."

"I **owned** half these cars," Tony-From-Down-The-Block said, and Feet smiled.

"We better get to work," Mr. DiNunzio said, finishing his coffee and wiggling the empty cup. "Wait, what're we doin' with our trash?"

"Just throw it on the ground," Tony-From-Down-The-Block said, but Mr. DiNunzio shook his head.

"That ain't right. You don't throw litter on the ground."

"It's a **junkyard**, Matty."

"It still ain't right," he said. He folded his empty cup carefully in two and stuffed it into the pocket of his brown cardigan.

"Let's get it done," Judy said. She scanned the cars, whose rows extended unevenly to the sky, inevitably reminding her of a mountain range. "Feet, you and Penny take the far end. We'll all space ourselves along and start looking. It's a red Volkswagen pickup with a Mason's emblem. There can't be many of them here."

Feet nodded hopefully. "True. I remember it was

a pretty unusual thing. I don't think they made a lot of 'em. Frank, he loved that little truck."

Tony-From-Down-The-Block put a comforting hand on Judy's shoulder. "We'll find it, Jude. Anybody can find it, we can."

Mr. DiNunzio chimed in, "Sure we will. Red is easy to see."

Judy forced a smile, from the foothills of the junked-car mountains. "How hard can it be?" she asked.

Only Penny had the sense to look doubtful.

Four hours later, the noon sun burned high in a cloudless sky, and its heat reflected on the discarded metal everywhere, transforming the scrapyard into a furnace. Judy sweated through her suit, even with the jacket off, and Penny lapped bottled water from Mr. DiNunzio's unfolded coffee cup. But all of them forgot the heat when they discovered the short red truck in the middle, third from the bottom, in the stack of junked vehicles.

"You think this is it?" Judy asked, checking her excitement. Mr. DiNunzio had been the one to find the truck and had let out a yelp at the discovery, but she didn't want to jump to any conclusions.

"Sure, it is!" Mr. DiNunzio answered, pointing at the smashed grille. "Got the VW circle and all. It's smashed and burned but it's there."

Judy looked. The VW logo hung in a circle from the truck's broken black grille, and its red paint was visible only in dull splotches that weren't blackened by fire.

"Look!" Feet shouted from the back of the truck, and Judy's heart skipped a beat as she remembered the bomb that Tullio had found under her bumper. She hurried over to Feet, who was almost jumping with happiness. "It's got the Mason thing and all! This has gotta be the truck! See it?"

"Jeez," Judy heard herself say. A Masonic emblem, its fake gold charred, could barely be identified by its embossing. It seemed that the truck was the Lucias', and seeing the wreck this close saddened Judy. She couldn't see the driver's side, and the only obvious point about the wreckage was that nobody could have walked away from it alive. And as odd as it felt finding the truck without Frank's knowledge, she was glad he hadn't been here to see it. "Nobody tell Frank we found this, okay?" Judy said as a reminder.

"Okay," Mr. DiNunzio said, and the others nodded gravely.

She surveyed the situation. She had a junker that had been confiscated by court order, three very tired but victorious senior citizens, and a puppy shredding a paper cup with vigor. "Now all we got to do is get the truck out of here," she said, thinking aloud, and Tony-From-Down-The-Block brightened.

"Piece a cake. We snip the chains and yank—"

"NO!" Judy said. Instantly Penny dropped the

cup, but Judy considered her obedience as temporary insanity. "We can't just take it. It's here under court order."

Mr. DiNunzio frowned. "Can you call the court?"

"It's not that easy, especially bankruptcy court. You have to petition for it. And we can't get it out by police order unless we're willing to go public with it, which I'm not."

"You don't want Frank to know." Feet nodded.

"I don't want the Coluzzis to know either. If this was murder and not an accident, I don't want them to know we're onto them." Judy tried to think, but Tony-From-Down-The-Block kept talking, tempting her like a devil with a Macanudo.

"All it takes is a crane operator," he was saying. "Crane's right over there. Drive it over, pick the cars off the top, and pull out the red truck. Friend of mine can work a crane, and another friend got a flatbed."

Judy shook her head. "It's illegal."

"We won't get caught. This place is friggin' deserted. Both of my buddies are in the club. They'd be glad to help Pigeon Tony out, and they won't say nothin'. Be done in five minutes."

Judy shuddered. "I took an oath."

"People get divorced all the time. Look at me and Feet."

Mr. DiNunzio snorted. "You two make a bad couple. I wouldn't a given it ten minutes."

Feet laughed, but Judy didn't. "It's not the same thing," she said. "And if we get caught, it's my license."

"So don't be there. What we need you for?"

Judy shook her head. "Maybe we can bring the expert to the truck, instead of the other way around."

"How's he gonna test it, like a pancake in a stack?"

"Gimme a minute." Judy bit her lip. "There has to be another way."

"You think too much, even for a lawyer."

"Okay, gimme a day. I'll come up with something and let you know."

Feet laughed. "This is like that joke where the rabbi shoots a hole in one, but he's playing golf on a high holy day."

Judy smiled. Gazing at the car, she couldn't completely disagree.

"Not that I tell Jewish jokes," Feet added.

"Never happen," said Tony-From-Down-The-Block.

Judy didn't have to fight the press to get to the door of her office building. There were fewer reporters clogging the sidewalk than usual, and she was guessing it wasn't her new perfume, Eau de Scrapyard. Judging from their questions, they had deserted her for the Coluzzi Construction offices.

"Ms. Carrier, what do you say to today's news that Marco has thrown his brother John out of the company offices?" "Ms. Carrier, do you have any comment on the feud between the Coluzzis?" "Judy, where are you hiding Pigeon Tony and why?"

"No comment," she said, suppressing her excitement as she hit the building, grabbed an elevator, and punched the button for her floor. She could hardly wait for the doors to open so she could jump out. "Is Bennie in?" she called when she hit the reception area, but the receptionist was leaving, bag in hand.

"Uh, Bennie?" the receptionist asked. She was apparently a temp, a tall, thin woman with a long, dark braid and too much makeup; but then to Judy, everybody but Marlene Bello wore too much makeup. "Bennie Rosato? She said she went on an emergency TRO, whatever that is. On a First Amendment case. She's in court."

Damn. No wonder Bennie hadn't answered her cell phone. Judy had wanted to talk to her about the red truck before she got arrested, not after. "May I have my messages and mail? Also the newspapers."

"Hold on a minute." The receptionist turned reluctantly back to the desk, rooted through the papers to locate Judy's phone messages, correspondence, and today's newspapers, and handed them all to her. "Your name is Judy Carrier, right? Where's the dog?"

"With a man named Feet. Thanks for the mail." Preoccupied, Judy flipped through her phone messages. WCAU-TV, WPVI-TV, ABC, NBC, CNN, Court TV and an array of newspapers. "You a temp, by the way? Where's Marshall?"

"Gotta go. Late lunch and all."

"Have fun." Judy grabbed the papers and her correspondence, chugged to her office, and ignored everything but the front page of **The Daily News.** IT'S OVER, JOHNNIE, read the tabloid headline, and Judy flipped the page to read the story.

In a major power grab, Marco Coluzzi, chief financial officer of Coluzzi Construction Company, this morning blocked his brother John's entrance to the company offices. The surprise move almost caused a riot on this tiny block of South Philadelphia. Private security guards apparently employed by Marco Coluzzi were able to keep John Coluzzi, chief operating officer of Coluzzi Construction, and others from reporting to work without violence. Philadelphia police arrived quickly on the scene, and one highly placed company official commented that they had been called in advance to keep a lid on any potential disturbance.

Neither Coluzzi brother could be reached for comment, but Coluzzi Construction has issued a press release stating that, "Effective today, Marco Coluzzi has been named president and CEO of Coluzzi Construction. All previous contracts made under prior management will remain in force and be honored."

My God. So Marco had made his move. What sort of king waited to be crowned, when he could crown himself? Judy read the tabloid's account, then the next newspaper's and the next, sinking into her desk chair in her sunny office, soaking it all in. It couldn't have gone better if she'd planned it. She flipped the page to continue reading the story, and next to it was a sidebar that was even better.

Coluzzi Construction, considered a shoo-in for the construction contract for the new waterfront shopping complex, was today denied the nod. City officials state that the contract was offered to Melton Construction instead because of "their high quality of workmanship and price, of course," but insiders say that the recent racketeering lawsuit against Coluzzi Construction over the nearby Philly Court

Center was behind the upset. The contract was valued at $11 million.

Judy was stunned. She had cost the Coluzzis a fortune. The timing of Marco's takeover was no coincidence. If John had been responsible for the Philly Court debacle, it had to have been the final blow against him. Judy changed her plans. She had come back to the office to press her lawsuit against the Coluzzis, to prepare and file the first wave of interrogatories and document requests, but the takeover became instant priority. Marco had declared war, and she could only guess how John would react. Judy had no way of knowing. Then she thought about it. Yes, she did.

The tapes, between Fat Jimmy and Angelo Coluzzi. They were her only way into the inner workings of the Coluzzis, and she hadn't finished listening to them yet. They'd been a dry hole for the murder of Frank's parents, except for the fact that Angelo and Fat Jimmy had been together that night. But what could the tapes tell her, if anything, about the warring brothers?

Judy considered it. John Coluzzi and Fat Jimmy were allies now, maybe they had been for a long time. Maybe there had been discussions of Marco on the tapes. It was likelier than not. She tossed the newspaper aside and hurried to the conference room, where she had left the box of tapes.

But when she got there, they were gone.

# 33

Judy couldn't believe what she was seeing. The conference room was the way she'd left it this morning, minus the lo mein cartons, the dog dish, and the big cardboard box of tapes. "**Who took my tapes?**" she shouted.

She turned on her heels, but the office looked empty, normal for lunchtime. Nobody would have gone into the war room and taken evidence from it. It was an unwritten rule, observed by everyone. Who was new on the scene? Then Judy remembered. There had been a temp at the front desk. The temp was the only possibility. And she had been on the way out when Judy came in.

One of the secretaries appeared behind her. "The temp was in there this morning," she said. "She told me you told her to clean up the food and all—"

"Thanks, but I didn't do that." Alarmed, Judy sprinted from the conference room, past the astonished expressions of the lawyers, including Murphy, who was escorting clients to the reception area. Judy didn't care. "Murphy, call Marshall's house and check on her!"

"Why? What?"

"Our regular receptionist, Marshall. Just do it!" Judy called over her shoulder, and took off for the reception area. "Where's that temp?" she shouted, but the reception desk was empty.

"You just missed her," one of the associates said, waving a brief. "But don't use her, she's terrible. She's been trying to go home all morning, but I needed her to type something for me. Look at it! She types worse than I do."

But Judy was already hustling for the elevator. The steel doors were sealed closed but she heard the cab **ping** downstairs as it landed on the ground floor. She couldn't wait for it to return. She ran for the staircase next to the elevator, banged open the fire door, and ran down the concrete steps, her clogs clumping on the steel tread of each step. She wound down the one flight, then hit the fire door and slammed into it, banging it open.

"Where'd that woman go, with the braid?" she called to the alarmed security guard, who pointed to the service entrance of the building.

"Out the back. Said she wanted to avoid the press. Is there a problem?"

Judy was off and running, down a short corridor, past a green time clock with white cards in slots underneath, and out the back exit, which dumped her into an alley. She looked down the street just in time to see the receptionist's dark braid flying around the corner.

Judy darted up the alley after her and found herself on a hot sidewalk crowded with businesspeople coming back from lunch. She looked left. The dark braid wasn't in sight. She looked right. Up ahead, running now against the current of the crowd, sprinted the woman with the dark braid. She was tall enough that her head bobbed above the crowd.

Judy barreled through the crowd, keeping a bead on her. The temp had on running shoes, but they were no match for clogs. Judy could do anything in clogs. She could leap tall buildings. Running down a fake temp was a no-brainer.

Her heart beat faster. She sweated through her days-old suit. Questions flew through her brain. How had they known about the tapes? Had they been watching her? Who had sent this woman? Judy kept her eye on the dark braid, who swerved around a corner toward Chestnut Street, heading into the heart of the business district, clearly hoping to lose Judy in the crowd.

Judy put on the afterburners, becoming breathless, and the dark braid picked up her pace, too, tearing down the street. Startled passersby jumped out of the way and looked on curiously. The distance between Judy and the woman was widening. The crowd thickened. Judy was losing her. Clogs were stupid. Then Judy got an idea. If the dark braid could use the crowd, so could she.

"Stop that woman, she took my purse!" Judy called out, dimly aware that Bennie had tried that trick once, with success. But nobody stopped. They just let the woman run by. Damn. Judy charged ahead and got another idea.

"Stop that woman, she took my baby!" Judy shouted, louder, but nobody stopped the woman with the dark braid, who tore down the street, slipped through traffic and made it to the next curb, and took off. So much for the City of Brotherly Love. Judy got another idea.

"Stop that woman—it's **Cher**!" she screamed, but this time a ripple of excitement went through the passersby and they stopped and stared at the woman with too much makeup and a long black braid. One thrust a pen and paper at her for an autograph, and a young man started chasing after her. Bingo! "Hey, everybody!" Judy hollered at the top of her lungs, to anyone who would listen. "That's CHER!"

In no time a small crowd was running after the tall woman with the dark braid, and Judy trailed them by a furlong. They chased the woman into an alley, where they cornered her and had her backed against the brick wall, panting like a dog. Judy peered over their heads, blocked the alley, and waited for the inevitable.

"That's not Cher!" "She's not Cher!" "You don't

even look like Cher!" "Wannabe!" "Poser!" called the crowd, and after some commotion they dispersed, filing disappointed out of the alley, leaving Judy and the temp alone.

Judy went to the back of the alley and faced the woman, who didn't even try to run past her but looked plainly exhausted, her head to one side, as if she were nodding out. She didn't even move as Judy approached, and up close Judy could see that the woman was just a girl, with heavy black eyeliner, greasy from exertion, and her hair dyed black as midnight. She couldn't have been more than nineteen or weighed more than a hundred pounds in tight Guess jeans and a thin white sweater. Her skin was pale, her cheekbones too prominent to be healthy, and her pupils pinpoints. It wasn't because of the sun.

Judy grabbed the girl's skinny arm and pinned her against the  wall with ease. "Where are my tapes?"

"Don't hurt me. I put them in the incinerator, in the basement. They're gone." The girl's eyelids fluttered and her green eyes filled with tears of fear, which disarmed Judy. She had never acted this way before. Nobody was afraid of her. She could barely housebreak a golden. Nevertheless she tightened her grip. Her tapes, gone.

"Why'd you burn the tapes?"

"Because they made me. They said they'd beat me up if I didn't. Please don't turn me in. Please lemme go."

"Who said they'd beat you up? One of the Coluzzis?"

The girl pursed her lips, as if to resist Judy's prying out the answer, so Judy tried hardball.

"You destroyed critical evidence in a murder case. That's obstruction of justice. If I call the cops to arrest you right now, that's federal time. Who made you do it? Was it Coluzzi? Jimmy Bello?"

"I can't say." The girl shook her head, jittery against the rough brick. "I'd rather do the time than end up dead."

"You think they'd kill you?"

"I know they would."

Judy shuddered, thinking about Marshall. "Did they hurt our receptionist?"

"No, they said they'd **detain** her is all."

"Did they hurt Marlene Bello?"

"Nobody hurts Marlene." The girl grinned crookedly. "Lemme go, please. I didn't have a choice."

Judy considered it. There weren't a lot of alternatives. She felt too sorry for the girl to turn her in. If the girl told the police who'd sent her, she'd be in danger herself. Judy flashed on Theresa McRea, who had to flee the country in fear. Judy was suddenly tired of causing so much pain, even in the name of justice. She was becoming her enemy and that she couldn't stand. Let the bad guys do the bad things from now on. If Judy was a good guy, she had to do the good things. Her karma reserves were already in the red zone, from the scrapyard.

Judy released the girl's arm. "Go. Run. Get clean. Learn to type. But do me one favor. Tell them you think I copied the tapes."

The girl's eyes narrowed with street savvy. "You didn't make copies."

"You're not Cher, but those people thought you were. And look what happened."

The girl giggled, and then the laughter disappeared as quickly as it had come. "They're trying to kill you, whoever you are. Lawyer with a dog."

"I know, the car bomb gave them away," Judy said, forcing a smile she didn't feel. The threat by the Coluzzis was a constant now, gnawing at her stomach. "But why didn't they send you to do it? You could have killed me as easily as burned my tapes."

"Me?" The girl put up her palms. "Oh no, I don't go **there**. Not me. No. Besides, they do that themselves."

Even Judy's fraudulent smile vanished. "Better go now. Before I change my mind."

The girl broke free and ran off, without looking back.


"Hey, kids," Judy said, rushing into the reception area at the office, worrying about Marshall and

Marlene Bello. Murphy and the secretaries were standing around the front desk talking. Judy gauged the scene instantly and relaxed. They wouldn't have been loafing if the receptionist were in trouble. "I gather Marshall is okay?"

Murphy nodded. "She got stuck in an elevator. It broke, they think. She's on her way in."

"Great." Judy smiled with relief. The Coluzzis were killing only when necessary. They must have been off their game. "I gotta go make some calls. Thanks for your help."

"You didn't catch the temp?" Murphy asked, surprised, but Judy shook her head.

"Bennie woulda caught her, but I couldn't."

"Damn!" Murphy turned to Letisha, one of the secretaries. "I owe you a tenner."

Judy laughed, on her way to her office. She was liking Murphy more and more. She reached her office, shut the door, and punched in Marlene Bello's number, holding her breath while the phone rang one, two, three, and finally four times before Marlene picked up. "You're alive!" Judy said.

"Last time I checked." Marlene laughed in her throaty, smoke-cured way. "Very alive, in fact."

"Oh, yeah?"

"Yeah, you want to talk to Tony?"

Judy raised an eyebrow. "Tony? Tony who?"

"Tony-From-Down-The-Block. He's paying me a visit, for lunch. He says to tell you hi."

Judy smiled. So he hadn't been as tired as she'd thought. She filled Marlene in on the story of the tapes and told her to watch her back.

"Don't you worry about me, sugar. I keep a Beretta in my purse."

"Great, I guess." Judy wondered fleetingly how many Mary Kay reps carried concealed. "You didn't make copies of those tapes by any chance, did you?"

"No way."

"You think the PI you hired did?"

"Doubt it. He died anyway, three months ago."

Judy paused, suspicious. "How'd he die?"

"Kidney failure." Marlene put a hand over the phone, then came back on the line. "Hold on. Tony's buggin' me for the phone. He wants to tell you something."

"What?"

"First, he says, 'Don't be mad.'"

Judy knew instantly what he meant. "Damn him! Put him on!"

# 34

The detective at the front desk was on the phone, but Judy wasn't waiting for him to get off. She passed the desk and entered the squad room, where most of the Homicide Division looked up without surprise. Their ties loosened and their jackets off, they'd been eating lunch and waiting for jobs. Yellow Blimpie's cups dotted the messy desks and the oily papers left over from take-out hoagies remained, many with a pile of shredded onions scenting the air. The detectives had undoubtedly been alerted to Judy's visit, since she'd called Wilkins before she came, and she wondered if they'd been taking bets on whether she'd come bare-legged or not. She had. No panty-hose could withstand the way she lawyered.

"Miss Carrier," Detective Wilkins said, standing and hitching up his slacks on slim hips. His white shirtsleeves were rolled up and his tie was on and knotted tight. "You came to file another complaint."

"Let's review. A bomb on my car, my apartment broken into, and now a fake temp in my office. Call me crazy, but I think someone's trying to kill me."

Detective Wilkins smiled without mirth. "We don't think you're crazy. We take all of your calls and complaints very seriously, and I'm glad you came down to talk to us about it."

It sounded like the policeman-is-your-friend lecture they gave in third grade. Evidently Judy couldn't have this conversation in an open squad room. "Is there someplace we could talk in private?"

"I'll do you one better," he said, lifting his jacket from behind his chair. "Come with me."

Ten minutes later she was sitting in the beat-up passenger seat of Detective Wilkins's ancient blue Crown Victoria, telling him everything that had happened over the past two days, with the exception of that silly little felony at the scrapyard. She felt vaguely hypocritical, seeking police protection after she'd conspired to boost a junker. In the law, this was known as "unclean hands." Judy tried to put it out of her mind. In the law, this was known as "denial."

There was almost no traffic, it being the lull between the lunch and the evening rush hours, but Detective Wilkins drove as if there were, rushing even to red lights and gunning the engine when they turned green. They were heading toward her apartment in Society Hill, and Judy was glad it wasn't far.

"So we're checking out my apartment?" she asked, and he nodded. He kept his gaze straight ahead and his hands loosely on the wheel. His eyes were flinty in the sun coming through the windshield.

"I heard your message when I came in. You said your apartment door was open, but so was the front door downstairs. You said there were no signs of a break-in or forced entry of any kind."

"There wasn't, but someone got in there. I'm not imagining this, Detective."

"I didn't say you were. But isn't it possible that you left your apartment door open?" The Crown Vic lurched to a red light.

"I didn't. I never leave my door open. And the front door wasn't open when I left yesterday. I had to unlock it to get in last night."

"We'll do a walk-through together when we get there and you'll tell me if anything is wrong."

"Okay." Judy thought a minute. "What about the guys who were shooting at us and then wrecked? Is there anything new on that?"

"No new leads. We're still canvassing the neighborhood. Talking to the neighbors. Trying to get a description of whoever stole the car. So far, nothin'."

Judy sighed. "What about the bomb on my car bumper? What did they say about it?" It was like a laundry list of calamities.

"It's a pipe bomb. Homemade, nothing fancy."

"That's a relief. I wouldn't want a fancy bomb."

Detective Wilkins's eyes went flintier. "We don't have enough to charge anybody for it. We dusted the car bumper for prints and got nothing."

"What do you mean?"

"No matches to any known felons. No matches to anybody with a history of arrests for making bombs or incendiary devices. No matches to any of the Coluzzi family members or even their associates. That enough for you?"

Judy remembered what the fake temp had said, about the Coluzzis liking to commit their own murders. It gave new meaning to the term do-it-yourselfers. "Does John or Marco Coluzzi have a criminal record?"

"Not your business. But no."

"So you have no record of their prints?"

"No." The Crown Vic sped past the new federal prison, rising like a grim, gray nail next to the huge, redbrick United States Courthouse, and Judy gazed out the window in frustration.

"All this law and order, and it's not protecting anybody."

"Yo, enough of that. I don't do this for everyone, you know. I'm not even on this tour. I got ten uncleared cases on my desk right now. My partner's in court for four days. I'm doing it because of the car bomb and the case you're involved in. The department has done more than its part for you. There's no flies on us, dear."

"But I'm no safer. That temp could have killed

me today. I'm a defense lawyer, and I spend all my time defending myself."

"Well, you don't make it easy, do you?" Detective Wilkins's tone sounded testy, and he fed the big engine more gas. "Filing lawsuits. Holding press conferences. Thumbin' your nose. What did you think was gonna happen?"

Judy's head snapped around. "You saying that makes it right?"

"I'm saying that you gotta expect that. You can't have it both ways, lady."

The argument had some force, but she still had a problem. "Did you question the Coluzzis about any of this? The car chase? The bomb? The apartment?"

"I paid them a visit this morning, but I couldn't find Big John. Marco was otherwise occupied, and his secretary said he'd call me back."

"Can he just say that? That he's too busy to see the police?"

"When he's in the middle of a riot, I cut him some slack. He's not a suspect, not officially, and you don't know what those offices were like today, after he took over. It coulda been a riot. We put twenty uniforms on it just to keep the peace." The Crown Vic zoomed down Sixth Street, with Independence Mall on their left. A dappled draft horse, sluggish in the heat, carted tourists past the Constitution Hall, with its ivory spire and cupola.

"So what should I do? Should I hire protection?"

"You could do that. But if I were you, I'd get off the Lucia case."

"No," Judy said reflexively, but something made her stop. She had a fleeting suspicion that Wilkins could be involved with the Coluzzis, but dismissed it as paranoia. Maybe. "Why do you think I should get off the case?" she asked, fishing.

"Your client's going down, and I don't think a killer's worth gettin' killed for."

"Do you know the Coluzzis?"

"No." The Crown Vic shot down Market Street, past the Greek restaurants, gentrified coffeehouses, and junky storefronts of Old City selling men's clothes, gold jewelry, and Liberty Bell thermometers.

"You never met John or Marco?" she asked.

"No."

"You never had any dealing with them?"

"No, and I don't care to be cross-examined, counselor."

Judy reddened. She never was good at fishing. She didn't know how to be anything but blunt, so she went with that. "I'm not accusing you, Detective, but you can't blame a girl for asking."

"Yes I can." Clenched teeth strained his voice, but Judy wasn't sorry.

"Gimme a break, Detective. My life is on the line, as is my client's, and the police don't do anything. My client's house has been trashed, he's in hiding, and the police don't do anything. At some point, you start to wonder, and it's not out of the question, with the Coluzzis. They bribed half of L and I, not to mention whoever gives out the construction contracts at City Hall. The Philly cops haven't been immune from corruption in the past." She didn't give him the particulars, because the Crown Vic was already screeching to an extremely pissed-off stop in the middle of Market Street, blocking a full SEPTA bus, with no red light in sight.

Detective Wilkins turned to face Judy, his dark eyes glowing with anger. "Please don't even **think** that I'm dirty, or that any of the men in my division are dirty, when I am driving you around **like a cabbie** and **kissing your ass**. Got it, lady? I have only so much restraint."

Judy nodded. Judging from his vehemence, he was telling the truth. Either that or he was in "denial." Her neck whipped back as he stomped on the gas pedal and the Crown Vic took a right by her favorite storefront, Mr. Bar Stool, and zoomed down Second Street until he reached the cobblestone streets of Society Hill. Judy felt vaguely guilty while he fumed. Oh, what the hell. She was supposed to be a good guy. "I'm sorry if I insulted you," she said, meaning it. Sort of.

The Crown Vic bobbled on the bumpy gray cobblestones. The detective said nothing.

"I do appreciate what you're doing." Judy managed not to say, what **little** you're doing.

The Crown Vic swerved right and headed west. Colonial townhouses whizzed by. The detective had fallen mute.

"Look, I don't have to kiss your ass either."

The Crown Vic pulled up in front of Judy's apartment house and Detective Wilkins cut the ignition, yanked up the emergency brake, and got out of the car and slammed the car door, all without a word.

So be it. Judy got out of her side of the car, slammed her door even harder, walked to the front door of her apartment, and dug in her backpack for her keys. It took her fully ten minutes to find them, which proved her karma had dipped to an all-time low, and during that time neither she nor the constabulary spoke. She let them in the front door, and they tramped up the stairs, with Judy in the lead.

Her stomach tensed as she climbed to the first-floor landing, then went up to the second. What if someone were there? What if someone had come in since this morning? She would have asked Detective Wilkins to lead but she'd rather be dead than break the silence first. Lawyers call this "pigheaded." She reached her apartment door, unlocked it, and let it swing wide open.

The living room looked just as she'd left it, as a first impression. She entered the room, listening for commotion, but it was dead quiet. She walked around the sofa, the coffee table, and past the windows, looking for anything amiss. She went into the adjoining galley kitchen, but the dishes were still soaking in the sink and nothing was disturbed, then she hurried to her bedroom. The bedclothes were a happy tumble, the bureau drawers hung open with overflowing clothes, and the disarray on the bureau top looked normal. She walked to her jewelry box and saw that nothing had been taken.

Judy sighed. Maybe she had left the door open. Maybe no one had been here. She went through the bathroom, but it looked fine, and then went on to the studio. She froze on the threshold.

It was her painting on the easel, the one she'd started not too long ago. It was a self-portrait, the way she'd looked that night when the moon was full and she was changing the way she painted. No more landscapes from a nomadic childhood, long ago and far away. Judy had been starting over, with herself, so her first painting had been a self-portrait as she had been that night, in the nude.

But the painting horrified her now. A knife gutted her portrait, running from the base of her neck, slitting her chest between her breasts, and ending between her legs. The knife jutted crudely from her pubis. Vermilion paint the color of fresh blood had been smeared all over her knifed body. The meaning was unmistakable.

"Jesus H. Christ," said a voice behind Judy. It was Detective Wilkins, and his stricken expression as he stared at the painting matched her own. She didn't know which was worse, that a complete stranger was seeing a painting of her nude or that he was seeing a painting like **that**. Blood rushed to her cheeks and she turned away from the image.

"Please don't look," she said, her voice choked. She didn't know why she felt so shaken. Somehow this was worse than a car bomb. More terrifying, more personal. It threatened the heart of her. And it showed her that whatever war was being waged between the two Coluzzi brothers, they weren't too distracted to scare the shit out of her.

Detective Wilkins put an arm around her and led her from the studio. "Judy, we'll look into this. I'll follow up, I promise you. I will personally do everything I can to nail whoever did this."

"Thanks."

"But I'm not charging the Coluzzis on this evidence, not yet. You're a lawyer, you know that. I'll follow up, but all this is is vandalism."

"I know that."

"And you have to be realistic, even though you're upset. You're gonna want me to dust this whole place for prints and I'm gonna tell you we don't have the manpower for it, and even if we did, it wouldn't yield anything. I'll ask the Coluzzis where they were last night, and there'll be twenty witnesses to swear that they were having three-pound lobsters at The Palm."

Judy knew it was true but her heart beat harder just the same. This was sick and twisted and scary. She didn't want to live here anymore. She never wanted to come home again. She tried to think of a way to fight back. What could she do, legally? There had to be something. "How about a TRO, a restraining order, against the Coluzzis and members of their family? None of them could come within a hundred feet of me, the apartment, or the offices. I could prepare and file it this afternoon."

"A restraining order? Could you get one on these facts? With no proof?" he asked, but his tone told her he knew the answer, and so did she, thinking about it.

"Probably not. No proof that the Coluzzis are behind it. It's the same problem, every time. And the Coluzzis wouldn't heed a court order anyway." She felt herself begin to shake uncontrollably, and Detective Wilkins's arm steadied her.

"Don't let this get to you. Whoever did this, even if it is the Coluzzis, they're playing mind games with you. Don't let them win."

She liked the sound of it, but she still couldn't get in control. The law was no help. Had Frank been right? She found herself missing him suddenly, when she hadn't thought about him in so long.

"Judy, listen," Detective Wilkins said, his voice gentler, "I have a daughter of my own, younger than you, and that's why I told you to get off this case. Not because I'm dirty. I'm just telling you what I'd tell her. No job is worth your life."

Judy almost found a smile. "What do you mean? You're a cop. You get shot at for a living."

Detective Wilkins had no immediate reply.

# 35

It was all Judy could do to act natural in front of The Two Tonys, Mr. DiNunzio, and Penny, lying in a furry but sleeping pile. Judy didn't tell the old men what she'd found at her apartment for fear of worrying them. She had to keep moving forward and concentrate on the task at hand. She skimmed the books on the expert's shelves to get her thoughts back in order. **Low-Speed Automobile Accidents, Basic Collision Investigation and Scene Documentation, The Traffic Accident Investigation Manual, Engineering Analysis of Vehicular Accidents**. Judy's mind kept wandering back to the self-portrait. She folded her arms, aware that she was practically hugging herself, and looked elsewhere. Anywhere but in her own mind.

The room was windowless but immense, appearing bigger because of its walls of white-painted cinderblock. It was actually a converted garage in West Philly; gleaming red tool chests sat against

the far wall, and the near one was lined with text-
books, accident-reconstruction newsletters, and
chrome tools mounted on brown pegboards in
carefully calibrated size order. The back end of the
room contained a built-in work counter with three
black microscopes, a fax, a printer, a Compaq computer with a twenty-one-inch monitor, and file
cabinets, also in white. Fluorescent panels overhead illuminated the room so it was brighter than
most operating rooms.

Judy, Feet, Tony-From-Down-The-Block, and
Mr. DiNunzio watched as Dr. William Wold circled the charred wreck of the Lucias' red truck in
silence. The Two Tonys and Mr. DiNunzio had
taken it upon themselves to steal the junked truck
from the scrapyard, having cut a hole the size of a
whale in the Cyclone fence. They were quite proud
of themselves, but Judy was considering sending
them to bed without their cigars.

She felt terrible that they had done it and somehow worse that she had deniability for it. But once
Tony-From-Down-The-Block had told her what
they'd done, she'd asked him to bring it here on the
flatbed. Judy didn't know if she could still be a good
guy and benefit from a bad act. She was less and less
certain she wanted to be a good guy at all. She used
to think she was hard-wired to be ethical, but her
wires had gotten crossed and were sparking, especially after the self-portrait with the nasty incision.

She gazed at the Lucias' wreck, which rested on

its blackened chassis in the middle of an unwrin-
kled white tarp. The tarp had been placed atop a
spotless white linoleum floor, in order to catch any
debris the truck "shed," as Dr. Wold had
explained. Dr. Wold was turning out to be big on
explanation, a prerequisite for an expert witness.
He had testified on "accident reconstruction" and
"automotive forensics" in 135 cases, which proved
that, in America, there was an expert on everything. For a price.

Dr. Wold made a note on his metal clipboard with
a silver Cross pen and cleared his throat. "You are
quite right, Ms. Carrier," he said finally. "This is, or
was, a Volkswagen Rabbit pickup. These trucks
were manufactured here in Pennsylvania from 1979
through 1983, and were later produced in
Yugoslavia. They came with a diesel or a gasoline
engine, and about eighty of them were produced in
the United States in 1979, then the figure jumped
to 25,000 in 1980, and 33,000 in 1981. This model
is definitely a 1981."

"How do you know all that?" Judy asked, her
voice echoing off the hard surfaces in the large,
open space.

"I looked it up after you called." Dr. Wold
pushed his heavy, steel-framed glasses up his small
nose. An apparently humorless engineer—which
could well be redundant—he wore a fresh white
short-sleeved shirt and pressed navy pants. "It's
not as important to keep information in your head

as much as to know how to retrieve it. I know how to retrieve it."

"I bet," Judy said, just to make him feel that she was participating in the conversation, which was proving completely unnecessary. Dr. Wold didn't care if she participated or not, which The Tonys and Mr. DiNunzio must have instantly perceived, because they remained uncharacteristically quiet.

Dr. Wold walked around the front of the truck, which was bashed in and eyeless. Its hood had buckled almost in two. "You see that the head-lights are gone. This model had the square, four-by-six-inch sealed halogen beams. It also had turn signals to the immediate outer corners of the truck, resembling the 1983 to 1984 Rabbit. Of course the accident has demolished most of the truck's front end; it clearly absorbed most of the impact." Dr. Wold looked up. "I understand it fell off the overpass onto the highway below."

"I think so, but I don't have the police file on it. There must be one."

"Of course there is. I'll obtain it from the AID, the Accident Investigation Division. It's public record. I've already begun to gather articles about the accident, and I will visit the scene. I should be able to reconstruct the way the accident occurred and make you a computer-animated video of it, should you need it for the jury. They are usually quite effective." Dr. Wold made another note. "Of course, as we discussed, I'll also examine the wreck from stem to stern. I provide that as part of my service. Many accident reconstructionists don't."

Judy nodded, and Dr. Wold consulted his notes.

"From my specs, the vehicle was 4.46 meters in length, 1.64 meters in width, and 1.43 meters in height. I can tell you, just eyeballing the wreck, that it's no longer than 3.2 meters at this point, and much of the distortion is at the front, although there is some damage here."

Judy nodded again, but Dr. Wold didn't notice.

"You have asked me to determine if there was evidence of tampering of any sort to the truck, and that I can do. I generally run a complete battery of tests, mostly in products liability cases and wrongful death matters, but I suppose I can do it in a murder case as well."

"I'm sure."

"Of course, you made mention I should determine if the engine had been tampered with, but that would be difficult." Dr. Wold laughed shortly, a loud **ha!**

Judy reddened. It had turned out the truck had been junked without its engine. She hadn't realized it. It was a sore point. "Of course not. No engine. I guess it was sold for parts."

"Or scrap. Either way, cars are rarely junked with engines. They're too valuable."

"I knew that," Judy said. She could hear Feet laugh softly beside her. "You can check if there was a bomb used, can't you?"

Dr. Wold cocked a furry eyebrow. "Of course, but that's not likely, given that the wreck is basically intact."

Judy sighed. This wasn't her day. "Can you test anything, and everything, just to see if there is evidence of any kind of tampering? Maybe the brakes would be messed up. They're still there, right?"

Dr. Wold frowned. "In part."

"Okay, so check that. Check everything. I need to understand everything about how the accident happened. Why do two people drive off an overpass in the middle of the night? We have only the truck to go on."

"As you wish." Dr. Wold nodded. "I should tell you that I will render an expert opinion based on the facts as I see them, not as you wish them to be. I'm not one of those experts who tells you what you paid to hear, do you understand?"

"Understood." Judy hated experts like Dr. Wold. She liked experts who told you what you paid to hear.

"Excellent. Then you won't mind if I tell you that, from my preliminary examination of the wreck, and the information I have retrieved, I find the explanation for this accident fairly obvious, and simple. In fact, it is one of the most common types of traffic accidents, given the conditions."

Judy had to bite her tongue. She couldn't tell him what Pigeon Tony had told her, not in front of the others. She knew the conclusion but had to get the proof. A murder case in reverse.

"Step over to my computer, if you will," Dr. Wold said, and led them to the workstation, with Penny waking to trot happily behind. "Since I had some time this afternoon, I took the liberty of retrieving some of the articles on the accident in question, from the online archives of the Philadelphia newspapers. One of the photos was particularly instructive." He hit a key on his keyboard and the enormous monitor crackled instantly to life.

Judy couldn't help but stare. It was a huge black-and-white photo of a highway overpass, with the guardrail bent out like a bow and the Cyclone fencing ripped apart. The power of the image came from what it didn't show, rather than from what it did; from the fact that Judy knew that the couple who had gone through the gaping hole had crashed to their death. It reminded her sadly of the photo of the **Challenger** astronauts, waving as they boarded the rocket that would kill them.

"The articles report," Dr. Wold was saying, "that the truck flipped over the guardrail, which, as I said, is one of the most common types of highway accidents, particularly in the tri-state area. It crashed onto the underpass below and burst into flame. You can see here," he pointed with the silver pen, "that this guardrail is a vertical concrete bridge rail, an older design. It lacks a rubrail, the double section of W-beam on the top rail, and extra posts, and it has been crash-tested with catastrophic results. No doubt it contributed greatly to the ease with which the truck went over the side."

Judy shuddered.

"In addition, the article reports that the accident took place on January twenty-fifth, and I took the liberty of researching the weather that day." Dr. Wold scrolled down to find the article. The newsprint filled the screen. SOUTH PHILLY COUPLE DEAD IN TRUCK ACCIDENT. Dr. Wold went on, "It was well below freezing most of the afternoon, plummeting to ten degrees at night. It had rained only that morning, in fact, and there had to be icy patches everywhere on the roads, making them treacherous, especially at that hour. I believe it was one in the morning when the accident occurred, according to the article."

Judy nodded.

"This, too, is significant. The Better Sleep Council estimates that about ten thousand auto deaths occur each year due to drowsy drivers. Sleepiness seriously impairs reaction time, awareness of surroundings, and ability to discern potential roadway and traffic conflicts. And the danger is greater if alcohol is involved. A drowsy driver is as potentially dangerous as the drunk driver. The combination is lethal."

"Yo, they weren't drunk," Feet said defensively. "Frank had two beers at a shot, tops. Gemma never touched the stuff. She was a lady."

Dr. Wold's eyes fluttered at the interruption. "I wasn't suggesting your friends were drunk, sir. I was suggesting that if he had even a single drink at that late hour, such as one would have at a wedding, and drove on such an unsafe highway, it is extremely likely that this fairly light truck would meet with catastrophic accident."

Judy wasn't buying. Pigeon Tony had told her different, and she couldn't doubt him now, even with the facts going against her. And the attacks against her were giving her a new insight into why Pigeon Tony had killed Angelo Coluzzi. He was a good man, driven to a bad act. Judy was starting to feel exactly the same way. She was understanding how vendettas got started, and once started, took on a life of their own.

"Your decision, Ms. Carrier?" Dr. Wold asked, interrupting her thoughts. "Do you want me to go ahead, or do you want to save your money? I'm being honest with you. I think my findings won't be greatly different from those of the police."

Judy met his eye evenly. "Get it done, Doctor. Somebody's counting on me."

Part of her knew she was talking about herself, and even Penny looked up, not recognizing the new tone in her mistress's voice.

# 36

It was dark by the time Judy got back to the office, alone except for Penny. The Two Tonys and Mr. D had offered to stay with her while she worked, but she knew they had homes and lives to return to and hied them off. She'd spend the night at a hotel and tell them about the dog when she checked in, but she had a long night of work ahead. Judy had kept Penny for protection and made sure security downstairs was alerted to the fact that she was alone in the office.

She sat at her desk finishing a motion in the Lucia case. The office was empty. The window behind her was a square of black. The only sound was the clicking of her keyboard. She'd had the idea for the motion on the way back; she had decided to ask the court for an expedited trial in the Lucia case, in view of the string of lethal events directed at her and her client. It seemed the only thing Judy could do legally that had any chance of success, and she had been enthused about it when she'd started.

But as she reread the finished product, her mind grew restless and her bare foot tapped constantly. She couldn't remember when she'd eaten last. She hadn't had a good night's sleep in days. She was too antsy even for coffee, and Penny, sensing her mood, watched her alertly, her head between her paws, at the threshold to Judy's office. Judy thought of returning Frank's many calls to her cell phone, but she didn't want to talk to him yet, not in her present mood, and she didn't want him to know what had happened at her apartment. Bennie was unreachable and had left a message she would be at her client's until midnight, in settlement negotiations. Judy considered calling Mary but didn't want to worry her either. Even Murphy wasn't around. It left Judy feeling isolated, cut off, and more homeless than usual.

She tried to focus on the brief and read: **As the attached affidavit will show, it is undisputed that since leaving his preliminary arraignment, Mr. Anthony Lucia and his family have been the target of a riot at the Criminal Justice Center and an attempted murder in the form of a shooting and high-speed pursuit through the streets of South Philadelphia. Mr. Lucia's home and property have been completely . . .**

Judy shifted in the chair. The more she read, the angrier she got. It had barely been a week since she took his case and already there had been a litany of violence against Pigeon Tony, Frank, and her. The cops couldn't do anything until they were all dead. The situation was insane. Out of control. Which was close to the way Judy felt. Beneath the veneer of professionalism, she was off the reservation. Slightly deranged. She realized now that it had been brewing all day, since she'd seen her self-portrait smeared with blood. A hunting knife between her legs.

Judy stopped reading, shot up from her seat, and began to pace. Penny watched from between her paws, her large brown eyes rolling back and forth. The office was small and there wasn't far to pace; even that frustrated her. Her own defense could barely get off the ground, the accident reconstructionist was telling her she couldn't prove murder against Angelo Coluzzi, and the tapes had been incinerated. Jimmy Bello would be testifying that he had heard Pigeon Tony say, "I'm going to kill you." All of it was going down the toilet in a hurry. And the violence against her could end only one way, inevitably, on a case she refused to quit.

Judy paced this way, then that, in endless motion, like the proverbial loose cannon, rolling back and forth on a ship's deck. She paced forward. Wishing she could see her car again. Back. Wishing she could go home again. Forward. Wishing she could do something—**anything**—more effective against the Coluzzis than filing lawsuits and briefs. It may have gotten them angry, it may have distracted them, it may have pitched one against the other, but it wasn't making them **stop**.

Then Judy came to an abrupt stop. She wiped her brow, suddenly damp. Penny lifted her head, sensing something new.

It struck Judy that there was something she could do. Something she hadn't tried yet. It was undoubtedly a little crazy, it was equally danger-ous, but it sure beat writing briefs. She ran to her computer and sent an explanatory e-mail to Ben-nie, then resolved to do it. She had a rented Sat-urn. She had a golden retriever. She felt her sense of humor returning. What else did a girl need?

Judy grabbed her backpack and the dog, caught the elevator downstairs, took the back entrance to her waiting Saturn, and drove off, her eyes on the rearview mirror. Penny sat in the passenger seat, very upright and looking straight through the windshield, the way she always did. Judy always thought of it as the date position, but tonight it felt different. Tonight Penny was riding shotgun.

Judy pointed the Saturn in the usual direction and in no time was threading her way through the streets of South Philly like a professional Italian, instead of an amateur. Like a native she didn't notice the illegal double-parking, the little shops, or the cool brick colors. Girl and puppy were on a mission.

She took a right on McKean Street, traveled down the number street, then took a turn on Rit-ner. The traffic was slight. The beach chairs were empty. The Phillies were playing a double-header, but South Philly watched it on TV. The seats were better and the beer was cheaper. It actually made sense to Judy, now that she had changed citizenship. After all, these were the people who gave the world Michelangelo and Mike Piazza. Maybe they knew what they were doing.

Judy took another left and cruised down the street until she saw the sign. This was the place. The offices were red brick, with slitted anti-burglary windows on either side of plate-glass doors. She could see the large outline of a security guard through the glass, but the guards and crowd of the morning had died down. The coup of Coluzzi had been accomplished.

Judy parked the Saturn across the street from the offices of Coluzzi Construction, cut the ignition, and turned off the lights. She inhaled deeply to slow her breathing and calm her nerves. She was sweating profusely, odd for her, and she pushed clammy bangs from her forehead. She scanned the street, up and down.

It was dark, with only one of the four mercury vapor streetlights working. It made a purplish halo in the humid night air. The street was typically narrow, with room for parking on only one side. There were no residences in this part of South Philly. Small businesses, closed at this hour, lined the street, their lights off and their buildings empty. Nobody was out, but a light was on inside Coluzzi Construction. Given the events of the day,

Marco and his people had to be working late. Judy had hoped as much.

"This is it, Penny," she said aloud, and the puppy looked over and shifted closer to Judy, the better to lean into her shoulder. Penny was the Lean Machine in the car, but Judy never pushed her away, despite the traffic hazard. And tonight she could use the comfort, however furry.

Judy was supposed to be getting up and going inside, but she was having second thoughts. Why had she come here? She'd been planning to go in and confront Marco Coluzzi. Tell him to call off the dogs. Convince him to let the jury decide the case. Explain to him that if they got her off the case, or killed her, another lawyer would take her place. God, there were hundreds of them, everybody knew that.

Judy set her jaw. She had intended to look the man in the eye and confront him. If Bennie was negotiating a settlement, so could Judy. Lawyers convinced. Cajoled. Compromised. Wheedled and manipulated. And she had a bargaining chip. In return for Marco's stopping the violence, Judy would withdraw her lawsuit. It was costing the Coluzzis big money, and the loss of the waterfront project was only the beginning. She could make that end. The bleeding would stop on both sides. And if anything happened to her, her laptop would tell everybody where she had gone and who had done it.

Cold comfort. Very cold. Judy flashed on the morgue and felt the chill of refrigeration wreathing the black body bags.

It seemed like a crazy plan now that it had become real, and she sat in the car in front of the building, reconsidering. Judy was unarmed; Marco was not. She had a fuzzy puppy; he had uniformed guards. He may have been a Wharton grad, but he could still shoot her and dump her in the concrete foundation of a shopping center. She could be a Blockbuster Video by morning. And that was the best-case scenario. There was always the hunting knife. Eeek.

Judy scratched Penny behind the left ear, where her fur had matted in clumps, and told herself she wasn't stalling. Puppies needed quality time. It was so quiet she heard the digital clock tick to 11:50 and she sighed deeply. She should go back to the office, erase the last will and testament on her laptop, and talk to Bennie, who would be back soon. She would file her motion for an expedited trial, find a hotel room, and feel better in the morning.

Judy had no business here. It wasn't just a crazy idea, it was a stupid idea. She'd be lucky to get the hell out of here with her life. She reached for the ignition and was about to switch it on when the skinny street filled with light. The bright high beams of a dark sedan, which was roaring suddenly down the street.

Judy frowned in confusion. The car would crash

at that speed. It was barreling her way. She reached for the dog in shock.

The sedan screeched to a stop in front of Coluzzi Construction. Reflexively Judy looked for the license plate, but there wasn't one. The car was big and dark. Its four doors sprang open simultaneously and four men in ski masks jumped out, carrying huge assault rifles. Judy's lips parted in horror. Her heart pounded in her ears.

Suddenly the front doors of the construction office exploded. The sound was deafening and thundered in Judy's chest. Orange flame flared to the sky. Smoke clouded the entrance. Plate glass fell to the sidewalk in a shattered sheet. It looked like a movie scene but Judy could smell the burning in the air. Penny yelped in fear and began barking. Judy grabbed the dog's muzzle to silence her. She couldn't believe what she was seeing.

The four men charged through the smoke and rushed over the broken glass of the office entrance. The lights blinked twice, then went off inside, plunging the place into darkness. Rapid **pop-pop-pops** like firecrackers sounded from inside the building. Gunshots, a fusillade of them, all coming at once.

Judy could only imagine what was happening inside. Had they come to kill Marco? Was John in one of the ski masks? Would John go so far as to **kill his own brother**? Judy knew they were bad guys, but this was true evil. She had to do something.

She dived to the car floor for her backpack, dug inside for her cell phone, found it, and hit the 911 button. She shoved Penny down so the dog wouldn't get shot. Judy's eyes were glued to the entrance, which was still smoking when three men ran out through the fog and jumped back into the sedan, which took off with a scream.

The operator picked up but Judy couldn't wait for the may-I-help-you or whatever they said. "Please, come quick! The offices of Coluzzi Construction, in South Philly. There's been an explosion! A shooting! Hurry!"

"Did you see the shooter, miss? Can you give me any description?"

"There were four of them. They wore masks. Hurry! Come. Send an ambulance!"

"How many did you say?" asked the dispatcher, but Judy held the phone to her ear and leaped from the Saturn. Maybe she could do some good. She didn't know CPR, but the dispatcher could talk her through it.

She raced across the street, put her hand up to screen the smoke, and ran over the broken glass. She fell once on the slippery shards, then got up and darted inside the building. She found herself in a darkened and destroyed reception area that had been intact only seconds earlier. All she could see was that the front counter was splintered and smoldering from the blast. A huge framed picture on the wall had been blown to smithereens.

"Don't shoot! I'm here to help!" Judy screamed, but realized in the next second that it wasn't necessary. The reception area was deadly silent. The smoke on the tile floor was lifting. Judy felt something at her feet and looked down.

It was a security guard, his stilled eyes staring wide in death. Gunshot wounds strafed his chest, shredding his blue uniform in a soaked red line. Judy's hand flew to cover her mouth and she forced herself to move on.

Ahead lay a dark, smoke-filled corridor, and she ran a hand along the wall for guidance. In her path lay two more bodies, in uniform. Guards. Judy scrambled from one to the next, pushing up their tight cuffs and feeling for a pulse. Their wrists were still warm with life, but their pulses had ebbed away. Three men dead. How could this be? It was awful. Judy felt her gorge rise but willed it back down. She couldn't lose control now.

"Marco!" she shouted through the smoke, without knowing why. Yesterday she had wished him dead. Today she wanted to save his life. She ran down the corridor and heard moaning when she reached an office at the end of the hall.

It was large, dark, windowless. Judy couldn't see anything but she guessed the desk would be on the back wall, with Marco behind it. A moan confirmed it and she ran in its direction, then fell to her knees and fumbled for the body lying on the floor. The outline of Marco Coluzzi was faintly visible. But it had stopped moaning. Wetness gurgled dark from the corner of his mouth. Judy could feel it hot under her fingers. Blood.

She went into autopilot, tucking the cell phone under her ear and pressing rhythmically on Marco's chest. "Tell me what to do!" she called to the 911 dispatcher, but the connection was breaking up. She pumped frantically up and down. A siren blared nearby, joined by another. They were on the way. They had gotten her message.

"Marco, Marco!" she called out, but no sounds came from the body on the floor. She leaned on his chest with all her might, let off, then did it again. He still wore a knotted tie, even at this hour, and somehow that touched her. But he wasn't coming around. She couldn't save him.

"Operator, what do I do?" she called, panicky, but the dispatcher's voice vanished into static.

"No!" Judy dropped the cell phone and gathered Marco in her arms. His head fell back instantly, and Judy could see the glistening black blood staining his neck. His shirt was soaked. He had lost so much blood. He was bleeding to death. It was her fault. She had pitted one brother against the other. She never realized it would come to this. She should have known.

"Help!" Judy shrieked, cradling her enemy in her arms, but she knew they would come too late. He was already gone and she couldn't do anything but hold him.

"No! Please! Stop! This has to stop!" she heard herself cry out and she didn't know if she was talking about the blood or the killing or the vendetta. And Judy was relieved when she felt the warm tears fill her eyes and stream down her face, because they told her she was still a human being, with a heart, a conscience, and a soul, and nobody could take that away from her, least of all the poor man who was dying in her very arms.

The next hours blurred paramedics and gurneys and uniformed police asking her questions. There were Mobile Crime techs in jumpsuits and booties and Dr. Patel from the coroner's office, acknowledging her with a grim nod, and then there was yellow crime-scene tape and bodies being carried out in bags. Then came TV cameras and klieg lights and anchorpeople in orange makeup and Judy's cell phone ringing nonstop.

She said "no comment" to anybody who didn't wear a badge, and she must have said it at least a hundred times. Someone handed her a paper towel, and she wiped her face with it. When she pulled it away, it was streaked with blood redder than any oil paint.

Judy bore up under all of it and answered the police questions numbly, describing to Detective Wilkins, who came later, what she had seen and why she had been there, racking her brain for details of the sedan and the men and anything that could help him prove who did it, though they both knew it had to be John Coluzzi. He didn't make her go down to the Roundhouse because Bennie arrived and scared him and the press off, scooping Judy up like a lost child and hurrying her back to the Saturn and sitting her in the driver's seat next to a completely agitated Penny, who became frantic sniffing the blood on Judy's clothes.

"How are you?" Bennie asked, kneeling down in front of the open door on the driver's side, so that she was eye level with Judy. "Do you want to go to a hospital?"

"No, not at all. I'm fine. I really am fine." Saying it seemed to make it so, and Judy could feel herself coming back to herself, in a way. Penny scrambled over and licked her face. Judy laughed, despite the situation. "Dogs are good."

"Dogs are essential." Bennie grinned. "Now, I want you to get out of here. Do you want to stay at my place tonight?"

"No, I have a hotel reservation and everything. I'm fine. I really am fine."

"A hotel? You want me to take the dog? She can play with mine. Have a sleepover."

Judy considered it. It only made sense. It was in the best interests of the golden. "No. I want her with me."

Bennie laughed. "Meet me in the office at nine. We'll talk then. Take the back way in. I'm hiring two new guards downstairs and two upstairs, every day until this trial is over."

"Good. Thanks."

"Now get out of here. Here comes the press."
Bennie peered over the hood of the Saturn.
Anchorpeople were advancing, with bubble
microphones and whirring videocameras, and
Bennie fended them off like a mother grizzly. Her
concern remained with Judy. "Are you okay to
drive?"

"Okay enough to lose those clowns," Judy said,
and Penny assumed the shotgun position.

"Then go, girl!" Bennie stood, rising to meet the
press, as Judy gunned the Saturn's engine, backed
out of the space, and took off, leaving the orange
makeup, the blue uniforms, the yellow tape, and
all the other colors behind.

Judy had lost the last of the two press cars
twenty minutes later, mainly because their pursuit
was only half-hearted. She switched on the radio
news, KYW 1060, and it was all Coluzzis, all the
time. The big story was at the crime scene and
apparently the home of Marco Coluzzi. Judy sym-
pathized with Marco's wife and small children.
John Coluzzi couldn't be reached for comment.

Judy felt a wave of guilt. She should have foreseen this. She had underestimated John's ruthless-
ness. Killing his own brother. Three other men
dead. Innocent men. Their blood stained her
hands and clothes. Judy stopped at a red light but
didn't notice when it changed. A van driver
honked her into motion, and she cruised down

Broad Street toward the hotel. Exhaustion was catching up with her, as was sadness. Would the killing end now? Would it only get worse? Would John assume power? The questions bewildered her.

She cruised to another traffic light, barely concentrating on her driving, letting her thoughts run free, and they brought her to an insight. The Coluzzis had waged a war against her and had pushed her to the extremes of irrational behavior, namely driving over to the Coluzzi offices to confront Marco. So she was no different from Pigeon Tony. If they had pushed her as far as they had pushed him, killing someone she loved, would she have killed in return? It was at least conceivable, but she hadn't known that before. It made her understand what she had been wondering about from the beginning of the case. Bennie had asked her to decide whether Pigeon Tony was innocent or guilty.

Well, she had decided.

He was innocent.

The knowledge, or at least the certainty, brought Judy a sort of peace. The events of the day, as heinous as they were, ebbed away. She rolled down the windows and drove through the quiet city in the dark of night. In time the air cooled and a light rain blew up, dotting the windshield, and she drove to the sound of the beating wipers, gliding past the hotel. She didn't think twice. Didn't stop to go back.

Judy took a left onto the expressway and put on the cruise control. There was no traffic at this hour. The decorative lights outlining the boathouses on Boathouse Row reflected in wiggly lines on the Schuylkill River, its onyx surface disturbed by the shower. Judy turned smoothly on the curve past the West River Drive, heading out of the city.

It was a straight shot out the expressway to Route 202 and off at Route 401, winding through cool, forested streets. She slowed to permit a herd of deer to leap nimbly over a post-and-rail fence and smiled at Penny's astonished reaction. In time the streets turned into lonely country roads without stoplights or streetlights. There was nothing to guide Judy but the stars and she couldn't navigate by them at all, though her father had tried to teach her. But the Saturn found its way through Chester County to the abandoned springhouse, navigating by something much more reliable than the stars, though an equally natural phenomenon.

The human heart.

Judy pulled up on the wet grass, but Frank was already there to meet her, rushing toward the car and lifting her into his arms, warm and so powerful. She didn't have to say a word because he was kissing the blood and pain from her face and soul, and when she asked him finally if she could spend the night, he said:

**"I thought you'd never ask."**

# BOOK FIVE

*La massima giustizia è la massima
ingiustizia.*
Extreme justice is often extreme injustice.

> —Italian proverb

Justice must follow its regular course.

> —BENITO MUSSOLINI,
> to a journalist, December 10, 1943

"Calm down, old man! You will see, it will
be nothing at all."

> —A member of the firing squad to one of the
> Fascists he would execute on January 11, 1944,
> among them Mussolini's
> son-in-law, Count Galeazzo Ciano

# 37

The piazza in Tony's village was small, a single square of gray cobblestones bordered by the church, a bakery, and a butcher shop. Beside the butcher's on the corner squatted a tiny coffee shop where Tony took his little son Frank every Friday at four o'clock, early so as not to ruin his dinner, as Silvana had asked. Tony didn't mind occasionally being bossed around by his wife, especially as it concerned their child. Silvana was a devoted mother, tempering her rules with tenderness, and for that reason Tony felt especially guilty that he was sitting outside the coffee shop having an espresso with a two-year-old.

"Espresso is not good for young children," Tony whispered, as if Silvana would hear him, even with the house kilometers away. His guilt didn't stop him from his practice, however, and, weather permitting, father and son occupied the front table, sipping their coffees and watching the townspeople walk by. "Take little sips, son."

"Si, Papa." Frank nodded, held the tiny white demitasse in two sets of chubby child's fingers, and concentrated mightily to bring the cup to his little lips. Tony watched his son with pride and pleasure in even this small act, taking in the soft fringe of Frank's black eyelashes as he looked down, the rosiness of his cheeks, and the pinkness of his lips. The summer sun, low in the sky now that the farmer's work was done, shone on Frank's coal-black hair, finding strands of earth brown and even dark gold. Tony marveled that he never grew tired of looking at his son, drinking in all the details of him, even when Frank made the face he always did at his first taste of the hot coffee.

"Is hot, Papa," Frank said, lowering the cup partway to his saucer.

"What do we do then?" Tony asked, for he was teaching Frank the manners of gentlemen in society.

"Watch, Papa." Frank formed a little circle with his lips, not easy for him, and blew across the surface of the hot espresso. "See?"

"Yes. I see. Very good. Just like the wind. Pretend you are setting a boat sailing across a large, blue ocean," Tony said. He had never seen a boat, much less a large blue ocean, but he hoped his son would someday leave the farm and see the ocean, for it wasn't very far away. Unlike his own father, Tony wanted his son to grow up better than he, to go to school, to learn to read and write, and associate with city people without feeling like their servant. "Very good job, son."

"See, Papa." Frank blew so hard he made ripples in the tin cup. "Do you? See?"

"Very good. Blow gentler, son," Tony said, keeping the harshness from his tone, for he knew children needed praise more than they needed lessons on coffee drinking or good manners.

Frank stopped blowing, his face now quite red. "Can I drink?"

"Yes, yes. Good job."

Just then Signora Milito walked by, carrying her brasciole from the butcher shop in a cloth bag on one arm and her heavy purse of needlepoint in the other arm. She was a wealthy woman, with her face made up and expensively powdered, but she was kind, and she paused at the table and smiled at Tony and Frank. "Good day, gentlemen," she said, which was what she always said.

"Good day to you, Signora Milito," Tony replied, and both adults waited while Frank lowered his demitasse slowly to his saucer. It was a long descent for a two-year-old, and only after the cup had been nestled in place did Frank look up eagerly.

"Good day, Signora Milito," he said in perfect imitation of his father, and Signora Milito nodded with approval.

"No **biscotti** today, for such a good boy?" she asked, and Tony smiled.

"Not today. Today is Frank's birthday, and Silvana has a special dinner planned, with cake. We mustn't ruin his appetite."

"A birthday!" Signora Milito's purse slipped down her arm as she reached over and pinched Frank's soft cheek. "Happy birthday, little one!"

"Thank you," Frank said, pleasing Tony.

Signora Milito was equally delighted. "And what a lucky boy you are, to have a cake on your birthday. Your mother must have saved her sugar rations."

"She did," Tony said. The whole family had saved for the cake, for with Italy entering the war, so many things had been impossible to get. The coffee shops produced only the watered-down coffee they now drank and NO COFFEE signs hung on many espresso machines. Gasoline was short, and in the city a special permit was required for use of the cars. Meat could be sold only on Thursdays and Fridays. Farmers like Tony often had no electric light or running water. The telephone worked only when it wanted to. Everybody said soap, fats, rice, bread, and pasta were next to be restricted. Tony couldn't imagine it. Italy without pasta?

"Have you read the notice, posted on the kiosk near the church?" Signora Milito asked, but Tony shook his head, no. He didn't add that he couldn't read, though part of him suspected Signora Milito knew as much and was saving his face by informing him. "It says **Il Duce** needs our copper, from our houses. Pans, pots, tools, whatever you have. They need it for the war effort."

"Then we must turn it over," Tony said, in case anyone was listening. You could never be sure. The Blackshirts held absolute power, and those who spoke against the regime were as good as dead, the massacre of partisans well known. Tony, who hadn't been conscripted because of his feet, thought Italy was fighting only to serve Mussolini's vainglorious needs and abhorred the war. Nevertheless he said, "We will do what is necessary according to **Il Duce**."

"We must." Signora Milito nodded without enthusiasm, and Tony knew from their encoded conversations that she loathed the Blackshirts as much as he did. Signora Milito and her family had been prominent in Veramo for generations before the Fascists came. Everything that went on in Veramo, she knew. "Well, I must be on my way. Don't let the boy drink too much coffee."

"I won't. Don't tell Silvana, should you see her."

"It's our secret," Signora Milito said, and with a wink, hobbled away on her dark shoes.

"**Ciao**, Signora Milito," Tony called after her, and didn't add that it was not only their secret, but a secret many of the townspeople shared, a vast but benevolent conspiracy.

The piazza began to fill with townspeople, strolling to this store or that, or hurrying home to change into their best clothes for the **passeggiata**. A group of Blackshirts rushed by, black tassels on their corded caps jumping with each step, their leather boots clattering across the cobblestones.

Fascist presence was conspicuous in Abruzzo, with war wounded and party officials returning from the Ethiopian and Russian fronts. One of the passing Blackshirts caught Tony's eye, then quickly looked away.

It gave Tony a start. Who was that man? Tony knew him from somewhere. Then he remembered, with a bolt of fear.

The day Tony was beaten, the day of the Torneo. The man was one of his assailants. He had been on the dais, whispering into Coluzzi's ear. He was Coluzzi's lieutenant. Tony found himself rising to his feet at the table, his eyes trained on the Blackshirt, and he felt as if he were back on the narrow vias of Mascoli, writhing like a whipped dog.

"Papa?" Frank asked. "Papa?"

Tony looked down and the sight of the child brought him back to the present. He had a son; he had won Silvana. But his thoughts raced ahead. If Coluzzi's right-hand man had returned, had Coluzzi himself? It was likely. Holy God. Coluzzi was still a threat. Bad things had happened to the Lucias when Coluzzi was home; directly after Tony and Silvana's engagement, but before Coluzzi had gone to the war in Ethiopia, Tony had found his beloved pony gutted in the pasture one morning, and his first car had been set afire one night. Tony knew that Coluzzi had done these criminal deeds, but he was too terrified to tell the police, who were all good Fascists. The crimes had stopped when Coluzzi had gone. But was he back? Reassigned? In Mascoli? In **Veramo**? **Here?**

"Papa?" asked the child, his round brown eyes clouded with worry, and as much as Tony wanted to, he couldn't dismiss his anxiety. Suddenly it filled him, setting him trembling.

"We must go, son." Tony reached for his wallet, pulled out the lira, and left it crumpled on the table. "Come, now. We go."

"But Papa, my coffee. Is not all gone."

"We'll have coffee at home." Tony came around the table and took Frank's hand as the child slid obediently out of the chair. "Special for your birthday."

"At home?" the boy asked, bewildered. "Mama says no coffee." Frank raised his arms to be lifted from the seat, and Tony grabbed him more quickly than usual. The mention of Silvana's name had reached his heart. **At home?** Could Coluzzi be back? The fear in Tony's stomach was undeniable.

"We must go," was all Tony could say, his voice unaccountably choked, and he carried Frank along to his bicycle, set him on the middle bar where he always sat, jumped on the bike and pedaled off.

"Whee!" Frank squealed, delighted at the unaccustomed speed, but Tony kept a steadying hand on the boy's chest. Tony's fear powered his feet. His thoughts were on Silvana. This would be the perfect time for Coluzzi to strike. Everybody in town knew that Tony and the boy had coffee on this day, at this time. In fact, it was the only time all week Silvana was alone. And it was the boy's birthday. Tony picked up the pace, as fast as safety allowed.

They pedaled through the town, dodging farmers, cars, horses, carts, and other bicycles, into the countryside, with Tony fueled by sheer terror. Tony's breath came in labored gulps. His legs began to ache. Sweat dampened his forehead.

The child screamed gleefully on the middle bar. "Yiii!"

Tony avoided each large rock as the paved road turned to dirt, swerving dangerously, and one time Frank yelped in fright. Then came another rock, and another yelp. Frank was becoming frightened, sensing his father's mood, and with a child's wisdom realizing that something was going very wrong. His hands reached up for his father, and Tony held fast to him. The bicycle barreled ahead, flying past a stray sheep, on a momentum of its own. Silvana was alone, unprotected. Silvana. Coluzzi. Tony's feet raced around the pedals. Silvana. Coluzzi. Silvana. Coluzzi.

"Papa! Stop! Papa!" On the bar, Frank was crying fully now.

"Hang on!" Tony called to him. He couldn't stop now; the road led to home.

"Papa! Stop! Please! I said **please**!"

"Hold on!" Tony yelled, as the bicycle turned down the road to their farm, and as soon as he got home in his sight he found a reserve of strength and pedaled faster. The ache vanished from his thighs and the sweat evaporated from his brow. Even his child's screams seemed far away. Home. Silvana. Coluzzi.

They zoomed toward the house, and when they reached the front door, Tony slowed the bicycle on the soft grass, scooped Frank in his arms as he let the bike fall, and ran with the boy crying under his arm into the house.

"Silvana!" he cried, charging over the threshold with the sobbing child.

"Papa! Papa!" Frank wailed, squirming from Tony's arms to collapse in a crying heap on the floor.

"Silvana!" Tony looked wildly around the living room, gaily decorated with flowers and homemade notes for Frank's birthday. The lace tablecloth had been put out, and a white cake sat in the middle of the table with noisemakers, pieces of nougat, and a large wrapped present. Silvana had readied everything for Frank's celebration, to surprise him when they came home, according to plan. But she was nowhere in sight. Tony's heart was seized with a fear he had never known.

"Silvana!" he screamed, the sound so unaccustomed coming from the gentle farmer that baby Frank began to cry even harder, covering his ears in horror amid his birthday decorations.

"Silvana!" Tony ran to the kitchen. No Silvana. He ran to the bedroom and through the small house, yelling. "Silvana!" He ran outside to the pasture.

"Silvana!" Only the sheep looked over, peering

with their slitted eyes. He ran to the olive groves, hill after hill of flowering trees, their fragrance usually intoxicating to Tony. But not tonight. Where **was** she?

"Silvana!" he bellowed, cupping his mouth with his hands, but only her name came back, a hollow echo. "**Silvana!**"

Tony's thoughts were panicky. Where had she gone? She had few friends, her sister had moved and she had lost both parents. Silvana never went anywhere alone. What woman did? He racked his brain. What hadn't he checked? The pigeon loft? Perhaps she was visiting them. She liked them as much as he did.

Tony sprinted for the loft and threw open the wooden door. Birds fluttered on their perches at the intrusion, sending pinfeathers into the air. No Silvana. Tony ran from the loft for the house, but then he heard the sound of the horses neighing.

He stopped in his tracks.

The stable. It was the only place he hadn't checked, for Silvana never went in there. She was afraid of horses. Still. Tony ran for the stable and yanked open the rolling door.

The only sight worse than the one before him was the one behind him.

"Mama?" asked the boy, his eyes wide with shock at the body that lay lifeless in the hay.

# 38

"All rise!" announced the court crier, and every-one packing the largest courtroom in the Criminal Justice Center rose as one. "All rise for the Honorable Russell Vaughn!"

Judy stood up next to Pigeon Tony, dressed in a dark blue suit that fit him better than the last one and matched her regulation courtroom wear, with navy pumps. In the four intervening months, she had sprung for a boring new wardrobe and her first pair of lawyer pumps. In her view, it wasn't progress.

Judge Vaughn, a tall man, gray-haired and ruddy-faced, whose voluminous judicial robes couldn't conceal the power of his frame, swept into the courtroom from a pocket door, ascended the walnut dais, and took his leather seat as if he were born to it. In fact he was. His father had been a common pleas court judge before him, and both were equally respected. Judy considered his assignment to this case a good sign.

"Good morning, all," he said. "Please sit down. Court is now in session in the matter of Commonwealth versus Lucia. This trial has been expedited on request of defense counsel, and it's already taken two weeks to pick a jury, so let's not waste any more time." Judge Vaughn glanced at the bailiff. "Please bring them in, Bailiff."

Judy watched as the jury filed in through another pocket door and took their seats, in bucket swivel chairs of black vinyl. The jury consisted of two rows of seven, including alternates; there were an equal number of men and women. Judy felt lucky to have gotten five people over age sixty-five onto the panel, in the hope that they'd be sympathetic to Pigeon Tony. But since it was a case of murder in the first, they had been death-qualified. So as sympathetic as they seemed, every one of them had sworn that he or she would be able to sentence Pigeon Tony to death.

Judy gazed at them now, one by one, behind a sleek panel of walnut veneer. In time she would come to know their faces and they hers, in the oddly remote familiarity that occurred in every jury trial. But right now the jurors sat as stiff as the courtroom furniture, avoiding meeting anyone's eyes, almost blending in with the beige acoustic panels on the wall, a wool carpet of a graphite color, and walnut pews of the gallery. The only odd element of the courtroom's modern decor was the expanse of bulletproof glass that separated the gallery from the bar of court.

Judy glanced back at the gallery through the clear shield. In this case, security would be in order. The two guards Bennie had hired sat solidly in the front row; they had become Judy's new best friends, shadowing her everywhere, advising her when it was time to change hotels. They'd even followed her to her few visits with Frank, and between the guards and Pigeon Tony, ensured that the affair remained unhappily chaste. Judy sought Frank out in the gallery, and he was sitting in the front row next to Bennie, Mr. DiNunzio, Tony-From-Down-The-Block, and Feet, wearing new glasses. Judy tried to catch Frank's eye, but he was watching the Coluzzi side of the aisle.

John Coluzzi, in a black suit and tie, sat on the right side of the gallery with his meaty arm around his mother, who was also dressed in black, next to Fat Jimmy Bello. No one had been charged in the death of Marco, and the police said they still had no leads. Like Frank, Judy found herself glaring at John, unable to look away. Flashing on the image of Marco, dying in her arms. Judy hadn't been able to get far even in her lawsuits against them, without a live witness in Kevin McRea, but he was still nowhere to be found.

"Let's get started. Mr. D.A., Mr. Santoro?" Judge Vaughn was saying, and Judy turned around. The judge was slipping on a pair of black reading glasses, with half frames. "Your opening statement?"

"Yes, sir." Joe Santoro drew himself up, buttoned his well-made Italian suit at the middle, and strode to the podium facing the jury. His dark hair glistened in moussed waves, and his fingernails shone with nail polish, but his self-important grooming belied the time he had to have spent on case preparation. Judy knew it had matched hers, and she picked up her pen to take notes. The Commonwealth had turned over its evidence, which was predictably overwhelming. Given the evidence, the case was his to lose.

"Ladies and gentlemen of the jury," he began, "my name is Joseph Santoro, and I represent the people of the Commonwealth. I'll keep this short and sweet, because I prefer to let my witnesses do my talking for me, as you will see."

Santoro took a breath. "In my view, lying at the core of every murder case is a simple story. This case is no exception. This case is a story about defendant Anthony Lucia, a man who has hated Angelo Coluzzi for sixty years and has harbored malice against him, going back all the way to when they both were young men in Italy. The reason for this hatred? Defendant Lucia mistakenly believed that Angelo Coluzzi killed his wife sixty years ago and even killed his son and daughter-in-law in a traffic accident. Of course, this is pure fantasy, the imaginings of an angry man, who lives alone, with nothing but his malice."

Next to Judy, Pigeon Tony emitted a low growl, but she put a hand on his to calm him. She had warned him to behave during the trial, as she had Frank and The Tonys. She couldn't afford another courtroom war between the Lucias and the Coluzzis. It would play right into Santoro's opening argument. Santoro had been clever to bring the vendetta into the case, recasting it as one-way grudge, or pure malice.

"Defendant Lucia's hatred for Angelo Coluzzi has been brewing for all of these years. And the defendant carried his malice with him when he immigrated to America, where Mr. Coluzzi built a successful construction company in his adopted homeland. In contrast, the defendant's construction company, essentially a one-man bricklaying business, failed to thrive, feeding his hatred for and jealousy of Angelo Coluzzi. It was then that the defendant began planning to kill an innocent man."

Pigeon Tony's mouth dropped open in offense, but Judy squeezed his hand, though she was equally outraged. None of what Santoro was saying was true, but she couldn't disprove it. The proof of Silvana Lucia's murder was long gone, and the accident reconstructionist who had examined the Lucias' charred pickup had reached a disappointing conclusion: **Negligent driving, poor weather conditions, and a substandard guardrail resulted in the lethal accident involving the Lucia family on January 25.** The report also noted that the crash had killed the Lucias instantly, and found no evidence of tampering with the truck, as only residues of engine oil, diesel fuel, and gasoline appeared, not unusual in accidents involving construction vehicles.

"Acting on this mistaken belief, defendant Lucia took his brutal revenge, and after lying in wait for decades, killed Angelo Coluzzi on April seventeenth. That morning, which was a Friday, defendant Lucia entered the back room of a pigeon-racing club that both men belonged to. Angelo Coluzzi was inside the room alone. You will hear that a fellow club member was sitting nearby and heard the defendant shout at Mr. Coluzzi, 'I'm going to kill you.'" Santoro paused for dramatic effect, and the jury looked predictably surprised. One of them, an older woman in the front, glanced at Pigeon Tony, then looked away.

"You will hear, ladies and gentlemen of the jury, that this same club member heard a scream, then a crash coming from the room, apparently the sound of a bookshelf falling over. He ran into the room. Too late, unfortunately. Defendant Lucia had gone into that room, attacked Angelo Coluzzi, and broken the poor man's neck with his bare hands."

Judy set down her pen. The opening worried

her, if she wasn't already worried enough. She had prepared for something more conventional and had outlined a complete defense, described witness by witness in black notebooks. But Bennie had warned her to try the case that went in, from word one. She struggled not to panic.

"By the end of this case," Santoro said, "the Commonwealth will have proven beyond a reasonable doubt that the defendant murdered Angelo Coluzzi and that he is guilty of murder in the first degree. That is how the story of this murder case will end. It can by no means be considered a happy ending, for it will never bring Angelo Coluzzi back to his loving wife and family. Nor will it be an unhappy ending. What it will be is an ending that serves justice. Thank you." Santoro left the podium, crossed to the prosecutor's table, and sat down.

Judge Vaughn looked at Judy. "Your turn, Ms. Carrier," he said, and nodded.

Judy stood up and took the podium, after a thoughtful moment. "Ladies and gentlemen, my name is Judy Carrier, and I stand before you to defend Anthony Lucia. I will keep it short as well, because I want you to be clear on the one and only question in this case, which is this: Has the Commonwealth proved beyond a reasonable doubt that Anthony Lucia is guilty of murdering Angelo Coluzzi? The Commonwealth must prove that answer beyond a reasonable doubt, and that is the one question before you. I heard nothing about such proof in Mr. Santoro's opening. And proof is the only thing that matters."

Judy came out from behind the podium and, when Judge Vaughn didn't rebuke her, leaned on it. "As you listen to the evidence that follows, please keep your focus on the question at hand. Has the Commonwealth proved beyond a reasonable doubt that Anthony Lucia is guilty of murdering Angelo Coluzzi? And I submit to you, the answer to that question will be no. My client, Anthony Lucia, is not guilty of murder. And finding him not guilty is the only just ending to this case." Judy looked at the jurors for a moment, but they seemed attentive, which was the best she could hope for. She left the podium and sat down.

"Call your first witness, Mr. Santoro," Judge Vaughn called out, and Santoro gestured to the court officer through the bulletproof glass to the gallery. Judy half turned, expecting to see Detective Wilkins or Jimmy Bello getting to his feet, but entering the courtroom through the double doors at the back was an elderly, frail woman she didn't recognize. Her face was wrinkled and her cheeks gaunt behind plastic glasses with upside-down frames. Her hair was as poofy as Mrs. DiNunzio's.

"The prosecution calls Millie D'Antonio to the stand, Your Honor."

Judy didn't recognize her name, but the witness

list had been endless, covering most of South Philly. Judy had interviewed as many as she could and only vaguely recollected a Millie D'Antonio. She leaned over to Pigeon Tony. "Who is that?"

"She live next door," he whispered, and gave the woman a happy wave as she walked by. Judy forced herself not to grab his hand away, but Pigeon Tony kept smiling at his neighbor even as she was sworn in and took the stand. She wore a flowered dress with a worn red cardigan over the top, and Judy remembered speaking with her. But why would Santoro call her? Their conversation had been innocuous.

"Mrs. D'Antonio," Santoro began, "please tell the jury where you live."

"I live next to Pigeon Tony." Mrs. D'Antonio's hand trembled as she adjusted the microphone. "I mean, Anthony Lucia." She smiled apologetically.

"And how long have you lived there?"

"All my life. It was my mother's house. When she passed, she left it to me, may she rest." The woman crossed herself, and Judy caught the jury's approving reaction.

Santoro nodded. "How long has Mr. Lucia lived next door to you, if you know?"

"I lived next to him since he came to this country, I guess. A long time ago. Seventy years ago, maybe sixty."

Judy half rose. "Objection, Your Honor. This is completely irrelevant to this case."

Santoro looked up at Judge Vaughn. "Your Honor, the relevance of her testimony will become clear in just a few questions."

"Overruled," Judge Vaughn said. "Better make good on that, Mr. Santoro."

Santoro held up a finger. "Mrs. D'Antonio, have you ever had conversations with Mr. Lucia about his late wife?"

Judy half rose again. "Objection, relevance, Your Honor," she said, but Santoro barely waited for her to finish.

"It's relevant to the defendant's motive, Your Honor."

"Overruled." Vaughn eyed the lawyers. "But this fighting stops now, counsel. There are no cameras in this courtroom. This is too slow a start on testimony for me. Let's get on with it."

"Yes, sir," Santoro said, then addressed Mrs. D'Antonio. "Now, as you were saying, what was the substance of these conversations?"

Judy wished she could object. What conversations? When? But Vaughn wouldn't like it, and a hostile judge could be lethal to a defense. It was always a choice between not pissing off a judge and not sending a client to the death chamber. To Judy's mind the Constitution guaranteed rights to the defendant, not the judge. But she had to be practical.

"The substance?" Mrs. D'Antonio asked, confused.

"What were the conversations about? Take the most recent one, for example. The last conversation you had with the defendant, which was six months before Angelo Coluzzi was murdered, I believe."

Objection, leading, Judy wished she could say. But she was picking her battles.

Mrs. D'Antonio nodded. "They were about Angelo Coluzzi."

"And what did Mr. Lucia say about Angelo Coluzzi?"

"That he hated him, and that Angelo Coluzzi killed his wife and his son."

Judy sat stoically. Pigeon Tony looked unsurprised. It was undoubtedly the truth, but it didn't look good at all for the defense. And Santoro kept casting the hatred as one-way. Should she do anything about it? It was risky.

"Mrs. D'Antonio, was that the only time Mr. Lucia said those words to you, or words to that effect?"

"No, he said it all the time. Everybody knew it. He made no bones about it."

"So it is your sworn testimony that Mr. Lucia said that Angelo Coluzzi killed his wife, son, and daughter-in-law?"

"Well, yeah."

Santoro paused. "Mrs. D'Antonio, to the best of your knowledge, have any of these alleged murders ever been prosecuted by police, either in Italy or in the United States?"

Pigeon Tony started to speak, but Judy shot up instantly. If Santoro wanted to prove it wasn't murder, he'd have to do it another way. "Objection, no foundation."

"Sustained," Judge Vaughn ruled, and Judy sat back down.

Santoro nodded quickly. "I have no further questions. Your witness, Ms. Carrier."

Judy was on her feet, fueled by an anger she couldn't hide from the jury. She couldn't let this testimony go unanswered, even for a minute. "Mrs. D'Antonio, do you know anything about the events of Friday, April seventeenth, the morning on which this alleged murder occurred?"

Mrs. D'Antonio wet her lips. "No."

"You didn't see Mr. Lucia that morning, did you?"

"No."

"You weren't at the pigeon-racing club that morning, were you, Mrs. D'Antonio?"

"No."

"So, in truth, you don't know anything about the murder for which Mr. Lucia is now standing trial, do you?"

"Uh, no."

Judy considered stopping there. No lawyer was supposed to ask a question she didn't know the answer to. But these were friendly witnesses, asked only for half the story. She decided to take the risk. "Mrs. D'Antonio, you testified that Mr. Lucia hated Angelo Coluzzi, is that right?"

"Yes."

"Isn't it well known that Mr. Coluzzi hated Mr. Lucia as well?"

Santoro jumped up. "Objection, Your Honor. Mr. Coluzzi's motives are irrelevant here. The poor man is dead!"

Judy stood her ground. "Your Honor, it is extremely relevant to the defense that there was ill will between the two men. It's important for the jury to see both sides of the story."

Judge Vaughn said, "Sustained, but let's dispense with the speaking objections, counsel. I give the speeches in my courtroom, not you." The judge turned to the witness. "You may answer the question, Mrs. D'Antonio."

The witness nodded. "It is true. Mr. Coluzzi hated Mr. Lucia, too. They hated each other."

Judy wanted to ask why, but she let it be. It was tempting but was too risky. She sat down. "Thank you, ma'am. I have no further questions."

Santoro was up in a minute. "The people call Sebastiano Gentile to the stand," he said, and Judy turned, almost recognizing the old man entering the door in the bulletproof panel. Sebastiano Gentile, a small, wizened man wearing a white shirt, baggy dark pants, and a cabbie's hat of sky blue, came in shyly and approached the witness stand. He took off his hat when he was sworn in, leaving wisps of white hair like cirrus clouds around his pink head. His eyes were blue as his cap, magnified by thick bifocals.

Judy leaned over to Pigeon Tony, to confirm her suspicion. "Is Mr. Gentile another neighbor?"

"**Si, si,**" Pigeon Tony said, nodding happily at the stand. The anger caused by Santoro's opening argument had left him. It had become old home week, and Pigeon Tony was having the best time anyone could have at his own murder trial.

Santoro faced the witness after he was sworn in. "Mr. Gentile, where do you live?"

"Across the street from Pigeon To— I mean, Mr. Lucia."

"And have you ever discussed his late wife or his son with him?"

"Yes. All the time."

"And when was the most recent of those conversations?"

"Uh, last spring, after his son passed. He was washin' his stoop, and I was puttin' out the trash."

"And what did Mr. Lucia say on that subject, as you recall?"

"He said Angelo Coluzzi killed his wife and his son. And his daughter-in-law. He told everybody that."

Pigeon Tony remained pleased, evidently glad the facts of the murders were stated as truth, but his lawyer's head began to throb. Judy knew what Santoro was doing. He was beefing up the evidence of Pigeon Tony's motive, even front-loading the witness line-up with it, because his evidence of intent to murder and his physical evidence were borderline. If the jury knew Pigeon Tony's avowed motive, it would make it easier to find that he had killed Coluzzi in that room.

"Mr. Gentile, did you hear Mr. Lucia say this on more than one occasion?"

The witness didn't even have to think twice. "Sure. All the time."

Santoro nodded. "Thank you, Mr. Gentile, I have nothing further." He crossed to counsel table and hit a key on his laptop as Judy stood up.

She lingered at the podium. "Mr. Gentile, were you present at the pigeon-racing club on the morning of April seventeenth of this year?"

"No. I'm allergic to animals."

Judy smiled, as did the jury. But it was important to stay on message. "So isn't it a fact that you don't know anything about the murder for which Mr. Lucia is now standing trial?"

"I really can't say nothin' about no murder. I don't know."

Judy nodded. So far, so good. "Mr. Gentile, you testified that Mr. Lucia hated Mr. Coluzzi. Isn't it true that Mr. Coluzzi hated Mr. Lucia, too?"

Mr. Gentile smiled, revealing even, white dentures. "Oh, yeh. Angelo hated Pigeon Tony. I mean, Mr. Lucia. There was bad blood between them, very bad."

"I have no further questions." Judy sat down, pleased.

As Mr. Gentile left the stand, Judge Vaughn looked over his glasses. "Next witness, Mr. Santoro?"

Santoro nodded. "The Commonwealth calls Mr. Guglielmo Lupito to the stand."

Judy could see where this was going. The cavalcade of Italian senior citizens, all of whom had heard our hero announce his hatred of the deceased, would continue. The cumulative effect would hurt the defense, even given whatever small points Judy made on cross. She had to do something. She half rose. "Your Honor, the defense objects to the repetitious nature of these witnesses."

Santoro's glistening head snapped around. "Your Honor, it is important that the jury see the witnesses, and how many there are."

"Your Honor, it's a waste of the court's time and resources for a tangential line of questioning. Perhaps I could save time if I stipulate—"

"No, Your Honor," Santoro interrupted. "The Commonwealth will not stipulate. I think the jury should hear this from the horse's mouth."

Judge Vaughn sighed. "Go ahead, Mr. Santoro, but restrain yourself shortly. You've made your point, and Ms. Carrier's made hers."

Judy sat down and scribbled for the sake of scribbling, but she was too stressed to write any jokes in capital letters. Pigeon Tony's life was at stake and yet another neighbor was taking the stand. As much as Pigeon Tony warmed to see his old friends, she knew each one was driving a nail into his coffin. She considered asking them if they thought Coluzzi had committed the past murders, but she knew she'd draw a legitimate objection. Neither lawyer could prove or disprove the truth of the past murders, but Santoro was using them to advantage. She vowed to do the same before the case was over.

They sat through the testimony of Mr. Ralph Bergetti, Mrs. Josephine DiGiuseppe, Mr. Tessio Castello, Miss Lucille Buoniconti and, oddly, an Anne Foster, before Judge Vaughn granted Judy's objections. Santoro asked all the same questions and got all the same answers, as did Judy on cross. But she was concerned. The jury would remember these witnesses, whose demeanor was so credible and whose testimony was undisputed. It would lighten Santoro's burden on proving reasonable doubt. By lunch recess, Judy had serious doubts.

She had to turn it around, or Pigeon Tony was a dead man.

# 39

"That was the worst thing Santoro could have done, for us," Judy said as she, Pigeon Tony, Frank, and Bennie sat at the round table in the courthouse conference room. It was a small white room, dominated by a fake chestnut table and ringed with four black leather swivel chairs. Right now the table was covered with a large pizza box, filled with leftover crusts.

"Agreed," Bennie said. Her unruly hair had been swept back into a ponytail, which looked professional with her trademark khaki suit. Her face was pale, the result of hard work and worry; she had backstopped Judy on trial prep as if **she** were Judy's associate and not the other way around. "You know what he's doing, don't you? Setting up the physical evidence."

"I know. How'd I do, on cross?"

"Fine. You know what they say. When you have the facts, pound the facts. When you have the law, pound the law. When you don't have either, pound the table."

Judy grinned. "Got it. I'll just keep pounding and hold up until it's our turn."

Pigeon Tony set down his half-eaten pizza crust. "Then I talk to judge?"

Judy shook her head. They had discussed this only about twelve hundred times before the trial began. "No. Then we put on our witnesses. I thought we agreed, you should not testify. It wouldn't help your case. They have no good proof of what happened in that room except through you."

Pigeon Tony's face went red. "But they lie! They say Coluzzi no murder Silvana. Or my Frank. And Gemma! I hear! I know! **Lies!**"

"If you got up on the stand, you would tell the truth. You would say that Coluzzi did all those things, but we couldn't prove any of it, which would make you look just like the man they say you are. An angry old man, full of hate. Legally, it's your decision, but I am telling you not to go up there and let me handle it."

"I tell truth! Millie tell truth! Sebastiano and Paul! They all say truth!" Pigeon Tony went red in the face, waving a finger. "I **hate** Coluzzi! He **kill** my family! **That** is truth!"

Frank started to explain to him, but Judy held up a hand. This was between lawyer and client, since the decision to testify in his own defense was strictly the client's.

"Pigeon Tony, listen to me. All they can show is that you meant to kill Coluzzi, or even that you **wanted** to kill Coluzzi. But what they have to prove is that you did it. You don't go to jail in this country because you want to kill somebody."

"But I **kill** Coluzzi! I **do** it!"

Judy winced. It was still hard to hear. Plus it might not help the defense if he screamed it throughout the courthouse. "But they have to **prove** that you did, and that's a lot harder. If they can't prove it, you win. If you get up there, they can prove it easy, and you lose. Understand?"

Pigeon Tony's features went rigid, his mouth an unfamiliarly unhappy line, and Frank put a reassuring hand on his grandfather's shoulder. "Pop, Judy knows what she's doing. She's the lawyer, and she cares about us. She knows what's best for you. Let her do her job, okay?"

Pigeon Tony blinked in response. His mouth stayed set, giving a new meaning to Italian marble.

Judy locked eyes with Frank and she didn't have to tell him what she was thinking. They had become lovers the night she'd gone to him, but since then the relationship hadn't had a chance to blossom into a warm, rich, full-blown love affair. The law was a jealous mister.

Frank squeezed Pigeon Tony's shoulder. "Pop,

she's right. She's trying to save your life here. Tell her you agree."

Pigeon Tony sighed shallowly, his concave chest rising and sinking with resignation. "**Si**," he said quickly.

"Thank you." Judy patted Pigeon Tony's other shoulder, skinny even in shoulder pads. "Now let's go back in. And remember, it's gonna get worse before it gets better. Nobody feels good during the other side's case."

"Amen," Bennie said, but Pigeon Tony was losing his religion.

Detective Sam Wilkins made a professional counterpoint to the down-home ragtagginess of Pigeon Tony's neighbors. His dark eyes were alert and grave, and he was dressed in a neat blue suit with a cop-issue patterned tie. Wilkins didn't so much sit behind the microphone as address the courtroom, and his demeanor was natural and professional. Judy knew the jury would respect him. He reeked of integrity, which she valued in everyone but the opposition.

"Now that we have your background, Detective Wilkins," Santoro continued, "please tell us what you did the morning of April seventeenth." Santoro stood taller than he had before. Like most D.A.s, he sucked up to real live cops but wouldn't ever be one himself. Guns were involved, and somebody could get hurt.

"I was on the day tour and was called to seven-twelve Cotner Street, at eight-thirteen in the morning. About." Wilkins smiled, and so did the jury. The only person who didn't was Pigeon Tony. Judy remembered he no like police, and he was baring his dentures.

"Is that the address of a pigeon-racing club?"

"Yes, it is. The South Philly Pigeon Racing Club."

"What did you do and see there?"

"I was directed to the back room, where I found the body of the deceased, Angelo Coluzzi."

"Could you describe exactly what you saw, for the jury?"

"Mr. Coluzzi was partly underneath a bookshelf that held various veterinary supplies. I knelt beside him and determined that he had no pulse. It was clear to me his neck had been broken, and—"

"Objection," Judy said. "Detective Wilkins is not a medical expert, Your Honor."

"Sustained," Judge Vaughn said, and Judy felt vaguely satisfied. She didn't know if she had accomplished anything, but it didn't hurt to remind the jury that Detective Wilkins wasn't Superman. Again, Pigeon Tony was the only one who didn't need the reminder. He glared at the detective so fiercely that Judy clamped her hand on his arm. Oddly, he seemed angrier than he had during Santoro's opening and resisted her soothing.

Santoro nodded. "Perhaps you could explain what you saw, Detective."

"Mr. Coluzzi's neck was lying to the left, loosely, at a skewed, unnatural angle. He lay on the floor near a bookshelf, which was partly on top of him, and many of the items on the shelves had spilled out. The room showed signs of a struggle, but I concluded it was a brief one. From my investigation it appeared that the defendant had entered the room and attacked the deceased."

Suddenly Pigeon Tony jumped to his feet. "Scum! Coluzzi kill my wife! Coluzzi kill my son! You do nothing! You **know** he kill him! I spit on you! Pig! **Dog!**"

"Pigeon Tony, no!" Judy leaped up and grabbed Pigeon Tony as the judge's gavel started pounding. This outburst could get him killed. The jury was with Detective Wilkins, and Pigeon Tony was going berserk on the man.

**Crak! Crak! Crak!** "Order!" Judge Vaughn shouted. "Order in the Court! Ms. Carrier, get your client in control."

"Liar! Scum!" Pigeon Tony kept screaming, and then he segued into Italian. Struggling with him, Judy understood only the word Coluzzi, screamed at least five times at an only mildly surprised Detective Wilkins.

"Order! Order!" Judge Vaughn roared, banging

the gavel again and again. The bailiff and court-room security rushed over. The gallery rose to its feet. Frank looked anguished. All hell was break-ing loose.

Judy wrestled Pigeon Tony into his chair and caught sight of the jury. Even though they didn't understand Pigeon Tony's words, they understood his meaning, and he looked every inch the angry, violent man Santoro had told them about in his opening. Judy dug her nails into Pigeon Tony's shoulder and forced him to stay in his seat, but he was still yelling in Italian.

"Your Honor, may we conference?" she shouted, over him.

**Crak! Crak! Crak!** "We damn well better!" Judge Vaughn thundered. "Bailiff, dismiss the jury! Officers, subdue the defendant! Counsel, into my chambers! **Right now!**"

Judge Vaughn was so furious he didn't bother to take off his robes but swept into his huge leather desk chair and let them billow around him like the silken mantle of a king. His large chambers were elegantly appointed, with a polished walnut desk, which was faced by navy leather chairs so large they made even Judy look small. Santoro's Italian loafers barely grazed the sapphire-and-ruby-patterned carpet, and hunter green volumes of Purdon's Pennsylvania Statutes Annotated lined the walls of the chamber, as well as tan-and-red volumes of the Pennsylvania reporters and an entire shelf of detective fiction. It didn't bode well for the defense.

"Ms. Carrier," Judge Vaughn said, his tone exasperated and his face ruddier than usual. "What the **hell** is going on out there?"

"Your Honor, I apologize—"

"My courtroom is a zoo! The gallery is the Hatfields and the McCoys! I have double the usual number of men on security. We're already taking from the Williamson case upstairs." The judge gestured wildly, his sleeves flying out like an eagle's wings. "How am I going to explain this to the court administrator? What the **hell** is the problem with your client?"

"Your Honor, I apologize, but let me explain. My client—"

"Do. Please. Now." Vaughn simmered while Judy hatched a plan. She could still get Pigeon Tony out of the mess he'd gotten himself into.

"First, I am really sorry."

"Really sorry?" Judge Vaughn ripped off his glasses and held them poised beside his face. "**Really** sorry? Can't we do better than really sorry?"

"Very sorry. Extremely sorry. So very sorry." Was this a game? Judy stopped guessing. "The problem, as you can see, is that my client is very emotional about this matter and is obviously under a great deal of strain. I apologize for his outburst, especially coming as it did, in front of the jury."

"Disrupting my trial!" Judge Vaughn said, snatching a tissue from a box on his desk and wiping his forehead with it.

"Exactly, which brings me to my point." Judy cleared her throat. "The fact that it occurred in front of the jury makes me concerned that prejudice has occurred, and I doubt the ability of this jury to fairly evaluate the facts of the case. Because the incident occurred so early in the trial, it would not be so great an imposition of the judicial system if the Court were to grant a mistrial at this point, and the defense so moves."

Judge Vaughn's blue eyes widened and a thick vein expanded in his neck. "Are you crazy?"

Judy hoped it was rhetorical. "Your Honor, I'm as unhappy about it as you are, but I see no alternative, given the outburst."

Santoro fairly waved his hand. "Your Honor, the Commonwealth opposes any such mistrial. It is a terrible waste of resources. I have ten murder cases back at the office, and here we are, already on trial in this one, after it took almost two weeks to pick a death-qualified jury. In addition, Your Honor, I think defense counsel has incredible nerve, making this request after her own client acted out. How could there be any prejudice, when her client did most of his screaming in Italian? The jury has a right to evaluate this man for what he is, and he's obviously not shy about his conduct."

Judge Vaughn was shaking his head, and Judy knew it would be the fastest ruling in judicial history. "There will be no mistrial in this matter, and the defense request is denied. The defendant brought this on himself and he won't benefit by it." The judge pointed directly at Judy, his robe slipping back to reveal a white French cuff with a gold cufflink. "Ms. Carrier, tell your client to straighten up and fly right. I'll give him the night to cool down, and we're back in session at nine on Tuesday morning. Get your act together. **Capisce?**"

"Yes, Your Honor," Judy said. She **capisc**ed just fine.

But would Pigeon Tony?

# 40

"I go to judge, I tell him police do nothing! Nothing! Pigs! Scum! Bullies!" Pigeon Tony wasn't any calmer three hours and two cartons of take-out lo mein later, and Judy wasn't completely surprised. Bennie had gone back to her office, leaving Judy and an unusually quiet Frank in the main conference room at Rosato & Associates, which Judy had claimed as her war room. An expanse of windows, now black with night, reflected her agitated client.

"Why judge mad at **me**? I tell truth! I know truth!" Pigeon Tony's face was still red with emotion. He couldn't sit still in his tan swivel chair, in front of an oak credenza stuffed with accordion files for the Lucia case, mounds of legal research, and Judy's notes. None of it had proved any help in the face of an Italian client. It was the English common law, after all, and had stood only for centuries.

"Pigeon Tony, please." Judy glared at her client across the table. "You keep up what you did today, and that jury will turn against you. You're playing with fire. The judge is already very unhappy with you, and the jury can sense that too."

"Lies! All liars! No can believe!" Pigeon Tony's eyes had gone bloodshot and he began to get winded. Judy was worried he'd have a stroke and passed him a can of Coke across the table.

"Take a sip. Please. Calm down."

Pigeon Tony ignored her. "You tell judge. I tell judge! Liars! You hear what they say? All lies! He kill my son! My daughter-in-law!"

Judy's stomach tensed as she watched Frank's reaction. He was standing behind his grandfather, his forehead buckled with strain at the mention of his parents' death. Judy had had enough. She stood up and folded her arms. "Pigeon Tony, quiet! Enough! Stop!"

Pigeon Tony startled, evidently accustomed to being the only temper tantrum in the room.

"We'll go to court tomorrow and you will shut up! I almost got killed for you. You **owe** me."

Pigeon Tony opened his mouth, then shut it.

"Now do I have your attention?"

Pigeon Tony fell silent, his leathery skin mottled. He hadn't lost his tan from months of working outdoors with Frank, building a wall. Judy wished for just one rock.

"I promise you. The next peep outta you in that courtroom, you don't have to worry about the jury. I'll kill you **myself**."

Pigeon Tony stopped fussing in his chair.

"You promise?"

"Promise."

"Good." Judy glanced at Frank, who forced a smile. She knew him well enough to know he was concerned by what had happened in court. "Now, time for you to go home." She checked her watch. "It's almost ten. You both need some sleep for tomorrow, and I have work to do, to prepare."

Frank touched his grandfather's shoulder. "Come on, Pop, she's right."

"S'allright," Pigeon Tony said, rising as if he were suddenly weary, and Frank helped him to his feet, then stopped.

"Pop, gimme a minute alone with my girl, would you?" he asked softly, and Pigeon Tony nodded. Frank walked him out of the conference-room door, undoubtedly left him with the security guards, then came back in and closed the door behind him. When he returned, Frank's brown eyes looked washed out, not with fatigue, but with something Judy couldn't identify.

"What's the matter?" Judy asked. "Besides the obvious?"

"Siddown a minute," Frank said, but he didn't meet her eye. He took a seat on one side of the table, and Judy sat across from him. She watched him loosen his tie, tugging it from one side to the next.

"Are we having sex again? I really liked it the

first and only time." Judy smiled, but Frank didn't.

"No." He rubbed his chin, running his finger pads over his dark stubble. "But this is hard to talk about."

Judy didn't feel like joking, which left her speechless. "What?"

"My grandfather, today in court. He yelled at the detective."

"Right."

"First he yelled in English, then in Italian. You didn't understand the Italian, did you?"

Judy felt a wrench in her chest. Suddenly she sensed where this was going. "No," she said, but it wasn't an answer. It was a wish.

"In Italian, what he yelled at the detective was 'Coluzzi told me he killed my son, and that's why I killed him. But you did nothing.'" Frank's voice sounded soft, almost hoarse, as if the very words choked him. "At least that's what I think I heard. I may be mistaken. The microphones to the gallery distorted his voice. And he was facing away from me. And my Italian isn't **that** good."

Judy didn't breathe. "So then it probably isn't what he said."

"But it could be."

Judy wanted this conversation to be over. "You know your grandfather thinks it was murder. You told me that."

"But now he's saying that Coluzzi confessed to

it. Admitted it, that morning." Frank looked at Judy directly, his dark eyes boring into her, making the connection between them real, reminding her again of their lovemaking. It mattered to her. "Do you know what he was talking about?"

Her thoughts raced. She didn't want to hurt Frank but she didn't want to lie to him either, and she had kept so much from him. Finding the junked truck. The accident expert. The useless report. If the truck accident was murder, it couldn't be proved. It could only drive Frank crazy, for the rest of his life. He would become another Pigeon Tony, haunted by sorrow and rage. But she owed Frank an honest answer, so she gave it to him.

"I told you when we first met that I was your grandfather's lawyer. The fact that I am now your lover doesn't change that. If you want the answer to your question, you have to ask him."

Frank nodded, but it was a jerky movement, almost a spasm, as if the very notion that it could be true was a shock to his senses. "If it's true, I have a right to know."

"You should talk to him."

"But I'm talking to you. They were my parents, not his. And not yours either." Frank's tone went bitter, and Judy could taste the sourness in her own mouth, like a kiss at the end of an affair.

She rose, her knees weak, because if she stayed sitting a moment longer she would tell him. And she didn't want them to end before they had even started. "You really should go, Frank. Your grandfather needs to sleep."

Frank stood up and straightened with some difficulty, and Judy could tell from the way he moved that he knew he had heard right, that Coluzzi had killed his parents.

"Frank—" she said, but she caught herself before she finished the sentence. Because she both did and didn't want to tell.

"Judy, my love," Frank said, but his tone wasn't loving. He walked to the conference room door, then paused. "Someday it won't be about my grandfather anymore, or about his case. Someday it will be about you and me. And I hope we're still together when that happens."

Judy was left standing, jelly-kneed, long after he had gone.

Judy spent her last few hours of alertness at the office laying out her cross-examination of the Commonwealth's witnesses, then working on her own defense case. Her strategy taxed her brain and her talk with Frank tugged at her heart, and long after coffee had stopped working, fear wasn't even doing the trick. The security guards rested in the firm's reception area, awake because they were the night shift, and protecting her and Bennie. She checked her watch.

Midnight.

As tired as Judy was, there was something she liked about being at work at this hour. The city was so still outside, the night so dense it was hard to believe it would ever fade to light, setting cars cruising onto highways, coffee dripping into glass pots, and jurors coming to court to decide if another human being should live or die.

She got up, stretched, and made her way to Bennie's office. She took it as a measure of some sort of personal growth that she had stopped thinking of Bennie as the boss. The only boss Judy had ever known was her father, and she suspected that every boss after that was just a stand-in for him. But at some point, when she wasn't looking, Judy had become her own boss. Maybe it happened when someone had entrusted his life to her.

"Hey," Judy said from the threshold, and Bennie looked up from the brief she was editing, her hair falling across one eye. She pushed it away.

"Hey back at you."

"I forget what my dog looks like. Do you remember?" Judy sat down in the cushy chair across from Bennie's desk.

"It's yellow. That's why they call them goldens. Is your puppy still with Tony Two Feet?"

"Si, si. The hotel isn't having her." Judy sighed. "Boy, do I feel sorry for myself tonight. My case is in trouble, my client freaked in open court, and I just lost a boyfriend I didn't have."

"Count your blessings. Your best friend is alive and well."

"But still not back at work"

"You've survived the Coluzzis."

"Only so far."

"You're **suing** the Coluzzis."

"We're bogged down in paper."

"Also you know your client is innocent, even though he did it. Which is a neat trick."

"The neatest." Judy nodded in agreement. "I am Cleopatra, queen of denial."

Bennie sipped undoubtedly cold coffee. "Also you can win this case."

Judy blinked. Had she heard her right? It was late. Her Italian was poor. "**What** did you say?"

"Or more accurately, you can win this case if you figure out how."

"What do you mean? Why do you say that?" Judy edged forward, and Bennie leaned back in her chair, which creaked in the silent office.

"I've tried lots of murder cases, back in the day, as you know. And there's one thing that I have learned, and every criminal defense lawyer should know it."

"Hit me." It reminded Judy of Santoro. **Every murder case is a simple story**. If Judy were going to try murder cases for a living, she had to get a generalization of her own.

"Every murder case is about two questions." Bennie held up an index finger. "One, did the guy who got killed deserve to die?" She added another finger. "And two, was the defendant the man for the job? If the answer to both questions is yes, then the defense has a shot. Which is the most you can ask, especially in this case."

Judy blinked. It was a helluva theory. Better than Santoro's. But so was Bennie.

"In this case, the answer to both questions is yes, but you have to give the jury something to go on. Hand them a defense they can talk themselves into believing. You're all set up for it. You did a great job with the neighbors today. The jury will go for you if you just give them the chance."

Judy frowned. "Think I can do it?"

"I know you can."

"Think I can fail?"

"Of course."

Judy blinked. "Ouch."

"I'm a lawyer, not a cheerleader," Bennie said, but Judy couldn't manage a smile.

# 41

"No comment!" Judy shouted, putting her head down and plowing through the press outside the Criminal Justice Center. Two musclemen in suits flanked her, serving double duty against bad guys and reporters. Umbrellas covered the TV anchors, and videocameras whirred through thick plastic bags. Despite the rain, there were more reporters than yesterday, attracted by Pigeon Tony's courtroom tarantella. The morning headlines had made her shudder: TONY'S TIRADE. ITALIAN CURSES COP. GRUMPY OLD MAN. THE DIATRIBE AND THE DETECTIVE.

"Ms. Carrier, just one picture!" "Ms. Carrier, you gonna put him on the stand?" "Judy, any comment on Judge Vaughn's ruling against you?" "Ms. Carrier, what happened in chambers? Did he read you the riot act?"

Judy ignored them and climbed the slick curb to the courthouse entrance, almost tripping over wet TV cables that snaked along like pythons. If the

Coluzzis didn't kill her, the press would. The newspapers had reported Pigeon Tony's outburst, but nobody could translate it, and the courtroom stenographer hadn't transcribed the Italian. Judy could only hope that Frank remained as uncertain as everybody else. He hadn't called to say good night last night and wasn't answering his cell phone. She'd be meeting them upstairs in court, since they entered through the secured entrance.

"Judy, what are you gonna do to Jimmy Bello on the stand?" shouted one of the reporters just as Judy reached the revolving door, where she stopped.

"Best question of the morning," she called back, and entered the courthouse.


Judge Vaughn was wearing a light blue shirt under his robes, with a dark blue tie whose knot peeked through the V at the neck, and he spent most of Detective Wilkins's routine testimony glaring at Pigeon Tony from the dais, which worked for Judy. Pigeon Tony fidgeted a little but, as promised, didn't make a peep, so Judy didn't have to kill him. The courtroom was over-air-conditioned, to keep the humidity low on this rainy day, and Judy felt chilled even in her navy blazer and skirt. Or maybe it was the way Frank had looked this morning that left her cold. She glanced back at the gallery through the bullet-proof shield.

Frank met her eye only briefly, then focused again on the witness. His face was pale beneath his fresh shave, and there were circles under his large eyes, emphasized by the darkness of his corduroy suit and knit tie. He kept stealing looks at John Coluzzi. Obviously Pigeon Tony had told Frank about his parents. Judy didn't know what would happen next, but she had to put him out of her mind. She was trying to save his grandfather's life. She returned to the testimony, taking notes while Detective Wilkins spoke, but it concluded quickly, with Santoro taking his seat at counsel table.

"Ms. Carrier, your witness." Judge Vaughn shifted his icy gaze from Pigeon Tony to Judy, and she stood up and went to the podium.

"Thank you, Your Honor." She faced Detective Wilkins, who eyed her with remoteness. If he remembered that day in her apartment, when he was so nice to her, it didn't show. Today they were adversaries and they both knew it. "Detective Wilkins, we have met, haven't we?"

"Yes, we have, Ms. Carrier." The detective's blue-eyed gaze met Judy's levelly, and his demeanor remained steady. He even wore the same suit as yesterday; the jury would like that, Judy knew. And they'd already be on his side, after Pigeon Tony's display. She had to defuse it.

"Detective, you have my client's apologies for his conduct yesterday, as well as my own apology," she said, meaning it, even though she could see two jurors in the front row smile.

Detective Wilkins nodded graciously. "All in a day's work."

Judy laughed. Touché. Maybe it would help put the incident behind them. "Now, as you have testified, you were the detective on the scene the morning Angelo Coluzzi was killed, right?"

"Yes."

"And you were called to the pigeon-racing club?"

"Yes."

"And you examined the back room carefully, where the killing occurred?"

"Yes."

"And you testified there were signs of only a brief struggle?"

"I did."

"Excuse me a moment." Judy turned to counsel table, grabbed the exhibit mounted on foamcore, brought it to the witness stand, and placed it on a metal easel. The jury looked at the exhibit while she moved it into evidence, without objection. "Let the record show that the exhibit is a black-line diagram of the first floor of the pigeon-racing club, including the back room." Judy had reconstructed it from her memory and with the help of The Two Tonys. "Detective Wilkins, does this depict the first floor as you remember it, including the back room and the furniture?"

Detective Wilkins scanned the exhibit. "It does."

"The exhibit shows a large entrance room, let's call it, with a bar on the west side of the room, the left-hand side. The entrance to the back room is on the north wall, through a wooden door. Correct?"

The detective nodded. "Yes."

"The back room contained a blue card table in the middle of the room, with four chairs around it. Referring again to brief signs of a struggle, didn't you notice that the table had been out of square?"

Detective Wilkins thought about it. "I did."

"So the table had been moved," Judy summarized for the jury's benefit. "Would you say it was clearly out of square?"

"Slightly." Detective Wilkins knew just where Judy was going, and he wasn't going with her, which was to be expected.

"But clearly, correct?"

"Correct."

"Thank you." Judy pointed to the black-line chair in the diagram. She could have proved this easily through use of police photos, but they showed Angelo Coluzzi dead in the center of the picture. "Now, Detective Wilkins, there were four chairs around the table, all of which are brown metal folding chairs. Do you recall them?"

"Yes."

"Isn't it true that the chair on the east side of the table was knocked over?"

"Yes, but it was on the path of travel, from the door to the bookshelves."

Judy held up a firm hand. "I'm not asking why or how you think it was knocked over, only that it had been knocked over. And it had, hadn't it?"

"Yes." Detective Wilkins's mouth became a hard line.

Judy pointed to the exhibit again. "Now, the metal shelves we have been talking about that you said had been pulled down, they had been standing against the east side of the room, opposite the table, correct?"

"Yes."

"And they had been pulled down. To the floor, correct?"

"Yes."

"And the contents, which were pigeon supplies, had fallen to the ground. Had bottles broken?"

"Yes."

"Pills spilled out?"

"Yes."

"Bands for pigeons' legs had fallen from their boxes?"

Detective Wilkins thought a minute. "Yes."

Judy collected her thoughts. She had almost accomplished what she needed to, setting up her closing. She couldn't get much more out of a hostile witness. But she needed to make her point. "Detective Wilkins, your credentials are very impressive, your having worked for twenty-three years as a homicide detective. How many crime scenes do you think you have examined in that time?"

Detective Wilkins sighed. "Thousands, unfortunately."

Judy let it be. There were roughly two hundred murders in the city in a year, and she didn't want to do the grisly multiplication either. "I would gather that most of those murders involve a weapon—a knife or a gun—am I correct?"

"For the most part, yes. That is the typical situation."

"So you are very familiar with the signs of a struggle that occur in such situations?"

"Yes."

Judy took a breath—and a risk. "Have you ever investigated a killing that took place without a weapon, between two men over the age of seventy-five?"

Surprised, Detective Wilkins reacted with a short laugh. "No."

"So how much of a struggle do you want?" she asked with a throwaway smile, and Wilkins smiled, too. "Thank you, I have no further questions." Judy grabbed her exhibit and sat down before Santoro could object. That had gone as well as it could, and Santoro stood up and approached the podium.

"Your Honor, I have redirect," Santoro called

out, but Judge Vaughn was already nodding over his half-glasses. Santoro addressed his witness. "Detective Wilkins, you said you have investigated thousands of murder scenes, is that right?"

"Yes."

"And you have a set of skills and experiences that you bring to bear in every murder scene you investigate, is that right?"

"I like to think so."

"And so you can be presented with a new situation in a murder scene and you can bring to bear your skills, experience, and instincts, honed over twenty-three years?"

Judy thought about objecting but let it go. The jury could see how self-serving it was, and she wouldn't get points by tearing down Detective Wilkins.

Detective Wilkins nodded slowly. "Yes, I think so."

Santoro rocked on his loafers a minute, evidently thinking about pressing it, and Judy shifted in her chair. If he went too far, she would object and she would have to be sustained. It was the lawyer's equivalent of the cowboy's hand hovering at his hip holster. Santoro made a decision. "I have no further questions. Thank you very much, Detective," he said, and sat down.

It was always high noon in a murder trial, but only one man took the risk of getting dead.

Santoro's next witness was a woman from Mobile Crime, a tall brunette with a black suit, a severe ponytail, and thick glasses, who testified that she had collected fibers from the clothes of Angelo Coluzzi that came from Pigeon Tony's clothes. She was absolutely credible, and Judy barely objected, since it wasn't inconsistent with her case for the defense. And her thoughts were elsewhere, as she tried to figure out what Santoro was doing and ways she could meet whatever it was in her case.

It was clearly the morning for police testimony, because his next witness was another crime tech, a red-haired young man who had taken photographs of the scene. Santoro's only purpose was to show the photographs of Coluzzi's body to the jury, over Judy's objection. She could do little but watch them as they looked uncomfortably at the grim photos, which Santoro had enlarged on a projection screen in the front of the courtroom. They swallowed hard at the sad sight, and Coluzzi looked horrible in photo after photo, his dark eyes sunken, his body as small and frail as Judy had remembered. The slides weren't bloody, but somehow their very ordinariness spoke with a more subtle eloquence. Two jurors looked away, and even Pigeon Tony blinked.

But Judy was suddenly grateful for the bullet-proof sheet muting the reaction of the gallery. Out of the corner of her eye, she could see Coluzzi's widow crying and John Coluzzi holding her as she sobbed. The entire Coluzzi side of the courtroom was red-faced and teary, but the Lucia side remained still. Sketch artists drew madly, kept busy not only by the scene in the courtroom but by the one in the gallery, and the reporters scribbled their squiggles of old-fashioned shorthand. The Tonys had no reaction, and Frank kept eyeing the Coluzzis. Judy would have to talk to him at the noon recess and find out what he knew.

For the first time in her life, she wasn't looking forward to lunch.

# 42

The courthouse conference room suddenly felt smaller than Judy remembered, but maybe that was because she was facing off against her lover. She stood on one side of the table and Frank on the other. The fluorescent lights were harsh and glaring. An uneaten pizza sat steaming in its box on the table. In two swivel chairs sat Pigeon Tony and Bennie, reduced to a captive audience.

"You didn't tell me, Judy," Frank said, his tone an accusation and his mouth tight with hurt. Pain filled his eyes, which looked bloodshot from a night without sleep. "You knew Coluzzi killed my parents and you didn't tell me."

Judy felt her face flush. "Your grandfather told you what Coluzzi said."

"Yes. He didn't want to, but he did."

Pigeon Tony was shaking his head with regret. "Sorry, Judy. He no stop. He ask, ask, ask, ask. He scream and yell. He no give up. Like father."

But Frank ignored him. "He also told me about

my parents' truck, which you found, and **have**, incredibly enough—and the report you got from an expert who examined the wreck. You know more about my parents' death than I do, Judy. You knew all along. And you didn't tell me!"

"I couldn't. It was privileged."

"Bullshit!" Frank raised his voice, then glanced nervously at the conference room door. "You could have told me! I don't want to hear about this privilege shit!" Frank caught himself and lowered his voice. "You're not my lawyer. You're supposed to be my lover. My friend. Everything. I took that seriously, but evidently you didn't."

Judy went hot with embarrassment. She didn't want to be having this conversation in a courthouse, in front of other people, much less Bennie, so she said as much.

"This **is** the time and place, Judy, and you didn't tell me about my parents' murder because you were afraid I'd retaliate. You both were!" Frank cast a scornful glance that managed to encompass both Judy and Pigeon Tony. "That's why you two kept your mouths shut. You both decided what my reaction should be, and it wasn't the one you wanted, so you didn't tell me. But that wasn't for either of you to decide. They were **my** parents! I am their **only** son! I had a right to know they were murdered."

"But we don't know that they were!" Judy couldn't help but shout. "Think logically. Coluzzi told your grandfather he killed them, and I didn't tell you that. Granted. But before you go off half-cocked, you should understand that there's no proof that Coluzzi was telling the truth. I don't think he did it."

Pigeon Tony was nodding. "He did it."

"He did it!" Frank agreed.

"You don't know that," Judy said. "In fact, I have, or had, tapes of Coluzzi discussing the night your parents had the accident. There's not a word on them about the murder or your parents. Nothing."

"**Tapes**, from where?" Frank demanded, and even Pigeon Tony looked over. She hadn't mentioned the tapes to either of them. "What tapes? Videotapes?"

"Phone tapes."

"**Phone tapes?** Of Coluzzi? Who was he discussing it with?"

Judy thought better of it. She didn't want Frank attacking Jimmy Bello, not before she had her chance with him on cross-examination. "It doesn't matter. But I had them, and they said nothing. And the expert I hired said the accident was only an accident, as did the cops. They can't all be wrong, Frank. Use your head, not your heart."

But Frank's anger became unfocused. "Who was Coluzzi on the phone with? Who? And where did you get the tapes?"

"I'm not telling you that, and you have to trust me. They don't prove anything. Nothing proves anything. I think it was an accident. I didn't think it before that accident expert, but now I do."

"I don't need proof. Coluzzi admitted it."

"That doesn't mean anything. Think about it."

Frank threw up his hands. "Why would he say it if he didn't do it?"

"To drive your grandfather crazy. To make him nuts. To take credit for something he didn't do, with false bravado." Judy felt calmer. The more she thought about it, the more sense it made. "There are a million explanations, Frank. Coluzzi was a sadist."

"He did it!"

"He did it," Pigeon Tony echoed, and Bennie shot him a dirty look.

Judy got fed up. "Look, Frank, I'm in the middle of a murder trial right now. So this isn't about you **or** your parents, as sorry as I am for their deaths. Right now it's about your grandfather, who is charged with murder, and it doesn't look so good for the good guys. Or the bad guys. Whoever we are." It was a little confusing.

Frank swallowed, visibly dry-mouthed, and Judy saw her opening and went for it, as much as it hurt her to shut him down.

"You want to know the truth, Frank? You can read it. I'll give you the files tonight. My file, the police file, the whole thing. You want to, you can even talk to the expert. He's completely impartial. He said the guardrail was too low to be safe and there was no foul play. But right now I have a client to defend and you are not helping him—or me—in the least."

Frank's features went stiff and he looked down at

Pigeon Tony, whose tiny face sagged between his hands. Frank stood still for a minute, then his sigh was audible. "Fine. We'll discuss it later."

Judy figured it was the closest an Italian man could come to an apology. "And you won't get crazy until we do."

"I didn't promise that."

"It wasn't a question," Judy said, and let it drop. Frank wasn't nuts enough to be thinking about murder, was he? And who would he kill? Angelo Coluzzi was already dead. "Now let's get back to court, where all I have to fight with is the Commonwealth of Pennsylvania." Judy glanced at Bennie. "You have anything to tell me before we go back in there?"

"Nope. You're the boss, boss," Bennie said, with a relieved smile, and Judy breathed in the encouragement.

"Then let's go kick some ass."

On the witness stand in a three-piece suit of light gray wool, Dr. Patel made the same professional picture Judy remembered from the medical examiner's office. Glossy black hair, large brown eyes behind glasses, a pleasant smile, and a British accent that enhanced the impressiveness of his qualifications. He could have ordered a cheese pizza and sounded smart.

"Now, Dr. Patel, you were the assistant medical examiner who examined the body of Angelo Coluzzi, were you not?" Santoro asked.

"Yes."

"And you prepared a report of that postmortem examination, did you not?"

"I did."

Santoro approached the witness stand. "May I approach, Your Honor?" he said needlessly, as Vaughn nodded. "I am showing you a copy of your report on the examination of Angelo Coluzzi, and I ask you to identify it, Dr. Patel."

"It is mine."

Santoro moved the report into evidence without objection and addressed the witness. "Please describe briefly for the jury your examination, in layman's terms, if you would."

"Briefly, the first step in an autopsy is the external examination," Dr. Patel began, then described in detail the procedure that Judy had witnessed at the morgue, beginning with the inspection of the deceased's clothes, and ending with the weighing and sectioning of the internal organs. It sounded even more revolting in description, with the imagination working its wizardry. By the time Dr. Patel was finished, Santoro was pulling out autopsy photos like a proud father.

Judy half rose. "Objection, Your Honor, as to prejudice."

"Overruled," Judge Vaughn said. It was by now established law that the Commonwealth had the right to gross out the jury.

"Thank you, Your Honor," Santoro said, and he

moved the exhibits into evidence without further objection. He set the first one before Dr. Patel and broadcast it on the overhead projector. "Dr. Patel, you see before you Commonwealth Exhibit Ten. Is this, in fact, the body of the deceased, Angelo Coluzzi?"

"It is."

"Dr. Patel, did you form an opinion, to a reasonable degree of medical certainty, as to the cause of death of Angelo Coluzzi?"

"I did."

"What was your opinion, Doctor?"

"I found that it was homicide, and that the cause of death was a fracture to the spinal column, at C3, in the cervical vertebra."

"And how did you determine this, Doctor?"

"By inspection and by X ray."

Santoro looked grave, and Judy had the sense that he'd practiced. "What was the mechanism of death, sir?"

"Death resulted from a blunt-force injury, that is, a rapid forward snap that broke the neck. Death was instantaneous."

Santoro nodded. "Dr. Patel, just so the jury understands, when is this type of injury often seen?"

"This injury is similar to the whiplash type of injury one sees in auto accidents, when a car is struck from behind, or even in child abuse cases, with so-called Shaken Baby Syndrome. In this family of injury, undue stresses are placed on the cervical spine, and it ruptures, as it did in the case of the deceased."

Judy made a note. She should have objected but she hadn't seen it coming. She didn't want Angelo Coluzzi equated with a baby in the jury's mind.

Santoro changed to a slide of the top half of Angelo Coluzzi's body, showing the neck and shoulders. The head was hideously askew. The jury reacted instantly. "Dr. Patel, I show you Commonwealth Exhibit Eleven. What does this view tell us?"

"It shows the looseness of the neck, which is clearly at an abnormal angle, as it is now severed from the shoulders. A broken neck can be difficult to detect. There is often little bruising, so X rays are indicated to confirm the conclusion."

Santoro showed the slide of an X ray, which he moved into evidence, and Judy didn't object, as repetitive as it was. She would lose anyway, and in fact the X ray was abstract in a way the photographs weren't, reducing the whole human being to a black-and-white segment. If anything, it was a relief from the autopsy photos, and the jury returned to the fold. Judy bet Santoro wouldn't have it up there long.

"Dr. Patel, I now show you Commonwealth Exhibit Twelve. What does this teach us?"

Dr. Patel shifted around and lifted a steel pointer from the witness stand. "As you can see, the human vertebrae interlock almost like a thick chain, except that one of the links has been broken." He pointed to a break in the chain. "It determines positively that the spinal column has been broken."

"Thank you." Santoro nodded. "I have no further questions."

Judy stood up, armed with notes and a report from an expert osteopath she had worked with in preparation for trial. "Good afternoon, Dr. Patel. My name is Judy Carrier, and if you recall, I was present at the postmortem of Mr. Coluzzi."

"Yes, hello, Ms. Carrier." Dr. Patel smiled.

"I have only a few questions for you. Dr. Patel, do you recall the age of Angelo Coluzzi at the time of his death?"

Dr. Patel nodded. "He was eighty, I believe."

"In your opinion, how are the bones of an eighty-year-old man different from those of, let's say, a thirty-year-old man?"

"Well, the bone mass of older people is, in general, markedly different from that of younger people. Bones become more brittle as we age. They lose mass and resiliency." Dr. Patel cleared his throat and shifted uncomfortably in his chair when he looked in Santoro's direction. Judy could guess that the D.A. wasn't happy with the lecture, but Dr. Patel was his own man, a dangerous thing in an expert.

"Specifically, how is the spine of an eighty-year-old man different from that of, let's say, a thirty-year-old man?"

"Like other bones, the spine weakens with age in general, becoming more fragile. This is because the vertebrae lose some of their mineral content, making each bone thinner. Also, between each pair of vertebrae, the intervertebral disk, a gel-like cushion, loses fluid gradually, making these thinner as well. The spinal column therefore becomes curved and compressed. In addition, as we age, the likelihood of arthritis and osteoarthritis increases."

Bingo. Judy paused. She had hired an expert of her own, a gerontologist she hoped she didn't have to call, if she could get the evidence now. "And is it true that Angelo Coluzzi's cervical vertebrae shows these typical signs of aging?"

"It is."

"And isn't it also true that he had signs of osteoarthritis in his cervical spine?"

"He did. The deceased had signs of arthritis in his neck and also signs of osteoarthritis, which is not uncommon in that age group. By age sixty-five, most people experience pain and stiffness in their joints. Osteoarthritis occurs with equal frequency in men and women. The hands and knees are more commonly involved in women and the hips in men. But it can exist in the neck, too, as in Mr. Coluzzi's case."

"And isn't it true that these conditions—his age, his arthritis, and his osteoarthritis—would make it easier to break his neck than the neck of a younger, healthier, man?"

Santoro was on his feet. "Objection, relevance," he said, but Judge Vaughn was already shaking his head over his papers at the dais.

"Overruled." The judge returned to listening to the testimony, his chin in his large hand.

Judy nodded at Dr. Patel. "You may answer."

"Yes, Mr. Coluzzi's age and his osteoarthritis would render his neck fairly susceptible to such an injury."

Judy decided to press it. "Before, Dr. Patel, you testified that his injury was like a whiplash injury from a car accident or Shaken Baby Syndrome from child abuse. Did I hear you correctly?"

"Yes."

"But, just so the jury isn't confused, isn't it true that it would take far less than both of these examples to break the neck of Angelo Coluzzi, especially given his ailments and his age?"

"Yes, of course." Dr. Patel turned to address the jury directly, as Judy was praying he would. "I didn't mean to confuse anyone. I only meant to say this was in the same **family** of types of injury, not that it was caused the same way. The injury to the deceased could occur with very little force or violence, and it could happen in an instant."

"As if, in a scuffle?" Judy offered, but Santoro was on his loafers.

"Objection, Your Honor, as to relevance."

"Overruled," Judge Vaughn said wearily, and Santoro sat down. It was more than Judy had hoped for.

Her karma banks were kicking in. It must have been the pantyhose. Anybody who had to wear pantyhose every day deserved a break from the cosmos.

"You were saying, Dr. Patel. Could this type of injury, on an eighty-year-old man with osteoarthritis and arthritis, have occurred in a scuffle?"

"Yes."

"Thank you, Dr. Patel," Judy said, and meant it. She wouldn't even need to call her own expert later. She had gotten what she needed from the Commonwealth's. "No further questions." Judy grabbed her notes and sat down as Santoro got up hastily and commanded the podium.

"Dr. Patel," he asked, "could this injury also be caused by a violent push from the front, as in an attack?"

Judy let it lie. She knew the answer. It was what had happened, but it wasn't the only thing that **could** have happened, which was all that mattered for reasonable doubt.

Dr. Patel thought a moment. "Yes, this injury could also have occurred from a violent push from the front, as in an attack."

Santoro exhaled, obviously pleased. "Thank you, Dr. Patel."

But Judy was pleased, too. She could be on her way to saving Pigeon Tony, if she could put a hurt on Jimmy Bello, who undoubtedly would come next.

# 43

Jimmy Bello wore a dark silk tie, a bright white shirt, and a shiny gray suit for trial, which looked remarkably like Santoro's. Judy assumed it wasn't the thug aspiring to be a lawyer, but the other way around, and she hoped that everyone would stop wanting to be mobsters soon. She was completely over Mafia chic and was considering boycotting **The Sopranos**.

"Now, Mr. Bello," Santoro was saying, "you have worked for the Coluzzi family for thirty-five years, correct?"

"Yeh."

"And while Angelo Coluzzi was alive and running the construction company, you worked directly for him?"

"Yeh."

"You knew him well?"

"Very."

"He was a friend?"

"Yeh."

Judy smiled to herself. If Santoro was trying to wring some emotion out of Fat Jimmy, he'd have to wring harder.

Santoro twisted his neck to free it from his tight collar. "Now, moving directly to the events on the morning of April seventeenth, you were with Angelo Coluzzi that morning, correct?"

"Yeh."

"It was just the two of you, by the way?"

"Yeh."

"Where did you go?"

"I drove Angelo to the club, 'cause he needed to get some bands."

"Bands, what are they?"

"Steel bands, for his birds. His pigeons. For the next race. They're numbered, like that, so you can't cheat at the races."

Judy noticed two of the jurors chuckling, and Santoro decided to move on, with good reason.

Santoro continued, "Mr. Bello, please tell the jury what happened at the pigeon club that morning."

"Well, me and Angelo opened the place and Angelo went in the back room while I went to make some coffee. Instant, at the bar. That's right near the back room. They got like a coil, you know. You plug it in and stick it in the mug, with the water."

Santoro sighed, almost audibly. "Then what did you do?"

"I went to the bathroom while the water was gonna boil."

"Then what happened?"

"When I came out I seen Tony Pensiera and Tony LoMonaco standing there and the water boiling in the mug. So they see me and they say, what are you doin' here, and I say what are **you** doin' here, and we both figure out that Pigeon Tony, I mean Tony Lucia, went in the back room to get his bands, where Angelo already was."

Santoro raised a hand. "Did you hear anything at that point?"

"I heard Tony Lucia yell, 'I'm gonna kill you,' in Italian."

Judy eyed the jury, which reacted instantly. A juror in the front row gasped; a homemaker, from Chestnut Hill. Judy prayed she didn't end up as foreperson.

Santoro nodded. "And then what did you hear, Mr. Bello?"

"A big crash and then like a scream, a real bad scream. And then we ran in the back room and there was Angelo lying there dead near the shelves, and they were spilled onna floor."

"What was defendant Lucia doing?"

"Tony Lucia was standing over Angelo, and then his friends got him outta there and then I called the cops."

Judy glanced again at the jury, and several in the back looked upset. But out of the corner of her eye she glimpsed her client, and to her surprise, there were tears shining in his eyes. His lashes fluttered

in embarrassment, then he focused quickly elsewhere.

Judy's mouth went dry. So Pigeon Tony felt
remorse at the killing. She should have expected as
much. She tried to reach for his hand, but he
pulled it away and blinked his eyes clear. Judy
would never understand this little man. He wasn't
ashamed to tell her that he killed Coluzzi, but he
was ashamed to let her see him crying about it.

"Ms. Carrier," Judge Vaughn was saying, "your
witness."

Judy looked up at the dais to find Santoro sitting
down at counsel table, the court personnel staring at
her expectantly, and Jimmy Bello examining his fingernails. She was on deck. She grabbed her pad and
her exhibit and went to the podium.

"Mr. Bello, you testified that you worked for Mr.
Coluzzi for thirty-five years, is that right?"

"Yeh."

"You were his personal assistant, isn't that
right?"

"Yeh."

"So you were with him, performing tasks for
him?"

"Yeh."

"How much of the time where you with him?"

"24-7."

Judy lifted her legal pad so Bello could see that she
was reading from her notes. In time he would figure
out that they were her notes of the phone tapes.

Bello had to know the tapes had been destroyed by the fake temp, but he couldn't be sure Judy hadn't made copies of them. Lawyers who planned better would have. Boring lawyers, who liked pumps. "Let's briefly go through those types of tasks you performed. You drove him around, right?"

"Yeh."

"He would tell you when to pick him up and even items to bring, right?"

"Yeh."

"If he needed, let's say, 20,000 square feet of plywood, builder's grade, you would bring that, right?"

Bello blinked. "Uh, yeh."

"If he needed extra groceries, like the Cento clam sauce his wife liked, you would bring them, right?"

"Yeh." Bello glanced at the gallery, but Judy couldn't afford to turn and see the reaction of Coluzzi's widow.

"If he needed malathion and baby oil, so his pigeons didn't get mites, you would bring it?"

"Yeh."

"If you got him the wrong thing, let's say, normal peanuts to feed the pigeons instead of the raw Spanish peanuts, not roasted, no salt, you would go and get the right kind?"

"Yeh."

"If he wanted you to bring him a Coke when you picked him up, you did that, too, am I right?"

"Objection," Santoro said mildly, not bothering to rise. "Asked and answered, Your Honor."

"I'll move on," Judy said quickly. Santoro wouldn't understand the significance of the questions, but Bello would. He was already shifting in his chair. Judy checked her notes, which had run out of tapes and read, I'M SLEEPY. "So, Mr. Bello, since you were a friend of Mr. Coluzzi's, you probably know a lot about who he liked and disliked, isn't that right?"

"Yeh."

"Isn't it true that Mr. Coluzzi hated Tony Lucia, because Mr. Lucia's wife had chosen to marry him instead of Mr. Coluzzi?"

"Objection!" Santoro shouted, jumping to his loafers. "Assumes facts not in evidence."

"Your Honor," Judy said, "it's cross-examination."

Judge Vaughn was shaking his head. "Sustained. There's no foundation, counsel."

Judy nodded. She didn't need the foundation, she had just laid one. As the law books said, you couldn't unring the bell. "Thank you, Your Honor, I'll rephrase. Mr. Bello, isn't it true that Mr. Coluzzi hated Tony Lucia?"

Bello ran a tongue over his thick lips. "Well, uh, yeh."

"Mr. Bello, you testified that when you came out of the bathroom, Mr. Pensiera and Mr. LoMonaco were standing there, and then you heard the yell, is that right?"

"Right?"

"Would you say that five minutes passed while you were standing there but before you heard the yell?"

"I dunno."

Judy paused. "Let's figure it out. You testified that you came out of the bathroom, and they said, 'What are you doing here,' and then you said, 'What are you doing here?' It would take less than a minute for this to happen, wouldn't it?"

"Okay, right."

"And then you heard your water boiling, is that right?"

"Yeh."

"It takes about two minutes for an immersion coil to boil water, doesn't it?"

"Uh, yeh."

"So that's two minutes for sure." Judy paused. "And you had to go around the counter to unplug the immersion coil, is that right?"

"Yeh."

Judy reached for her exhibit and placed it on the easel. "Mr. Bello, I show you Defense Exhibit One, a diagram of the first floor of the club. The counter is here, approximately fifteen feet long. Please show the jury, where is the plug you used for the coil?"

"At the far end." He pointed, and Judy nodded. She knew the answer from The Two Tonys, who had told her it was the only outlet at the club that worked.

"Let the record show that the witness is pointing to the west end of the bar. Doesn't that mean that you had to go the length of the bar **twice** to unplug the coil?"

"Uh, yeh."

"Wouldn't it take you another two minutes to go around the counter, unplug the coil, come back again to where you were?" Judy didn't refer to his weight. She didn't need to.

"Yeh, prolly. I don't move that fast, ever. And I wasn't in no rush." He laughed shortly, but the jury didn't. They were listening, which gave Judy heart.

"So that's four minutes, at least. Then how much after you came back from unplugging the coil did you hear the yell?"

"Right then."

Judy paused. "So the two men were in the back room together for at least four minutes, maybe five."

"Objection, that's not what the witness said," Santoro said, half rising.

"Overruled." Judge Vaughn frowned.

"I'll move on, Your Honor," Judy said, as if it were a concession. She was on a roll. She had just proven that two men who hated each other had spent almost five minutes in a small room together. Who could say for sure who pushed whom first? It was Judy's best hope for saving Pigeon Tony. The slender reed of reasonable doubt. But there was a big problem, and she went for it. "Mr. Bello, didn't you testify that you were standing at the bar when you heard Mr. Lucia allegedly yell, 'I'm gonna kill you,' in Italian?"

"Yeh."

Judy paused. "Mr. Bello, have you ever spoken to Mr. Lucia?"

"No."

"Have you ever even heard him speak?"

"Uh, no."

Judy could see one of the jurors reacting with a half smile in the back row. He was the electrician from Kensington and he got her point. If she pushed it further she'd lose it. "Mr. Bello, I'd like to move back in time for a moment, to the night of January twenty-fifth. That is the night that Tony Lucia's son and daughter-in-law were killed in their truck, in an alleged truck accident. Do you recall where you were—"

"Objection, relevance!" Santoro said, rising, but Judy was already addressing Judge Vaughn.

"Your Honor, may we approach the bench?" She didn't wait for him to nod his approval, though he did, and both lawyers went to the dais. "Your Honor," Judy jumped in, "I know these questions seem unrelated but I have to ask the Court for some latitude, particularly in view of the fact that my client is on trial for his life. If I am permitted just a few questions to follow up, I think I can show the Court the relevance of the questions."

Santoro was beside himself. "Your Honor, the defense is trying to muddy the waters here and distract the jury!"

Judy almost laughed. "Your Honor, the Commonwealth opened the door. Mr. Santoro is the one who raised the issue of the defendant's belief about his son's alleged accident, in the prosecution's opening argument."

Santoro stood on tiptoe. "Your Honor, I mentioned it but I haven't called a single witness regarding the accident. It wasn't important whether it was an accident or not, only that the defendant thought it wasn't an accident. If Ms. Carrier goes forward with this point, I'll be forced to bring in a witness to refute these allegations and prove that it was indeed, an accident."

"So do it," Judy said, but Judge Vaughn was nodding slowly.

"I'll have to overrule the objection, for the time being. You did open the door, counsel." Then he glanced at Judy. "But don't travel too far afield, Ms. Carrier. No frolics and detours."

"Thank you, Your Honor," she said. She returned to the podium as Santoro took his seat and started tapping on his laptop, trying to act casual, which wasn't working. Judy felt a little nervous herself. She couldn't get any guilt-stricken admissions from Bello, but she could rattle his cage. Because Bello didn't know what she knew, or what she could prove, and therefore would only overestimate both. It would set up her defense, and it was all she had.

"Mr. Bello, do you recall where you were at midnight, the night Anthony Lucia's son and daughter-in-law were killed in an alleged truck accident?"

"No." Bello's lips set firmly, as did Santoro's, opposite him.

"Do you recall if you were with Angelo Coluzzi on that night?"

"No."

"Even though you were with him, as you testified, 24-7?"

"No."

"Do you keep any calendar, datebook, or the like that would remind you of where you were that evening?"

"No."

"Mr. Bello, you are aware, aren't you, that your telephone conversations from your home, including conversations with Angelo Coluzzi, were being taped at that time?"

"Objection!" Santoro erupted. "Irrelevant and prejudicial!"

Judy's eyes were trained on Bello, whose upper lip twitched slightly. The jury was watching him, intrigued. They would remember it. He would remember it. And he wouldn't be sure what was on the tape, especially after the opening questions, and could only assume it incriminated him. Judy figured it was time to get the hell out of Dodge. "I have no further questions, Your Honor."

"I demand that the record be stricken, Your Honor!" Santoro shouted. "This is a bald attempt to smear a completely credible witness and confuse the jury!"

Judge Vaughn waved him into silence. "Relax, Mr. Santoro. I'll sustain your objection, but we're not striking the record over it."

"Thank you, Your Honor," Judy said, grabbing her exhibit. She felt flushed and happy until she headed back to counsel table and caught sight of Frank, in the front row of the gallery.

His skin had gone gray and he focused on Bello with fresh anguish. He had just found out that it had been Bello on the telephone with Coluzzi that night. He believed he was looking at his parents' murderer. And his dark eyes told Judy, in that moment, that he was capable of murder himself.

She sat down at counsel table, and she was shaking.

# 44

It was after six o'clock at night by the time they got back to the office, and almost everyone had gone home. Judy had just gotten Bennie and Pigeon Tony into the war room at Rosato & Associates when Frank put a gentle but insistent hand on her suit sleeve.

"Can I see that file now?" he asked, his voice quiet. He had been silent all the way back from the courthouse, stuck in the cab with one security guard and Judy.

"Sure." Judy wasn't surprised, and set her briefcase and purse down on the polished walnut table. She opened her briefcase and retrieved the complete file, including the police file and the report of the accident reconstructionist. It would be awful for him to read. Judy couldn't get its gruesome conclusion out of her mind, and the Lucias weren't even her parents. "You sure you want to read this?"

"Yes."

"Okay." Judy stacked the computer-animated videotape on top of the report. It had convinced her, and she hoped it would convince Frank. "You can read in the other conference room, which also has a TV with a VCR in it. It's down the hall and to the left. You probably don't want me to send you in dinner, do you?"

"Thanks, but no." Frank met her eye, but his gaze was disconnected, and Judy suppressed comment. It made sense he'd feel distant.

"You go ahead," she said. "I want to talk to your grandfather anyway, explain to him what we'll be doing tomorrow."

"Okay, thanks." Frank palmed the files and tape and left, closing the door behind him, as Judy settled Pigeon Tony at the table and Bennie went to the credenza at the far end of the room, picked up the phone, and began checking her voicemail.

"Frankie okay?" Pigeon Tony said, and Judy shrugged.

"I hope so."

"I no like." Pigeon Tony hung his head. "Not good. Not good for Frankie."

"No, it wasn't."

Pigeon Tony looked up, his eyes dark and sad. "No, not. Not a good day for him."

Judy felt a twinge. It was clear Pigeon Tony wasn't talking only about Frank. She told herself to slow down. Dialed herself back a little. "You want some coffee, Pigeon Tony?"

"Got Chianti?"

Judy laughed. "No. But you won't need it. You want water?"

"Si, si."

"No problem." Judy got up and grabbed the pitcher of water from the back of the credenza, where Bennie was still on the phone. The woman must have 2,543 phone messages. Judy brought the pitcher back to the table, poured Pigeon Tony some in a Styrofoam cup, and handed it to him. "Here, handsome."

"**Grazie**, Judy." Pigeon Tony took a sip, and Judy watched his knobby Adam's apple travel up and down, as if it had been hard to swallow. "My wife, Silvana. You know?"

Judy nodded, wondering where this was coming from. But she had noticed that when Pigeon Tony got tired or stressed, he became confused or talked more about the past. Judy could only guess at what memories this case was dredging up for him. She couldn't imagine what it was like to live through a war, or to lose people you loved. She poured herself a cup of water, kicked off her pumps, and eased back to let him talk.

"Silvana, she gotta hard head. Baby Frank, he gotta hard head. Me, I'ma no hard head." He smiled, and Judy smiled with him.

"No, not you. You're a piece of cake."

Pigeon Tony laughed then, a little **heh-heh-heh** that fit his size perfectly, a custom-made laugh.

He finished his thought, shaking his head. "Silvana, she beautiful!"

"I'm sure she was."

"I tella judge how beautiful!"

Judy sipped her water as Pigeon Tony's eyes began to shine, his thoughts transported to another place and time. Judy had seen her grandmother do this, without the depth of feeling. Or maybe Judy had never given her grandmother the chance to talk over a Styrofoam cup of lukewarm water. She should have, and now it was too late.

"I tell judge when I first see Silvana, I meet Silvana, onna road with Coluzzi, atta race. How beautiful she is! Onna cart! She wear"—Pigeon Tony's small hand went to his lips and he patted them, fumbling for the word—"she wear, you know. **Rossetto per le labbra. You** wear, when I see you, at jail."

"Lipstick?" Judy offered.

"**Si, si!**"

Judy smiled. And here she thought she didn't speak lipstick.

"Red, like **wine** she wear! Onna **mouth**! How we kiss!"

"Ooh!" Judy laughed. "Can't tell that in court!"

Pigeon Tony held up a finger. "No! No! We kiss with a **tomato**! **Si, si!** Yes! A tomato!"

Judy didn't get it, but Pigeon Tony was too wrapped up to stop and explain.

"So many tomato! Many, **many** tomato! Until

she love me! Alla my tomato!" Pigeon Tony went **heh-heh-heh**. "Alla time, my mama, she say, 'Where my tomato? I no have tomato, for make salad! Why I no have tomato?' I laugh and laugh."

Judy smiled, her throat unaccountably tight. She didn't know exactly what Pigeon Tony was talking about, but she could get the gist. And somehow the feeling.

"Then Silvana, she eat lunch, make picnic, with me. You know, make picnic?" Pigeon Tony looked at Judy for verification, and she nodded. "In woods. Alla time. We talk and talk and we kiss."

"No tomato?"

"No tomato. Kiss! **Kiss** a woman! **La bella femmina!** Ha! Aha! So sweet!" Pigeon Tony clapped his hands together once, his face alive with the memory. "Such a kiss! Such a woman! **Sweeter** than tomato! I say to myself, Tony, you marry these woman! You be happy **forever!**"

Judy smiled, forgetting for a minute the way it had all turned out, but Pigeon Tony leaned over and touched her hand.

"I tell judge, I tell him how she marry me, and choose me, he will see." Pigeon Tony's voice grew urgent, and deep. "Alla Coluzzi, I tell judge, how Coluzzi beat chemist, beat **me**, in street, at **Torneo**. You know, **Torneo**?"

"No," Judy said. It sounded like tornado.

"I tell judge, he know. I tell people—how you say, **jury**—they know. I tell, I make them see how

Coluzzi murder, **murder** my Silvana. **Murder** my baby Frank. **Murder** Gemma, his wife. I make them see!"

Judy shook her head. He wanted to testify so much, she couldn't reason with him. "Pigeon Tony, you'll tell them all about Silvana and how wonderful she was, and then you'll tell them all about Coluzzi and how terrible he was—"

"**Si, si!** And how he kill her, how I find her, inna stable, with baby Frank." Pigeon Tony's breathing began to quicken. "Baby Frank **see** his mama! Like **that!**" Pigeon Tony's eyes filled with tears, and Judy jostled his hand, trying to bring him back to the present day, to a different country.

"And then you'll tell the judge and the jury what? How you went into the back room at the clubhouse and Coluzzi told you he killed Frank and Gemma and then how you ran at him and broke his neck?"

"**Si!**" Pigeon Tony nodded. "I tell! I do it! I make them see no is **murder!**"

"But it is! It is, here! If you tell them that, they will lock you up. Don't you see?" Judy heard herself shouting in frustration, and she became aware that Bennie had hung up the telephone and was staring at her with disapproval. Judy stopped and looked over. "Uh, hi?"

"Uh, no." Bennie managed a smile. "You might want to stop screaming at your client."

Judy relaxed back in the chair. "Good point."

Pigeon Tony glanced from one lawyer to the

other as Bennie came over, pad in hand, sat on the edge of the conference table, and looked down at him.

"Mr. Lucia," she said, "you and I haven't talked much during this case because Judy is your lawyer. She is doing a wonderful job for you. She has a defense that the jury can understand and believe in. Depending on what she does tomorrow, she may win this case for you, which is a very difficult thing to do. She is advising you not to testify, and I would listen to her if I were you. You should also know that in the United States very few defendants like you take the stand and testify. I have defended many murder cases and never had a defendant on the stand."

"Si, si."

"But as she told you, it is your right to testify if you want to. So here's what I think. Tonight you sleep on it." Bennie caught herself in the idiom when Pigeon Tony's forehead crinkled. "You rest tonight and you can decide tomorrow. If you still want to testify tomorrow, then you and Judy can discuss it again. Okay?"

"Si!" Pigeon Tony said quickly, pumping his head with vigor.

"Judy will discuss it as much as you want to, because it is a very important decision. It is the single most important decision in every defense. And it is your decision. Understand?"

"Si, si." Pigeon Tony seemed to back down.

Judy exhaled. "Okay, I agree."

Bennie shot her a look. "It doesn't matter whether you agree."

Uh, oh. Judy smiled. "But it's a good thing that I do, huh? Makes it nicer, all around."

Bennie rolled her eyes and smiled at Pigeon Tony. "Mr. Lucia, you see, Judy gets a little excited, and she cares about you. Also she's young. Not like you and me."

Pigeon Tony burst into laughter. "**You** young woman, Benedetta!"

"I'm forty-five, sir. I stopped being young forty years ago." Bennie hopped off the table and nodded at Judy. "Maybe you should order your client some dinner before you start talking business."

"Okay, sure." Judy reminded herself she had to do better in the care-and-feeding department. She had even lost custody of her puppy, she was such a bad mother. "Pigeon Tony, you want me to order dinner before we talk?"

"Dinner, **si**."

"You want Chinese? You had the plain lo mein."

Pigeon Tony wrinkled his tan nose. "Bad pasta."

Judy smiled. "Want pizza?"

"Si, si."

Judy nodded. It was only the 3,847th time they'd had pizza delivered in the past week. "Okay, pizza it is." She went to the phone to order when the conference room door opened suddenly, and everybody looked up.

Frank came in and tossed the file on the table, where it slid across the smooth surface. His face was grim but oddly relieved. "My parents **were** murdered in their truck that night," he said simply.

Judy's mouth dropped open. "What do you mean? Didn't you read the expert's report?"

"I did. That's what proves it to me."

"How? The expert found it was an accident."

Frank managed a half smile. "But I know something he didn't."

Judy put the phone back down in surprise.

# 45

"You may sit down," Judge Vaughn said as he entered the courtroom and ascended the dais. His manner telegraphed that he was ready to move along, which was just how Judy felt. She couldn't wait to put on her case, now that she believed she had a winner. But a lot depended on what happened with the Commonwealth's last witness.

Judy shifted forward on her seat. It had occurred to her, as she worked through last night preparing questions and making phone calls, that the tables had turned in this case. Until this morning it had been Pigeon Tony on trial, but from now on it was Angelo Coluzzi's turn to be tried for murder. And Judy didn't want him to get away with it, even in death, though she still didn't know if she could convict him with the evidence she had. But she had a better chance than before Frank's discovery. And Judy was glad that it was Frank who had found the key. It was fitting.

She glanced over at Pigeon Tony, who looked

intent now that the truth would finally come out about his son's death. In the front row of the gallery, Frank was on the edge of the pew. The rest of the gallery settled down, with only the reporters and courtroom artists working away. The judge had seated himself and cleared a stack of pleadings from the center of the dais.

"Good morning, Ms. Carrier, Mr. Santoro. Mr. Santoro, you may call your first witness."

Santoro rose, in a new dark suit with deep vent. "Good morning, Your Honor. The Commonwealth calls Calvin DeWitt to the stand."

Judy looked back as the door to the courtroom opened and the bailiff escorted in a middle-aged African-American man with a little goatee and rimless glasses. He wore a neatly pressed suit and carried himself with confidence as he walked to the stand, was sworn in, and sat down.

Santoro took his place at the podium. "Mr. DeWitt, please identify yourself for the jury."

"I am an officer with the Accident Investigation Division, or AID, of the Philadelphia Police Department. I have been with AID for fifteen years, during which time I have investigated over five thousand traffic accidents in Philadelphia County. Basically our mission is to determine how a traffic fatality occurred."

"Officer DeWitt, what is your training to perform such a complex task?"

"We are schooled in the most modern methods

and technology of accident reconstruction, including courses in physics, crash investigation, bridge and highway construction, human anatomy, drug and alcohol impairment in the driver, and computer-animated graphics."

Santoro nodded. "And do you receive accreditations, sir?"

"We do. We may be certified by ACTAR, which is the Accreditation Commission for Traffic Accident Reconstruction. I am so certified."

Santoro flipped a page in his legal pad. "Your Honor, I move to have Officer DeWitt qualified as an expert."

Judy nodded. She needed his testimony, too. "No objection."

"Granted," Judge Vaughn said, and Judy cast a glance at the jury. They appeared to be listening quietly, and she hoped they were anticipating the testimony about the accident, after yesterday with Jimmy Bello. Judy had subpoenaed him so he'd be in court today, and he sat coolly near John Coluzzi, who was himself stern-faced.

Santoro addressed the witness. "Officer DeWitt, are you the AID officer who investigated the traffic accident that occurred on January twenty-fifth, involving the deaths of Frank and Gemma Lucia, of Philadelphia?"

"I am."

"And please describe briefly what you did to investigate that accident?"

Officer DeWitt looked up. "May I refer to my report?"

"Of course." Santoro located a paper in his stack and distributed copies to Judy and the court personnel, who gave one to the judge. "Your Honor, I wish to move into evidence Commonwealth Exhibit Twenty-three, which is Officer DeWitt's report of the accident in question."

"No objection," Judy said. She set the report aside to signal to the jury that she had seen it already. In fact, she'd memorized it last night, but there was no way she could signal that, as much as she wanted the extra credit.

Officer DeWitt thumbed through his report. "This refreshes my recollection. I visited the accident that night at one o'clock in the morning, less than one hour after it occurred. I examined the truck involved, a VW pickup. I also examined the guardrail on the overpass where the truck went over, as well as the point of impact on the underpass beneath."

"Could you briefly describe how the accident occurred?"

"Yes. The truck, a light, old-model pickup, was traveling west on the double-lane overpass when it skidded on a patch of ice, due to driver error and road conditions. The truck collided with the guardrail, tipped over the side of the overpass, and landed upside down on the underpass below, where the fuel tank ruptured and burst into flame.

The occupants would have been killed on impact, if not by the fire that consumed the vehicle's passenger cab, though their bodies had been removed by the M.E.'s office by the time I arrived at the scene."

"So it is your expert opinion, to a reasonable degree of scientific certainty, that the crash of the truck was an accident, pure and simple?"

"Yes." Then DeWitt added, "Though no accident that involves loss of life is simple. But yes, it was an accident."

"I stand corrected. You are quite right." Santoro nodded. "Officer DeWitt, I take it from your explanation of how the accident occurred that no other vehicles were involved?"

"No other vehicles."

"And there were no other fatalities as a result of the accident?"

"No."

"As a result of your conclusion that it was an accident, no charges of any kind were issued by the police, correct?"

"Yes."

"And the case was considered closed by the Philadelphia Police Department?"

"Yes, it was and is."

"No further questions," Santoro said. He returned to his seat as Judy stood up, went to the podium with her papers, and introduced herself before her first question.

"Officer DeWitt, you said you examined the Lucias' truck an hour after the accident and that it had caught fire. What caused that fire, in your opinion?"

"The fuel line ruptured and the tank was compromised when the truck overturned. The interior of the vehicle was filled with fuel and then consumed by fire."

Judy hoped Frank wasn't visualizing this. "Officer DeWitt, did you perform any tests to determine the residue left by the fire on the interior or exterior of the truck?"

"No, there was no reason to."

Judy made a note. THAT'S WHAT YOU THINK, SMARTYPANTS. "In your opinion, Officer DeWitt, what caused the fuel to ignite?"

"Many things commonly cause such fires, such as sparks from an electrical connection, the heat of an engine in contact with fuel, and often when steel and concrete collide, sparks result."

"So it's your testimony that the Lucias' pickup truck left the overpass because of the ice and driver error, rolled over the guardrail, and crashed onto an underpass, and that the impact of the crash or the fire from the ruptured fuel tank killed the Lucias?"

"Yes."

Judy didn't pause. "What kind of fuel was it?"

"I don't understand the question."

"Do you recall the type of fuel it was that ignited, in the cab?"

"Diesel."

Judy made a fake note. EUREKA! She asked the question she needed the answer to: "How do you know that it was diesel fuel, if you performed no tests on the residue left behind?"

"The truck had a diesel engine." Officer DeWitt glanced at his report. "I examined the engine of the vehicle and contacted Harrisburg to determine its registration. It was a 1.6-liter diesel engine. Fifty-two horsepower."

Judy thought a minute. Had to cover all the bases. "So is it your testimony that the ruptured fuel tank in the pickup was the only fuel container in the pickup?"

The witness cocked his head. "What other kind of fuel container could there be?"

"Well, was there a lawn mower in the truck, or a chain saw, or just a spare gas can?"

Officer DeWitt reflected on it, then shook his head. "No. Nothing like that. The back bed was empty, as was the cab, except for minor debris and some broken glass."

"If you had seen something like that, you would have noted it, would you not?"

"Yes. I take careful notes."

"And does your report contain any such notation?"

Officer DeWitt thumbed through the exhibit. "No."

"Thank you," Judy said, and remained at the podium, as the witness stepped down. She was halfway home. And she was saving the best for last.

"No redirect, Your Honor," Santoro said, rising at his seat. "The Commonwealth rests."

On the dais Judge Vaughn nodded smartly. "Ms. Carrier, looks like you're up, for the defense."

"Thank you, Your Honor. The defense calls Dr. William Wold to the stand." Judy looked expectantly toward the double doors, feeling oddly like a groom awaiting a bride. Dr. Wold strode past the bar of court in a dark suit, walked to the witness stand, and was sworn in. "Dr. Wold," she began, "please tell the jury who you are and what you do."

"I am an accident reconstruction expert. I was an officer with the Accident Investigation Division of the Philadelphia Police for thirty-two years until my retirement, and now I consult full-time. I determine how a traffic accident occurred in order to testify at trials, like this one."

"Dr. Wold, what is your training to perform such a complex task?"

"I teach courses in accident reconstruction, including courses in crash investigation, guardrail construction and renovation, bridge and highway construction, anatomy, drinking and driving, physics, the sleep-deprived and drugged driver, forensic sciences, and computer-animated graphics."

"And are you an accredited accident reconstructionist?"

"Yes, by ACTAR, as well as by agencies in Pennsylvania and New Jersey."

Judy looked at the judge, who was skimming

papers on his desk. "Your Honor, I move to have Dr. Wold qualified as an expert."

Santoro nodded. "No objection," he said, and Judge Vaughn nodded.

"Granted," he ruled. "Please continue, Ms. Carrier."

Judy smiled to herself. Santoro was stuck. He didn't dare object in front of the jury, not after he'd opened the door with the AID man. Judy had hoped he'd go for it, after Jimmy Bello, and he had. She deserved extra-**extra** credit. "Dr. Wold, did there come a time when you examined the wreck of the Lucias' pickup?"

"Yes, about four months ago, at your request. You asked me to determine how the accident had occurred."

Santoro was on his loafers. "Objection, Your Honor. Where's the chain of custody for the vehicle? How do we know he examined the right vehicle?"

"Your Honor," Judy said, waving the papers, "I was just about to introduce these documents into evidence. They are the bill of sale and the receipt for the Lucias' truck. The VIN, or Vehicle Identification Number, matches the wreck that Dr. Wold examined at my request."

Judge Vaughn motioned for the papers, and Judy handed them to the bailiff, who brought them to the judge. She held her breath while the judge read the documents, hoping he wouldn't wonder where the junkyard release was, since all she could offer into evidence was a wire cutter and a couple of senior citizens.

Judge Vaughn handed the documents back with a grunt. "Go for it, counsel."

"I move these documents into evidence as Defense Exhibits Twenty and Twenty-one," she said, handing Santoro the copies, and he read them quickly.

"No objection," he said, and Judy returned to the witness.

"Now, Dr. Wold, more paperwork. Did you prepare a report in connection with your findings?"

"I did." Judy located the copies of the report and distributed one each to Santoro, the judge, and the bailiff. "Your Honor, I move this report into evidence as Defense Exhibit Twenty-three."

Santoro, reading, put up a hand. "No objection," he said after a moment, but he kept reading.

"It's admitted," Judge Vaughn ruled, and went back to skimming his papers.

Judy paused so the jury could focus. "Dr. Wold, please tell the jury what you investigated to determine how the accident occurred."

"I examined the wreck, measured it, researched the make and model of truck, which was a 1981 VW Rabbit. I visited the scene, obtained the AID report from the police, and also ran a number of residue tests on the exterior of the vehicle and the interior of the passenger cab."

"What were the results of those residue tests?"

"Well, I found a number of residues in the burned wreck, primarily residue of burning plas-

tic, residue of burned and partially burned diesel
fuel, and residue of gasoline."

Judy noted it. RESIDUE CITY. "Were these
residues—diesel, oil, and gasoline—found in
equal amounts?"

"No, not at all. By far the greatest amount of
residue, particularly in the passenger cab, was
residue of gasoline. Both unburned gasoline and
gasoline-impregnated ash were all over the interior of the passenger cab."

Judy made a note. YOU GO, GIRL. "Dr. Wold,
what is the significance of that gasoline residue in
the passenger cab?"

"It is extremely significant. It tells us that it was
a gasoline fire that engulfed the passenger cab."

"I see." Judy paused. "Dr. Wold, is there any reasonable explanation for the gasoline inside that cab?"

"Yes, of course. As I said in my report, it is very
common for construction vehicles to be carrying
all sorts of fuel, even in their cabs. In fact, I
assumed that the Lucias' truck was, since it was a
working truck. In addition, if the truck was carrying gas cans, a lawn mower, a chain saw, or the
like, gasoline could come from there."

Judy nodded. "But what if the truck wasn't carrying any of those things?"

"What do you mean?"

Judy sighed. The toughest expert she ever met.
Biting the hand that feeds him. She could only hope
it increased his credibility, because he was busting

her chops. "I mean, do you have an explanation for a diesel-powered truck, carrying no container of gasoline, to be engulfed in a gasoline fire during a crash?"

"No."

"Nothing in your examination could explain why a diesel truck with no gasoline in it had a gasoline fire?"

"That's what I just said."

Judy made a note. I AM NOT PAYING YOU, NO MATTER WHAT. "Dr. Wold, I direct you to the conclusion of your report. Could you please read it to the jury?"

"Certainly." Dr. Wold flipped to the last page of his report. "I concluded that 'negligent driving, poor weather conditions, and a substandard guardrail resulted in the fatal accident involving Mr. and Mrs. Lucia on January twenty-fifth.' I also noted that 'petroleum residues included engine oil, diesel fuel, and gasoline, not unusual in a construction vehicle crash.'"

Judy paused. Was it insane to refute the conclusion of your own expert in a death case? Not when it was this expert. It was a pleasure to prove him wrong. "Dr. Wold, is it possible that the gasoline fire caused the crash, instead of the crash causing the gasoline fire?"

Dr. Wold cleared his throat. "I never looked at it that way, but it's possible. And if the truck was not carrying gasoline, then the presence of the gasoline remains unexplained."

"So I ask you, do you still agree with the conclusion in your report?"

Dr. Wold thought for a long time. "I don't know."

"I have no further questions," Judy said, and she walked to counsel table and sat down next to Pigeon Tony. She didn't dare look at him or Frank, who was the one who had known the truck had a diesel, not a gasoline, engine. It was good stuff, and she didn't want to jinx anything.

Santoro was already at the podium, his expression tense. "Dr. Wold, didn't you in fact conclude that the Lucias' deaths were the result of driver error, bad weather, and a low guardrail?"

"That's what I concluded, yes."

"Thank you." Santoro stormed to his chair and sat down, and Judy hid her satisfaction.

"No redirect, Your Honor," she said. Her stomach was a knot. She thought she was making headway, but she was too focused to have any perspective. On the dais, Judge Vaughn was making notes, probably I LOOK GOOD IN BLACK. She glanced at the jury, which remained impassive, watching Dr. Wold step down and leave the courtroom.

It was time for Judy's last witness.

# 46

"The defense calls Marlene Bello to the stand," Judy called out. She turned to face the double doors, and the gallery was craning their necks to see, particularly on the Coluzzi side of the aisle. Jimmy Bello's mouth had dropped open, and Tony-From-Down-The-Block looked like a man in love. He had been Judy's secret weapon, though Marlene was such a class act, she didn't need to be convinced to testify.

Judy smiled at her as she entered the courtroom, and she smiled back, sashaying down the aisle in a red knit dress that caressed every curve, with matching red pumps. She even made pantyhose look like a damn good time. Marlene took the witness stand as if she owned it, was sworn in, sat down, and crossed a great pair of legs.

Judy was at the podium. "Please tell the jury who you are, Ms. Bello."

"My name is Marlene Bello and I used to be married to Jimmy Bello." She pointed a crimson-lacquered nail at him. "Right there."

"How long were you married to Mr. Bello?"

"With time off for good behavior?" she asked, and the jury laughed. "Almost thirty-two years."

"And when were you divorced?"

"Cut him loose about a year and a half ago, almost two."

"Now, Ms. Bello, did there come a time when you began tapping your own telephone, without your husband's knowledge?"

Santoro shot up. "Objection, relevance, Your Honor."

"May we approach?" Judy asked, and Judge Vaughn gave them the go-ahead. Judy reached the dais first. "Judge, as you will see in just a few questions, Ms. Bello is here to make statements against her own interest, which bear directly on the matter at hand."

Santoro was shaking his head. "Your Honor, the matter at hand is the murder of Angelo Coluzzi. If she doesn't speak to that, she has no business testifying. She's just the ex-wife of a prosecution witness!"

"Your Honor," Judy said. "Again, the Commonwealth opened the door on the deaths of Frank and Gemma Lucia."

Judge Vaughn sighed. "I overrule the objection, but keep the questions in control, or I will." Santoro went back to counsel table and Judy to the podium.

"You may answer the question, Ms. Bello."

"I did tap my own phone. I hired a private detective to do it."

"And why did you do this?"

"To see if that pig was cheatin' on me, which he was."

"Objection, relevance, and prejudicial, Your Honor!" Santoro shouted, but Judge Vaughn waved him off.

"And did the time period you tapped cover last year, commencing on January first?"

"Yes. It was my New Year's resolution. Throw the bum out."

"So I take it you were tapping your own phone through January twenty-fifth of that year, the date on which Frank and Gemma Lucia were killed?"

Santoro simmered but evidently thought better of objecting, since even Judge Vaughn was listening intently to Marlene. Judy almost managed to relax, but she was still a lawyer and it proved impossible.

"Yeah, I was tapping our phone on the twenty-fifth."

"Ms. Bello, did you also overhear some of these conversations, as well as having them recorded?"

"Yes, because we taped all calls, even legit ones and ones when I was there. Half the tapes is me talking to my psychic." Marlene turned to the jury. "Talk about a rip-off." The jury laughed.

"Did you ever overhear any conversations Mr. Bello had with Angelo Coluzzi?"

"Puh-lenty." Marlene chuckled. "Jimmy was on the phone with Angelo all the time, taking orders."

"Do you recall that Mr. Bello had a conversation with Mr. Coluzzi on the evening of January twenty-fifth, the evening that Frank and Gemma Lucia were killed in their truck?"

"I do."

"And where were you when this conversation occurred?"

"I was in the kitchen doin' my reports for my business, and he was on the kitchen phone."

Judy flipped her legal pad to her notes of the tapes. After she had found out about the gasoline in the truck fire last night, she had gone back to her notes of the tapes. Then she had called Marlene and told her about the note and the gasoline fire. Only one thing could explain both, and only Marlene could explain that one thing. "And what did you hear Mr. Bello say?"

"Objection, hearsay," Santoro said, but Judy would have begged if she had to.

"Your Honor, it's coming in for the fact that he said it, so it's not hearsay."

"Overruled," Judge Vaughn said, motioning Santoro into his seat at counsel table.

Judy skimmed her notes. "You may answer, Ms. Bello. What did you hear Mr. Bello say to Mr. Coluzzi on the night of January twenty-fifth?"

"It sounded like they were making a date for Jimmy to pick Angelo up, since he was his driver, and I heard Jimmy say to Angelo, 'I'll bring the Coke.'"

"And what did that mean to you?"

"It was like code they used, the two of 'em."

"Code for what?"

"It meant, 'I'll bring a Molotov cocktail.' "

"Objection!" Santoro bolted out of his chair. "Relevance and extremely prejudicial! Your Honor!"

Judy was desperate. She needed this one piece of evidence. "Your Honor, this is absolutely relevant to the death of the defendant's son and daughter in-law."

"But it has nothing to do with the death of Angelo Coluzzi, Your Honor!"

Judge Vaughn shifted forward on the dais, his expression concerned. "I want to hear what this witness has to say, Mr. Santoro," he announced, and Judy knew from his tone it had nothing to do with Marlene's charms. He turned to her. "Ms. Bello, it is incumbent upon the Court to warn you that you may be making a statement which could incriminate you, since tapping a telephone conversation without a party's knowledge and consent is unlawful in this Commonwealth. Are you represented by counsel at this proceeding?"

Marlene smiled shakily. "I already talked to a lawyer. He's sittin' in the back, and I'm ready to deal with whatever they do to me. I lived with Jimmy Bello, I can live with prison."

Judge Vaughn hid his smile with a respectful nod. "Fine, Ms. Bello." He pointed at Judy. "Ms. Carrier, do go on."

"Thank you, Your Honor," Judy said, then stole a glance at the jury out of the corner of her eye. Each one was listening, many leaning forward urgently. Judy turned to Marlene. "Ms. Bello, what is a Molotov cocktail, by the way?"

Santoro threw up his arms. "Your Honor, is the witness a qualified expert on incendiary devices now?"

On the stand Marlene burst into laughter. "I'm from South Philly, pal. You think I don't know from Molotov cocktails?"

"Overruled," Judge Vaughn said, glaring Santoro into his chair. "Please answer the question, Ms. Bello."

"Sure thing." Marlene brushed a sprayed curl from her eye. "A Molotov cocktail's a bottle with gasoline in it, and you put a rag in it and light it. Then you throw the bottle and it breaks and makes a gasoline fire."

Bingo. Judy would have felt happy, but the words "gasoline fire" made her shudder. The Lucias had been burned alive. What a way to die. And what must Frank be feeling? She couldn't look at him and stayed focused on Marlene. "Ms. Bello, what time did Mr. Bello leave the house that night?"

"I know it was late, maybe about nine-thirty at night."

"Did he tell you where he was going?"

"No, just that he was going to pick up Angelo."

"And did he bring the Coke with him when he left?"

Marlene wet her glossy lips. "I'll tell you what I

saw him do that night, after they talked. He took a Coke out of the fridge, in one of those glass bottles he always bought. Then he emptied it out in the sink. The whole bottle. Without even sippin' it."

Judy paused as the jury reacted. "Did he leave the house with the empty bottle, Ms. Bello?"

"Yeh." Marlene bit her lip. "I didn't say anything, but I should have. I knew he was up to no good but I didn't think he'd kill somebody with it, least of all the Lucias."

Suddenly Judy felt for her, for the Lucias, for Frank and Pigeon Tony, even for Jimmy Bello and the Coluzzis. So much death, so much killing. She gripped the side of the podium. "Ms. Bello, why didn't you come forward to the police with this information before now?"

"I didn't put it together until you called last night and told me about the gasoline, in the diesel truck. I didn't know. I'm sorry." Marlene turned directly to Frank and Pigeon Tony, her eyes glistening. "I really am so sorry."

Judy held back her emotion. She was almost home free. She had done it. Proved who murdered the Lucias. Raised reasonable doubt about the Coluzzi murder. She felt her knees go weak, from exhaustion and relief and sheer joy.

Crak! Crak! Crak! banged the gavel suddenly, and Judge Vaughn began shouting, his eyes filled with alarm at the gallery. "Order! Order! Stop that man!"

Judy stood stunned. Pigeon Tony grabbed her arm in surprise. Santoro was on his feet, his face a mask of dismay. The bailiff reached for a telephone. The court stenographer cried, "Holy God!"

The gallery had erupted behind the bulletproof divide. Jimmy Bello was making a break for it, barreling full steam toward the exit doors. Frank was running after him, his tie flying. A cadre of court security charged behind them both. Spectators leaped out of the way in fear. Reporters scribbled like mad. Artists couldn't sketch fast enough. Behind the bulletproof plastic, the scene was an action movie on mute.

**Crak! Crak! Crak!** Judge Vaughn kept banging the gavel. "Security! Security! Bailiff, call downstairs!"

Bello hit the double door at speed, with Frank and court security right on his heels. There was no way he would get out of the courthouse. There were layers of cops, police personnel, and courthouse security between him and the elevators, much less the exit downstairs. Bello's only hope was that the cops got him.

Before Frank did.


The judge had declared a lunch recess, but nobody in the courthouse conference room was interested in food. Judy held Frank close, unembarrassed even in front of Bennie and Pigeon Tony. She breathed in the smells of him, the sweat from the dash after Jimmy Bello, and the fresh grief at his parents' death. His corduroy jacket was soft in her arms, though his sleeve had been ripped in the melee. Judy hung on until Frank broke the embrace and wiped his bruised cheek. "At least we got Bello," Frank said, his voice soft.

"We sure did." Judy grinned. "One of the cops told me they'll hold him for questioning. I turned over copies of my file and asked the expert to send the wreck over to police impoundment, so they have something to go on."

"Think they'll charge him?"

"We won't let 'em rest until they do, will we?" Judy peered at Frank's bruise. "How's that feel?"

"Okay. After I tackled him, he kicked out. But I got a few good licks in." Frank straightened up and actually broke into a smile. "The bailiff let me be the one to bring him down."

"Good," Judy said, meaning it. "What better use for my tax dollars?"

Frank smiled, then hugged Pigeon Tony, rocking him slightly. The little old man seemed to burrow into Frank's broad chest, and Frank flashed Judy a grin over his grandfather's bald head. "You and Bennie can hug now. I think we won."

Judy laughed. "I think so, too."

Bennie looked over. "No hugging, though. Lawyers don't hug."

"Agreed," Judy said. She was too happy to stop

smiling. She felt great. It was a miracle. She had to have been a galley slave in a former life to cash in on this karmic payload.

Then Pigeon Tony emerged from Frank's arms, his brown eyes bright. "I talk to judge now," he said, and Judy's good mood vanished.

"You don't have to. It's over."

Pigeon Tony turned slowly, shaking his head. "No. I talk to judge. I talk to judge now." A surprised Frank stood behind him, but Judy was aghast. He couldn't mean it. This wasn't happening.

"Pigeon Tony, we're ready to go to the jury now, just as it is."

"No! You say, today I say. I say. I go to judge. I tell truth!"

Judy wasn't hearing this. Maybe he didn't understand, even though she'd explained it 236,345 times. "Let me explain. Again. I have proved that Angelo Coluzzi hated you, and that you and he were in a small room together for maybe five minutes. During this time Angelo Coluzzi's neck got broken, but I proved that that could have happened easily in a man his age, in even a scuffle."

"I broke! I did!"

Judy checked her urge to grab Pigeon Tony by his scrawny little neck and shake some sense into him. "But the only proof they have that you started the fight and not Coluzzi is that somebody who **never** heard you speak heard you yell, 'I'm gonna kill you,' in Italian."

"Me! I said! I **did**! But no é murder!"

Judy wanted to kill him, in English. "But they can't prove that, and they haven't. They **lost**. I bet you ten to one that the jury is going to come back for you, Pigeon Tony."

"I tell judge! I tell them! I tell about Silvana! And tomatoes! And kiss!"

Judy's head began to throb. Tomatoes and kisses wouldn't do it, in a court of law. Maybe if she explained more. "I am going to argue to the jury in my closing that it's just as likely that you pushed Angelo Coluzzi in self-defense as that you attacked him. That is demonstrably true."

"What means mons——?"

Judy was losing patience. "It's true, leave it at that. In addition, we have also proved, fairly conclusively, that Angelo Coluzzi and Jimmy Bello killed your son and daughter-in-law by throwing a Molotov cocktail in their truck, which set fire to their cab and caused what everybody thought was an accident." Judy knew she was talking too fast for Pigeon Tony to follow, but she couldn't stop herself. He was threatening to snatch defeat from the jaws of victory. Never mind that he could end up dead. "And if the jury thinks Coluzzi really killed your son, and not just that you believe it for no reason, then they will feel less sympathetic for him and less inclined to convict you for his murder. Don't you get it? Shut up and win!"

Frank had gone white, his hands on his grandfather's shoulders. "Judy, you're hollering at him."

"I have every right to holler at him! I'm trying to save his fucking life!" Judy shouted, and realized she had lost it. She didn't need the expression on Bennie's face to tell her, but it was there just the same.

Bennie was holding up her hand, like a stop sign. "Judy, enough. You're upset. Get a grip." She turned to Frank, almost formally. "Frank, does your grandfather understand what Judy is saying? Because she's right."

"I know he does. He understands more than people think."

"I don't want to take any chances. His life is at stake, and my liability. I want you to explain to him everything Judy just said, in Italian. And tell him if he chooses to testify, tell him he does so against his attorney's advice."

"Fair enough," Frank said. "But I'm telling you. He understands fine. He just doesn't agree."

"I no agree!" Pigeon Tony chorused.

Frank began speaking to Pigeon Tony in rapid Italian, and Judy watched, feeling utterly helpless. She couldn't believe it was happening. Her emotions went from complete frustration to stone cold fear. She looked at Frank and Pigeon Tony, then to Bennie. Was Bennie going to let this happen? "Bennie, they could kill him! They could give him the death penalty!"

"I know that." Bennie was calm, which only made Judy crazier.

"We can't just let him walk into it!" In the

background was the sound of Italian, too musical for the grim occasion.

"We have to, if that's what he wants."

Frank looked up, grimly, his hands on his grandfather's arm. "He wants to do it. He wants to tell the truth. He wants his day in court. He says he's innocent, and he wants the jury to find that he's innocent."

"What's the difference?" Judy exploded at Pigeon Tony, but Frank answered for him.

"You know what it is. He doesn't want to think he got away with murder, because to him, it's not murder. It's not just that he's not guilty—he's innocent."

"Then it's done," Bennie said simply, cutting Judy off with a chop and checking her watch. "We have two minutes until we go in."

Judy couldn't stop shaking her head. She grabbed Pigeon Tony by both of his hands. "Pigeon Tony, do you understand that after you testify, Mr. Santoro can ask you questions? All sorts of questions?"

"Si, si." Pigeon Tony nodded, unfazed.

"Mr. Santoro will not be nice to you, he will be very mean. He will try to make you look like a very bad man. He will ask you, 'How did you murder him?' He will say, 'Tell the jury exactly how you broke poor Angelo Coluzzi's neck.'"

"I tell. I kill. No murder."

"It will be awful! Santoro will tear you apart! He

can keep you up there for days! You hardly even speak the language!" Judy wanted to cry, but she had to keep a tenuous grip or she couldn't save him. "The jury won't like what you say! They will say, 'This man is a killer. Let's give him the death penalty. Put him to death!'"

"Si, si." Pigeon Tony half smiled, and his eyes, hooded with age, met Judy's with a sort of serenity. Behind them Judy saw a strength she hadn't noticed before, but also a folly. The bravest men got themselves killed. The pioneer was the one with the arrows in his chest.

"Pigeon Tony, please don't." If she had to beg, she would. "I am begging you."

"Judy, no worry." Pigeon Tony squeezed her hands. "You ask questions, inna court? Si?"

Judy blinked back tears. She couldn't imagine it. She would have to take him through it on direct examination. "Yes," she said, but her eyes filled up anyway. She didn't want to see him dead, or even in prison. She didn't know it until now, but she loved him.

"Ask me, I tell Silvana. Ask baby Frank. Ask tomato. Ask how Silvana die, inna stable. I tell. Like before, yesterday. I tell."

Judy remembered. She had been transported by his stories. But she wasn't a jury. And nothing had been at stake, least of all Pigeon Tony's life. A tear rolled down her cheek, and she let go of his hand to brush it away.

"Everything okay, you see, Judy. Judge see. Jury see. Alla people see. Say me, how you see Silvana, Pigeon Tony?"

Judy's lips trembled and she couldn't speak. Bennie had fallen silent.

Frank sighed audibly. "Juries can do whatever they want, can't they, Judy?" he asked.

Judy wasn't holding any false hope. "At least they can't kill him twice."

Bennie shot her a disapproving look. "Yes, Frank. Your counsel should be telling you that there is something called jury nullification, which means the jury simply ignores the law and does what it thinks is just. It happened first a long time ago in the Old South, where white juries wouldn't convict white men who lynched black men. Since then it has occurred, only rarely, in mercy killing and domestic abuse cases. But it is very rare."

"**Very** rare," Judy echoed. "Like winning-the-lottery rare."

"**Andiamo!**" cried Pigeon Tony abruptly, clapping his hands together in excitement. His eyes were shining and his face was bright, and for a minute he looked positively victorious.

Judy knew it couldn't last.

# 47

"Pardon me, Ms. Carrier?" Judge Vaughn asked, trying to hide his astonishment as court resumed after the recess. Even the judge's eyebrows curled like question marks. Tugging at his robes, he leaned over the dais, as if he had heard Judy wrong. "**What** did you say, counsel?"

"The defense calls Anthony Lucia to the stand, Your Honor," Judy repeated, and Judge Vaughn blinked in surprise. Judicial decorum prevented his commenting, **That's what I thought you said, bozo.**

Santoro wasn't half as polite. At the prosecutor's table he didn't bother to hide his glee. He was smiling and alert, rejuvenated after the melee with Jimmy Bello. Santoro had gone from the nadir to the zenith faster than you can say vocabulary words. If he took fake notes he could write, WHAT ARE YOU, STUPID?

Pigeon Tony rose next to Judy at counsel table, and she helped him to the witness stand, where he sat down behind the Bible and was sworn in by a rather startled clerk. Judy returned to the podium, holding her head high and trying to regain her professionalism after the waterworks in the conference room. If Pigeon Tony was determined to do this, she was determined to mitigate the damage, even if this murder trial had become an assisted suicide.

Judy took the podium, gripped the edges, and found herself face-to-face with the tiny man who looked like a bird, in the cage that was the witness box. Her throat caught at the sight and she remembered the day she had first met him. How cute he was. How little. She prayed the jury would see him that way. It was almost all he had going for him, and she started feeling emotional again.

"Judy?" Pigeon Tony whispered from the witness stand, and the jury reacted with soft laughter. Even the court personnel were smiling.

Only Judy was on the verge of tears, looking at him. Nobody would tell him it was against the rules to talk to your lawyer from the box. He was on his own now. His fate was his own, and his karma. Judy believed in it, and it gave her heart. If anybody's past could redeem his future, it was Pigeon Tony's. But his lawyer still couldn't chase the tears from her eyes.

"Ms. Carrier?" Judge Vaughn said, moving his hand from underneath his chin.

"Sorry, Your Honor." Judy wiped her eyes and

bit her lips to control their tremor. God! What an idiot! She was a lawyer! In a courtroom! Ask a question, dufus! "Mr. Lucia, please tell the jury where you are from, originally," she blurted out, then realized it was only the stupidest question in the world.

Pigeon Tony turned slightly toward the jury, as relaxed as if he were conversing over Cynar in a piazza café. "I am from Italy," he said. "Abruzzo, Italy. You know, Italy?" He pronounced it Eeetaly, his accent flavoring his words as strongly as sweet basil, and the front row of the jury smiled collectively. One juror, an older schoolteacher in the front, even nodded. Judy remembered she was Italian and had family that were Abruzzese. Most of the Italians in South Philly were Abruzzese.

Judy wiped her eyes with the back of her hand. She had to get it together. "And Pigeon Tony— wait, can I call him Pigeon Tony?" Judy wondered aloud, but didn't wait for the judge to rule. Why the hell not? Her motto had always been, Don't ask permission, apologize later. She was making up her own rules as she went along. After all, she had already called an expert witness whose conclusion she disagreed with. It was a slippery slope.

"Sure," Pigeon Tony answered with a grin. "Alla people, alla people here calla me Pigeon Tony." He looked up at Judge Vaughn, who had been peering at him from behind his knuckles with a mixture of bewilderment and delight, neither of which

Pigeon Tony noticed. "I have pigeons. Birds, you know, birds? They race, my birds. The Old Man, he come back. Soon. This, I know."

"That's nice," Judge Vaughn said politely, then hunched toward Pigeon Tony. "Mr. Lucia—"

"Calla me Pigeon Tony! Alla people calla me Pigeon Tony! Even judge!"

Judge Vaughn laughed. "Okay, Pigeon Tony, I heard you say that you are from Italy. Do you feel the need for a translator? We can have one brought in here very quickly."

"No, Judge. I no need. I know. I hear. I unnerstand." Pigeon Tony pointed to his temple. Judy wanted to cover her face with her hands, but the jury burst into laughter.

"Uh, Pigeon Tony," Judy said, but when she had his attention, was too upset to think of a question. Talk about a slow start. She tried to remember her client's coaching in the conference room. Every lawyer needs a smart client, to give them advice. **Everything okay, you see, Judy. Alla people see. Say me, how you see Silvana, Pigeon Tony?** Judy translated. "Pigeon Tony, please tell the jury how you met your wife, Silvana."

Pigeon Tony swallowed, his Adam's apple moving like an elevator. "I was young, but a man, I go to race. In Mascoli, with birds. You know, Mascoli?" He paused, and only when one of the jurors shook his head no, did he respond. "Is city, near Veramo, where Pigeon Tony live. Mascoli big city." He spread his arms wide, which for his wingspan meant three feet. "**Rich** city. Not like Veramo. Veramo small, very small city. Alla farmer, in Veramo. You know, farmer?"

The front row nodded and smiled. Yes, they knew farmer. Santoro was frowning. Judy made a real note on her legal pad, trying to recall the stories Pigeon Tony had told her the other day, and at other times. FIRST KISS, WITH TOMATOES. PICNIC IN THE WOODS. FIRST REAL KISS. THE DAY AT THE TORNADO.

On the stand, Pigeon Tony was saying, "I see Silvana, onna cart, and her hair, it **shines**. Shines in the sun! Only dark, brown. Soft. Like earth. **Rich**." He rubbed his fingers together, crumbling imaginary soil in his hands. "So beautiful. A woman, like **earth** she is beautiful!"

Judy noticed that the front row of the jury, five of them older women, were engrossed in what Pigeon Tony was saying. Santoro's frown had grown deeper. It got Judy thinking. If Santoro was hating it, maybe it was good. Maybe there was hope. She made another note. THE DAY PIGEON TONY KILLED ANGELO COLUZZI.

Then again, maybe not.


After three hours of direct testimony of Pigeon Tony, Judy was down to her least favorite story. The others had gone in beautifully, but this one couldn't. She straightened at the podium and let it rip. "Pigeon Tony, let's begin with you walking into the back room of the pigeon-racing club on the morning of April seventeenth. Where was Angelo Coluzzi when you came into the room?"

"Near shelf."

Judy didn't bother to fetch the exhibit. They were beyond exhibits now. Beyond laws. "Did you know Mr. Coluzzi was in the room when you opened the door?"

"No."

"So you were surprised to see him?"

**"Si, si."**

"You mean, yes?"

"Yes." The word sounded strange coming from Pigeon Tony's mouth, and he managed to stretch it to two syllables, like Yays-a.

Judy thought about the best way to couch the story. "You opened the door, and Mr. Coluzzi said something to you, didn't he?"

"Yes."

"What did Mr. Coluzzi say to you?"

"He laugh. He say, 'Look who come in! A buffoon! A weakling! A coward!'"

On the dais, Judge Vaughn was listening alertly. The court personnel, who usually did paperwork while court was in session, were listening, too. Santoro was taking rapid notes. Judy didn't have to see the gallery to know what it looked like. She kept her focus on Pigeon Tony.

"Please explain to the jury why he said that, Pigeon Tony."

His face flushed. "I no avenge Silvana. I go to America. I no make vendetta."

Judy thought it might be time for the short course. Vendettas 101. "What was wrong with that?"

"Man must honor vendetta, must take eye for eye."

The schoolteacher on the jury gave a slight nod, and Judy knew she had at least one vote. Maybe the schoolteacher would be foreperson, please God. Judy kept an eye on the jury as she asked the next question. "Pigeon Tony, why didn't you honor the vendetta? Why didn't you take an eye for an eye?"

"I no want to kill," he answered, after a moment. "I no want to kill nobody, never." He turned to jury. "I grow olives, in Italy. Tomatoes. Zucchini. I no want to kill. I grow."

Judy breathed a relieved sigh. "What did you do next, after Mr. Coluzzi called you a coward?"

"I say to Coluzzi, you pig. You scum. You worse coward than me, for you kill defenseless woman." Pigeon Tony turned to the jury. "My wife, Silvana," he said, needlessly. Judy knew the jurors would never forget his account of the day he found Silvana in the stable, with his little son standing behind him. Two in the front row had wept openly.

"Then what did Mr. Coluzzi say to you?"

"He say, 'You are a stupid, you are too dumb to see I destroy you. I kill your son and his wife, too. I kill them in truck and soon I kill Frank and you will have nothing.'" Pigeon Tony trembled, newly anguished, and several of the jurors gasped. The schoolteacher's eyes narrowed with Abruzzese anger. Even Judge Vaughn shifted in his leather chair.

"Then what happened?"

"My heart is so full, and I say, 'I kill you,' and I run and I push him. I run at him, fast. I no think, I run, and I push, I shove. I no can believe how hard! He falls and shelf fall, and I make noise, and alla things offa shelves."

Judy focused on something she hadn't before. "So, the scream was you, and not Mr. Coluzzi?"

"**Si, si**. Yes, and alla people come in—Tony, Feet, Fat Jimmy. They say, 'You break his neck,' and I see, **é vero**, I break his neck!"

Judy paused. It was death, after all, and it deserved its moment. It wouldn't serve Pigeon Tony to gloss over it, and he looked stricken on the stand. The jurors' faces were uniformly grave and several of them were looking toward the gallery. Nobody had to tell Judy that Coluzzi's widow and family would be crying. She had to deal with it.

"Pigeon Tony, are you saying, in open court, that you broke Mr. Coluzzi's neck?"

"Yes."

"In your opinion, was that murder?"

Santoro was on his feet. "Objection! Your Honor, the witness is not a lawyer. His opinion about whether his act constitutes murder is a conclusion of law, irrelevant and prejudicial!"

Judy shook her head. "Your Honor, the defendant is entitled to state his own personal belief about his own actions. His state of mind is always at issue in a criminal case."

Judge Vaughn mulled it over, looking from one lawyer to the next, then returning to Judy. "You may proceed. Objection overruled."

"Pigeon Tony," Judy said, facing him directly. "Is it murder?"

"No! Is killing, no is murder. Is no murder because Coluzzi kill my wife, Silvana. And my son and **his** wife, Gemma."

Judy watched the jury, but they didn't react one way or the other. There was nothing left to tell. That was it. Pigeon Tony had told the truth, the whole truth, and nothing but. She hoped to God it didn't kill him. But a detail was nagging at her.

"Pigeon Tony, I have one last question. In the back room, after you pushed Mr. Coluzzi, why did you scream?"

Pigeon Tony blinked. "I no know," he answered quietly.

But Judy did. "You don't know?"

"No."

Judy let it go, for now. "I have no further questions. Thank you, Pigeon Tony."

"**Prego,** Judy," he said with a polite nod, but this time the jury remained unsmiling.

She left the podium only reluctantly, aching inside as she took her seat at counsel table. She had done the best she could, and so had Pigeon Tony. There was no way she could predict what the jury would do. It would depend on how Pigeon Tony held up on cross-examination. Santoro was already on his feet with his notes and stalking to the podium, filled with the righteous anger that was regulation-issue to prosecutors. But this time, even Judy thought it was justified.

She tried to relax in her chair. The only thing harder than assisting a suicide was watching one.

In slow motion.

Santoro glared from the podium at Pigeon Tony. "Mr. Lucia, is it your testimony that you believe Angelo Coluzzi killed your wife?"

"**Si, si.**" Pigeon Tony straightened in his chair, which still brought him only six inches over the microphone. "Yes."

"Did you report this to the Italian authorities?"
"Yes."

"Did they bring charges against Angelo Coluzzi for this alleged murder?"

"No. No do nothing."

Santoro raised a warning finger. "Confine your answers to yes or a no, Mr. Lucia, do you understand?"

"Sure." Pigeon Tony nodded, and Santoro clenched his teeth.

"So the Italian police brought no charges against Angelo Coluzzi?"

"**Coluzzi** the police."

"Mr. Lucia!" Santoro shouted so loudly that Pigeon Tony startled at the witness stand. "Only yes or no is proper! Do you understand me?"

Pigeon Tony fell silent.

"Do you understand me? Answer the question!"

"Yes."

"Do you want a translator? Yes or no, Mr. Lucia!"

"No."

On the dais Judge Vaughn shifted in his leather chair, and Judy considered objecting but made herself stop when she saw the jury's reaction. A few eased back in their seats, which she read—she hoped correctly—as distancing themselves from the scene. If Santoro was going to yell at Pigeon Tony, maybe it wouldn't be the worst thing for the jury to see. For the jurors who liked him, it would increase their sympathy. For the jurors who hated him, at least they see him get some comeuppance. It was in Pigeon Tony's interests for Judy to shut up, so she did.

"I'll ask again, Mr. Lucia, you do understand me, don't you!"

"Yes." Pigeon Tony's face fell, deep parentheses around a mouth that loved a smile, fissures on a forehead remarkably unfurrowed most of the time. The browbeating changed Pigeon Tony's demeanor on the stand, and to Judy's eye he seemed to shrink, his shoulders sloping, his eyes becoming opaque and guarded. Pigeon Tony knuckled under on the spot, and Judy wondered if it was an ingrained response, from growing up under Fascist rule.

If anything, it encouraged Santoro. "Now, I'll ask this again," he said, his tone stern. "The Italian authorities ruled your wife's death an accident, did they not?"

"Yes," Pigeon Tony answered quietly.

"They came to your house and investigated her death, did they not!"

"Yes."

"And they decided that it was an accident, did they not!"

"Yes."

"They decided that she fell from the hayloft, didn't they!"

"Yes."

Santoro's fingers tightened around the podium. "Now, your wife died sixty years ago, isn't that right!"

"Yes."

"And you loved your wife very much!"

Pigeon Tony's eyes fluttered. "Yes."

"And you thought she was a wonderful mother!"

"Yes."

"And for sixty years, you have **hated** Angelo Coluzzi, because you believe he killed your wife, isn't that true!"

"Yes."

"You have hated him because you believe he took your wife from you and the mother from your child!"

"Yes."

Judy bit her lip not to object. Her client was being berated before her eyes, all of it legally. She could see that it was wearing Pigeon Tony down. She didn't know how much more he could take. She had to suppress her best instinct as a lawyer to protect her client. She picked up her pencil to take fake notes, but couldn't write anything remotely funny.

"Mr. Lucia, isn't it true, haven't you wished, for every day of the past sixty years, that you could kill Angelo Coluzzi?"

Pigeon Tony thought a minute. "Yes."

"You thought Angelo Coluzzi deserved to die?"

"Yes."

Santoro leaned over the podium, his fingers tight on its veneer edges. "Mr. Lucia, please move forward in time to the present day, if you can. With reference to the murder at issue here, which you have admitted committing—"

"Objection," Judy said, half rising. "Your

Honor, again, whether Pigeon Tony's act constitutes murder is for the jury, not Mr. Santoro, to
decide. Pigeon Tony's state of mind is relevant,
not Mr. Santoro's."

Santoro's brown eyes widened in personal
offense. "He did it, Your Honor! **An intentional
killing!** He admitted as much!"

Judge Vaughn motioned to both lawyers to
come toward the bench. "No speaking objections,
counsel. Please approach, now," he said gravely,
and they complied. He addressed only Judy, the
full weight of his blue-eyed intelligence boring
into her. "Ms. Carrier, I am going to overrule Mr.
Santoro's objection, for the time being, because
your analysis is legally correct."

Santoro scoffed under his breath, but it didn't stop
Judge Vaughn.

"But I warn you, Ms. Carrier," the judge continued, pointing a finger like a gun at her, "if you are
going for a jury nullification here, be forewarned.
If you make one improper reference in a question,
objection, or closing argument, which suggests in
any way that these jurors ignore the law, I will
hold you in contempt, dismiss this jury, and
declare a mistrial. So watch your step. For your
sake, and for your client's."

"Yes, sir." Judy didn't want a mistrial. She didn't
know if Pigeon Tony could go through another
trial. "Thank you."

"Thank you," Santoro said quickly, and he

returned to his podium while Judy walked to counsel table. It was one of the longest walks she'd ever taken. Her knees felt weak again. She wobbled in her pumps. Had they moved the table when she turned her back? She took her seat and pushed her pad away. She should have prevented this from happening. She should never have let Pigeon Tony take the stand.

Santoro cleared his throat. "Mr. Lucia, please answer yes or no to the following questions, as before. Do you understand!"

"Yes."

"Now, there came a time, on April seventeenth of this year, when you went to the pigeon-racing club and opened the door to the back room, isn't that right!"

"Yes."

"And isn't it true that you rushed at Angelo Coluzzi and grabbed him by the shoulders and whipped his back with such violent force as to break his neck from his very shoulders!"

"Yes."

Santoro didn't break stride. "When you ran at him, you intended to kill him, did you not!"

"Yes."

"You **knew** you were going to kill him!"

"Yes."

"You **wanted** to kill him!"

"Yes."

"You **hoped** you could kill him!"

"Yes."

"You had wanted to kill him **for sixty years**!"

"Yes."

Santoro stopped suddenly. The courtroom was utterly quiet. Judy, the judge, and the jury all waited for the next question. "Well, you did," Santoro said, very quietly.

Judy rose to object, then shut her mouth. It would look heartless. But she finished rising and went to the podium. If Santoro was finished, it was time for redirect.

Judge Vaughn seemed to come out of a reverie, and, like everybody, he was visualizing the awful scene in the back room and looking at Pigeon Tony with new, cold eyes. "Mr. Santoro, do you have any further questions?" the judge asked crisply.

"No, Your Honor," Santoro answered, and Judy went forward.

"I have a single question on redirect, Your Honor," she said.

"Good," Judge Vaughn replied grimly, which Judy took as a bad sign. Santoro's cross had hit home. He had emphasized all the worst parts of Pigeon Tony's story. The jury looked restless and unhappy. She couldn't hope to bring them back to the warmth they'd felt for him when he started testifying. There was only one thing she could do, but it needed to be done, and she didn't know if she could get it from Pigeon Tony.

She cleared her throat. "Pigeon Tony, I have one question for you."

On the stand, Pigeon Tony raised his small chin, but his eyes remained opaque.

"Pigeon Tony, are you sorry that Angelo Coluzzi is dead?"

Pigeon Tony breathed shallowly, his concave chest rising once, then twice. His mouth moved into a firm, tiny line, and he blinked once, then twice. "Yes, I am sorry," he said softly.

Judy permitted the word a hang time, as she had with Angelo Coluzzi's death, and her gaze met Pigeon Tony's. She locked eyes with him for a minute, keeping him in that moment, remembering the day he'd welled up in court, and his eyes grew shiny again, with remorse restrained enough to ring true. Then she said, "I have no further questions, Your Honor," and returned to counsel table.

But Santoro was stalking to the podium. "Likewise, I have only one question on recross, Your Honor," he said, but didn't wait for Judge Vaughn to nod him on. He reached the podium and fixed a glare at the witness stand. "Mr. Lucia, are you sorry you killed Angelo Coluzzi?"

Pigeon Tony paused only a second. "No."

"Thank you," Santoro said quickly and went back to counsel table.

Judy kept an eye on the jury. A juror in the back row looked shocked. Another juror, next to her, had knitted her brow in confusion. Judy considered going up to the podium to mitigate the damage, but she knew Pigeon Tony would tell only the truth: He was sorry Angelo Coluzzi was dead, but he wasn't sorry he had killed him. Whoever said that the truth, while plain, was easy? Or that human behavior was ever black and white? It gave her an idea.

"Ms. Carrier?" Judge Vaughn asked, cocking a questioning eyebrow, but Judy had arrived at a decision and held her head high, with a confidence she didn't feel.

"The defense rests, Your Honor," she said.

They were the hardest words she had ever said, and also something of a lie. Because she was already hatching another plan.

# 48

Judy stood at the head of the table in the courthouse conference room, pitching Plan B to her
client. "Pigeon Tony, listen to me. We can still
save your life. You know you are charged with
murder in the first degree, which is the worst kind
of murder there is."

"**Si, si,**" he answered wearily, almost slumping in
the chair across from Judy. He was clearly exhausted
from testifying, and the grind of the trial had taken
its toll. Frank sat next to him, his expression tense,
with an arm around the back of his grandfather's
chair. Bennie listened as she stood with folded arms
against the side wall. She had given Judy her blessing for this last-ditch effort.

"We can move the Court—ask the Court—to
charge you on a lesser crime. For example, murder
in the third degree. I have the definition right
here. Murder in the third degree is when someone
kills someone else"—Judy read from her pad—
"'without a lawful justification, but acts with a

sudden and intense passion, resulting from serious provocation.'"

"What means voca—?" Pigeon Tony asked.

"It's like when Coluzzi told you he killed your son and his wife. He provoked you."

**"Provocare,"** Frank translated, and Pigeon Tony nodded, seeming to perk up.

"Coluzzi provoke me, **è vero.**"

Judy nodded, encouraged. "He did provoke you, and you did kill him with a sudden and intense passion. It fits! Now is the time the Court charges the jury, or tells them what the law is. If we ask the Court to charge the jury on murder in the third degree, I think they won't convict you on murder in the first degree."

Frank brightened. "What's the difference, Judy?"

"One big difference. No death penalty. The mandatory minimum for third-degree murder is ten to twenty years."

"Hmm." Frank shook his head. "That might as well be life in prison for him. But at least it's not death."

"Exactly," Judy said, heartened. "It gives the jury a compromise. They want to punish him, they can convict on the lesser crime. It's not all black and white."

Frank nodded. "I like it."

"So do I," added Bennie, still leaning against the wall.

Judy felt relieved. "It's your choice, Pigeon Tony, but I advise that you let me do it." She checked her watch. "I meet with the judge in five minutes to go over the charge, and after that we have our closing arguments. Then he charges the jury and they go out to deliberate. You have to decide now. Say yes."

Pigeon Tony blinked, his lids slower than usual. "Say again."

"Say what?"

"Say what you say before." He motioned at Judy's legal pad. "What you read."

Judy looked at her pad. The definition of third-degree murder. "Killing someone without lawful justifi—"

"What means?"

"It means the killing wasn't legal. There was no legal reason for it."

Pigeon Tony's eyes flared open. "Is no murder! No! No! No!"

"Pigeon Tony—"

"No!" he erupted.

It was over. Judy knew she could move Mount Vesuvius sooner. There was no Plan C. And it was time to go.


At the podium, Judy stood for a moment before the jury, thinking of what to say in her closing argument. Events had obviously mooted her neatly outlined reasonable-doubt closing, with Points A through F. She was on her own.

She looked up and eyed the jury, and they looked refreshed and eager. The schoolteacher smiled at her, but Judy had to speak to the back row, which had already decided that Pigeon Tony was guilty. She had thought that once, too. Maybe it was a good starting point.

"Ladies and gentlemen of the jury. You have heard something extraordinary in this courtroom, in Pigeon Tony's testimony. I heard it for the first time myself, when I met my client. You all heard him tell you, because he insisted on taking the witness stand to talk to you and tell you the truth. He didn't hide behind me, an expert, or even his rights under the Constitution. But when Pigeon Tony told me that story of what happened in the back room, the same way he told it to you today, I was appalled. I didn't know if I should represent him. After all, he had killed someone. In my mind then, he was guilty."

Judy paused, thinking aloud. "But I came to know him, and to hear about his life, much as you did through the stories he told you when he testified today. I began to understand what he had gone through. First, his wife murdered in a stable, on his young son's birthday, and then his son and his wife burned alive in a truck that went flaming off a highway overpass. Pigeon Tony Lucia is a man who has had his entire family taken from him." Judy was choosing her words carefully, because Santoro was on the edge of his seat, waiting to object. She couldn't say Angelo Coluzzi had committed the murders because he hadn't been convicted, but she didn't have to, she hoped.

"And as time went on, I began to understand what would happen to a normal person, if pushed to that length. What would happen to me, or to you. And if I, or you, were provoked the way Pigeon Tony was, had lost the people we loved, wouldn't we behave the same way, in that one instant when we are taunted, teased, and provoked, with the source of our greatest pain? Remember Angelo Coluzzi's words: **I killed your son and—**"

"Objection, irrelevant!" Santoro said, and Judy's head snapped around. Most lawyers would never interrupt another's closing, especially with an objection that lame.

"Your Honor," Judy said. "That was Pigeon Tony's testimony, and I'm entitled to argue it."

"Overruled." Judge Vaughn looked askance at Santoro, who sat down.

Judy paused to collect her thoughts. If Santoro was trying to break her stride, she wouldn't let him. "And hearing that, Pigeon Tony flew at Angelo Coluzzi and pushed him, breaking his neck. And after that he screamed. At the horror of what he had done. You heard him say he was sorry that Coluzzi was dead. He was, and is, sorry."

Judy drew herself up. "But you are here to judge Pigeon Tony, and Judge Vaughn will charge you on the law, and he will tell you that you are the ultimate finder of the facts in this case. You alone will decide what is truth. You alone will decide whether Pigeon Tony committed murder when he killed Angelo Coluzzi."

Judy paused, eyeing each juror. "Your best guide in that deliberations room will be this question: What is justice? Because it is justice that brings the lawyers here, and the court personnel, Judge Vaughn, and the Lucias and the Coluzzis and all of the spectators, the reporters, and most of all, each of you. Juries are convened for one purpose only: to do justice. Justice is the reason for this system, and for objections, and for opening and closing arguments. Justice is, in fact, the entire point of the law."

Judy thought about it, clarifying her own thoughts as she spoke. "Pigeon Tony has never had justice in his life, and he is seventy-nine years old. He grew up under Fascism, in prewar Italy, and he doesn't expect justice. He has learned not to expect justice. But he remains hopeful. It is time for him to have justice now." Judy paused. "Show him what this country was built on. Teach him what we are all about. Grant him, finally, justice. And find him not guilty of murder. In so doing, you will not be ignoring the law. You will be fulfilling its highest and best purpose."

"Thank you." Judy nodded at the jury, then made her way to her seat. She didn't look anywhere but straight ahead as Santoro hurried to the podium and slapped his legal pad on it with a resounding **thwap**.

"I cannot believe what I just heard," Santoro said angrily, eyeing the jury. "I had expected that the defense would play on your sympathy, but I never thought I would hear her call upon **justice**. Is it justice to kill an innocent man, in cold blood, while he is doing nothing but practicing his hobby? How can that possibly, by any stretch of the imagination, be called justice?"

Santoro held up a finger. "Ms. Carrier told you that the point of the law is justice. She is correct. But the law that governs this matter has already been decided and the law on this subject is clear. Please listen while I read it to you." He picked up his pad. "'A criminal homicide constitutes murder of the first degree when it is committed by an intentional killing.'" Santoro slapped the pad down again, startling the jurors in the front row. "That is the law of this Commonwealth. And if you follow the law, as you must, you can only find defendant Lucia guilty of murder in the first degree."

Santoro didn't break stride. "The defendant **admitted he killed** Angelo Coluzzi. The defendant admitted he **intended** to kill Angelo Coluzzi. The defendant admitted he **hoped** he could kill Angelo Coluzzi. And semantics aside, the defendant **isn't** sorry that he killed Angelo Coluzzi. Which means to me, he'd do it again if he had the chance. Ms. Carrier wants you to imagine yourselves as Mr. Lucia, but on the contrary, please imagine yourselves as Angelo Coluzzi. Because that's who you would be if we permitted people to kill each other for reasons they think are valid but that have no basis in reality. To kill for imagined slights. To kill for unsubstantiated revenge. To kill because they think they have the right to. To kill because of an ancient grudge. To kill for their cultural beliefs."

Santoro paused. "Ms. Carrier spoke personally, and so will I. I am an Italian-American, and I must tell you, I am absolutely offended by this defendant. Because this is not prewar Italy; this is America. This is not a time of war and disorder; this is a time of peace, and order. We in America are not about tyranny, we are about democracy and the law. We Americans all must abide by the law, for the safety and good of the whole. When the defendant came to this country from Italy, as did my own grandfather, he took on the responsibility to accept our laws. Just as he accepts our benefits and our riches."

Santoro eyed the jury, the front row and then the back. "In the beginning of this case, I told you that every murder case is a story. Now we are at the end of this one. All of us are here to hear it and witness it, except for one man. Angelo Coluzzi. The law will guide you, and Judge Vaughn will charge you on it. And when you follow it, you will be doing justice, not only for all of us, but for Angelo Coluzzi.

"Thank you," he said, and left the podium.

Judy couldn't ease the tightness in her stomach as Judge Vaughn began reading the law to the jury, taking them through the early paragraphs of the charge, regarding the jury as the ultimate fact finder. Though the boilerplate had always sounded like a bar- review course before, it took on a special significance now. Pigeon Tony listened to every word, sitting upright in his chair, and Judy was sure that Judge Vaughn was reading more slowly so he could understand it. Until the judge had heard Pigeon Tony's admission on the stand, he had liked him. Judy hoped the jury wouldn't feel the same way.

She stole a glance at them as the judge read. Each face was grave, and from time to time many of them glanced over at Pigeon Tony and Judy, then at Santoro and back again, as if trying to reach a decision visually. Judy took a mental head count. The Abruzzese schoolteacher would vote for Pigeon Tony, and maybe the older woman next to her. Everyone else was against, and the back row wanted him drawn and quartered—with his lawyer. Judy stopped counting. It was a guessing game anyway.

Her head began to throb, as the judge segued into reading the jury the definition of first-degree murder. It would be the only degree of guilt that went to the jury, on Pigeon Tony's insistence, even though Judge Vaughn had raised a question about it during their earlier conference. Judy had told him this was her client's wish, and he'd acceded to it. Legally the judge couldn't add a lesser degree of guilt to the charge without a request from the defense or the Commonwealth. It had been obvious at the conference that Santoro was too confident of victory on murder one to do so. The case would go to the jury as all or nothing.

It set Judy's teeth on edge. She blamed herself, she blamed Pigeon Tony, then she blamed Italy and Mussolini, and then came back to herself again. She glanced over at Pigeon Tony, but he was listening to the charge. It was impossible for her to keep a professional mask for the jury, so she looked away.

In the front row of the gallery, beyond the bulletproof divider, sat Frank, his eyes as worried as Judy's. He caught her glance and forced a tense smile, but Judy couldn't find one. She could only imagine how Frank would react when his grandfather was sentenced to death, or life in prison. Or what would happen between them, when Judy became the lawyer who had put him there. She faced the front of the courtroom, where Judge Vaughn was finishing the charge and dismissing the jury to deliberate.

"I am giving the bailiff a verdict sheet for you to

take with you into your deliberations," the judge said, handing several pieces of paper to the bailiff. The bailiff then brought one sheet to the jury, walked to the Commonwealth's table and handed one to Santoro, and finally carried one to Judy, leaving it on counsel table in front of her. "Thank you in advance for your time and your best efforts. Court is now adjourned." He banged the gavel as the jury rose and filed out of the pocket door beside the dais.

Only then did Judy's gaze fall to the verdict sheet, which contained but a single interrogatory:

**Murder (1st degree)—Guilty or Not Guilty?**

# 49

Judy sat with Bennie in the courthouse conference room. The small room was dead quiet.
The lighting was harsh. Nobody was talking.
They were all talked out. They had spent the first
two hours of the jurors' deliberations psyching
them out, comparing notes on the raise of an eyebrow or a sniff of contempt. Extrapolating from
stereotype and anecdote and sheer guesswork
which way they would go. Who would be the
foreperson? Who the holdout? How long would
they be out? Would they come back with a question? Or worse, an answer?

Judy checked her watch. 6:30. The jury had
gone out at 3:13, but who was counting? When
would they come back? How would they decide?
Judy's anxious gaze roved over a table cluttered
with briefcases, papers, newspapers, and a copy of
the charge, which she had explained to Pigeon
Tony, just for something to do. He hadn't seemed
all that interested, and truth to tell, neither was

she. They had rolled the dice and were waiting for them to stop.

Judy checked her watch. It was 6:31. Pigeon Tony looked down at his lap, silent but not dozing. He couldn't even if he wanted to, because Frank, sitting next to him, had an arm around him and was rubbing his back, jiggling Pigeon Tony with each stroke. They had been doing this for so long, Judy wondered if Frank would wear a hole in Pigeon Tony's new jacket, but she didn't say anything. Nobody acted normal when a jury was out, least of all the client, whose life, or money, was at stake. And for the lawyers it was a limbo of the worst sort. Because whatever happened, they would be responsible for it, and the words of that closing would be a refrain of sleepless nights to come, causing a cringe of regret, or even a tear, in a dark bedroom.

Judy sighed inwardly. Looked nowhere and everywhere. Tried not to think about it but failed. Every profession had its moments, moments only insiders experienced, and lawyering was no different. But for all the highs and lows of being a trial lawyer, Judy thought this was the most incredible moment the law had to offer. A moment that turned a job into a profession, and a profession into a love. A moment when life hung in the balance. A moment when human beings struggled together to govern themselves, to make sense of conflicting facts, and to discover and determine the most elusive of ideals. Justice. Truth. Fairness. Law. Morality. A moment to fix and define ideas that refused to be charted, that defied definition.

Judy marveled at it, truly, anytime any jury went out, but in this case realized something for the first time. The law really wasn't found in the green casebooks that contained the Pennsylvania Statutes or the pebbled maroon books that spelled out the United States Code. It lived in this moment, in the hearts and minds of the jurors who decided it day by day, in courtrooms big and small, everywhere across the country, under a system of law that had become a model for nations around the world. And even though it dealt with such lofty ideals, it always came down to one thing—

A knock at a conference room door, a startled lawyer jumping up to open it, and a solemn bailiff standing at the threshold.

"They're back," he said simply.

In the courtroom the jurors filed from the pocket door into the jury box. Judy struggled to read each face, but they were all looking down as they found their seats. Courtroom lore held that it was bad news when the jury didn't look happy, but Judy never got that. All verdicts were bad news for one side. She prayed it wasn't her side, this time. Pigeon Tony's side.

She watched, almost breathless while the

foreperson, a reserved older man in the front row that nobody had bet on, handed the verdict sheet to the bailiff, who delivered it folded to Judge Vaughn.

Judge Vaughn was collecting himself behind the dais, his features falling into somber lines and his dark robes drawn about him. He reached over and accepted the verdict sheet, opened it slowly, then closed it and handed it back to the bailiff without reaction. Judy almost burst with frustration. Didn't these people have any emotions? Wasn't there an Italian among them? Pigeon Tony fidgeted in his seat. She didn't dare look at Frank, in the gallery. Or Bennie, The Tonys, and Mr. DiNunzio. The bailiff gave the verdict sheet back to the foreperson, who nodded as he took it, seated.

The bailiff addressed the jury. "Mr. Foreperson, would you please rise?"

It was time for the verdict to be read. Judy found herself reaching for Pigeon Tony's hand. He would need the support. She would need the support. They would get through this together.

The bailiff spoke again. "Ladies and gentlemen of the jury, on the charge of murder in the first degree in the matter of Commonwealth versus Lucia, how do you find?"

The foreperson cleared his throat. "We find the defendant not guilty."

Judy thought she'd heard it wrong. Pigeon Tony closed his eyes in thankful prayer.

An outraged Santoro jumped to his feet. "Your Honor, please poll the jury!" he demanded, and Judge Vaughn stoically complied, asking each juror what was his verdict, guilty or not guilty.

Judy remained stunned as each juror repeated "not guilty," and it took twelve "not guilty"s for her to believe it was really true, and that they had really won, and that Pigeon Tony had finally gotten justice for all he had suffered, and that nobody could take it away from him.

And then her tears came.


Once Judy and Pigeon Tony were outside the bulletproof barrier, courtroom security took over and ushered the Coluzzis out, but nobody could easily restrain the Lucias. Bennie, Frank, The Tonys, and Mr. DiNunzio surged joyously toward Judy and Pigeon Tony, enveloping them both in their embrace and crowding with them out the courthouse doors, clapping and shouting.

Judy was almost out the door when she caught sight of a woman in the back of the gallery. She did a double-take when she recognized her. Strawberry-blond hair, bright blue eyes, and a big Irish grin. It was Theresa McRea, sitting next to her husband Kevin, the subcontractor. If they were here, it must mean he would testify against the Coluzzis.

Judy saluted them, with karma to spare.

# 50

It would have been nice to take off for Bermuda after the trial, but Chester County was looking good to Judy right now, as she zipped under the cool oak trees covering the wooded country road, in the cutest lime-green VW Bug ever made. Penny occupied the passenger seat, characteristically erect, her brown eyes focused out the windshield. A girl, her dog, and her car. It was good to be reunited.

Judy drove with the windows open, and the wind fluttered through her hair, levitated Penny's raggy ears, and ruffled the newspapers on the backseat of the car. Judy turned right and downshifted as she pulled onto the property, headed for Frank's construction site, and parked near his tool bag, of worn sailcloth. She cut the ignition and opened the door, and Penny bounded onto her lap and jumped out of the car into the mud. Judy retrieved the newspapers and got out of the car. Good thing one of them could retrieve.

Penny sprinted for Frank, who looked up from the wall-in-progress and caught the golden as she plastered muddy paws on his khaki shorts. Rocks lay in piles around his Timberlands, which were fringed with orangey mud, and Penny deserted Frank to sniff each one, her tail wagging. Moths fluttered from her in confusion, disturbed in their wandering from one dirty puddle to the next, where the topsoil lay soaking from last night's rain. This morning had dawned muggy and hot, atypical for spring, and Judy had gotten out of the office as soon as she could, to bring the news in person.

Penny darted off to get into trouble, and Judy walked over to the wall, watching a shirtless Frank pick up a large tan stone, brace it against the thick cotton of his shorts, then strike it with the long tip of a rock hammer, making an almost musical **chink**. The impact sent fine dust blowing into the air, setting the breeze aglitter in the summer sun.

Judy was in no hurry to rush the moment. She sat down on a rock with the newspaper. "How do you know where to hit it?" she asked, curious.

"Rock has a grain, like wood. Particularly sandstone does. Look for the cleft, find the grain, and smack it so it breaks with the grain."

"Of course." Judy had no idea what he was talking about, but it didn't matter. She liked the sound of his deep voice and the movement of his shoulder muscles under a thin veneer of perspiration. She tried not to leer, so Frank didn't think he had become a sex object, which would have been a completely reasonable assumption given the last few days.

"The old guys, like my father, they could tell you exactly how the rock would pop. He could even send the chip where he wanted it to go." A chunk of the rock fell to the ground, and then Frank holstered the hammer and wedged the smaller piece under the end of the rock, filling in a space Judy hadn't seen.

"Why do you do that?"

"Shim it? Supports the foundation. The little ones do most of the work. It's just that the big ones get all the credit." Frank grinned and wiped his brow, leaving dark streaks on his forehead. "As in life."

Judy scanned the wall, which curved sinuously across the top of the gentle hill. It was almost seventy-five feet long and made only of tan, gray, and iron-streaked fieldstones. No mortar at all, in the rural style of a dry retaining wall. "It looks wonderful."

"Thanks." Frank paused. "I own it now, you know. Settlement is next month, before it gets too cold to break ground."

Judy didn't get it. "Wait. What do you own? The wall?"

Frank nodded, with a grin. "I bought this property as of yesterday, from my client. Ten acres, most of it uncleared, but it's still land."

"You're kidding!"

"So now it's my wall." Frank turned and pointed behind him, to lower ground. "The house will be there."

"House?"

"I can build it."

"By yourself?"

"Nah." Frank turned and pointed toward the oak grove, where Pigeon Tony began the long trek toward them. "I got the little stones to help, like that one."

Judy smiled. "Jeez! And I thought I had news."

Frank cocked his head. "What's your news?"

Judy opened the newspaper, held it up, and showed him the headline. She knew what it said. JOHN COLUZZI ARRESTED FOR MURDER OF BROTHER MARCO.

"They announced today, huh?" Frank set down his hammer and accepted the paper.

"The proverbial good news and bad news." Judy winced. "Jimmy Bello turns on John Coluzzi in return for a lighter sentence on your parents' murder. Bello even produced the ski masks and bloody clothes, which he was supposed to stash after they killed Marco. The D.A. said he has John nailed."

Frank's lips parted as he read the story, and Judy waited for his reaction. In the background she could see Pigeon Tony getting closer, in his baggy pants and blousy white shirt. After a minute Frank looked up from the paper. "They don't say how light the sentence will be," he said, dry-mouthed.

"It won't be that light, they told me, and it'll run consecutively, so he's locked up for a good, long time."

"I can meet with the judge when the time comes, as victims' family, right?"

"Right. I'll go with you."

"Good." Frank squinted against the sun. His broad chest heaved up and down with a deep sigh. "Not the worst thing in the world. Justice, in a way."

"In a way. And Dan Roser's lawsuit goes forward, against John and the company. With Kevin McRea's testimony, Coluzzi Construction is out of business."

Frank handed her back the newspaper. "Sometimes that's the best the law can do," he said quietly. "Maybe it's time to end all this, huh?"

"You mean the hate part? The hostility and the war?"

Frank smiled. "The vendetta."

"So the vendetta ends. Excellent. From now on there will be only peace, stone walls, and houses in the country."

"And love," Frank said. He leaned over and kissed Judy gently, without her even asking.

"Judy!" came a shout, and Judy managed to unlock her lips. Behind Frank, Pigeon Tony was walking, with Penny dancing circles at his side. He carried a Hefty bag, and Judy knew it had to be full of lunch and laundry. But Pigeon Tony's straw hat was tilted at an unusual angle, and something she couldn't see clearly was on his shoulder.

"How do you think he'll take the news?" she asked, shielding her eyes to see Pigeon Tony better. Something appeared to be sitting on his shoulder, and Penny kept jumping up to get it.

"I told him we'd have to make the deal, and he's okay with it. He's stronger than both of us and this wall put together." Frank turned and waved at his grandfather. "He's already talking about rebuilding his loft, at home, so he can get ready for race season this summer. He loves you forever for saving his birds."

"I didn't do it. The Tonys did." Judy stood up and waved as Pigeon Tony approached, swinging his Hefty bag, and when he got close enough she could see what was driving the dog nuts. Perched on Pigeon Tony's shoulder, riding happily under the brim of his hat, perched a slate-gray pigeon. Judy burst into laughter. "Is that a **pigeon** on his shoulder?"

"That's no ordinary pigeon. That's The Old Man."

"He came back?"

"Naturally, to South Philly. Where else can he get fresh mozzarella?"

Judy laughed. "So what's he doing here?"

"Tony-From-Down-The-Block brought him,

and my grandfather won't let the bird out of his sight. They're both single, and they go everywhere together now."

"Judy!" Pigeon Tony was pumping his hand with a familiar vigor. "Thank you, Judy. Thank you! Look! See! He come back!" The motion unsettled the bird, which began fluttering its wings, and suddenly Penny leaped into the air at the pigeon.

Judy was about to shout in warning, but the aged pigeon, who had survived dangers greater than mere puppies, took easy flight, flapping its wings in a gentle rhythm, swooping in unhurried spirals into the cloudless blue sky. The bird climbed higher and higher as they all watched from the meadow, until finally it soared into the light of the sun, safe and free.

# ACKNOWLEDGMENTS

I know something about the law and about golden retrievers, but that's about it. For this novel I had to understand homing pigeons and prewar Italy, so I was, in at least two areas, flat out of luck. Also the writing part never comes easy, but that's another story. This is where I say thank you for the help, and kindly forgive my length. I'm a big fan of thank you. People should say it more often. Only goldens are exempt.

First thanks to my agent Molly Friedrich and my editor Carolyn Marino, for their guidance, support, and good humor during the writing and editing process. Thank you to HarperCollins CEO Jane Friedman, who watches over me, my books, and even their covers, and to Cathy Hemming, who is the best publisher in town. Thank you to Michael Morrison, for his expertise and kindness, and to Richard Rohrer, for all of the above, plus great taste in wine. Thank you to the Amazing Paul Cirone and to Erica Johanson, for everything.

Special thanks to Laura Leonard and Tara Brown, for putting up with me.

Thank you to my wonderful family, The Flying Scottolines, here and in Italy, who let me mine them and their memories relentlessly. Thank you to my *compare* Rinaldo Celli and his family, who helped me understand something about life under Mussolini. Also helpful in this regard were several excellent works: Mussolini, *My Rise and Fall* (Da Capo, 1998); Moseley, *Mussolini's Shadow* (Yale University Press, 1995); Whittam, *Fascist Italy* (Manchester University Press, 1995). For background, see Juliani, *Building Little Italy; Philadelphia's Italians Before Migration* (Penn State University Press, 1998), and Mangione, *Mount Allegro* (Syracuse University Press, 1998). Like most Italian-Americans, I grew up in a proverb-spouting household, but I hear that not everybody learns *what goes around, comes around* or the ever-cryptic *I cry, or you cry* at age three. Those of you who escaped childhood without this experience, or even those of you who survived it, may want to read Mertvago, ed., *Dictionary of Italian Proverbs* (Hippocrene, 1997). Thanks to my friend Carolyn Romano.

Thank you to Anthony and Rocco LaSalle and his family, who invited me into their home, loft, and friendship. I am forever grateful. Thank you to the members of a certain local pigeon racing club, for letting this rookie attend. For further reading about pigeon racing, see Rotondo, *Rotondo on Racing Pigeons* (Mattacchione, 1987) and Bodio, *Aloft* (Pruett, 1990). Thank you to Wil Durham, for his expertise and kindness, and to Marty Keeley, Sebastian Pistritto, and Chris Molitor.

Thank you to Paul Davis, friend and master stonemason, for answering countless questions and for letting me watch him pick up rocks and put them down again. Fot the zen of dry-laid walls, see Allport, *Sermons in Stone* (Norton, 1990) and Vivian, *Building Stone Walls* (Storey, 1976). Thank you to Dr. Anthony Giangrasso, for his forensic expertise and kindness. Thank you to my dear friends criminal defense lawyer Glenn Gilman and detective/whiz Art Mee of the Office of the District Attorney of Philadelphia.

Most of all, thank you to my readers, who have been so supportive to me and my books over the years. I think of you every sentence, and am grateful for the time you spend to read me and even write to me. I am both honored and cheered by your very kind letters and e-mail.

Finally, a personal thank you to my husband and family, for their love and support, and to three goldens I know, for just being you.